Susan Willis Fletcher

Twelve Months in an English Prison

Susan Willis Fletcher

Twelve Months in an English Prison

ISBN/EAN: 9783744756136

Printed in Europe, USA, Canada, Australia, Japan

Cover: Foto ©Andreas Hillbeck / pixelio.de

More available books at www.hansebooks.com

IN AN

ENGLISH PRISON

BY

SUSAN WILLIS FLETCHER

"I was sick, and ye visited me: I was in prison, and ye
came unto me." — MATT. xxv. 36.

BOSTON
LEE AND SHEPARD, PUBLISHERS
NEW YORK
CHARLES T. DILLINGHAM
1884

TO

MY DEAR HUSBAND AND SON,

AND

DR. AND MRS. T. L. NICHOLS

OF LONDON,

WHOSE DEVOTION AND LOVE SERVED TO STRENGTHEN ME DURING
WEARY MONTHS OF PERSECUTION AND SUFFERING,

THIS VOLUME

IS AFFECTIONATELY INSCRIBED

BY THE AUTHOR.

PUBLISHERS' NOTICE.

THE reader of this book, whether a believer in Spiritualism, or one who rejects its claims as delusive and impossible, will be struck by the clear and frank confidence shown in the narrative, especially of the circumstances that preceded the criminal trial, and will soon find his feelings drawn into sympathy with the tender, faithful, and courageous spirit of the writer. The heart of the book is the heart of a noble woman.

After a consideration of the whole case, there cannot remain a doubt of her innocence of the crime for which she suffered; and it must be a continual reproach to the jurisprudence of the foremost among nations that such an injustice could be done under the forms of law.

A strong cry has been heard of late from the wretched precincts of "outcast London;" and it is deplorable to see in the account of the women's prison, as here given, how most of the victims of the law as now

administered are educated for evil, and are graduated
as criminals for life.   If the wise and humane suggestions of the author should aid in bringing about a
change in discipline for the restoration of fallen women,
her unmerited imprisonment will not have been without
recompense.

CONTENTS.

CHAPTER XIX.

CHAPTER XX.

CHAPTER XXI.

CHAPTER XXII.

CHAPTER XXIII.

CHAPTER XXIV.

CHAPTER XXV.

CHAPTER XXVI.

CHAPTER XXVII.

CHAPTER XXVIII.

CHAPTER XXIX.

CHAPTER XXX.

CHAPTER XXXI.

CHAPTER XXXII.

CHAPTER XXXIII.

CHAPTER XXXIV.

CHAPTER XXXV.

CHAPTER XXXVI.

CHAPTER XXXVII.

CHAPTER XXXVIII.

APPENDICES.

APPENDIX I.

x

TWELVE MONTHS IN AN ENGLISH PRISON.

TWELVE MONTHS IN AN ENGLISH PRISON.

CHAPTER I.

MY STORY.

In the summer of 1880, while visiting my mother in the United States, I was arrested on a charge of obtaining jewels and clothing of great value, by undue influence or false pretenses, from a lady known as Mrs. Juliet Anne Theodora Heurtley Rickard Hart·Davies. After having been kept one night in prison, I was released on bail, and, on the hearing of the case, honorably discharged.

Learning that the same charge had been made against me in England, and a warrant sworn out for my arrest, I left America just before Christmas, and came to England to meet my accusers. I came alone; because my husband was suffering from lung and heart disease, and his physician would not consent to his making the voyage in mid-winter. As I expected, I

1

was arrested before leaving the steamer, arraigned at Bow Street, and was in due time tried at the Central Criminal Court, Old Bailey, found guilty, and sentenced to twelve months' imprisonment.

All this time *my own story* of the matters connected with my accusation, trial, and imprisonment, *has not been told.* Condemned without a hearing, undefended at my trial, my witnesses uncalled, and, by the criminal procedure then in force, not allowed to tell my own story to the jury, I now, in the first hours of my freedom, after undergoing the full sentence of the law, desire to tell the whole story of my life to all whose love of truth and justice may make them willing to read it.

Because the right of every person accused of crime to tell his or her own story to the jury was not allowed to me, and because the witnesses who would have proved my innocence, and shown the perjuries of my accusers, were excluded from the witness-box by being included in the indictment against me, or were not called upon to testify, I was condemned unheard. Therefore I claim the right to tell the story of my life, — how I became a Spiritualist, and discovered myself to be a medium; how it came about that I was accused of crime, convicted, and punished.

Let me begin at the beginning. I was born in Lowell, Mass., a manufacturing town on the River

Merrimac, " the Manchester of America," on the 25th of March, 1848.

Alvah H. Webster, my father, was one of the numerous New-England family of Websters, which has produced a famous lawyer and statesman and a great lexicographer.

My parents were religious people, and belonged to the denomination of Baptists, which is one of the largest of the numerous sects in America, where, in the absence of an established church, there are no nonconformists or dissenters.

My mother was gifted·with the " second sight," or clairvoyance, which is a not very unfrequent accompaniment of deep religious feeling. When her first child, who died two years before I was born, was lying ill, she saw three angels appear, one after the other, floating around its crib. As the last one disappeared, the child held up one of its little feet, and said, " Kiss it, mamma," and immediately passed away.

I was born in the same year that saw the advent of modern Spiritualism. Of two brothers born after me, one died; and I have a sister, younger than myself, still li,ing.

About the year 1850 my father, leaving his family in Lowell, went with his brother to seek their fortunes in the gold-fields of California, and there remained for several years. In travelling from one miner's camp to another, my uncle was overwhelmed by a sudden snow-storm, during which he perished, and was buried sixteen feet deep in the snow. For six weeks my father vainly sought to find him or his dead body. One day, snow-blind, and groping about to find his way, he fell; and when rescued he was found close by the frozen body of his brother.

Returning to Lowell, my father bought a small place in the country, where we lived peacefully for several years, and I grew strong in childish plays and the innocent enjoyments of a country life. I remember that I was so fond of dolls as to make them of potatoes by the dozen, all dressed and named; while my cruel uncle John, in his boyish contempt for such playthings, cut their throats, and hung them on the clothes-line. After this horrible murder, John went off to his Sunday school, while I was in a great passion of grief and anger. On his return he found me crying, and became very penitent. To console me he proposed a funeral service for the twelve dead dolls. They were all laid out for burial; and we were to have singing, Bible-reading, praying, and preaching. But John, though very penitent for his crime, wanted to do more than his share of both praying and preaching. I told him to hurry up, and we sang a hymn. As I began my sermon, I seemed to be in the open fields among the flowers, and the air was full of angels. Mamma and grandmamma, who were listening to me, called grandpapa, who brought with him one of the elders, who was visiting us. We closed our services with the Doxology, when the door opened, and we discovered our audience.

My grandfather came to me. "Elder Hinckley," he said, " don't you think she was born to preach?" He took me in his loving arms, and with tender emotion said, "The Holy Ghost has descended upon this house. O God, make her strong to do her work!"

From that day he always encouraged me, and I had at times the feeling that I had a work to do. When about seven years old, walking alone in the fields one day, I climbed upon a rock for my pulpit, and began to preach; and it seemed to me that when I looked up into the trees I saw them full of hands applauding me.

My father's adventure in California, and the strange manner of his finding the body of my uncle in the snow, led to his conversion to a belief in Spiritualism. The manner of my uncle's death was known only to the party that found the living and dead so near together. To save the feelings of the family and friends, my father had kept the secret; and it was generally supposed that he had died of some ordinary disease.

Dr. Kenney, an old friend of papa's, had been in California at the same time, and came to see us at our country home. He asked papa if he had heard any thing of Spiritualism. Father said he thought it was perfectly absurd, and had no belief in it.

" Well," said Dr. Kenney, " I can't agree to that ; for I have just seen a lady at Lawrence who professes to be a medium, and she told me all the particulars of your poor brother Charles's death. I came here on purpose to talk with you about it."

He went on to tell some of the things he had heard from the medium, until father said he would go and see her. So they drove together to the lady's house.

To avoid the possibility of any collusion, he asked to see the medium alone. When he entered the room, she began to shiver, and said, " There is some one belonging to you who was either drowned, or frozen to death, and who wishes to speak with you."

Passing suddenly into a state of trance, she stretched out her hands to him, saying in accents of delight, " Why, Alvah dear, how glad I am to see you! I am your brother Charles, who was frozen to death," giving the date. He proceeded to give my father the most minute details of the whole affair, describing the manner in which his body had been found, and told him that the spirits had made him temporarily blind. so that they could lead him to the spot where his brother's body lay buried in the snow.

" Don't you remember what a dreadful finger I

had?'' The medium held up the forefinger of her right hand.

My father remembered that his brother had a bad whitlow on the *third* finger, which he had often dressed for him. At the instant the medium, or the spirit through the medium, said, "It was not the first, but the third finger, you will remember."

After giving my father many proofs of my uncle's identity, the medium was controlled by one of her "guides," who told him, that, if he wanted proofs of the reality of spiritual manifestation, he need not go to mediums, for he had in his own daughter one of the most remarkable mediums in the world. He had only to sit with his wife and daughter at home to get communications from spirits who might wish to come to us. The spirit gave him some predictions as to my future, saying that I should become a wonderful medium; that I should travel nearly the world over, be very successful, and also meet with dreadful trials. "Something will happen to her," she said, "at the age of thirty-three; but I cannot tell its significance, or whether it portends her death. But I see her raised upon a pedestal in front of a man with silvery hair, robed in scarlet and black, with a great assembly of people. I see two men — one with a gray beard, the other younger — who seem to support her, and through whose efforts she seems to be raised to a life of higher aims and nobler uses."

On his return home, my father told every thing to mother, who was strongly prejudiced against Spiritualism, and believed that it was all either rank imposture or the work of the Devil. But at my father's earnest desire she consented to sit with him at the table.

I was also invited, but refused to come near them. I was afraid. At length my father placed me on a little couch near them. They sat a long time, but nothing came of it, and mother said, —

"Well, Alvah, if you care to go on with this folly, I don't." And she got up, and left him. I also thought it was nonsense, and said, "Well, papa, if the table won't move, why don't you try my rocking-chair?"

He took the suggestion seriously, and said, "Well, little one, we will try it;" and, lifting up my little chair, he placed it upon the table. He and mamma put their hands on the rockers, and I jumped up, and put mine on the table. The little chair began to turn round, so that they got up from their seats to follow its movements. Mother accused father of causing the movements. She thought he had done it. Both denied having any agency in the matter.

Father then asked if the spirit of his brother was present, and wished to communicate. He was answered by a shower of raps made by the rocker of the chair on the table.

Father solemnly turned to my mother, and said, "Truly we are in the presence of the angels."

I said, "O dear uncle Charles, I am so sorry you were frozen in the snow! I loved you so much! Won't you come to me now?"

As I spoke, the chair turned completely round, and leaned over to me, so that I could have put my arm around it.

This was the beginning of the experience of my parents in Spiritualism, and I may now proceed to relate some of my own early experiences.

CHAPTER II.

SOME VERY CHILDISH MANIFESTATIONS.

I HAVE said that my parents were Baptists; and we, of course, attended the Baptist church. In America all chapels are churches: in earlier times they were "meeting-houses." There was a baptistery in our church,—a tank of water under the pulpit,—in which persons who had "experienced religion" were baptized by immersion. The minister and candidate, dressed in baptismal robes, went down into the water. This scene greatly impressed me; and when the minister raised his loosely draped arms, as he came up from the water, and said, "Come unto me, all ye that labor and are heavy-laden, and I will give you rest," two beautiful women seemed to me to come through the window opposite, and bend over, and touch his hands, as if to bless him.

Once, after seeing this appearance, I was impressed to go to his robing-room, and tell him how much I loved and revered him. I knocked at his door, and was bidden to enter. I told him that I had come to

10

tell him how I loved him and the beautiful ladies who came to him in the church.

" Ladies ! " he said. " What ladies? "

I told him of the two who always came at the baptismal service, describing them, and telling him that one was dark and the other fair, and that the younger and fairer had said, " Remember Ida," and that she had placed a wreath of beautiful orange-blossoms on his head, and said, " Separate in life, united in death."

I shall never forget his troubled look and tearful eyes, as he said, —

" Little one, this is witchery. Have your parents ever spoken to you of Spiritualism? "

" Oh, yes ! " I said. " And we sit at the table together."

" My child," he said earnestly, " never do so again. It may be true that spirits come to you ; but it is the Devil who comes to tempt people, and get possession of their souls. Pray to God to forgive you ; but, if you continue, you will surely go to hell."

I was horrified ; but I asked, " What is hell? "

" It is a dreadful place, where people are burned for ever and ever."

I went out : and, feeling that I had been a great sinner, I wanted to punish myself ; so I took off my shoes and stockings, and walked home (two miles) barefoot, on the sharp gravel. Then, to get an idea of the dreadfulness of hell, in my childishness I put my finger on the hot stove-pipe, first high up, then lower down, until it was burnt to a blister, and I almost fainted with the pain.

My mother came in, took me on her lap, and asked what was the matter.

I said, "Dear mamma, if I were a dreadful wicked girl, and you were God, would you send me to hell?" She said she would not. "Then I will never love God any more," I said; "for I love you better than God."

She soon got from me the whole story of my visit to the minister, and soothed and comforted me.

Years afterward the minister confessed that he had been engaged to be married to a young lady named "Ida," who died a few weeks before the day appointed for their nuptials.

It was not uncommon for me at this period of my life to see the spirits of beautiful men, women, and children, who seemed as real as the people about me, and who came and talked to me and my mother, while others could neither see nor hear them.

Behind our house, and a little separated from it, was a coach-house with a hayloft; and it was my delight to clamber up into this huge loft of fragrant hay, and lie down to sleep upon it. It was dimly lighted by a lattice; and when I closed my eyes I saw beautiful angels come through the lattice, and bend over me; and then I felt an ecstatic happiness, and a sense of inflation or extreme lightness. After a time I seemed to float up and up, until I came to the roof, when the roof would open, and I seemed to see throngs of beautiful angels coming to me. Some of them talked with me; and one day I said to them, "May I bring you some flowers the next time I am made so happy?"

They gave me leave to bring them; so the next day, when I went to the loft for my little *siesta*, I carried a great bunch of flowers, which I cuddled closely in my arms before shutting my eyes. Very soon the feeling of happiness, as I called my ecstasy, came over me; and I floated up and up, until I came to the roof, which seemed to open as before, and I asked the angels to take the flowers. They seemed to take them, but would not carry them away, and said, "We will put them where you can see them, and remember us." And then they placed them on the spikes that came through the roof, and could not be reached without a high ladder.

When I awoke from my sleep, my flowers were gone. Looking up, I saw them hanging on the spikes. I remembered then, that "the ladies," as I called them, had said that they would carry the spirits of the flowers to heaven, but would leave their material forms where I could see them.

CHAPTER III.

Our family *séances* were kept up, with varied manifestations, until, in 1860, when I was in my twelfth year, we removed to Lawrence, Mass., a new manufacturing town, and rival to Lowell, situated farther down the River Merrimac. Here my father engaged as his business assistant Mr. William M. Willis, a son of his first medium, to whom I was afterward married. It became known at Lawrence that I was a medium, "a wonderful medium," it was said; but all mediums are wonderful, and the smallest manifestation of spirit-power is a marvel.

I had a great repugnance to sitting in circle, as it is called, and to any spiritual manifestations, except in my own family or with friends: but we were soon importuned for sittings; and our home was flooded with eager visitors, for whose benefit I was with some difficulty induced to sit.

It was at one of these *séances*, when I was twelve years old, that I fell into a deep trance, and my body

14

became possessed by, or came under the control of, an Indian spirit, who gave such tests to our visitors, that the notoriety I got became a great torment to me ; for I was stared at in the streets by strangers, and pointed at as a witch.

I became a writing as well as a trance medium ; that is, I was controlled to write unconsciously, or without my own volition. Even my school-exercises were so written, to my own great relief, and somewhat to the wonderment of my teachers.

One day my hand wrote, "Get a covered slate." I told my father about it ; and he found for me what is called a book-slate, in which I could conceal my writing. I cannot tell whether it was the best way. I do not think all spirits are wise : I only record the fact, that they saved me from the labor of study, did my sums, wrote my exercises, and that I got many prizes, and stood at the head of my class. This seems to me unjust to those who worked much harder, but perhaps no more unjust than when prizes are given to, or successes are gained by, those who are gifted with extraordinary talents or genius.

The spirits who assisted, and at times controlled me, wished now to develop my mediumship so as to make it of the greatest use in carrying out what seems to be their great object or mission, which they declare to be the conversion of the world to a knowledge of spirit existence, of the great fact of immortality. When I refused to sit at *séances*, the manifestations went on in the night. These were often very unpleasant to me. We were living in a country which had been once thickly peopled by the North-American Indians. Our beautiful River Merrimac, and my native State, Massachusetts, had Indian names; and my poor little body was taken possession of, greatly against my will, by fierce Indian warrior-chiefs.

When I resisted, my bed was lifted up, and violently shaken. A heavy table was drawn across the floor, the clothes violently taken from my bed, and I lifted up, and seated upon the table.

These manifestations, which may have been exercises for my development as a medium, went on to the period of my marriage, at the age of fourteen. Mr. Willis had become very fond of me, as, truth to say, I also had of him. My parents gave their consent to our engagement, — a consent not always asked in America, where young people, often at an earlier age than in England, are accustomed to make their own matrimonial arrangements.

Of marriage and all that belongs to it, no child was ever in more profound ignorance. My first child was born when I was sixteen years old. I had the discipline of terrible suffering; and I had to wonder, like many others, why my guardian angels did not protect me against what may have been necessary for my progress, and a preparation for the work I had been chosen to perform. I believe it was " for the best ; " but I do not understand why it has been necessary for me to endure so much suffering.

This reminds me of a fact I had forgotten. I got poisoned while at school ; and my voluntary nerves became so completely paralyzed, that I could move only my little fingers. Medicine had no effect upon me ; but my mother-in-law, who was a healing medium, mesmerized and gradually cured me. The mesmerism, or magnetism, differed from the usual kind in this : being a medium, she was under the control of some spirit ; and it was the controlling spirit who really magnetized and cured me. The cure began where movement often ends. It began with the power to move my toes, and in a short time I had the control of the entire voluntary system.

CHAPTER IV.

DURING the first year of my marriage all my manifestations ceased, and I believed and even hoped that they had ceased forever. But at the age of fifteen I became acquainted with a Mr. Morell, who was about sixty years old, and husband of the first trance and inspirational medium in the city where I resided, — indeed, the first medium of any kind I had ever known. With much persuasion he induced me to sit with him. I was reluctant; but the result was my development in a similar phase of mediumship, which soon made me known to a larger public, and engaged me in a broader work.

A Spiritualist society had been organized in Lawrence, as in almost every considerable town in America. Some called it a Spiritualist Church. They had a hall for Sunday meetings, and regular exercises, services, and lectures. Mr. Morell wished me to speak under spirit-influence at their meetings. Under their direction I was placed on what they said was a regimen

18

which would strengthen me for my work. I had oat-meal and cream for my breakfast, fish and vegeta-bles for dinner, and brown-bread and milk for tea or supper.

After a fortnight of this diet I was to attend the Sunday meeting. On Sunday morning, at the break-fast-table, I fell into a state of trance, which contin-ued through the day. In it, and while unconscious of all that was about me, and fasting after breakfast, I was taken to the church, and gave two lectures, which seemed to have had great success. I had no conscious-ness, and no memory of them or of any thing that had occurred; and the secret was kept from me until one day a gentleman congratulated me upon my per-formance. I asked him what he meant; and I then found out that I had been speaking — with great power and eloquence it was said — on the subject of "Wo-man's Rights." I was deeply disgusted; because I did not believe in woman's rights, nor care for woman's wrongs, and I did not wish to speak in public. I said it was all the work of the Devil, and passionately declared that I would have no more to do with it.

I busied myself with my domestic and maternal duties, and in my eighteenth year gave birth to my second child. At this time we were living in the coun-try, at some distance from Lawrence. I had no mani-festations, and hoped and prayed that my mediumship might never come back to me.

One night, when my boy-baby was two months and six days old, I sat with him in my lap, and a flood of moonlight fell across me and my babe. As I sat looking at him, he seemed to turn from me, and, floating out on the moonbeams, vanished from my sight. Perhaps I had fallen asleep. I must have moved when startled with this dream or vision. My baby fell from my lap upon the floor, and went into convulsions.

This was on Saturday night. At ten o'clock on Monday the nurse thought he seemed better. I took him to my breast, and then placed him in his crib, and went into the next room, singing for joy. I soon went back, and fell on my knees to thank God for the hope that I could keep my darling.

He put out his little hand, — this babe of two months and eight days, — patted my cheek, and said, "Mamma, mamma!" and with one little gasp was dead. My aunt who was with me heard him as well. It was not my fancy. They tried to take me from the room in vain. To my agonized question, "Is my baby dead?" I got no answer. I was in convulsions all day, and seemed nigh to death.

It was in the month of December, which in New England is very cold; and the country, as usual at this season, was deep in snow. They buried my baby in a graveyard two miles and a half away. I did not know where it was situated. I cannot now remember that I had ever seen it. For weeks I was ill. Deep snow had fallen; and my one idea was, that my baby was under the snow, and that to keep him there was very wicked. Unbeknown to any one, I got out of the house, and walked through the snow, two miles and a half, to the little grave, from which I scraped the snow, and found a little pansy, a dear little heart's-ease, blooming as if angels tended it under the snow. I put my face down, and talked to my baby. Then I saw above me a cluster of little clouds, which gradually came near me, and then opened, and I saw a beautiful girl holding my baby in her arms, both of them radiant and happy.

"Do you want him back again?" the beautiful girl asked me.

"Oh, yes, yes!" I cried.

"Look at him," she said, and laid him in my arms.

I looked; and oh, how beautiful he was, and how happy!

"Look at me," she said. "Look at my face, so as to remember who I am. Tell your mother that Mary has him, and that we shall help to prepare him for what he has to do."

My selfish feeling was conquered. It would be too cruel to ask him back; and I said, "You may keep him."

"We have taken him," she said, "to save him

from the evils that would have come to him, and also to save your life for our best work. We will take care of him, but you must work for us."

" What can *I* do for you?"

" Resist our influences no longer. It was this resistance that brought you those horrible manifestations. Have no more doubts, ask no more questions. Go out into the world, put your hands in ours, and do as we shall direct you."

I gave her back my baby, put my hand in hers, and promised there, kneeling in the snow by the grave of my child, to do my appointed work. This was my dedication for what I have done, or may do or suffer.

She took my baby back into the clouds from which she had come. The vision ended.

I came to my senses, and found myself very cold and wet, and wanted to get home, but did not know the way. When I got out of the gate, I knew not which way to turn ; but a neighbor of ours, who was passing, carried me home in his sleigh, after which I had a long illness, and was carried to my mother to be better nursed.

From this time I never more resisted the influences which controlled my mediumship. I gave my pledge ; and I will, God helping me, keep it to the end.

CHAPTER V.

In 1867, when I was nineteen years old, my health failed, and I went with my husband to live in Lawrence, so as to be near my mother. With the loss of health I seemed to lose my mediumship. Not succeeding according to his wishes, my husband decided to go to the newer country of the West; and we found a home at Marseilles, Ill., seventy miles west of Chicago. Here there fell upon me a calamity which comes to so many women that it cannot be called a strange one. My husband got into habits of intoxication; and I had for nine months a life of such misery, that 'my mother, having a strong impression that something was wrong, came to see me, and, after trying vainly to make things better, advised me to return to my father's house, which I a few months after did. My husband followed us. Soon promising to do better, I tried to live with him again. Doubtless he tried to reform. He fell into greater evils; and I suffered from wrongs I do not wish to dwell upon, and had an expe-

23

rience which made me sympathize with every woman
who suffers. After an illness of seventeen weeks,
caused by his misconduct, I felt compelled to sue for a
divorce, and after a season obtained my legal emanci-
pation.

I was now employed for some years in giving inspirational addresses, speaking under spirit-influence in .
most of the towns of New England where Spiritualist
societies had been established. It was during this
period that I first saw and became acquainted with
Mr. John William Fletcher, a medium and trance-
speaker who had lectured in my father's hall. I was
not at home when this occurred; but my mother was
much attracted to him, and became warm in his praise.
I was, capriciously perhaps, prejudiced against him,
and even refused to be introduced to him, but out of
courtesy, and to please my mother, finally consented.
We had met at a lecture given by one of the earliest
and best-known of American advocates of Spiritualism.

I resisted the attraction I doubtless felt for Mr.
Fletcher, from a sense of duty also; for I was at this
time engaged to be married to a gentleman of New
York, and could not with any propriety have had
much to say to my mother's favorite. · '

We met, however, a little later, at a Spiritualist
camp-meeting. These camp-meetings are held every
summer in many parts of America, in imitation of

the Methodist camp-meetings, a century older. Some beautiful grove by a river, lake, or the sea or mountain side, is chosen; sheltering temporary buildings are erected, or tents. In some cases there are even large hotels built near the grounds for the accommodation of visitors. Mediums gather; *séances* are given in the tents; the grove resounds with singing; and there are lectures, trance-addresses, etc., at the appointed hours.

At the camp-meeting I attended, and in the services of which I took part, Mr. Fletcher was a favorite medium and speaker. We renewed our acquaintance, and in conversation wandered into a quiet and secluded little grotto, where he became controlled by his spirit-guide, "Winona." To test Mr. Fletcher's clairvoyance, I left off my engagement-ring.

"Winona" immediately asked me why I had taken it off. I evaded the question by asking, "How do you know that I have an engagement-ring?"

"Oh! I have seen it," said "Winona," and went on to describe it. "But," she continued, "you will never have any use for it. You will never marry that man."

"How can you tell that? Do you know him?"

"No, I don't know him; but I can find him." And in a few moments she described him and his house in New York with perfect accuracy. "You'll never marry him," she continued: "you will break off your engagement."

"For what reason, 'Winona'?"

"He will try to compel you to break off your work for Spiritualism. You will not consent. You will marry a medium."

"Can you describe the medium I am to marry?"

She described some one like her own medium, and said, "You will marry him. In five years you will tell me that my prediction was true."

My expected marriage, which from a worldly point of view was very advantageous, and was warmly approved by my parents, was broken off precisely on the grounds that "Winona" had predicted. Three weeks before the day appointed for our marriage, my affianced opened the subject in a letter. He wrote, "When you are my wife, I shall expect you to take your proper place in society. Of course you can no longer be known as a medium, or speak in public: all that I must strictly prohibit. Of course you can see that all that sort of thing would be entirely inconsistent with your position."

I had to make my choice. I sought counsel from my parents, who said, —

"Do what your angels tell you to do, my child. They have never advised you ill."

That night, when I had been half an hour in bed,

thinking of my position, and trying to see and feel what it was my duty to do, I fell, I suppose, into a trance. The roof of the house seemed to open, the clouds came down to me. A gentle spirit descended, and brought my child. He lay, a little baby, on the bed beside me. He put his little hand upon my face, and patted it, as he had done by the snow-covered grave, and said again, "Mamma, mamma!" as when passing away, and vanished out of sight.

It was enough. He had recalled the pledge I had given to the angels on his grave. Next day I wrote, returned the ring, and broke off the engagement. In a year and a half I was married to Mr. Fletcher, with the full and free consent both of his parents and my own.

We went to live with the parents of my husband. My father-in-law was opposed to my doing any more public work until rested, and restored to my usual health. Now that his son was married, he wanted us to live with him, and enjoy the property and sufficient income of which my husband, as only child, would be the heir. My mother-in-law said, "As well as you love my son, so will I love you." I am compelled to say that the very reverse of this has been true. There seemed to come a strange, jealous hatred in place of the love she promised, and which at that time she may possibly have felt.

For the year we lived with my husband's parents I was the child of my father-in-law. No man could love his own daughter more than he seemed to love me. But a sad domestic complication marred our happiness. He refused to give up the society of one whom he had known for years, and of whom his wife was furiously jealous. Husband and wife separated.

When my father-in-law, whom I truly loved, took his departure, I went to the door to see him off, and say good-by. He put his arms round me, and kissed me tenderly. I shall love him always for all his kindness to me then, and because of his love to me in the long-ago.

Three months after, the person who had been the cause of this separation died, and the husband and wife were reconciled and re-united. But my mother-in-law was jealous of me, as if the jealousy, for which she had cause, was transferred to me. She told her husband terrible stories about me. I believe she became the victim of malicious, lying spirits, who interfered, and kept us apart.

CHAPTER VI.

WE were compelled to leave this discordant home. The treatment I received was insufferable. The reconciled husband fell naturally completely under the influence of his wife, and could not protect me from her malice. When we went from their home, our worldly means were five dollars, and Mr. Fletcher was disabled by an attack of sciatica.

After a visit to a lady of our acquaintance in Lowell, we went to a Spiritualist camp-meeting at Silver Lake, near Plymouth, Mass. While here, being under control of spirits, we were told to go to Lake Pleasant, another camping-ground, near Greenfield, about a hundred and fifty miles north-west of Boston. We both gave *séances* there with such success, that, after paying our expenses, we had a little fund of a hundred and fifty dollars.

On the day we left Mount Pleasant, there came to us a remarkable vision. An Egyptian spirit, who seemed venerable and wise, laid before us the course of our

29

future lives, and the work we were to do for a consid-. erable period.

He said we were to go to Boston, and take an office together as test mediums, and stay there for some years; then I was to cross the Atlantic, and engage in a similar work in London, and, after encountering some difficulties, return to America. Mr. Fletcher would then go to London, and I would follow him. There we should find our home. We would meet opposition, but would overcome it. Mr. Fletcher would give public lectures, first in a small hall, and then in a larger one in a more fashionable quarter. At first this place would be refused to him, on account of the prejudice against Spiritualism; but influences would be used to overcome this prejudice, and secure the place. There would be a great success, and he would have a public testimonial.

"When you have had this triumph," the spirit continued, "then beware, the day of your trial will be at hand. From this time for two years will be the crisis of your life; and your whole future will depend upon the trust you place in us, your fidelity to us, and your courage. You will be publicly disgraced; you will be imprisoned for the truth's sake; but do not falter. Remember always that God understands, and that even in this world your rights will be restored, and your characters vindicated. Take this for your motto: —

"To-day — alone amid ruins:
To-morrow — victory and the people."

You will suffer for the truth as no medium has suffered. You will return to America, and remain for a time; but you will then go back to England, and receive a triumph to which the first was but a shadow.

This vision, now in so large a part fulfilled, came to us in 1873.

Afterward all this prophecy of our future was given again in a vision which both of us saw, in which the scenes of our future lives passed before us like a moving panorama. At its close there appeared a silver goblet, and over it were the words, "*Beware! The day of your trial is at hand.*"

After the triumphal presentation of the silver goblet to us at Steinway Hall in 1879, when we had retired from the brilliant stage and applauding assembly, into the artists' room, I took up the goblet, and the whole vision came into my mind, and also into my husband's. The subject of his last lecture at Steinway Hall was, "Beware of the Foes of your own Household."

CHAPTER VII.

A NEW HOME AND NEW MANIFESTATIONS.

LEAVING Lake Pleasant, we went to visit my parents, where we had some peaceful rest; but we had our orders to go to Boston. We held a *séance* for more specific directions. "Winona" came, and told us to go to the office of the "Banner of Light," the American Spiritualist paper.

We went to the office in Montgomery Place, and had a kind and hearty welcome from Mr. Rich, the business manager, who said he had a large room in his building which could easily be divided into three. Men were at once set to work, and we were soon in possession of a small but convenient home.

The "Banner" publishers had suffered heavily, some time before this, from a fire; and subscriptions were made by Spiritualists for their relief. I had done what I could to promote these, and had some success, which Mr. Rich had not failed to remember. But, aside from this small claim upon his good offices, he was and is, and I hope may long continue to be,

32

the large-hearted, liberal, and considerate friend of all honest and worthy mediums. When we spoke of business, and of the rent we were to pay, he said, "If you succeed, you can pay: if not, it don't matter." With this model landlord we staid a year and a half, and quite succeeded in paying our rent. Partly through his recommendation, no doubt, we were successful from the beginning. I have never in my life been more kindly treated than by Messrs. Colby and Rich of the "Banner of Light;" and I am glad to acknowledge our success was very largely owing to their kindness, which has continued through our darkest hours.

About this time I experienced a new development of mediumship. I became what is called a "flower medium." It came in this way:—

Major H. C. Dane, a gentleman well known in Boston, who was interested in Spiritualism, and thereby somewhat in us as mediums, said one day at a *séance*, "I have been hearing about Mrs. Thayer (the celebrated flower medium). Do spirits ever bring flowers to *you?*"

"No: they never have."

"I think they would," he said, "if we should ask them. Let us try."

So we closed the doors and windows, and sat round a table in the centre of the room, in total darkness. Soon we got raps upon the table, then views on the wall, of beautiful forms and colors changing like those in a kaleidoscope. These manifestations continued for perhaps half an hour.

We were then told to join our hands on the table, one over the other, so as to form a pyramid, or sort of living voltaic pile, and to sing. I was then told to make a mental request, which I did, and immediately felt something fall upon my arm.

"Shall we strike a light?" I asked. Three raps answered, "Yes."

Major Dane lit the gas; and there lay on the table the loveliest calla-lily I ever saw, with a stalk eighteen inches long, and two great leaves.

Major Dane burst into tears, and, taking a memorandum-book from his pocket, opened to one of its pages, and gave it to me to read. It was a communication from his departed wife. It said in substance, "You are to become acquainted with a medium through whom I can come to you, and I will some time bring you a lily."

One day a gentleman, an entire stranger, had what he considered a wonderful *séance* with me. He did not tell me what had come to him; and I, as usual, was entirely unconscious of what the spirits might have spoken through me while I was in a trance. He said only, "If what has been told me proves to be true, I will let you know what it is." Six months after, a stranger came to see me. At least I did not recognize him ; but my spirit-control, " Dewdrop," did.

When I came out of my trance, he said, " Six months ago I came to you disguised, so that no one should know me." And then he mentioned what he had said. I remembered it.

" I was in Providence," he continued, " where I heard of you, and came to Boston to see you. I was interested in what seemed to me a valuable invention, but I did not wish you or any one to know me or my business. But your spirit at once discovered my name, my address, and my business. You described my invention, told me how to perfect it, and where to take it. You told me to take it to one Col. Cushman at Chicago, who, you said, would assist me to bring it out.

" This was direct and specific. I had some business which made it convenient for me to go to Chicago, and when there I inquired for Col. Cushman. I got acquainted with him. He helped me to bring out my invention ; and I made a scientific and financial success, for which I am largely indebted to you and the spirit who came to me through you."

Here was one instance, at least, of some use in Spiritualism, and of a communication having some positive and tangible value.

On taking leave, the gentleman thanked me warmly,

and put in my hand an envelope, which he said contained his address. When I opened it after his departure, I found his card, and with it a bank-note of a hundred dollars (about £20), which was by no means unwelcome, but which gave me much less pleasure than his account .of the success of our former *séance*. When we sat this time, "Dewdrop" came to us. Her first words to him were, "*What have you done with that wig and beard ?*"

It was, I think, in the year 1873, that we sat one day for flowers. It was in the same room; and there were present Miss Mattie Houghton, Major Dane, and myself. We were sitting round a table in a faint light, when the raps came, and spelled out the word "l-i-g-h-t." Turning up the gas, we found in front of each person a beautiful carnation-pink, and two of them in the centre of the table.

"For whom are the two flowers?" we asked.

"Dewdrop" said they were all given to her and "Winona," and they had made a fair distribution of them.

We thanked the spirits, and put all the pinks in a vase of water.

In another room in the same building was Mrs. Maggie Folsom, a test medium. Next morning she came to my room bringing a large bouquet of carnation-pinks. She said she had been told to leave them

in an obscure place in her room, and thought they
might be wanted for Mrs. Thayer's *séance.*

"See," she said, "here are five pinks missing. You
see the places from which they have been taken. Now
I am going to Mrs. Thayer's to see if I can find them
there."

"Maggie, perhaps you will not need to go so far,"
I said. "Come and see the pinks we had brought to
us last night." She found that our five pinks were
exactly like hers, and fitted the vacant places ; but how
they came from her locked room into mine is a question
that materialists must settle for themselves.

On a visit to Lawrence, I called on Mrs. Wise, a lady
who lived at Methuen, and was telling her some of these
experiences, when a friend of hers proposed that we
should sit together, and see if any thing would come to
us. She was very sceptical, but not too bigoted to seek
to know the truth. So we darkened the room, and sat,
another lady who had called making a third sitter.

When we had been sitting round a table a few minutes, signal-raps came to tell us the *séance* was over.
We opened the shutters to let in the light, and found
sixteen white daisies lying on the table, as if some one
had hastily grasped a handful in the fields.

Raps came as we were expressing our surprise, and,
when we asked who wished to talk with us, they spelled
out "D-e-w-d-r-o-p."

" For whom are the daisies, ' Dewdrop ' ? "

" A-n-y-b-o-d-y."

" Where did you get them ? "

" M-a-m-m-a W-e-b-s-t-e-r's." ,

On going home I found my dear mother in great perturbation.

" What *is* the matter, mamma dear ? " I asked.

" Oh ! my beautiful pots of daisies on the veranda," she said, " that I have watered so carefully. Some ruffianly little wretch has stolen nearly all of them."

" That's very mean," I said. But we made an examination, and found that the daisies brought to us fitted the broken stalks in my mother's plundered flower-pots.

These were slight things compared with some which came to my knowledge. Mrs. Thayer sitting with Madame Blavatsky had birds brought from Philadelphia to Boston, some four hundred miles distance. One day we met Mrs. Thayer when we were out walking, and arranged to have a *séance* with her the same evening. My mother was with me, and the table at which we sat was covered with flowers. I think there was a bushel of them brought into our closed and darkened room ; but we thought it very strange that there were none for mamma.

" Let us put out the light again," said Mrs. Thayer. " I think the influence is not exhausted." We put out the light, and in a moment mamma cried out, —

"Oh! there is something so cold and wet in my hand. Why, I believe it is my bird!"

"It is not your bird," said Mrs. Thayer. "A spirit who says her name is Susie, daughter of Dr. Smith, has brought for her father some moss and a pebble from her grave. She says, 'Take it to him with my love. If he will examine my grave, he will see whence the moss and pebble were taken.'"

We lighted the gas. Close to one of mamma's hands was a little yellow canary-bird, and in the other a piece of wood-moss and a pebble.

Dr. Smith lived with us. He had buried a beloved daughter Susan; and her grave was a hundred miles away, in the State of Maine. On her grave he had formed a large letter S. with pebbles, and filled in the interstices with moss. He was so impressed with the circumstances of the *séance*, and the message to him, that he carried pebble and moss to his daughter's grave, where he found two spaces in the S. which the pebble and the moss he carried with him exactly filled.

CHAPTER VIII.

REMARKABLE TESTS AND SPECIAL PROVIDENCES.

ALL this time my husband was giving *séances*, as I was also. He was sought by some, I by others. His control, " Winona," faithfully served or used him, as " Dewdrop " served and used me ; and both were quite sufficiently employed by our numerous visitors.

A Mr. Low residing at Chelsea, a suburb of Boston, came pretty regularly to Mr. Fletcher for *séances*, and was anxious to get materializations. " Winona " told him what to do as a preparation for such manifestations, — as to the purification of his body by bathing, a simple, pure diet, and the avoidance of any hurtful indulgences.

" Go where you please for materializations," said " Winona." " Don't tell me where, but tell me when, you are going, and I will tell you what I will try to do." So she fixed upon the kind of dress she would materialize in, and some things she would do, such as carrying flowers to persons present ; then, meeting him after he had this *séance*, with some to us unknown

40

medium, for materializations, coming to Mr. Fletcher, she would tell him every particular. These things were perfect tests of the genuineness of these manifestations.

Spirits out of their earthly bodies, with all their extraordinary powers, seem to have much the same characters and dispositions as in the matter-enveloped earth-life. Of course this must be the case, as their feelings, thoughts, and will constitute their personality.

Now, my little spirit-friend " Dewdrop " was as fond of Mr. Low as was Mr. Fletcher's friend " Winona ; " and they were naturally a little jealous of each other.

One day " Dewdrop " said to Mr. Low, " I am going to weave the most beautiful scarf in colors to-night. I shall wear it round my waist, and I will twine it all about you." But at the *séance*, instead of " Dewdrop " there came " Winona," wearing a colored scarf, who walked up to him, and said, " Mr. Low, I like you perzackly as well as ' Dewdrop ' does : so I thought I would come and do the scarf instead."

As she lifted the scarf over his head to twine it about him, " Dewdrop " whisked out of the cabinet, snatched the scarf from " Winona," and twined it round and round Mr. Low. " Dewdrop's " revenge was to carry off a bouquet which Mr. Low had brought for " Winona."

Next morning Mr. Low came to see Mr. Fletcher ;

but, finding him absent, he asked to have a sitting with me. "Dewdrop" came, and complained bitterly of "Winona."

"I don't care if she *is* a spirit : she is a thief!"

"Why, Dewey dear," said Mr. Low, "what strong language!"

"Well, I know that 'Winona' is your favorite ; but if she had stolen your scarf, as she did mine, *you* would call her a thief. And the worst of it is, I took her flowers and dematerialized them, and now she has got them in the spirit-world ; *for in that world we always get what belongs to us!*

"I was awfully angry at 'Winona' at first ; but one of the bright spirits came, and said, 'What you in the earth-life call mistakes are penances enforced upon you for wrong doing, and generally result in restoring the rights of those you have injured.'"

Sitting one day with a stranger, I experienced a cold shivering, and said to him, "You must go at once and take her body out of the ice. It is detaining her spirit, and subjecting it to horrible suffering. She cannot speak to you. She says it don't matter about carrying her body home : she would sooner be buried at Mount Auburn. Never again put the body of any recently deceased friend in ice. It is torturing to the spirit before it is finally released."

The *séance* lasted not more than ten minutes ; and,

when I came to myself, the gentleman said, "You have never seen me before."

"No."

"I know it, because I left this country when you were a child. I have heard enough in these few minutes to perfectly convince me of the truth of Spiritualism."

He had formerly resided in Massachusetts, where he had married. Some years before, he had removed to Wisconsin, where his wife had just died. He had her body packed in ice, and came with it to Boston. Leaving the corpse at the station, he came to consult a medium to see if he could come into communication with his wife, and ask her where she wished her body to be buried.

I do not give the names of persons who visited me as a medium, unless I have good reason to believe they will not object to such publicity.

One of my frequent visitors at this time was Mr. George Proctor, the editor of the "Gloucester (Massachusetts) Advertiser." One day a spirit who gave the name of "Lucy" came to him, and begged him to go to her father and mother at Gloucester, and give them a message from her; and, to convince them of her identity, he was to tell them from her certain particulars, — as when and in what way she died, and what arrangements were made for her funeral. She said they were not Spiritualists : but she wished them to know that the old home and her dear parents were sweet to her, and that she begged them not to shut their door against her, or grieve for her, or think of her as dead ; for the grief of friends on the earth marred the happiness of the spirit-life.

On his return to Gloucester, Mr. Proctor found Lucy's parents, gave them her message, and, to his own satisfaction, learned the accuracy of all the particulars given him.

Another gentleman from Gloucester, Mr. Robert Tibbets, who came to me an entire stranger, got some very convincing tests. At his first sitting, the spirit of a young girl who called herself " Maggie " came, and, speaking by my lips, said to him, —

" I lived in Gloucester, not far from your home ; and my father, whom you knew well, was drowned when sailing in a vessel in which you were interested. He left my mamma very poor ; and she has no fire and no food, and is very ill. I have prayed that I might help her. I went to her last night. She thought she had been dreaming. I said, ' Mamma, cheer up. Papa and I will manage to help you.'

" Now, I want you to go to my mamma. She lives at (giving street and number), and tell her that Maggie sent you. Tell her she is a medium ; and, if she will try to believe, I shall be able to show myself to her, as I did last night. Give her my love, and tell her that papa and I, under the care of her guardian angels, will see that she never wants."

This gentleman, an old and honored resident of Gloucester, on his return went at once to the address given him to carry out Maggie's commission. It was in one of the poorest quarters of the town; and he found the poor woman exactly as described, — ill in bed, suffering from cold, with no food, or fire, or hope. He sat down by the bed to further " try the spirits."

" You seem very badly off, my poor woman," he said.

" Yes. My husband was drowned at sea, and I had no other help. I took in washing, and managed to get on while my daughter lived. She gathered the clothes, and carried them home for me; but when she died, three months ago, my health failed, and I have come to this.

" Sir, do you believe in angels? I do. Last night my little Maggie came to me in my dreams. But God must have permitted it. She said, ' Cheer up, darling mother. Papa and I will help you.' "

From that day until her death, eighteen months afterward, this friend took care that Maggie's mother wanted for nothing.

Maggie had said to him, " Every penny you give to mamma shall be returned to you tenfold." And from that day he said that he prospered more than ever, and every thing he touched seemed to turn to gold.

One day a gentleman called upon us, and asked if we knew the address of a certain medium he wished to find. We did not even know her name.

That night there came some signal-raps; and in answer to our questions, when we called over the letters of the alphabet, the raps spelled out, —

"I am 'Honto,' and I belong to Mrs. ——.

"Oh, you are 'Honto!'" I said. "Then, perhaps you will be so kind as to give me your medium's address for a gentleman who has been inquiring for her to-day."

"Honto" rapped out the required address, and also this message to us: —

"Take this money to my medium, who is in great need, and tell the gentleman who asked for her address to-day, that his money has not been stolen by one of the servants, as he supposes, but that we have taken it from his purse; and if he will call upon my medium to-morrow, at four o'clock, he shall have the money returned to him. Take this money to my medium at once, and you shall have the explanation of our apparently strange proceedings."

As this message was finished, a twenty-dollar bank-note fell upon the carpet at our feet.

We wrote at once to the gentleman, giving him the

address he sought, and "Honto's" message, and then called a carriage, and drove to the residence of the medium. On our arrival we found a cart before the door. The poor medium had been unable to pay her rent, and the cart had come to take away her furniture. The money we had brought her paid the rent, and the cart went empty away. The much-relieved woman told us that she had written to her friends for help, but for some reason had got no answer. But the expected letter and help came before the gentleman from whom "Honto" had borrowed the money called, as requested. She handed him the money; but, now that he knew her situation, he refused to receive it.

Such special providences are managed by our spirit-friends in multitudes of cases in which we do not suspect their agency.

There are a few instances which I remember; but a multitude, marked by no special circumstance, have faded from my mind. It is easy to see how I should remember such a case as that of Mr. Wilson, Vice-President of the United States. On his last visit to Boston, he came to consult Mr. Fletcher about his health. The controlling spirits gave him a diagnosis of his case, and told him that he could not remain six months longer in this life, unless he retired from all active work. To make their advice more impressive, they gave him some striking tests, showing their knowledge of some details of his life.

Mr. Wilson, a grand, self-made man, of whom Massachusetts was and is justly proud, said to me, —

" Well, Mrs. Fletcher, I suppose I must go and make my will. I don't know why I should try to stay here. There seems to be a great deal more of reality in the spirit-world than in this. Heaven is full of certainties, and for me death has no terrors."

These were the last words I heard him utter. In three months he had gone to test the realities of the world of spirits.

It was, I think, in 1875 that a stranger came to me for a medical diagnosis, — a tall, strong man, who seemed to be possessed of considerable magnetic power. He was, I found, employed as a medical rubber by a gentleman on Beacon Hill, Boston, who had been given up by his physicians. The diagnosis given by my spirit-guides quite differed from that of the physicians; but, as " doctors disagree," we need not be surprised when spirits differ from doctors. The medical rubber was directed how to treat his patient. He was told to use magnetized water and magnetized paper, and was shown how to magnetize them. Under these instructions he became a strong, effective magnetizer, or mesmerist: and his patient in a few weeks — I think three weeks — happily recovered. For three months I examined the cases of his patients, and gave, or rather the spirits gave through me, directions for their treatment; for which I received no compensation but that of being the means of relieving suffering, which is the best of all.

This mesmeric healer whose work I thus assisted was the James McGeary, *alias* "Doctor Mack," who afterward became one of the most virulent of my persecutors, and whose name, as of one returning evil for good, must, to my great regret, often appear in the course of this narrative.

CHAPTER IX.

WE had taken the house No. 7 Montgomery Place
until January, 1876, where we went on, day by day,
with our interesting but arduous work, which lasted all
day, and often deep into the night, and which, by
bringing us into contact with so many and often so
discordant spheres, and with persons in various states
of physical weakness and nervous disorder, wore upon
us. I bore it better than my husband, having a more
vigorous constitution. The worry of family troubles,
to which I have made allusion, hurt him more, perhaps,
than his work. New-England winters are very severe.
His lungs and heart were affected, and his life was
despaired of.

On the 7th of January, 1877, " Winona " came to
me, and said, " You had better get my medium's box
ready. He is going to London." This announcement
was a surprise to me. I could not credit it. Mr.
Fletcher seemed too ill to travel. But "Winona" per-

50

sisted in her assertion. "I tell you it is all that will save his life," she said; "and you must pack his box."

When Mr. Fletcher came out of the trance in which he had been speaking for "Winona," I told him what she had said. He laughed at the idea, and said it was "some of her nonsense." "I am as likely to take a trip to the moon as to London."

On the 8th of January, at about ten A.M., Mr. George Smith, a friend of ours, called to say good-by to us. He said, "I am going with my family to London." I told him what "Winona" had said, and suggested that she had made a mistake, and meant him instead of Mr. Fletcher. He said he had not known that he was going himself until the previous day.

That evening he brought his wife to say good-by to us. We four had a farewell *séance*. The spirits insisted that my husband should go to England. Our friends wanted to take him with them.

"Are you willing to let him go?" they asked me. "Let us know in the morning."

So we discussed the matter seriously between ourselves and also with our spirit-friends. There was the risk to an invalid of a winter-voyage. It was very hard to think of parting with him. But the spirits said he must go, that it would save his life, and that, moreover, he had a great work to do in England.

At ten A.M. on the 9th of January, our friend Mr.
Smith came for his answer. I packed my husband's
trunk, and on the 10th he left for London. They had
a good voyage; travelled together over the Continent,
and went to Egypt, and thence to Jerusalem and the
Holy Land; and Mr. Fletcher was treated by these excellent friends with unremitting kindness. The change,
the securing of rest, the strange and interesting countries, and the soft, dry atmosphère and sunshine of
Egypt and Palestine, restored his health.

While in Egypt, Mr. Smith, one day while out walking, lost a packet which he carried in the breast-
pocket of his coat, containing a considerable sum of
money in Bank-of-England notes. He missed the
packet when he came to the hotel, but had no idea
how or where he had lost it. He said nothing about it,
but soon after proposed to have a *séance.* "Winona"
came, and said to him, "Mr. Smith, you are awfully
worried about something. I know what it is. You
have lost some money. Don't fret about it. I will
find it, and bring it to you."

After the *séance* Mr. Smith went to bed, and found
the packet of money under his pillow. This did not
in the least lessen our obligations to our good friends;
but I think it had a pleasant effect on all of us, which
the reader perhaps can appreciate better than I can
describe.

Spiritualists are often asked what is the use of spirit-manifestations. The first and highest and all-important use is *to prove that spirits exist*, that Spiritualism is a reality, that there is no truth in materialism, that we are all to live on, and to show at least the probability that we are to live forever. Spirits may show us the means of health; they are often able to assuage our pains, and cure our diseases; in various ways they console and comfort us; they not seldom contribute to our material prosperity. But what are all these things to the demonstrations they are able to give us of *the sublime fact of individual immortality!*

In May, 1877, Mr. Fletcher returned to London, where he was told he must stay, and do his work. He took rooms in Southampton Row, and began to give free *séances;* but the crowd that came to him soon compelled him to fix a price. "The laborer is worthy of his hire;" and "they who serve the altar must live by the altar." If lawyers, doctors, and clergymen are paid, why not mediums?

As soon as he was settled to his work in London, Mr. Fletcher urged me to come to him; but I thought it better to wait until there was some assurance of success. He might return to Boston: there was the risk of failure. But in June he telegraphed to me to "Come." And very shortly afterward I joined him; and we lived at No. 2 Vernon Place, Bloomsbury, London.

The "Spiritualist," a weekly paper which for years did much good service to the cause of Spiritualism, and which also did us good service for a time, and then turned, with a great, and to me unaccountable, bitterness against us, announced in its issue of May 11, 1877, that "Next Monday week Mr. Fletcher, trance-medium, of the United States, will give a trance-address for the first time in this country in public, at one of Mrs. Weldon's weekly concerts at the Langham Hall, Portland Place, London."

The same paper of May 18, 1877, said, "If, instead of a trance-address, Mr. Fletcher could give to a large audience the evidence of spirit identity which he does to a small one, he would awaken considerable interest."

These evidences were soon given, not only to large audiences in Langham Hall and the Cavendish Rooms, but afterward to the still larger ones at Steinway Hall. Nearly every number of the "Spiritualist" during the year 1877 contained reports of public addresses or private *séances* given by Mr. Fletcher, and the highest possible testimony to the genuineness and value of his manifestations.

Brought into a circle of twelve or fifteen persons, — all strangers to him, some foreigners, or persons from distant parts of England, — he passed quickly into the trance-condition, and, controlled by "Winona," gave to each, in turn, the most convincing evidences of the personal presence and identity of their departed friends. The same was done for many persons also, under the probably more difficult conditions of a large audience in a public hall.

The first public lectures or trance-addresses, after those at Mrs. Weldon's concerts, were given in the Cavendish Rooms, Mortimer Street, Cavendish Square. Later, these meetings were continued in Steinway Hall, a larger place, in a more fashionable locality, near Portman Square.

CHAPTER X.

EARLY in the spring of 1879, needing more room and better accommodations than we were able to find in lodgings, we took a lease of a good house (but by no means the "palatial mansion" it has been called in the newspapers), No. 22 Gordon Street, Gordon Square. It seemed to us central, accessible, and healthy; the many neighboring squares giving us a purer air than is found in many parts of London.

It is proper for me to say here, that I had never been a professional medium in London. I gave *séances* only to intimate friends. Only once had I spoken in public, — at the celebration of the Anniversary of Spiritualism, at the Cavendish Rooms, April 2, 1879.

Among the public testimonies to the reality of Mr. Fletcher's mediumship, and the value of its manifestations, that of Mr. ALFRED RUSSELL WALLACE, the celebrated naturalist, will be to many persons of the highest interest. In the "Spiritualist" of Jan. 25, 1878, Mr. Wallace says, "My first sitting with Mr. Fletcher, a

56

few weeks ago, carried to my mind A FULLER CON-
VICTION OF THE REALITY OF SPIRIT-LIFE THAN ALL THE
PHYSICAL PHENOMENA I HAVE EVER WITNESSED."

It was such testimony as this, from a man of the
highest scientific reputation since the death of Charles
Darwin in England, which should have been given to
the jury that found a verdict of guilty against us both
at the Old Bailey. Mr. Wallace and a score of witnesses besides — of similar character, and some of
almost equal reputation — would have given similar
evidence. My feëd defenders, for reasons best known
to themselves, refused to call them. And that was
called a trial, in which my witnesses were uncalled,
and I was condemned unheard. But I am getting in
advance of my story, and must try to be patient to the
end.

The Sunday evening meetings at Steinway Hall were
very successful, perhaps *too* successful. It was a surprise to the public that we should be admitted into a
place so elegant and so aristocratic. The Hall was at
first refused; but influence enough was brought to bear
to induce the proprietors to reconsider the matter, and
we had ever after their cordial co-operation. The Anniversary of Spiritualism was celebrated there during
the progress of my trial in 1881.

I come now to the most painful, but most necessary,
portion of my story, — the events which led to our

prosecution and trial, and my imprisonment. Painful
as they are in many ways, justice demands that they
should be faithfully and fully related. The public has
had one side of the story, published in all the newspapers. I have to give, as best I can, the other side
of that story. If any editor of any newspaper in England takes the least notice of *my* side of the story, or
even admits that there is another story than that given
to the public on my " trial," conviction, and sentence,
and in the leading articles that echoed and amplified
the sentence, I shall be very happily disappointed.

I make my appeal to the sense of justice, said to be
so strong in Englishmen, with but little hope, because
so far I have had so little evidence of its existence.

In April, 1879, after we had taken the house No. 22
Gordon Street, of which we were to have possession
on the 25th of June, a Mr. Hart-Davies, residing at
Farquhar Lodge, Upper Norwood, who had been advised
by some friends to consult Mr. Fletcher, came to him,
and asked him to visit his wife, who was an invalid
requiring treatment; and, as she was too ill to come to
Gordon Street, he engaged Mr. Fletcher to go and see
her twice a week at Farquhar Lodge, for which the
price was to be three guineas per visit.

He went at the time appointed, and found a pale,
delicate-looking lady, with a highly nervous organiza-

tion, who appeared to take a great interest in Spiritualism, and told him that she had been in the habit
of seeing angels or departed spirits from her childhood,
and that she often held sweet communion with her
departed mother.

Mr. Fletcher made a clairvoyant examination of her
case; and she felt so much benefited by his magnetic
or mesmeric treatment, that she begged him to come
and see her every day, instead of twice a week, as
arranged for with her husband.

Mr. Fletcher did not see any need of such frequent
visits, as they would interfere with his other engage-
ments, and told her that it would be better that he
should come twice a week, which he continued to do
until the middle of June.

At Mr. Fletcher's second visit to Mrs. Hart-Davies
she told him of her domestic difficulties. She said she
was very unhappy. She was not living with her
husband as his wife: they were virtually separated;
because, from his past and present habits and his
debilitated condition, he could not be her husband.
Entering very fully upon her personal history, of
which, as we found later on, she made no secret, she
told him how her mother had forced her, at the age of
sixteen, to marry a man whom she detested, by whom
she had one child, and whom she left on account of his
immoralities. Her boy, she said, had inherited the

bad traits of his father, and was so entirely beyond her control, that she had allowed his father to take charge of him.

We found, later on, that much of this story was false, and that her first husband had sued for a divorce from her as an adulteress; which suit had been decided in his favor.

In Mrs. Hart-Davies' conversations with my husband she expressed a strong desire to see me, because he was doing her so much good. Mr. Fletcher told her that I made no visits. She then asked permission to write to me, and did write nearly every day until June. She often sent me flowers, and wished me to consider her a personal friend in whom I was also interested. Naturally I felt a sympathy for one who had suffered so much, and I was glad that my husband was treating her so successfully that she seemed to be steadily gaining in health from every visit he made her.

About the middle of June Mr. Hart-Davies invited me to dine with them, and spend the day. Mrs. Hart-Davies telegraphed the same invitation to us, which we accepted. He met us at the station, and attended upon me to Farquhar Lodge, where I for the first time saw Mrs. Hart-Davies. She warmly embraced me, expressed her gratitude for Mr. Fletcher's treatment and all his kindness to her, and said and did every thing she could to show her friendly feelings to us both. There was a *fête* at the Crystal Palace, where we spent the day, and dined; and as there was a great crowd, and it began to rain, we accepted an invitation to spend the night with our hosts at Farquhar Lodge.

The next day (Sunday) Mr. and Mrs. Hart-Davies came into town, and went with us to Mr. Fletcher's lecture, at Steinway Hall. By this time Mrs. Hart-Davies and I had had a good deal of conversation together. I found her intelligent and accomplished, and have seldom taken so much interest in any one of whom I had known so little. From circumstances in my own past experience I could sympathize with her in some of her troubles. I pitied her misfortunes,— deserted or abused by all her friends and relatives, living so uncomfortably with her husband, and in every way so desolate.

I wished to help her, and make her life more pleasant to her. She begged that she might come and see us often in London. I was too much occupied to see her always, but did see her about twice a week. Both Mr. and Mrs. Hart-Davies became seat-holders at Steinway Hall, and regular attendants at the Sunday meetings.

Mr. Fletcher was also, at this time, giving lectures at Mrs. Weldon's Institution for Orphans at Tavistock House, formerly the residence of Charles Dickens, where Mrs. Hart-Davies also went; so that I saw her about four times a week.

She seemed to become more and more attached to us, more and more fond of both of us. She talked with me very freely about her domestic troubles. She made bitter complaints of her second and present husband, who, she said, was an ignoramus; who had squandered his money; who had pawned her jewels, and spent the proceeds in debauchery; who drank to excess; and who was in no way fit to be her husband.

I was surprised and shocked at some of these revelations. I wondered how she could ever have married a man so little suited to her position, education, and habits. She said that she had hastily, inconsiderately married him for pity, and not for love. He was madly in love with her, and she was very desolate. She had sacrificed herself for him.

Afterward I heard another and a very different story, of the truth of which I shall give the necessary proofs. While living with her first husband in South America, she became acquainted with a young Swedish engineer, with whom she became very intimate. After her return to England, and after her divorce, — in respect to which he was not the co-respondent, — she wrote to him that she had come into a great property, and had many offers of marriage, but that she wished to know if he still loved her. Her friend replied in substance that he was not a marrying man. She invited him, however, to come and see her at Hampton Court; and he accepted her invitation.

One question must come into the mind of every reader, as it has so often into mine: —

Why had I no warning, no perception, no revelation, of the real character of this woman? Why did not our guardian spirits tell us all about her, as they did about so many others? It is easy to ask such questions, and impossible to answer them.

"'There's a divinity that shapes our ends,
Rough-hew them how we will."

We are protected from some misfortunes; others fall upon us. We are guided and guarded; but great calamities, or what seem to be such, come upon us without warning. My husband and I were both fascinated with this woman; and neither of us had any perception of her real character, nor were we in any way warned against her. Our guardian spirits were either as much blinded as we, or they were prevented, for a time, from giving us any information.

CHAPTER XI.

THE STORY OF THE JEWELS AND THE DEED OF GIFT.

ONE night when I was ill, and not able to go to the lecture at Tavistock House, Mr. Fletcher returned with a bouquet from Mrs. Hart-Davies, around which she had tied a lace handkerchief which had belonged to her mother, with this message: "Tell Bertie that I am mamma's little carrier-pigeon, and that I send this handkerchief and these flowers with mamma's love and mine."

This was the first present of any value she had made me, and for this there was an obvious reason. Up to this time she had paid Mr. Fletcher only five pounds for all his visits to her upon the agreement to pay him three guineas a week; and this five pounds was all the money she ever paid.

Soon after sending the bouquet she came to see me, and expressed great sympathy with me in my illness. After some expressions of affection she said, "Will you do me a great favor? I have not been able to pay Mr. Fletcher the money I owe him for all his

64

visits and his kindness to me; but I want to give you something I prize very much, that belonged to mamma."

Saying this, she took from her pocket a box containing a necklace of amethysts. They were of no great value, but were accepted in kindness, as they were offered. This was, I think, in the month of July; and up to this time the only jewels of hers I had ever seen were a heart-shaped pendant of diamonds, and ear-jewels to match, which she frequently wore.

On the night that Mr. Fletcher brought me the bouquet and lace handkerchief from Tavistock House, he said that Mr. and Mrs. Hart-Davies were going to leave Farquhar Lodge because they could not afford to keep it, and that Mrs. Hart-Davies had told him that she had an extensive wardrobe which had belonged to her mother, which was packed in boxes, and some furs, which would spoil if packed; but if she could only find some friend who had house-room, so as to keep them for her, she would be glad to leave them.

We had plenty of room, and I saw no objection to our taking charge of her things. There was box-room and a wine-cellar quite empty. The china vases, etc., could be placed in our rooms, and the furs properly taken care of.

She came to see us in a few days, when we arranged what was to be done to protect the clothing from damp, the furs from moths, and how the china should be placed so that she could see it when she called. I consented to take charge of her things on the condition that I should not be held responsible for loss or damage. She wrote a paper which held me free from any responsibility for careless servants, fire, or thieves; and I consented to receive and store her things. Nothing was said of jewels, and I had no knowledge of any but those I have mentioned.

About the last of July she seemed ill, and had a cough. A weakness of the chest had compelled her for several years to spend the winters in a warmer climate. She complained of her husband's drinking, and his cruel treatment of her. In the first week in August she came, and said she had been frightfully ill, and believed that her husband had attempted to poison her. He was deeply in debt, she said. He had borrowed all the money he could of his brother, and had pawned some of her valuable jewels for two hundred and fifty pounds, and still needed two hundred pounds more, and was teasing her for more jewels; but she had refused to let him have them. The night before, he had come home in a state of intoxication, and brought her a glass of port wine. She drank it, and was violently ill all night, — so much so, that she suspected poison, and found a white sediment in the glass. He sat in his room all night, intoxicated; and he allowed an escape of gas in the hall.

She declared that she could not and would not
endure this horrible life any longer: she would separate herself from her husband, and was determined to
leave Farquhar Lodge.

A few days after this conversation I received a
note from her, asking me to come to her at Farquhar
Lodge. Not feeling able to accept the invitation, I
asked Mr. Fletcher to write to her. I soon received a
telegram from Mr. Hart-Davies, saying that his wife
was very ill, and begging me to come and see her.

I went as quickly as possible. She said her husband had been drunk again, and had treated her most
brutally. He had even beaten her, she said: he had
actually struck her three times.

I was probably too credulous in believing these
stories. Mr. Hart-Davies had always seemed to me
a good-natured fellow, and very devoted to his wife.
Her greatest complaint against him was, that his vices
had reduced him to a condition of physical weakness
that made him an unsatisfactory husband. Looking
back upon the case, I can have no doubt that she was
a victim of a disease of quite a different nature, and
which sometimes gives great trouble to physicians.

Before receiving the articles which Mrs. Hart-Davies
wished us to store for her, we required that her husband, as the real owner of all his wife's property,
should either call upon us, or write and ask us to

receive it. He wrote and also called, and said he had heard of the arrangement, and would consider it a great kindness. We showed him the box-room and empty wine-cellar, and he seemed very grateful for our kindness to his wife.

This visit was on or about the 1st of August, 1879. About the middle of August, Mrs. Hart-Davies came, bringing a small travelling-bag, and said to me, "Mrs. Fletcher, I am going to ask a great favor of you. I want to make my will. I love you both better than anybody in this world. I have brought some things I wish to give you, not only for the love I bear you both, but because I want what I have to go for the support of Spiritualism, and to help your work. If you will accept of this free offering, you will be doing me the greatest possible favor."

I thanked her for her good feeling to us and to our work; but I said, "My dear, you have other persons to consider. There is your son."

"He is abundantly provided for. His father is immensely rich."

"But there is your brother and his wife."

"He is an equal heir with me to my mother's property, and his wife I detest. I could never rest in my grave if she had any thing that belonged to mamma. Besides, the jewels are not safe in the house. I have no peace about them."

"But," I said, "we have no safe. Our house might be robbed at any time. The best thing to do is for you to put them in some bank for safe-keeping."

"That is not what I want. If I live, I want to share the jewels with you, as if we were two sisters; and if I die I want you to have them."

Then she opened her bag; and showed me the jewels.

"How do you know," I asked, "whether your mamma would like to have you give them to me?"

She said she had had a vision the night before, in which her mother had appeared to her, and expressed her wishes.

I said, "Come, here is a good chance for a test. Mr. Fletcher knows nothing about them. Let's put the bag away, and call for him. If your mamma will come, we shall see what she has to say about it."

I sent for Mr. Fletcher. He came, and soon went into a trance; and Mrs. Hart-Davies recognized her mother as the spirit speaking through him, and said, —

"You came to me last night, mamma."

"Yes, my child."

"Do you approve of what I wish to do, mamma?"

"My child, the jewels are your own to do with as you please, — to let your husband have them, to throw into the street, to give as you wish. They are absolutely yours."

Mrs. Hart-Davies then brought out the jewels as

she testified at my trial, and laid them on Mr. Fletcher's lap. He, still controlled by the spirit of her mother, took up the jewels one by one, examined them, gave the names of their makers, saying, " I got this from " such a one; and gave, in short, a series of marvellous tests, which only a Spiritualist, or one who has witnessed such manifestations, can understand.

When Mr. Fletcher came out of his trance, the jewels were still lying in his lap; and she told him, as she had told me, what she wished to do with them. He said, " It is very good of you to wish to give them to Bertie, but of course she cannot accept such a gift. If you choose to wear them together, I see no objection, only that we have no safe place to keep them." But he left the matter to me, and Mrs. Hart-Davies insisted on leaving the bag in my keeping.

A short time before this, Mrs. Hart-Davies had spoken to me about some difficulty she had about some property in New York, and asked me if I knew any American lawyer who would understand about it. I told her that Mr. Morton, a Boston lawyer who was then staying with us, would know all about it. He was a gentleman of excellent character and good standing, and might be able to do what she would require, or would know of some one in New York who would attend to it. I asked her to stay and dine with us, and be introduced to Mr. Morton.

Mrs. Hart-Davies staid to dinner, and became very friendly with Mr. Morton, whom she called upon several times afterward on matters of business.

She used to wear at this period, at the Steinway Hall meetings, a necklace of pearls with a diamond pendant, and a pair of diamond ear-rings. One day I mentioned that I had been invited to a dinner-party the next Sunday evening. On the Sunday morning her servant came with a little box and a note from her, which she had been expressly ordered to give into my own hands, and refused to intrust to my servant. I went down into the hall to receive it, and the servant left before I had time to read the note. It said, —

" I send you a little souvenir of mamma and myself, which I beg you will wear at the dinner."

I wrote to thank her, saying I would wear the jewels with pleasure, but that they were much too valuable for me to accept as a present, and would be returned to her at the earliest opportunity.

This was about the middle of August, 1879. She continued her interviews with Mr. Morton, of which I knew more than I might have done otherwise by means of a curious habit she had of almost never having any money, so that we generally had to pay her cab-fares.

One day in the last week of August, at the end of a long interview with Mr. Morton, I was sent for and went to his study.

" I have sent for you," he said, " to read to you a paper I have been preparing at the request of Mrs. Hart-Davies." And he proceeded to read the following deed of gift: —

To Whomsoever it may Concern.

Upon the death of my mother, Anne Heurtley of Hampton Court House, Hampton Court, County of Middlesex, England, she left to me, Julia Anne Theodora Hart-Davies, her daughter, a certain quantity of jewelry for my own use and control. I the said Julia Anne Theodora Hart-Davies, now residing in London, in consideration of the love I bear to Susie Willis Fletcher of Boston, United States, America (now residing in . London), and for the many kindnesses shown by her to me, and for other good and sufficient considerations, hereby give and relinquish to the said Susie Willis Fletcher the said jewels which my mother gave me, for her own separate use and control, and have made this writing: first, that she may be fully protected in the possession of the said jewels; secondly, that I have made the gift of my own free will; and, further, to say that she has consented to accept the jewels, only upon my earnest request and solicitation, and upon assurance that it is my earnest wish and desire she should do so. The said jewels were very dear to my mother, and doubly precious to me; and I have made the above disposition of them in full conformity with my own wishes, setting forth my reasons for so doing, not only for her protection, but also for my own; and that at any time, now or in the future, there may be no question as to the right of the said Susie Willis Fletcher to the within-named jewels or property; the said gift being made by me without any reservation, with a desire she may wear the jewels during her lifetime, and make such further disposition of them as she may think proper. Furthermore, in view of my experience with trustees and other parties since the death of my mother, I have preferred to dispose of the property in the manner above indicated and during my lifetime, rather than it should be disposed of in a way repugnant to my own nature by those who might obtain possession of it upon my decease, or by disposing of it by will, as I might have done but for this gift of conveyance. In witness whereof, I have hereunto set my hand and seal this 25th day of August, 1870.

(Signed)
　　　　　JULIET ANNE THEODORA HART-DAVIES.

Witness:
FRANCIS MORTON.

I listened to the reading of this document, and said, "It is very kind; but I think Mrs. Davies will get her health, and live to wear these jewels herself."

With characteristic impulsiveness she knelt at my feet, and begged me to accept them. She said, "I am going to France. I feel sure I shall not live long, and I shall be happy if I know that they will be used as I wish them to be."

Mr. Morton, who had drawn up the paper at her solicitation, did not at all favor the project. He said, "I see a serious objection to your receiving these things. You are known as Spiritualists and mediums, and you will risk a prosecution like that of Home (alluding to the chancery case of Lyon vs. Home, in which the well-known medium D. D. Home was ordered to restore sixty thousand pounds forced upon him by a rich Jewish widow-lady, who, after receiving back the uttermost farthing of her own gifts, kept the rich laces which had been the property of Mr. Home's deceased wife).

" Knowing this danger," Mr. Morton continued, " I shall refuse to witness this deed until she has sworn solemnly, that in making it she has not been influenced by spirits or mortals."

She rose to her feet, raised her hand, and said, " *I solemnly swear that I have not been influenced by spirits or mortals.*" The document was then signed and witnessed.

The paper was then given to me. I held it a moment in my hand, and said, " I think Mrs. Davies will recover her health, and live a long time. I have no objection to keep these things for her if she desires it, but here is the paper (giving it to Mr. Morton). Do you keep it, so that, at any time Mrs. Davies wishes it to be destroyed, you can burn it." Mr. Morton took the paper; and I never saw it again until after we were arrested in America for stealing these jewels, or obtaining them by false pretences, when we telegraphed to Mr. Morton, who was then in Paris, to send over the deed of gift.

Four days afterward I received the following letter from Mrs. Davies : —

UPPER NORWOOD, Aug. 29, 1879.

DEAREST MRS. FLETCHER, — After my repeated and earnest solicitation, you have very kindly and generously permitted me to send my jewels, clothes, boxes, and sundry other articles, etc., to your house, where you have undertaken the charge of their safe keeping; these said jewels, clothes, boxes, and sundry other articles, being my sole and absolute property, and free from claim or interference from my husband, or any other person. I am aware that I have therefore the perfect right to deal with them in whatever manner I may think fit. Dearest friend, out of gratitude for all the unselfish and inestimable services of friendly kindness shown by you and your excellent husband repeatedly towards myself, thereby causing my love to reap daily blessings, I wish to notify you that it is my express wish and ardent desire to make over to you, as a humble and free gift from myself to yourself, the whole of the property above mentioned, and that it shall henceforth become by right of gift your sole and absolute property, to have, to hold, to enjoy, and ultimately to bequeath or dispose of as you shall of your own free choice deem suitable. These my intentions and acts I have purposely thus declared upon paper in order to effectually preclude any risk of future hostile dispute about your possession or right to the said property, and as a guaranty, moreover, that the declaration made by me to yourself is purely voluntary, and is evolved out of a spirit of the deepest affection and gratitude towards yourself and your husband, — you, who daily labor for the happiness and spiritual welfare of your fellow-creatures. May God shower over your two lives an ever-increasing meed of divine benediction! Such is the prayer of your faithful and devoted friend.

(Signed)

JULIET ANNE THEODORA HART-DAVIES.

This letter, she falsely claimed on the trial, had had been written partly by herself, and partly drafted by Mr. Morton. He had prepared the formal body of the letter, which she had copied, adding, as she said, " the head and tail."

CHAPTER XII.

Mrs. Hart-Davies had arranged with her husband to leave their residence at Upper Norwood, and come to London, where she had engaged apartments at No. 2 Vernon Place, Bloomsbury. She wished to pack her wardrobe herself, but was too ill to do so, and telegraphed to me to come and see that it was properly done. The things were hastily packed together, to be assorted afterward.

They came to live in Vernon Place in September, 1879. Mrs. Davies was ill; and I called to see her, and helped to settle her rooms. She came to Gordon Street every day, and had her magnetic treatment from Mr. Fletcher, always staying to luncheon or dinner, or to talk with me. She was still complaining of her husband, who, she said, had grown so brutal, that she had arranged with her landlady to come herself, instead of the servant, if the bell was rung violently, as he constantly came home intoxicated.

From the first she had wished to live with us; her

77

chief reason being that Mr. Fletcher would be near to assist her in her frequent and sudden attacks of illness. But she also professed to take great interest in Spiritualism. In July these intimations of a desire to live with us had become more frequent. I told her that I was too much occupied to give her the attention she required, and that Mr. Fletcher needed all my care. I opposed her idea of coming to live with us, but it was not from dislike. I was really fond of her. She was a slender blonde, very affectionate, intelligent, and with many talents. She had, certainly, grave faults of character and manners; but I attributed much of these to her unhappy conditions, and a state of nervous disease. I pitied her very much, and pitied her faults as well as her misfortunes.

One day toward the last of September she came in a cab, without her hat, and was shown into the drawing-room. The servant who came for me said that Mrs. Davies was so ill that she had taken her a cup of coffee. When I went to her, she seemed to be in a fit of hysterics. As soon as she could speak, she said her husband had got worse and worse until there had come a crisis. He had beaten her frightfully. She showed me her discolored wrists, and her dress almost torn off her. She said he had threatened to kill her, that she dared not go back to him, and she begged that she might stay with us, if only for a few days.

I sent for Mr. Fletcher to consult with him about it.
He said, that, if she were in danger, of course she
could remain, and tried to calm her excitement. I
thought she was nervously excited, and had exaggerated the matter, and proposed to go home with her.
However, she staid to dinner, and seemed much better.
The servants noticed the improvement; and at eleven
o'clock Mr. Fletcher went home with her. The house
was perfectly quiet, and her husband had gone to bed.
Mr. Fletcher talked with Mrs. Mayo, her landlady,
about the matter. He did not want any misunderstand-
ings, and thought, that, if there were no danger, Mrs.
Davies had better stay with her husband. Mrs. Mayo
smiled at the idea of danger. Evidently she had not
taken that view of the matter.

In about three days Mrs. Hart-Davies came again,
and with another fearful story.

"Oh! what do you think?" she said. "Mr. Hart-
Davies is plotting to put me into a lunatic-asylum."

"Nonsense! Impossible!"

"No. It is actually true."

Her story, told in her excited manner, was, that,
several weeks before, she had had a note from a friend,
warning her of a plot to secure her property. That
day she had a craving for some lager-beer, and sent a
servant to a public-house to get some. When the servant came with the beer, she said she had heard Mr.

Hart-Davies talking with two men at the public-house about her. One of them said, "How had we better do it? Suppose you ask her to take a drive, and send for a cab, and then" — But Mr. Davies said, "I had rather not be seen in it. You must manage it yourselves."

As soon as Mrs. Hart-Davies had heard this story, she came at once to tell us. She would never go back. If she could not stay with us, she would go to a hotel.

Mr. Fletcher could not think of turning her out of doors, and said she could stay with us, and he would send word to her landlady in Vernon Place. She preferred to go herself, and give notice that she was leaving; and Mr. Fletcher accompanied her. On the way she told him that she must soon be off to her usual winter-residence at Tours. He advised her to go at once, so as not to have the trouble of a double change, and suggested that she could come to us on her return in the spring, if she still wished to do so.

She proposed to come and stay with us all day, and go to Vernon Place to sleep; and finally it was so arranged.

Talking the matter over with my husband, I remembered that Mrs. Davies had an aunt. Why not make her a visit? Next morning I went to her, and proposed this as better for her own sake. She said she hated her aunt, but would write to her. The answer she got was not very gracious. Her aunt would not receive her. She did not approve of her conduct, and thought her present husband was much too indulgent. She might visit, but could not live with her; and she might be obliged to reduce her allowance.

Mrs. Hart-Davies showed us this letter. I advised her to go to her aunt, and tell her all the circumstances. She went, and then wrote us the most urgent letter, asking us to allow her to immediately return.

When she returned from this visit to her aunt, we thought it necessary to give her the protection of our home, to which it had been agreed she should come on her return from France; but we requested her to send for her trustee, the Rev. James Burroughs, vicar of Hampton. He came to see us, and we told him the circumstances which had compelled her to seek our protection. Mrs. Davies said to him, "Mr. and Mrs. Fletcher are the best friends I have in this world. I have given them all my little belongings, and their house is henceforth to be my home."

Whatever Mr. Burroughs may have thought of this arrangement, he did not withhold his consent to it; and so it was settled.

When, in the course of my trial, I went to see Mr. Burroughs, who was suffering with apoplexy, at Hampton; he said to me, "Mrs. Fletcher, don't give yourself the least uneasiness. My testimony will set this all right; for when I called on Mrs. Hart-Davies in September, at Vernon Place, your photos were on the mantel, and she spoke of you as being the best friends she had in the world. She said you moved in the most fashionable society, and she gave me a list of distinguished and royal personages who were among your visitors. She said, " I am going to do every thing in my power in order to live with them, so that I can get into the society I like, and from which I have been debarred by the character and habits of my husband."

" I fancied," continued Mr. Burroughs, " that, from Juliet's romancing and fault-finding ways, her friends the Fletchers would have a hard time of it."

This Mr. Burroughs was ready to testify; and this evidence, like so much beside, constituting the real facts of the case, was shut out by the determination of my counsel to call no witnesses.

On the 1st of October Mrs. Hart-Davies left London for Tours; and Mr. Morton, who was going to Paris, waited over two days, and saw her across the Channel, and on the train going to Tours. Her condition at this time no doubt made some escort or companionship desirable; and Mr. Morton, from his character, and relations to all of us, was a very suitable travelling-companion. He was a member of a religious and benevolent society whose members were pledged to a special fidelity to its objects. Mrs. Hart-Davies had been accepted as a member of this society. On my trial she testified that we had also formed a smaller society-group of three persons, consisting of Mr. Fletcher, herself, and me, constituting a "social trinity," in which she represented the principle of love; Mr. Fletcher, that of wisdom; and I, the department of work. Something of this kind may have been spoken of, but I think the whole credit of the idea belongs properly to Mrs. Hart-Davies.

On her arrival at Tours, there began that correspondence which figured so largely in my trial, of which more than seventy letters said to have been written by me were read, but not one from Mrs. Hart-Davies, that would have explained them. Her letters to us had been left in our house, 22 Gordon Street, when we went to America. When I returned, not one of them could be found. Though urgently demanded by Mr. Lewis, my solicitor, as necessary to my defence, they were not forthcoming. When Mrs. Hart-Davies went with Mack and a pretended search-warrant, and ransacked our house, she took care to secure all her letters, some of which I found, with others addressed to us, and a quantity of my property besides, among her things at the Bedford Pantechnicon, thirteen months later.

These letters, or our part of them, which constituted, perhaps, a quarter or third of the correspondence, were read as evidence of fraud upon the trial, and published in the newspapers. But neither judge, jury, editors, nor the public seem to have remembered, that the fraud, if one had been perpetrated, had been consummated, the deed of gift executed, the confirmatory letter written, and the will made, *before one of these letters had been written, and that the property was at that time in our keeping*, with "the honorable understanding," as Mrs. Hart-Davies testified on the trial, that it was to be given back to her whenever it should be demanded.

Why should we have written letters to get property which was already in our keeping, and had been formally made over and secured to us?

CHAPTER XIII.

WE GET MORE, NOT TO SAY BETTER, ACQUAINTED.

Mrs. Hart-Davies's letters written at Tours, if they could have been produced, would have shown that she was improving in health, that she had frequent communion with the spirit of her departed mother, who rejoiced with her in the safe disposition of her property, and that she expressed the most devoted friendship to us and the greatest interest in our cause and work.

She came from Tours to Paris, and wrote, begging Mr. Fletcher to come there and see her. I thought the change and rest would be good for him, and wished him to go. She telegraphed that she was very ill, and that her doctor said the illness was dangerous. Mr. Fletcher went to Paris, being absent one day and night, when he saw and talked with her, and took such care of her as her condition seemed to require.

This visit to Paris, of which more was made at the trial than was needful, was in January. In February I was ill from the effects, as my physician thought, of

too severe a climate, and he advised me to go to
Rome. I prepared to go, and wrote to Mrs. Hart-
Davies, proposing that she should accompany me. She
consented, and promised to meet me in Paris ; but she
failed to do so, and wrote to Mr. Fletcher that her
mamma wished her to return to London. Mr. Fletcher
wrote to her that it would be inconvenient; that there
were only the servants in the house besides himself,
and that her being there alone with him during my
absence would not be a proper arrangement. To her
repeated proposals he made the same answer, saying
that the house would be prepared for her reception on
the 3d of May.

I have mentioned that Mrs. Hart-Davies had introduced to us an old friend of hers, Capt. Lindmark.
On the 30th of March, though far from being a Spiritualist, — being, in fact, a scientific materialist of very
decided views, — he came to the anniversary meeting
(the Anniversary of the Origin of Modern Spiritualism
in America) at Steinway Hall, and afterward called
upon us at Gordon Street. We spoke to him of Mrs.
Hart-Davies and of the arrangements that had been
made for her residence with us, and showed him her
things in the house.

He did not seem very much pleased at the information. "Are you certain you will be happy with her?"
he asked. "A woman who has quarrelled with two

husbands, who has been divorced from one, and has separated from another, may not be more fortunate with you." As a gentleman, and one as yet but slightly acquainted with us, he was not in a position to interfere; but it was easy to see, that for some reason he did not quite approve of the arrangement.

When the 1st of May was at hand, and Mr. Fletcher had promised to go to Paris for Mrs. Hart-Davies, he was unwell, and not in a condition to make such a journey. I therefore offered to meet her at Dover, where she would most need me, coming from a possibly rough passage across the Channel; and Capt. Lindmark, as an old acquaintance of our coming guest and our adopted sister, kindly offered to bear me company.

I wrote of all this to Mrs. Hart-Davies, and told her we should meet her at the Lord Warden Hotel, and that Capt. Lindmark would receive her upon her landing, and make all the necessary arrangements for her at the hotel.

The boat came in, but no Mrs. Hart-Davies: so we waited for the night boat, and I engaged a porter and chambermaid to meet her, and had a warm room ready for her reception. She did not come. On inquiry, we found that the boat had landed at another pier; and at eleven o'clock we got a telegram from Mr. Fletcher to tell us that the unhappy and neglected woman had landed alone, and was staying in a cold room. We found her at last, and she went home with us; but, such is her fault-finding and malicious temper, she has probably never forgiven what she considered our neglect when we thought we had made every provision for her comfort.

We arranged as well as we could, however, to make her the pet child of the family. She had many amiable qualities. She was conversable, affectionate to excess, wrote with facility in verse as well as in prose, and had a considerable talent for drawing, as was shown by her questionable sketches which so interested Mr. Flowers, the Bond-street magistrate, and Sir Harvey Hawkins, at the Central Criminal Court.

But amiable, kind, generous as she could be and had been, she had not been an inmate of our family a week, before she showed very different and less desirable qualities. She became exorbitant in her demands, and extremely irritable in her temper, requiring every thing in the house to be changed to suit her. She increased the work of the servants by tardiness and disorderly habits, — coming to lunch in a morning-dress, and the same at five-o'clock tea, which, in a house where there were guests at almost every meal, was inconvenient, and scarcely respectful. She gave no assistance in our work. The servants could not endure her temper, and gave notice to quit. She did not receive as much attention as she desired from our visitors, and seemed very jealous of any attention that was paid to me. In fact, she seemed to think or feel, that, whenever we had company, it was her right to be the object of exclusive attention, and that she was defrauded if any notice was taken of any other person.

In a few weeks she showed great jealousy of Capt. Lindmark. Any kindness or gentlemanly attention he showed to me was deeply resented; and she showed so much irritation, and he so much indifference, for one whose manners toward ladies were generally so admirable, that when I had observed them a short time I suspected a previous intimacy. One day toward the end of June, as I was coming into the drawing-room, I heard Capt. Lindmark say, "That's absolutely horrible. Certainly it cannot be."

Capt. Lindmark is a gentleman of great self-possession, but he was evidently shocked and angry. He is an accomplished linguist; but his English is of course marked with a slight foreign accent, which makes it more emphatic. To my husband and myself, who were entering, he said, "Mr. Fletcher and Mrs. Fletcher, I must tell you something before I can ever visit you again." Then, turning to Mrs. Hart-Davies, he said, "Shall I tell them, or will you? We have no right to be here together until they understand."

"I prefer to tell them myself," she answered, and immediately left the room with Mr. Fletcher. They were absent for two hours. She then came and took me out, and made her confession. It was in general what I had suspected. I heard now, for the first time, some details of her past life, — the cause of her divorce from her first husband, her meeting Capt. Lindmark in South America, her wild and irrepressible passion for him, — the whole story, the old story (reversed, for the entreaties were hers), needless to dwell upon or repeat. It was told with many sobs and tears. It was, she declared, the one error of her life, for which, she also declared, she was truly penitent.

I had no right to judge the poor woman, and no desire to act harshly toward her, or punish her in any way. I had taken her into my home because she was in trouble. If she were more guilty than I supposed, she so much the more needed kindness. I was sorry that she had come under false colors as a chaste and ill-used wife. I forgave her, but Mr. Fletcher did not. He said she had come to us under false pretences, and that we had a right to know the extent of our responsibilities. Still he yielded to my wishes, and treated her with politeness, but never with the same cordiality as before. He was the same as formerly in company, but not the same in private. I wished to treat her as a sister, as I think one woman ought to treat another. Nor can I understand why women should be more unforgiving to each other than they are to men.

CHAPTER XIV.

OUR EXCURSION TO AMERICA.

WE had planned to make an excursion to America for our summer-holiday, and we forgot our troubles in the preparations for the voyage and in the visits we proposed to make. We spent some weeks in dressmaking and arranging our wardrobe, making up the new materials and trimmings which I purchased, and altering the old dresses which she had inherited, and which were now considered our common property. All was finished and packed up for the voyage; the dresses for both of us being, in some instances, in the same box.

Capt. Lindmark, who wished to inspect some government works and manufacturing establishments in America, proposed to join our party, as also did one of our frequent guests, Miss Spencer.

Mrs. Hart-Davies did not like this arrangement. The presence of Capt Lindmark embarrassed her; and she was jealous of the attentions paid to Miss Spencer,—not that they were in the least exclusive, for our two gentlemen scrupulously divided their attentions between us three ladies, I as the wife getting of course rather less than an equal share.

It was, however, a mathematical difficulty to divide two gentlemen among three ladies; and we could not avoid some vulgar fractions. Mrs. Hart-Davies, between Mr. Fletcher's brotherly coolness and Capt. Lindmark's dead ashes, with her natural tendency to jealousy, grew more and more fault-finding and disagreeable as the day of our departure approached.

We sailed for New York, July 29, 1879. On the steamer, where we were made as comfortable as people who are not good sailors can be at sea, our poor sister's bad temper was naturally aggravated. She had no one to rule, and she got no attention. No doubt it seemed so to her: for she would say at table, "Nobody will come for me; but, if Mrs. Fletcher is absent, everybody wants to tear after her."

Among our fellow-passengers was a young and talented clergyman, returning to America from a tour for health in Europe. He and Mrs. Hart-Davies seemed much attracted to each other, and got up a rather pronounced flirtation, seeking out retired places on deck for *tête-à-têtes*, and being discovered later at night than the regulations allowed behind the wheelhouse. This made some scandal; and Capt. Lindmark, with what may seem a cruel frankness, told her she was disgracing our party. Probably, from the fact that he had become acquainted with us through her introduction, and from his past relations to her, he felt more strongly than was necessary a certain responsibility for her conduct.

She very emphatically resented his interference; and, when Mr. Fletcher told her that one of the ship's officers had told him it was against the rules for passengers to be on deck after eleven o'clock, the breeze became a storm. She complained that Mr. Fletcher had neglected her, and declared that the minister had proposed to marry her. To this it might have been objected, that the clergyman was reported to be elsewhere engaged, and that she had already two living husbands, from only one of whom she had as yet been divorced.

I am sorry to be obliged to enter into these petty and scandalous details; but I do not see how I can avoid it, and yet give the reader a clear understanding of my story.

CHAPTER XV.

HEAD-WINDS made our trip to New York two days longer than we expected. Mr. Colby, editor of the " Banner of Light," had written to us that the Boston Spiritualists had arranged to give us a public reception on the 9th of August, and that Mr. Fletcher had been announced to speak at the Lake Pleasant Camp-Meeting on the 11th. I meant to take the first train after landing to visit my father and mother in Lawrence, Mass.

We arrived in New York on the 10th, too late for our reception at Boston (which, on the non-arrival of the steamer, had been postponed), and just in time to take our respective trains, — I to Boston, Mr. Fletcher to the camp-meeting.

After reaching Boston, being quite at home where I had lived so long, I went at once to the office of the " Banner of Light " for letters, and to shake hands with my old friends, Mr. Colby and Mr. Rich, and found that our reception was appointed for three o'clock that afternoon. The medium who gave regular *séances* at the "Banner" office had told them of our detention, and that we should arrive on the 10th. They had tried to telegraph to us the altered arrangements, but without success. I at once telegraphed to my mother and sister to come to me at the Parker House; and they went with me to the reception, where I had the happiness of being warmly welcomed by many old friends. Then I went home with mother and sister, and was once more in my dear father's arms, and the next day took the train to join my husband at Lake Pleasant.

On my arrival, loaded with the flowers given me at the reception and with many sent to Mr. Fletcher, as I walked up the veranda of the hotel, I saw sitting there Dr. Mack and his friend Signor Rondi. Dr. Mack arose, and bowed to me.

I did not return his salutation; because I would not be a hypocrite, and I knew he was my enemy. I do not know the reasons for his animosity. On coming to England as a mesmeric or Spiritualist healer, he took rooms in Southampton Row, near the office of the "Medium and Daybreak," a Spiritualist paper edited and published by Mr. James Burns. Mr. Burns, for some reason unknown to me, had been opposed to Mr. Fletcher and myself. It is difficult

to account for the animosity of persons engaged in
the same profession, or enlisted in the same cause.
There is a world-old proverb, "Two of a trade can
never agree." It is notorious that mediums are often
jealous of each other, as physicians, lawyers, possibly
clergymen, may be; as actors and singers and rival
beauties are; and as nobody in the world, and, least
of all, Christians and Spiritualists, ever should be.

However it was, Mr. Burns did not like us; and
Mr. James McGeary, now known as Dr. Mack, had
an evident interest in being in the good graces of Mr.
Burns, who, as able editor, and powerful champion of
Spiritualism, could render him important service. Mr.
Burns said I was the champion of Mrs. Woodhull and
of "Free Love," which he had a mission to trample
out; and, though Mr. Burns knew that Dr. Mack's
own life was not without stain, he seems to have listened to his stories about me. Mr. Fletcher, meeting
Mack at Doughty Hall, demanded an apology and re-
traction of all his scandalous tales about us, which
Mack made; but he kept up his slanders, and we had
no further intercourse.

I regret that it is necessary to speak of either
Dr. Mack or Signor Rondi, and I shall say as little
as possible of either. Signor Rondi is an Italian artist
of considerable merit: as a "red" revolutionist, he
served under Garibaldi, of whom he has painted an

excellent portrait. Being a Spiritualist, with some
gifts as a professed medium, he got acquainted with
Dr. Mack. Signor Rondi is a little man, and Mack
a very big one; and such opposites often attract each
other. On Mr. Fletcher's arrival in London, Signor
Rondi had some *séances* with him, and got remarkable
tests. They liked each other, and Signor Rondi was
very useful to him. This friendship continued until my
arrival in London, in July, 1876. Of course Signor
Rondi was soon presented to me, and we became
very friendly. For three years he was a constant
visitor at our house, and almost an inmate; for he
came in frequently to supper, and always staid late,
his own rooms being very near us. I find it hard to
understand the loss of Signor Rondi's friendship, and
the hostility he afterward manifested, his jealousy, his
revenge, and his joining with Dr. Mack to charge us
with fraud, and bring about my imprisonment. Mack
was wicked; poor Rondi was weak.

Signor Rondi knew all about our quarrel with Dr.
Mack. He wanted to go with us to America, and, because he could not join our party, was naturally a little
unhappy. He wrote from Liverpool, giving us notice
that he was going with Dr. Mack; and they preceded
us by a week. On their arrival at the Lake Pleasant
Hotel, after inquiring of the landlord, they secured
rooms commanding a view of those we had taken by
cable, and were ready for us when we came.

CHAPTER XVI.

WHAT HAPPENED AT THE CAMP-MEETING.

DR. MACK was acquainted with Miss Spencer professionally, and soon after our arrival she introduced him to Mrs. Hart-Davies. Possibly Mrs. Hart-Davies hoped to be benefited by his magnetic powers; but it was not in very good taste, to say the least, for her to be seen walking and talking with one whom she knew to be our enemy. We all noticed a change in her manner to us. From being merely irritable and rude, as she often had been, she became insulting and violent.

Through Dr. Mack, Mrs. Hart-Davies soon got acquainted with a clairvoyant medium and her husband from Saratoga. They had introduced themselves to us, and invited us to visit them. We were too fully occupied to see much of them, which occasioned us but little regret after we learned of their real character and standing. But Mrs. Hart-Davies was a good deal with them; and they seemed to have so bad an influence over her, that I spoke to her about it, and also of her

99

intimacies with persons whom she knew to be our enemies. It made no difference in her conduct. She spent much of her time with Rondi and Mack, and these unworthy people.

On the 17th of August, while writing at an open window in the corridor (and all windows are open in the warmth of an American August), I could not avoid hearing the peculiar voice and Italian English of Signor Rondi, who was holding a *séance* in his room with Mrs. Hart-Davies. Speaking as if under the control of some spirit, Signor Rondi was saying, —

"So far as Mr. Fletcher is concerned, he has in London a hundred sweethearts. You need not think he cares for you. He only cares for what he can make."

As this communication was evidently not intended for me, I went back to my room. An hour later Mrs. Hart-Davies came to me in a state of violent agitation, and said, —

"What would you do if a reliable clairvoyant were to tell you that your husband had been unfaithful? I have been told," she persisted, "by a most reliable medium, that Mr. Fletcher is very unfaithful; and it drives me mad to think that my brother, whom I thought so pure and good, is not to be trusted."

I did not care to enter into the subject, and tried to soothe her irritation. "If any person should tell me such a thing," I said, "I should consider him undeveloped, or in some way gone wrong; and, if a spirit said so, I should think it an undeveloped, and therefore evil spirit. If *you* listen to such things, and are influenced by them, what can we expect of the world about him? We who know him ought and do know that such talk is utterly absurd."

She seemed for the moment to feel better about it, but soon went to the Saratoga medium, and had a *séance* with her. I accidentally saw them sitting at a table; and Capt. Lindmark also noticed it, and remarked that it meant mischief.

"I ought to speak to you candidly about Juliet," he said, "even at the risk of offending you. I have observed her conduct here, and spoke to her about it yesterday. But first let me ask, Has Mrs. Hart-Davies made a will in your favor?"

"To the best of my knowledge, no."

"Then I will tell you what she said. She told me yesterday that she hated and despised you. It was you who prevented my return to her, and it was you who prevented Mr. Fletcher from paying her the attention she had a right to expect from him. She said she had given you all her property, and had made a will in your favor; but that did not amount to any thing, for the papers were at her disposal, and she could tear them up in five minutes. And raising her hand, and clinching her fist, she said, ‘ I will have my revenge upon her !’ ’’

‘‘ I don't attach any importance to her threats,’’ I replied.

Still, I *had* some anxiety, though not for myself ; for her conduct was spoiling Mr. Fletcher's holiday. But I could not see that there was any thing to be done, and said I thought we had better let it rest.

‘‘ No !’’ said Capt. Lindmark. ‘‘ Take my advice, and send that woman back to London, or she will certainly cause some disaster. She has been the ruin of every one she was ever connected with.’’

Mr. Fletcher joined us. Capt. Lindmark continued the conversation. He said, ‘‘ I want to speak to you plainly, Mr. Fletcher. This woman is unhappy, and she is bent on mischief.’’

‘‘ Well,’’ said Mr. Fletcher, ‘‘ what can she do beyond making us uncomfortable? That we are bound to bear as well as we can. When we return to London, she must take her property, and make a home for herself. The influence she has over our son is such, that we had decided before leaving London, were there no other reason, she could not live longer with us.’’

Our son Alvah, then fourteen years old, was in the university school, which was quite near our home, and getting on very well with his studies ; but the table-talk of Mrs. Hart-Davies was so far from edifying, that I was more than once obliged to ask him to leave the table, and finish his dinner elsewhere. She had a way of talking of things, and using expressions, that no child should hear. No doubt this was attributable to a morbid condition, a kind of mania well known to physicians, difficult to manage, and more difficult to cure. When I sent my boy away from the table to save him from such "evil communications" as I feared might "corrupt good manners," she was very angry, and said, "Boys of his age should learn such things." But to resume.

On the 17th of August, Alvah came to me, and said, "Aunty (as he called Mrs. Hart-Davies) wants papa."

"He is somewhere about the grounds," I said. She came out upon the veranda, and said she wanted to see Mr. Fletcher about going to Saratoga. He was the treasurer of the party, and she would require some money for her fare and expenses. I saw Mr. Fletcher approaching, and left them together. In a little while he came to me, and said,—

"Juliet tells me she is going to make a visit to Saratoga, and would like to take mamma's jewels with her. She has been told that their influence will be good for her."

"Well, there is no reason why she should not have them. Does she want those that are in the bank as well?"

All the most valuable of her jewels had been deposited in a bank on our arrival at Boston, as hotel-rooms are sometimes robbed in America, as elsewhere.

"Don't know," he answered. "I told her you would see that she had whatever she wanted."

After lunch I went to her room, and said, "Willie tells me you are going away, and want mamma's jewels. Do you want all of them, — those deposited in the bank at Boston? And when do you intend to go?"

"To-morrow morning, at half-past ten."

"Well, that can be easily arranged," I said. "We can telegraph to the bank for the box, and it will come by the night-train."

"I think I would like to take them all," she said. "Besides, I want to tell you that I have been disturbed and uncomfortable; and I think it will be better for me to go away for a week."

"I have noticed for several days," I replied, "that you were not like yourself; and it seems a pity, for it destroys your comfort and ours. You know how hard Mr. Fletcher has worked, and how much need he has of peace and rest. It *does* seem a little cruel that you or I should do any thing to destroy his happiness, and deprive him of the rest he so much needs."

"Nobody but you ever called me bad-tempered," she answered. "Everybody else has liked my pretty,

dainty ways. Besides, I may as well be frank with
you. I will no longer remain with this party if Capt.
Lindmark is to stay in it. He treats you always with
marked respect, and me with marked indifference;
and it is mortifying and humiliating. If he don't leave
the party, *I shall*."

I tried to quiet her. "It is only for a few weeks,"
I said. "I can understand how you feel. But you
should have thought of it before we left England."

We talked for two hours, and she seemed more reasonable. In the course of our conversation I told her
I thought Dr. Mack was not such a man as she should
associate with, and that I thought he had a bad influence upon her.

She replied that she had had frequent *séances* with
Signor Rondi and others, and that her mamma said
she ought to be with Dr. Mack; that his magnetism
was good for her, and that he would be her friend.

"Very well," I said: "I have nothing more to say.
If these communications are agreeable to your sense
of right, you must act accordingly."

At the end of our conversation, when I had risen to
go, she said, "Bertie, don't send for those jewels until
I see you again."

"Very well. Any time before seven o'clock will be
in season for the night-train."

At the *table d'hôte*, at six o'clock, she seemed in

better spirits than at any time since our arrival. Coming up to the back of my chair, she put her arms round me, and said, "Bertie dear, I have decided not to take the jewels; and, if you are disengaged after dinner, I should like to have a little chat with you."

There was to be a concert that evening, for the benefit of one of the mediums at the camp-meeting, at which I had promised to sing. Miss Spencer, who was going with me, had lost a brother the year before; and this was the anniversary of his death. She intended to wear a dress of silver blue, his favorite color, in his honor; and Mrs. Hart-Davies intended to wear the same, and proposed that I should join them. I had intended to dress, as usual, in black, but willingly consented to wear the blue for the occasion, if I could find the right shade. Mrs. Hart-Davies volunteered to assist me, found the dress, and laid out the jewels to match.

The concert was a great success. We all enjoyed it, and took home with us a party of friends, who staid late. I hoped for better times. Going from our cottage to the hotel, Mrs. Hart-Davies said, —

"Bertie dear, do you think our jewels are safe here? I fancy I have lost things from my room. Wouldn't it be better to send all of them to the bank?"

I readily assented to this prudent arrangement. "It

can easily be managed," I said. "Mr. Fletcher will take Alvah to Boston to-morrow, and can deposit all the jewels at the same time. This was on the 17th of August. We said good-night; and next Monday, on the 18th, Mr. Fletcher took the jewels to Boston, deposited them at her suggestion, and returned at nine o'clock the same evening.

The following morning Mrs. Hart-Davies complained of a violent headache, and said, "I don't feel able to travel, and I think I shall not go to Saratoga."

I said, "I am very glad you have decided to remain; for I think it would be very unwise for you to go off with people you have only known a week. They know nothing of you, nor you of them."

"They know, at least, that I am a lady."

"Unfortunately they do not. They may know that you have the manners of a lady. They can only judge of you as you can of them. But, aside from that, it seems to me a surprising arrangement."

After breakfast she went to her room, and sent for me to come to her. She had seen her friend Horne, the new medium, she said, and told her she did not feel able to travel then, but would come and visit her later. Madame was very angry, and her husband also seemed in a bad temper. "What shall I do?" she asked. "I don't want to make them angry."

This seemed very strange to me; but I asked if I

should go and speak to them. She wished I would; and I ran down, and tapped at their door. They were having a *séance* with Miss Spencer; and as I entered Mr. Horne was saying, " Well, she *shall* go ! "

I asked madame to step into the corridor, and gave her my message. I told her Mrs. Davies was very sorry to disappoint them, but felt too ill to travel.

" Well, she never knows her own mind five minutes at a time," she answered. " But, if she comes to us at all, she must come with us this morning."

" It is very strange that you should speak in this way," I said. " If you want her so much, I presume she will try to go. But, if she goes, I must tell you something about her. You are a stranger to her, and she is one of my family. She is subject to severe attacks of nervousness and neuralgia. If any thing happens to her, I beg that you will let us know of it as soon as possible." And I gave her our Boston address.

" Perhaps you think I am giving Mrs. Davies spiritual advice, but I am not. The real matter is this: Mrs. Davies formed a most unfortunate attachment coming over on the steamer. She thinks, that, after a little rest with us, she can go to Indiana and get a divorce, and then marry this young man."

" What is the dear child thinking of ! " I said. " But, as she has never mentioned this matter to me, she probably does not wish me to know it: so I think we will not talk any more about it. Good-morning."

I told Mrs. Hart-Davies the result of my interview, that she must go then, if at all; and, while we were talking, her friend came to see her, and I left them together. In a few moments Mrs. Davies came out with her hat on, and said, "There is nothing for it but to go."

I said, "Juliet, I don't understand this matter; but of course you must do as you like." She answered that it was only for three or four days, when she would come and join us.

"The sooner the better," I said. "Whenever you come, we shall be glad to see you." She caught me in her arms, crying and sobbing like a child.

I took her wraps on my arm, and went with her down to the veranda, where I handed them to Capt. Lindmark, who went with her to the station. The last I saw of her was when, at the top of the hill, she turned, and kissed her hand to me until she passed out of sight.

At half-past four o'clock that afternoon the sheriff came into the house with a warrant to arrest us.

Dr. Mack joined her on the train. The two left it at Montague, went before a justice of the peace, charged us with having illegal possession of property of immense value, and got a warrant for our arrest;

while Mrs. Hart-Davies gave Dr. Mack a power of attorney to prosecute us, and recover the stolen property.

When the sheriff came in the afternoon, he found that Mr. Fletcher was in Boston, and I heard nothing about it. Mr. Fletcher returned late in the night, and the matter was not mentioned to him.

At half-past seven next morning, feeling ill, I was having my breakfast in bed. There came a rap at the door. Thinking it was Mr. Fletcher, I said, "Come in," when entered the burly form of Dr. Mack, who said, —

"I have come for Mrs. Hart-Davies' property."

I supposed that he meant some things she might have left in her bedroom, and said, —

"Why do you come to me for 'her property'? And how do you dare to come into my bedroom?"

"Come, come!" said he with insulting importance. "This won't do. You have carried your head altogether too high the last five years. I'll see what I can do to bring it down."

I was getting angry; but, lying ill in bed, I could only say, "Dr. Mack, leave this room. If you have any business to transact, you can do it with my husband."

"Your husband has run away," said he. "Not much chance of finding him!"

"I think you will find him in the dining-room," I

replied as calmly as I could. "He left this room ten
minutes ago to get his breakfast. Dr. Mack, I have
not the least idea of what you are doing; but, knowing you as I do, I am sure it is some dreadfully dirty
business."

"We won't argue, Mrs. Fletcher," said Mack.
"If there is any thing I dislike, it is argument."

He left the room; and I locked my door, and
dressed myself. In a few minutes Mr. Fletcher came
with Dr. Mack, and said, —

"Dr. Mack says he has come for Mrs. Hart-Davies'
property."

"Well," I said, "he will find it in her bedroom.
You had best give him her key."

"Oh! it is not *that*. He wants the property she
has transferred to us."

"How can that be?" I asked. "There must be
some mistake. Most of it is in London. How can
we give that to Dr. Mack?"

"That is easily managed," interposed Mack. "She
will take what is here now, and go back to London
for the rest of it."

"I suppose what you mean is this," said Mr.
Fletcher: "Mrs. Hart-Davies has determined to leave
us, and wants her property. In that case, I am only
too glad to return every thing that ever belonged to
her."

He then gave Mack, who had shown his power of attorney, an order on the Boston bank for her jewels and the money she had given him to keep for her; and I searched our boxes to find any things that might belong to her. I even put out some of my dresses that were trimmed with her lace, and her dresses trimmed with my lace.

"She don't want any of the dresses," said he. "She says they are of no consequence."

I hung them on nails in the room, that they might be at her disposal. Dr. Mack took his order, and went with the sheriff to the bank, and got the jewels, with which he returned to the camp, and took them and the other things to Mrs. Hart-Davies. Having her power of attorney, he managed every thing to his liking, and said he wanted these matters settled quietly; that we had quarrelled in London, but here he was willing to let bygones be bygones, and wanted to be friends.

Next day he came again, with a list of things which Mrs. Hart-Davies said we had not restored to her, and which she demanded. She said that only about half her jewels were returned, and wanted her furs, India shawl, and such articles as she had herself packed to leave in London.

Dr. Mack went away, but came back for the dresses, which were given to him. Soon after, he came again with another list. Madame was not satisfied.

I was very ill. Mr. Fletcher was losing patience. He said, " Dr. Mack, Mrs. Fletcher is ill. Ask Mrs. Hart-Davies to come and look through the boxes, and take whatever she claims as her property." I suggested that he should write a note to that effect, " and be sure that she gets it."

He wrote : —

"DEAR JULIET, — Your more than strange conduct is wholly inexplicable to me, and all the more because you know, that, at any time you wished for your property, all you had to do was to ask me for it. Would it not have been wiser and more kind for you to have come to me personally, stating your wishes in the matter, and by so doing giving yourself less trouble, and me less pain and humiliation ?"

This note was taken by Dr. Mack, who refused to give her address. Of course we had no assurance that it was ever given to Mrs. Hart-Davies, and for several days we heard no more of her.

All this time Signor Rondi was with Dr. Mack, and apparently assisting him ; and reports came to us, that he was making statements not calculated to improve our reputation.

As soon as I was able, I went to Boston, and stopped at a private hotel, where I also engaged rooms for Miss

Spencer and Capt. Lindmark. Before I left the camp, Signor Rondi had been begging Mr. Barnard, the landlord of our hotel, to procure him an interview with me. I preferred not to see him. He was very unhappy. But one day he became quite radiant, and said to Mr. Barnard, "You do not need to ask Mrs. Fletcher any more to give me an interview. It is all right."

"Why, signor, what has happened?" said Mr. Barnard. "You seem triumphant."

"Nothing has happened. But soon you will know all."

The morning after my arrival in Boston, appeared the article in the "Boston Herald," written by the reporter from information furnished by Dr. Mack and Mrs. Hart-Davies, with sensational headings, in the American style, and full of the wildest exaggerations. These were not, of course, the fault of the reporter; though he did not, probably, make any effort to soften the picture. How many miscarriages of justice are due to sensational reports spreading a deep prejudice through a community, editors of newspapers have perhaps never considered. The spirit of English law, and American law derived from English, is to hold and treat every one as innocent until he is proven guilty; but the spirit of an excited public opinion is the exact opposite of this law of charity: it is to consider and treat every accused person as guilty until he can prove his innocence. That there are many lying in prison, and that many have suffered death, in consequence of an excited and violent public prejudice, created and fostered by sensational reports in newspapers, no one can doubt who has given the matter any consideration.

When the "Boston Herald" reached the camp, there was of course a great excitement; but we were in the midst of friends who had known us too long and too well to be carried off their feet by a report in a newspaper. The three thousand persons assembled at Lake Pleasant were, with a few individual exceptions, as one family. An indignation-meeting of the friends of Mr. Fletcher was held, and resolutions of confidence passed, and signed by seven hundred persons. Dr. Mack was forbidden the hotel, and Signor Rondi warned to leave the camp also, unless he wanted a coat of tar and feathers. He took the next train to Boston.

CHAPTER XVII.

MY FIRST NIGHT IN PRISON, AND WHAT CAME OF IT.

IN the first week of September Mr. Fletcher returned to Boston, and joined me at our private hotel.

The impression had come to me that I should be arrested that very day: it had come so strongly, that I wished Mr. Fletcher to go to Lawrence in order to escape the pain and excitement which I felt only too certain was approaching; so, having invented a pretext, I induced him to go. He asked Capt. Lindmark to pay me any attention I might require in his absence, and took the half-past two train.

At half-past three there was a rap on my door. "Come in!" I answered. Capt. Lindmark, who was in the adjoining room, heard me, and, thinking I had spoken to him, came into the room by one door just as Dr. Mack, Mrs. Hart-Davies, and three detectives came in at the other.

"Are you Mrs. Fletcher?" asked the chief detective.

"I am."

" I am an officer, and have a warrant to search your room."

" You are quite welcome to perform your duty, whatever it may be."

I was not in the least surprised by this visit. " Forewarned is fore-armed."

But Capt. Lindmark was not entirely satisfied, and was less gifted with the virtue of equanimity. He observed that Dr. Mack had kept on his hat, while the three officers had politely taken theirs off ; and he ventured to make a remark on the subject. He said, —

" How dare you keep on your hat in the presence of a lady? "

Dr. Mack replied offensively, that he generally wore his hat when he wanted to : thereupon Capt. Lindmark knocked it off. The three detectives were a little astonished at this assault committed in their presence by a very tall man in faultless attire. Of course it was their duty to arrest him. Their leader gave the order, " Put on the twisters." The twisters are of American invention, and are used instead of handcuffs. The men did not approach him. I sat down, and waited to see what would come of it. Capt. Lindmark was pale with passion, but quiet and resolute.

" It is an assault, sir, an assault," said the officer. No doubt it was, for there lay Dr. Mack's hat on the floor.

Mrs. Hart-Davies, apparently in a happier frame of mind, drew a little near Dr. Mack, no doubt hoping to encourage him by her support.

"In Sweden we consider it the duty of every gentleman to see that every lady is protected from insult," continued Capt. Lindmark; "but, in obeying the laws of gallantry, I see that I have disobeyed the laws of your free and progressive country. If you want to put your twisters on my wrists, pray proceed," holding out his arms to them.

The officers thought better of it, and one of them very civilly conducted him to the station-house.

They then, with the assistance of Mrs. Hart-Davies, very thoroughly searched my room. In about two hours she found and claimed property valued by her at THIRTY POUNDS, every particle of which belonged to me, with the exception of two night-dresses, which had been put in one of my boxes because her own were full, and which were so old she had intended to throw them away after the voyage.

When the search was finished, I said, —

"Now, gentlemen, I presume you want me to go with you."

"I have been used to this business for many years," said the officer; "but I never before have done any thing so painful as this."

One of the men, who seemed to be in the employ of

Dr. Mack, told me I could give him any letters I wished to write, or telegrams for bail.

I at once telegraphed to my husband, "Capt. Lindmark has been arrested. Secure bail for him." I also telegraphed to persons in Boston who I knew would at once give bail for me. When doing this, I asked Mrs. Hart-Davies to sit down, as she looked very tired and ill.

"You seem to be very fond of Mrs. Hart-Davies," said the officer to me.

"Yes," I answered. "I have a great pity for her, because I think she is acting under the influence of persons much worse than herself."

At five o'clock P.M. I was taken to the police-office in Court Square, and was treated, as I have been everywhere by the officers of the law, with all possible politeness. The officer kindly offered me his arm, but I declined it with thanks.

After I was seated in the clerk's office, the us· questions were asked, and entries made.

"Where were you born?" asked the clerk.

"In Lowell, Mass."

"Why, but you are English! Any one would know that by your accent."

"I beg to assure you that I was born in Massachusetts for all that."

The men standing about, hangers-on I suppose, were

making remarks upon my appearance, my dress, and my feet, while I sat in an easy-chair, answering the formal questions. This being ended, a woman was sent for, who searched me for any thing that I might have concealed in my dress. When this was ended, I was taken to the Tombs, where I was met by the jailer, a rough-looking, but, as I soon found, a most kind-hearted man, who said, " I suppose you have never been in a place like this before." He gave me the only cell there was vacant, sent to a neighboring hotel for my dinner (which was brought and nicely served by a colored waiter), got me a clean mattress for my bed, and treated me with every possible kindness.

"I can't give you what I would like," he said; "but you shall have the best I have got." And he brought me a glass tumbler to drink from, instead of the usual prison tin cup.

The doors of the cells were made of iron bars, through which all sounds could penetrate. In a short time a large, handsome black cat came to keep me company. I gladly accepted my room-mate, and shared my dinner with her; and as she staid all night, purring on my bed, I could not help thinking that she showed more humanity than did the merciless woman, who, for the sake of a miserably small amount of property, had placed me in my unjust position. I was very happy in thinking that my husband knew nothing about it.

At midnight the prisoners from the different stations were brought in; and the place became a bedlam of noisy, drunken men and women, drunken mothers, crying children, and coarse, boisterous young girls. They were shouting and singing the whole night.

I was not sleepy. At two o'clock I heard a steady tramp, tramp, in one of the cells, that sounded familiar. The jailer came past, and I asked him, "Who is this prisoner tramping so uneasily?"

"I don't know who he is, ma'am," said he; "but he is an awful swell. He is a Captain something." And my heart was none the lighter from knowing that my friend was sharing my misfortune.

In the morning my good angel, a rough-looking specimen of an angel certainly, but as kind as he could be, took me to his office, brought me hot and cold water, and towels, and left me to my ablutions. Then he came bringing a comb and brush.

"You need not be afraid of them," he said. "They belonged to my poor mother. I have kept them for her sake. Nobody has ever touched them since she died, but I kinder felt as if I would like to have you use them."

If there are many hard hearts among those who have charge of prisoners, I know that there are also

some most tender and kind. I can testify that I have
never found greater kindness or a more unselfish devotion than from this class.

In the morning I sent for a good lawyer to attend
to my case, and at ten o'clock I had my hearing before
the magistrates.

The letters I had written had not been posted, and
the telegrams for bail had not been sent; but, when I
entered the court-room, the first thing I saw was the
gray hair of my dear old friend Dr. Kennedy, a venerable man, who in the time of my trouble looked to
me like an angel.

The dock was cleared of the every-day offenders, —
those charged with drunkenness, disorderly conduct,
and petty thefts. The last prisoner was a little boy
whose head did not come above the dock. He had
been arrested for stealing cigars. "Stealing, ma'am,"
he said, when I asked him. "I wanted a smoke, and
it was nothing but a stub."

At last my name was called. Dr. Kennedy came,
and said, "Mrs. Fletcher, I have as much confidence
in your innocence as I have in my own, and I have
come to bail you." And he took a seat at my
side.

"But how did you come here?" I asked; for I
knew the day before that he was not in town.

"Well, I was up in Vermont, near Canada, and saw

an account of your affair in a Boston newspaper. I have travelled all night to come to you."

While we were talking, another gentleman came, one who knew me professionally, to ask if he could give bail for me, or supply me with money.

My friendly jailer had told me that the bail was fixed at fifty thousand dollars (ten thousand pounds). This was of course owing to the sensation reports in the newspapers, in which I was accused of swindling a beautiful young English girl of sixteen out of an immense fortune. It may be well to state here that Mrs. Davies was at least thirty-eight years old.

In a few minutes some of the facts of the case were stated by my lawyer, and the magistrate reduced the bail to three hundred dollars (sixty pounds).

When I drove home to our hotel with Dr. Kennedy, we found Mr. Fletcher. The telegrams had been delayed by the detectives ; and the writ had been obtained late, simply to keep me one night in prison. The better to enjoy the triumph, Dr. Mack and Mrs. Davies went to Lawrence, to my mother's house; and he walked up to my sick husband, brutally saying, "*Will Fletcher, I have come to tell you that your wife is in the Tombs, Capt. Lindmark ditto, and you will be there before to-morrow night.*"

Having perpetrated this outrage, they jubilantly returned to Boston. My husband had an attack of heart-disease, so that a doctor was with him all night. The feelings and the condition of my family may be imagined, but can never be expressed. Mr. Fletcher came to Boston in the morning, and, without waiting to be arrested, gave bail for his appearance; the case having been postponed for a fortnight to secure the presence of Mr. Morton, to whom we telegraphed at London, asking him to come with the papers by the first steamer.

The charge against us at this time was larceny. We were charged with getting the beautiful young English heiress into our power, and robbing her of her inheritance.

The case came on about the last of October, when such proofs were given of a conspiracy against us, that a warrant was issued for the arrest of Dr. Mack and Mrs. Hart-Davies. Mack was arrested, but I prevented the warrant being served upon his accomplice. She swore on my trial that no such warrant had been issued; though she was present with Mack when he was arrested, and knew that her name was also in the warrant. They were found together in a very low hotel in a not very reputable quarter of the New-England capital.

When Dr. Mack had his hearing before the magistrate, he was discovered to be one James McGeary, a leather-dealer who became bankrupt, and found it convenient to change his residence, his profession, and even his name. Of course he had a right to change all three, and to "better himself" generally, which I shall always be glad to see him do. As Dr. Mack, he came to England, and then spent some time on the Continent, I do not know in what capacity; but in 1875 he came out as a mesmeric healer, or healing medium.

Finding himself under arrest, Mack failed to get bail, and sent a note to Mr. Fletcher by Signor Rondi, proposing an amicable settlement. Mr. Fletcher consented, if it were done in such a way as to show our innocence of the charges brought against us. Finally the hearing of Dr. Mack's case was postponed to the 18th of November, while ours was to come on the following day; and Mack was bound over in his own recognizance of forty thousand dollars.

Next day our case was again postponed for the purpose of settlement. We had a meeting at the office of Dr. Mack's lawyer; and the terms of settlement were drawn up, by which Mrs. Hart-Davies agreed to return to us most of the property she had claimed in Boston; to make over to us a portion of that left in Gordon Street, London; to pay a hundred and forty pounds for expenses incurred in her behalf; and personally, or through her solicitor, to completely exonerate us from all the charges that had been brought against us. We agreed, on our part, to deliver up to her all other property belonging to her, and to abandon the legal proceedings.

This settlement is a *matter of record*, and was witnessed by all present. It was specially provided that the property seized should be delivered to me for my inspection; and within a certain date, I think the 29th of October, we were to deliver to Mrs. Hart-Davies her property in London, which she was to go and inspect, and then telegraph to us at Boston.

The next day we expected the property there to be given to us according to the terms of the agreement. It did not come, nor on the next. After waiting a few days, we heard that Dr. Mack and Mrs. Hart-Davies had sailed for London, by which proceeding Mack had forfeited his recognizances of forty thousand dollars, and become in some sense, or to that amount, a fugitive from justice.

It was expressly stipulated in the settlement that the property of Mrs. Hart-Davies at our house in London should be given to her or her order, and specially provided that it was not to be given to Mack, and that he should not enter our house. Our first news of them in London came by a telegram informing us that Dr. Mack, Mrs. Heurtley (as she now preferred to be called), and Mr. Abrahams her solicitor, had been to our house, and taken away all her property and much of ours.

According to the letters that followed the telegram, the house had been ransacked from cellar to attic, and our papers and private correspondence seized, including all the letters of Mrs. Hart-Davies to us, thus robbing us of our means of defence.

All this, of course, was in direct violation of the formal settlement made at Boston, and under all the circumstances an outrage which I cannot trust myself to speak of as I think it deserves. It was not only an invasion of our house much worse than an ordinary burglary, made in violation of a solemn agreement, but if there was, as pretended, a search-warrant, it must have been procured by downright perjury. In any case, there was robbery; for on getting an order to search the Bedford Pantechnicon, after the term of my imprisonment, I found there a bundle of letters addressed to Mr. Fletcher and myself, and quantities of furniture, dresses, and other articles, which it was utterly impossible that Mrs. Hart-Davies could mistake for her own. There were some articles, no doubt, difficult to identify. Whenever I had any doubt as to any article, I declined to claim it; but furniture, dresses, and jewels such as I found among the things removed by Mrs. Hart-Davies and her accomplices from my house, no one could mistake. My servants are able to swear to them.

We were bound over in the sum of six hundred

dollars (one hundred and twenty pounds), to remain until the 10th of November. Mr. Fletcher had been announced to resume his discourses at Steinway Hall in October. The whole matter seemed disastrous. Mack was busy using the English press against us; and we were bitterly attacked, not only in the "Spiritualist," but in a short-lived weekly paper, which was said to have been started by some friends of Mack, and certainly contained nothing of interest but its attacks upon the Fletchers.

Early in November I received a letter from Mr. W. Eglinton, the well-known medium, telling me that Dr. Mack had applied for a warrant against us in London. On the 7th of November I received a letter from our friends Miss S. E. Gay and Mrs. Maltby, who had charge of our house, informing me that Mrs. Hart-Davies intended to have me arrested on my return. So in the first week of November I had every reason to believe I should be arrested, as I was, before I landed in England.

The final hearing of our case in Boston had been set down for Nov. 10. On the 8th Dr. Mack telegraphed to Mr. Ives, their counsel, that ill health prevented Mrs. Hart-Davies from returning, and asking for a postponement. Mr. Ives sent an open letter to the Court, saying, that, as the settlement made by his advice had not been carried out, he must abandon the

case. We were accordingly honorably discharged ; and
on Nov. 15, 1880, I left New York by the steamer
"Anchoria" for Greenock, previously announcing my
departure by that steamer in the Boston papers, and
stating my object in going to London ; viz., to meet
the accusations against me. I marked newspapers
containing this announcement with a red pencil, and
sent copies to Dr. Mack, to Mrs. Hart-Davies, and to
the Bow-street magistrates, which I think disposes of
Mr. Abrahams' flourish about the herculean efforts of
the police, which had happily resulted in my arrest.

The following report of the final proceeding in the
Boston Municipal Court, which will best show the termination of the case in America, so soon to be revived
in England, appeared in "The Boston Herald" of
Nov. 10, 1880.

THE FLETCHER LARCENY CASE COMES UP IN COURT, AND IS DISMISSED.

In the Municipal Court, before Judge May, this forenoon,
the often continued and well remembered case of Mr. J.
William Fletcher and his wife Susan W. Fletcher was called.
This case is one where the defendants, who are well known
in Spiritualist circles, were charged with having obtained a
large amount of property from one Julia Hart-Davies by false
representations. When it was reached to-day, Major John W.
Mahan, of counsel for the defendants, read the following letter
from S. B. Ives, jun., counsel for Mrs. Davies: —

MY DEAR MAJOR,—I am actually engaged in the trial of a case here, and can't get away at present, perhaps not to-day. As you know, an arrangement was made between your clients and mine, in the matter of the complaint against Fletcher, for an adjustment of all matters in controversy, by which nearly all the goods claimed by my client were to be given up to Fletcher, and others surrendered by Fletcher to Madame Davies. I am sorry to say that this arrangement was not carried out, by no fault on your part or that of your clients, and that my client has fled the country. Under the circumstances I do not see that my presence in court can be of any service, as I could only say this, and that I could not ask that the proceedings against the Fletchers should be kept alive any longer.

Yours respectfully,

JOHN W. MAHAN, Esq.   STEPHEN B. IVES, JUN.

Joseph H. Bradley, Esq., also counsel for the defence, addressed the Court briefly, contending that the relations between Mrs. Davies and the defendants were of a friendly nature until one Dr. Mack, seeking revenge on the defendants, poisoned the minds of Mrs. Davies, and induced her to make this prosecution. At all times the defendants were ready to meet the charges against them; and finally, to show that they did not have any dishonest intentions toward the complainant, they consented to an arrangement whereby the property, which remains intact, would be restored to her, although the proof was positive that the Fletchers were in legal possession of it. Finding that they had placed themselves within the reach of the law for defamation of character, Mrs. Davies, and her adviser Dr. Mack, had left the country, and there is now no redress for Mr. and Mrs. Fletcher the defendants.

The Court asked if there was any one to appear and prosecute the defendants; and, being answered in the negative, he ordered the case to be dismissed.

Thus ended our prosecution in America, by our prosecutors running away to England to avoid the consequences of their own misdeeds, and to carry on their work where a stronger prejudice against Spiritualism might give them a better chance of success.

CHAPTER XVIII.

In these troubles, the health of Mr. Fletcher, always feeble, had utterly broken down; and his doctor would not hear of his facing a winter voyage across the Atlantic. I had concealed from him, and also from my parents, the fact of a warrant having been, in spite of the settlement on record in Boston, sworn out against us in London. It was only on the very eve of my departure that any of my family had a suspicion of the fate that awaited me. When the carriage was at the door to take me to the railway, my boy Alvah, who was to drive me there, came and put his hand in mine. " Mamma," he said, " you may deceive grandpapa and grandmamma; but you can't deceive me. I know that you expect to be arrested when you get to England, and that you are going over to take your trial."

Poor mamma was nearly mad with the grief of parting with me, and my little sister clung to my neck until I was forced to tear myself from her. My

132

father, calm and strong, said, "My child, is this true?"

"Yes, papa, I think it is. I thought it best to keep it from my husband, but I must go. I know all that will be said about it. They will call me foolhardy and crazy, and all that; but I could not sleep if I left one stone unturned to prove my innocence. And dearer than that is my desire to relieve Spiritualism from this scandal. Every friend we have in London has a right to demand that we clear ourselves of the stigma of these false accusations."

"My child," he said, "I am not going to oppose you for an instant. If you feel it to be your duty to go to London, *go*. In your defence of what you believe to be right I will stand by you, if it takes you to the scaffold."

This was all the help I had. These partings with my loved ones were my real trial. What came after was of no account, in comparison. I did not tell my husband that I should be arrested, but he did every thing he could to keep me from going. He came with me as far as Springfield on the way to New York, and bore it as well as he could until the moment came when he had to leave the train; then he broke down, and said, "O Bertie, Bertie! for God's sake don't go!" And there came into his face at that supreme moment the anguish of all that was to come.

For my part, I never had a greater evidence of supernatural assistance than the power that made me say, "*I must go*," and which sustained him through that dreadful farewell.

No one on the steamer recognized me as one who had become of late so notorious. The November gales gave us a rough passage; but I was less affected by them than usual, and was glad to be able to give some help to others. Toward the end of our passage we had one of the most frightful storms our captain had ever experienced. It seemed for hours as if we must go to the bottom. I was not in a condition to regard this as a calamity, for I knew that a much worse one awaited me. I cheered the women, and sang to them when it was possible to keep my seat at the piano-forte.

When we had steamed out of the cyclone, the captain said, "I believe I never saw a person so free from care as you are. All the way, you have been as merry as a bird. I think we should give you a vote of thanks, for I don't know what we should have done without you."

"Captain," I answered seriously, "you have been very kind to me, and I should like to tell you a little of my story. What would you say if I told you that I expected to be arrested before I leave your ship?"

"Well, I should say you were taxing my credulity."

"Captain, I *do* expect to be arrested; and I think I ought to tell you the fact and the reason why."

So I told him who I was, and what I had come to meet. He urged me to return to America, not to land at all. "It is preposterous," he said, "that you should be subjected to such an indignity."

"The warrant is out for me," I said. "My information is accurate on that point. I have not crossed the ocean for a pleasure-trip. I have come expressly to meet the charges against me."

He said I need not go on to Greenock. "Why not land at Moville? You can leave us there, and go to London when and how you please, if you *must* go."

Moville is the Irish landing-place for the Greenock steamers, as Queenstown is for those from Liverpool. When he found that I was determined to continue on my course, he only added, "Very well: then all you have to do is to tell me if I can do any thing to help you."

We arrived at Greenock about five P.M. I stood on deck watching for the officers. The captain came, and asked me if I saw them.

"None that I can recognize as detectives," I said.

"And no Mack?"

"No Mack, so far."

"Thank God!" said he fervently. and went to see to his visitors. I sat waiting where he left me.

Pretty soon the captain came again, and said, "Mrs. Fletcher, take my arm. The officers are in the cabin. Shall I bring them here?"

"No, captain. I will go to the saloon with you, and you can introduce my visitors."

The captain brought Mr. Shrive, one of the London detectives, and introduced me to him. "This is Mrs. Fletcher," he said. "She is a lady, and is on my steamer. I have been on this line for seventeen years, and you know me. I hold myself responsible for the treatment of my lady-passengers, and I shall hold you responsible for her treatment afterward."

The arrest was made so quietly and so politely, that though my fellow-passengers were all around me, and many came to say some parting words, not one of them knew what had happened.

I was taken in a cab to the police-station, and treated not only with consideration, but with real kindness. The men looked at me, of course. They were comparing me with a photograph which had been sent down from London. Photographs do not always flatter those who sit for them; and mine must have been very bad, for I was amused at a remark I overheard, "I say, Bob, bean't she handsomer than the pictur?"

I certified to my identity, and was politely shown to the room of the chief of police, where I sat writing letters till three o'clock A.M. Every thing was done

to make me comfortable.   In the morning I was taken
before the magistrate for some formality, and he did
me the honor of calling upon me during the forenoon.

Mr. Shrive, who had come to escort me to London,
did every thing he could for my comfort.   I was
struck with a remark of the female searcher, who was
of course obliged to perform her function.   She said,
" I knew there was nothing about you."   How well
they are able to read human nature !

On the way to London, Mr. Shrive was unremitting
in his kindness.   I was very tired after my sleepless
night, and he begged me to rest my head upon cush-
ions he had arranged.   An old Scottish lady sitting
opposite felt sure we were sweethearts, and was kindly
sympathetic, declaring that she had been young herself.

When we arrived at Euston, Mr. Shrive took a cab,
and did his best not to take me to Bow Street, where
the old lock-up, then nearing its last days, he knew
well was crowded and dirty and dreadful.   But the
better station to which he first took me was full.   The
cab went through Gordon Street.   My house was
lighted up, and the shadow of my bird-cage was pictured very prettily on the blind.   It was a little hard,
and very needless, I thought, to take me past the
home I so dearly loved, and through the Seven Dials
and the slums of Drury Lane, to those horrible cells

in Bow Street — as if I, who had come three thousand miles to be arrested, was likely to try to escape.

Capt. Lindmark, who left the United States for London early in November, met me at the Euston station, and, though not expecting me, came, as his angel directed, to the door of the railway-carriage in which I was. Later he came to Bow Street, where, in spite of the crowd, Mr. Shrive had managed to get me a cell all to myself. Capt. Lindmark, with his ever prescient, never failing, and always most gentlemanly kindness, got me a most comfortable rug, and ordered me a supper. I was made as comfortable as was possible in such a place ; and in the morning I made my first appearance in the famous police-court in Bow Street, before the bigoted, partial, and prejudiced Mr. Flowers, who had sentenced Henry Slade to three months' imprisonment as a rogue and vagabond, and where, sitting in the chair of Henry Fielding, he was destined to see me before him in the prisoner's dock through many weary sessions.

CHAPTER XIX.

·

ON the 3d of December, 1880, I made my first appearance at the ancient central police-court in Bow Street, close by Covent Garden Market and Opera House, — a gloomy, stuffy, wretched old place, which was soon after abandoned for the splendid and spacious new edifice then just completed.

Of ·this bad old place I am happy to testify, that from first to last I was treated by its officers with every possible kindness. I took my place in the prisoner's dock, in front of Mr. Flowers, who. happened to be the one of the three magistrates that day on duty, and who, having had the case of Henry Slade, had had some experience of Spiritualism.

The report of the proceedings in the "Times" of Dec. 4 occupies a column and a half, a very unusual space for a preliminary proceeding. It is headed "CHARGE AGAINST A SPIRITUALIST," a rather unusual kind of heading. How would "Charge against a Methodist," or "Charge against a Baptist," look, for

139

example? It displayed a prejudice at the beginning. A humane maxim of the law presumes the innocence of any one accused of crime until he is proved guilty. I was charged with fraud. The fact that I was avowedly a Spiritualist medium was, to the great body of the people, *prima facie* evidence of guilt.

The prosecutrix, Mrs. Hart-Davies, was " accommodated with a seat" in the witness-box, at the right of the magistrate. The pen in which the public is permitted to stand was packed, as is usual in interesting cases. As many of my friends were present as could get admission, and among them some enthusiastic ladies, who, with more zeal than discretion, brought me large bouquets of flowers.

Mr. S. B. Abrahams, described in the reports as a solicitor, is a Hebrew lawyer, whose practice seems confined to the alternate prosecution and defence of persons accused of irregularities in various police-courts. In New York he would be called a " Tombs lawyer." It is but just to say, that, whether he attacks or defends, he is equally energetic, and equally free from that bane of the profession, scruples. The maxim so often attributed to the Jesuits, " the end justifies the means," is necessarily the rule of the legal profession. According to Erskine, no barrister has a right to refuse a retainer, either to prosecute the innocent or to defend the guilty.

Mr. Abrahams, who solemnly puts on his shining silk hat whenever he takes an oath, had a few months before ably and successfully defended Miss Houghton, a healing medium whom I knew in America. She had been visited by that remarkable *protégé* of Lord Shaftesbury, and anti-spiritualist clergyman, Mr. Charles Stuart Cumberland, who pretended to consult her for rheumatism, took a box of homœopathic pillules, and, leaving half a crown upon her table, went and swore out a summons at Marlborough-street police-court for fraud. Mr. Abrahams was selected as the most fit and proper person to grapple with such an antagonist. He denounced Mr. Cumberland as an impostor, whose real name was Charles Garland, a butcher's clerk at Oxford, and got poor Miss Houghton out of the clutches of the law, and finally compelled Garland, *alias* "Charles Stuart Cumberland," the exposed exposer, to abandon the prosecution. Mr. Abrahams then proposed to prosecute him for perjury, and induced several Spiritualists to contribute a guinea each for this purpose. He has never brought the charge; but, as I presume the etiquette of the profession requires, he has carefully kept the guineas.

Mr. Abrahams, the reader will remember, headed the raid made on my house in Gordon Street in my absence, in which the property claimed by Mrs. Hart-Davies, including a quantity that never belonged to

her, and all our letters, disappeared, and a portion of
which I found later on stored at the Bedford Pantechnicon.

The formal charge against me at Bow Street was
for being concerned, with my husband, in unlawfully
obtaining three strings of Oriental pearls and other
jewelry, by means of false pretences, with intent to
defraud Juliet Anne Theodora Heurtley Richard Hart-
Davies.

"The prisoner having been accommodated with a
seat in the dock,"—I quote the report in the
"Times,"—"Mr. Abrahams proceeded to open the
case at very great length. He said the charge was
one of the most extraordinary nature. The prisoner
had conspired with her husband to defraud the prosecutrix of a great amount of valuable property, and
had obtained large quantities of jewelry and other
valuable effects. The prosecutrix was a married woman not now living with her husband."

Going on with the story, no doubt as told him by
Mrs. Davies and Dr. Mack, Mr. Abrahams gave a
highly colored account of the first acquaintance of
Mr. Fletcher with his patient at Farquhar Lodge.
"There was no doubt," Mr. Abrahams suggested,
"that Mr. Hart-Davies told many events of his life,
etc., to Fletcher, a point which it was important to
bear in mind, inasmuch as it solved the mystery of

the 'spiritual' messages which eventually came to the prosecutrix, and which had so much bearing on the prosecution."

It seems rather remarkable, if such was the case, that Mr. Hart-Davies was never, from first to last, called upon to testify.

"When Fletcher was introduced to Mrs. Hart-Davies," continued this son of Abraham, — "he having previously acquired a great deal of information respecting her mother, her antecedents, etc., from her own husband, — he knew she was the daughter of Mrs. Heurtley, a lady of very large fortune, who lived at Hampton Court House, Hampton Court. Mrs. Heurtley, at the death of her mother and brother, Mr. Sampson, came into property worth over one hundred thousand pounds. This was known to the man Fletcher, as would be proved by a memorandum in his own handwriting, setting forth the whole of the property which by and by, if she lived, the prosecutrix would inherit."

Let me pause in this romance to say, that the amount of Mrs. Davies's property, actual and prospective, is here exaggerated, perhaps twenty-fold, and that the late Mr. Sampson, formerly financial editor of the "Times," was not the brother of Mrs. Heurtley. They lived together, and he bestowed upon her a considerable amount of property; but there was no such lawful relationship.

Mr. Abrahams proceeded to read long messages, written down from memory by Mrs. Hart-Davies, which she said had been given her through Mr. Fletcher in their early interviews, advising her to seek genial society, and do what was needful for her health. It seems very improbable that one should remember so great a quantity of matter with accuracy, and highly probable, that, in any but a "Spiritualist" case, a magistrate would have hesitated to admit such matter as evidence.

Mr. Abrahams said, that, "as Mrs. Davies had never seen Mr. Fletcher before, she was simply astounded at these messages from her dead mother." It did not occur to her that her husband had been carefully coaching Mr. Fletcher in the history of her life. But why was he not in court? and why was he never called upon to prove it?

"On the fifth occasion," said Mr. Abrahams, "Mrs. Fletcher was introduced upon the scene, having, no doubt, also been made thoroughly acquainted with the history of the prosecutrix, to whom she was most affectionate. She would be charged with conspiring with a man not yet in custody [Mr. Morton] in obtaining jewelry, and, among other things, some lace worth four thousand pounds, and in fact every thing which she possessed. [This wonderful box of lace, which no one has ever seen!]

"It would be shown, that, under the influence of the Fletchers and the other man, the prosecutrix was induced to sign a will in the prisoner's favor. After signing the will, Mrs. Hart-Davies began to feel ill, especially after drinking some coffee and other things provided by the prisoner. Mr. Abrahams did not know to what this might lead, but he thought it sufficient to allude to the fact."

This charge of an attempt to murder made, as was intended, a strong impression upon the magistrate, and, no doubt, also upon the public. It justified Mr. Flowers in refusing bail; though it was urged by Mr. Flegg, who had been engaged by some friends to appear in my behalf, that, as I had crossed the Atlantic as soon as informed of the charge against me, it was highly improbable that I would wish to escape from an investigation I had come so far to meet.

But Mr. Flowers, in view of the immense robbery, and attempt to murder, with which I was charged, refused to admit me to bail.

"The prisoner was removed from the dock; and three ladies, each holding a bouquet, two of which were white, emblematic of purity, tried to get at her as she was removed to the cells." As if I were a cripple unable to walk, or some wild beast requiring as much force as poor Jumbo to remove me!

In spite of all Mr. Abrahams had said of my being

a robber, and probably guilty of an intent to murder, the magistrate, "Mr. Flowers, expressed *a hope that the prisoner would be properly treated while in custody.*"

As if prisoners simply accused of crimes, and presumed to be innocent until proved guilty, could ever be *im*properly treated!

CHAPTER XX.

THE worthy magistrate at Bow Street did not long
persevere in his determination to keep me safe in her
Majesty's prison at Clerkenwell. There was not much
to complain of there, only that it is a prison. A person accused of crime, still innocent in the eyes of the
law, should have every comfort consistent with safe-
keeping. No doubt this principle has been to some
extent lost sight of; and accused persons, poor debt-
ors, and even witnesses who were unable to find sureties for their appearance at trial to give testimony,
have been treated as if they were criminals.

After the charge had been made against me at Bow
Street by Mr. Abrahams, I sent for a solicitor recommended to me as an honorable man and a lawyer
of ability and experience in criminal procedure, Mr.
EDWARD DILLON LEWIS. He entered warmly and sym-
pathetically into the case in every respect but one. He
was not a Spiritualist. He had had no opportunity

147

of witnessing the phenomena, and had no belief in their reality. Filled as the age is with an utterly materialistic agnosticism, I could hardly expect to find an English solicitor or barrister who had any knowledge of the subject. There are a few, I believe; but it was not my good fortune to know them.

In the case of Mr. D. D. Home, the solicitor and barristers who defended him were Spiritualists; and many witnesses testified to the reality of his manifestations. But, nevertheless, he was compelled to give back to Mrs. Lyon the sixty thousand pounds she had forced upon him. In his case, however, though exactly similar to mine, there was only a civil suit in chancery. Mr. Home was never prosecuted as a criminal, was never a day in prison, and was condemned to no penalty but the restoration of the property. Had there been in England a law of adoption such as exists in every other civilized country, Mrs. Lyon, who had adopted him as her son, could not have capriciously abandoned him, and reclaimed her benefactions.

The first service Mr. Lewis did me was to make such a representation of my case to Mr. Flowers as to induce him to admit me to bail. Possibly the fact that I had come so far to defend myself and those dear to me from unfounded accusations may have had some influence: at all events, Mr. Flowers fixed my bail at two thousand pounds, my own recognizances in one thousand pounds with two sureties in five hundred each. Two steadfast friends who had known me for years came forward to bail me, — HENSLEIGH WEDGEWOOD, Esq., a man of property and scientific reputation, a relation by marriage of the late CHARLES DARWIN, and for fifty years a London magistrate, and Dr. T. L. NICHOLS, the well-known writer on sanitary and social science.

These gentlemen signed my bail-bonds, to the surprise, no doubt, of some who had listened to the rodomontades of Mr. Abrahams; and I was free to return to my house at 22 Gordon Street, and await the slow progress of my Bow-street examinations.

It was my misfortune, that, a short time before this case arose, the government had appointed a public prosecutor, an official to investigate complaints, and decide what cases should be prosecuted at the cost of the treasury. As this is and has been the practice in all civilized countries but England, nothing can be said against it. But at first it strongly prejudiced every case selected for government prosecution; because it was a novelty, and because people naturally thought a case selected by the government *must* be one of peculiar atrocity. The *selection* of cases must have this effect. The government should prosecute in *all* cases, as in America, France, and other countries, or not at all. Now the government takes up sensational cases, and leaves others, quite as bad, for private prosecution. The newspapers had made mine a sensational case. The police-reports were headed, " THE EXTRAORDINARY SPIRITUALIST CASE," and filled whole columns, while an ordinary felony passed with little notice.

From whatever motives or representations, Mr. Henry Vincent, chief of the Investigation of Crime Department of Home Office, Scotland Yard, decided to take up the case, and instructed Mr. Wontner, the solicitor of the treasury, to prosecute. So on Friday, Jan. 21, 1882, when I drove in the deep snow to Bow Street, I found the suave Mr. Wontner ready to re-open the case; while the belligerent Mr. Abrahams, with his long curved nose quite out of joint, yet insisted that he had a right to watch the case for his clients, and do what he could to assist the treasury. Mr. Wontner consented with a very bad grace, and snubbed his coadjutor contemptuously. All this I could watch very well from my commanding position in the prisoner's dock, where I sat wrapped in rugs, and with hot-water bottles at my feet, kindly brought me by a friendly policeman.

" The court," said the " Times " report, " was crowded in every part with ladies and gentlemen of ' Spiritualist ' renown, and well-known ' mediums.'

" Mr. Wontner, who now appeared on behalf of the public prosecutor, said he did not desire to again open

the case, but he wished to explain away some of the
statements made by Mr. Abrahams, particularly one
with regard to ' free-love.' Mr. Abrahams had mis-
understood what had been said.''

In his sense of '' freedom,'' and in his understanding of '' love,'' Mr. Abrahams, as doubtless instructed,
had been characteristically abusive ; but I think it
highly improbable that there was any '' misunderstanding '' in the matter. The object of the prosecution had been to blacken my character in every way,
which has also been done out of court by hideous and
persistent slander. Mr. Wontner thought it better not
to complicate the case with irrelevant matters.

In the same way the charge of attempting to murder the prosecutrix was quietly abandoned.

Mr. Abrahams having been snubbed, and these cob-
webs brushed away, Mr. Lewis desired to know what
the charges against me really were, — conspiracy, or
larceny, or what? Mr. Wontner declined to make any
specific declaration ; and Mr. Flowers decided that I
was there to answer to any charge that might be preferred against me, and expressed his intention to accept
evidence that was offered on any point.

Then Mrs. Hart-Davies was sworn in her own peculiar fashion. Listening to the rapidly uttered formula,
— in which '' you solemnly swear, so help you God ''
runs off like an alarum, — instead of kissing, or pre-

tending to kiss, the cover of an unknown book, she carefully opened it, and deliberately kissed some clean spot on the printed page. It was very carefully done, but it did in no way hinder her from making false declarations.

The testimony consisted chiefly of readings from Mrs. Hart-Davies's diary (in which she had recorded from memory spirit-messages purporting to come from her mother), and about eighty letters said to have been written by Mr. Fletcher or myself. Of course no proof of their authenticity was given but the oath of the principal, and really, as Mr. Justice Hawkins afterward acknowledged, the sole witness.

The following, from the report in the "Daily Telegraph," gives what the reporter considered most important and significant : —

"Witness was next handed her diary; and her attention was called to the following entry : —

"'Spirit flowers and gems. Mamma's spirit-flower, lily-of-the-valley; her gem, opal: Percy's spirit-flower, Lancaster rose; his gem, ruby: Juliet's (complainant herself) spirit-flower, gardenia; her gem, emerald: Julian's flower, moss-rosebud; his gem, moonstone: baby Juliet (in heaven), lily-of-the-valley; her gem, pearls. She wears a portrait medallion surrounded with pearls; Gasparde, tulip and carbuncle. Given by our angel-mother through the claraudient mediumship of Mrs. Fletcher.'

"This entry witness said she made at the dictation of the defendant, who was in a trance. In another letter Mr. Fletcher said he was writing a most interesting ghost-story, and the spirits kept interrupting with raps; one of their messages being to the effect that the spirits would never be happy till they had read his work. One of the most important of the other letters read contained the following extract, written in a constrained hand by Mrs. Fletcher: —

"'Mamma comes in just now, and says, "Burn all those letters, leaving not one vestige of them escape that has a word of this complication in it. I will satisfy my child's mind of the purity of Willie's mind, and also his complete trust in her. Tell her God bless her. I will take Willie's dear soul to her, and bring hers back to him, and love you all most tenderly all the time."'

"All together, about eighty letters and messages were read, among them the following, purporting to have been dictated by spirits: —

SPIRIT MESSAGES.
SPHERE OF REST IN THE SPIRIT WORLD.

MY LOVED CHILD, — My thoughts are ever with you, and the arms of my spirit infold you. I try to breathe life and strength into you, that you may yet feel the happiness of life. You are never alone unseen: ours watch and guard, and blend their life with yours. The struggles of life are passing. Soon the trials will be over, and then I shall bring all my loved of earth together for a season of sweet enjoyment. There were no tokens of love that I could give to my loved ones this Christmas time; but I breathed my blessing over each dear life, and treasured the pure blossoms of the spirit around them, for human loves seem very weak compared to that which now fills up my life and thoughts: and the old year is dying. With it may your pains cease, and your troubles pass away! May the new year bring happiness for my dear ones! Do not be troubled by the lack of sympathy aunt and others of her kind may manifest. They belong to a different world. It was always so. Heaven's sunshine face, warm and bright, around three.

Your loving mother,　　　　　　THEMIS.

22 GORDON STREET, GORDON SQUARE, W. C.,
January, 1880.

MY DEAREST JULIET, — Once more I raise the pen of a loved one to commune with you, and to try and give your poor heart hope and courage, that you may endure life's troubles to the end, that you may bear the cross uncomplainingly, and thereby be made ready for heaven's blessed rest and peace. Let your heart rest content. I am ever guarding and guiding you, and holding sweet communion with your spirit. As to aunt, why trouble? She is not an accountable being, and has never had any sympathy with us. To her we were another race of beings, and belonged to a different sphere, with which she has not the smallest feeling in common. We must not expect "figs from thistles." To a common-nature like hers the letter was only wasted. The vulgarity was not apparent. Remembering this, it is far better to ignore that which, as my daughter, you cannot condescend to notice. I am glad to find your heart happier. The warm spring-time will soon be here. May it bring happiness and health to all my loved ones! God's blessing be ever with thee is thy mother's prayer.

HAMPTON HOUSE, BUSHEY PARK, HAMPTON COURT, S.W.

Angels' greetings to you, my loved one. Sweet child of mine, I breathe forth my love and blessing; for I have felt your warm and true love about me, and knew there was one of my earthly children who remembered me, who treasured thoughts of the past, while Willie and Bertie have both held in sweet reverence the day and my memory. I fell to write to you upon this paper. But how the recollections flow in upon me as I see the well-remembered name!—joys that are past, friends lost to sight, sorrows whose stings still remain, all pass before me; then the blessed change from the land of winter to the land of summer sunshine, from darkness unto light; and then the long, weary nights of pain which followed, when my earthly loved ones were made to suffer and endure, and deceit and wrong seemed to rise up on every side; and then, blessed privilege! I was permitted to return to them, and breathe the thoughts and desires of my life upon them. Oh, sweet one, can I ever tell you how happy it has made me to be with you, and read your every thought and purpose! The cross laid upon you is changing, and ere long the tired head will find rest. Would that life could bring in the knowledge that comes after life! would that I could have understood you then as now! We shall one day stand side by side, and reap then the blessings and joys that were denied to us on earth. I know that Bertie and Willie will do all that loving hearts can suggest to make the sweet one happy and peaceful. I have looked upon Percy to-day: he lives in the present, not the past or the future. Sweet child, God's blessing fall upon you!

Mother's love will ever be about you and earthly friends. Show childish trust of future, and I will bear thee safely through with the love of Themis.

It is not to be forgotten that Mrs. Hart-Davies at this time professed to be, and appeared to be, an enthusiastic Spiritualist, and that she also believed herself to be a medium, and that she professed to have seen and had communication with her departed mother before she ever came to us. She was and is, no doubt, highly imaginative, with a poetical temperament.

I give these specimens of the testimony now, but will reserve the rest, as the whole case was necessarily and very tiresomely gone over again in the trial at the Central Criminal Court, which ended in my conviction.

CHAPTER XXI.

A CROSS-EXAMINATION.

On Jan. 22, 1880, the streets of London were almost impassable from the depth of snow. A favorite actress, unable to get cab or carriage, was taken to her theatre in a Pickford's van. With some difficulty I made my way to Bow Street in a brougham, provided by a friend whose kindness was the more watchful, the more it was needed; and I had my usual escort, a friend who stood beside me from first to last, — from the outer door through the dim crowd of curious spectators, to my place of honor, the prisoner's dock.

"THE EXTRAORDINARY CHARGE AGAINST SPIRITUALISTS" headed the attractive column in the newspapers with "world-wide circulation," or "the largest circulation in the world."

"The court was more crowded than on the previous day.

"On the sitting of the Court, the complainant was again placed in the witness-box, and her cross-examination by Mr. Edward Lewis at once proceeded with.

156

"Witnesses on both sides were ordered out of court."

Dr. Mack marched out unwillingly; while Mr. Harrison, editor of the "Spiritualist," who had secured a good place behind the government solicitor, refused to go at all. Mr. Lewis insisted; Mr. Abrahams warmly defended his right to remain; Mr. Wontner did not thank Mr. Abrahams for his interference. After a while Mr. Harrison indignantly marched out; and Mr. Lewis began his cross-examination, which I give as it was very much condensed in the report of the "Daily Telegraph."

Mrs. Hart-Davies, cross-examined by Mr. Lewis, said, I see no reason to modify the evidence I gave on the second occasion. It has been modified by Mr. Wontner, and I wish it to remain as it now stands. I adhere in all respects to my evidence given on the first occasion, when I was examined by Mr. Wontner, both as to the facts as to which I deposed and the opinions I then expressed. I then said that through Mr. Fletcher I had re-found my mother. That is the present state of my belief, very much modified. I still believe I had found my dear mother. I do not wish to modify that part of the statement. When I said I found my mother, I did not mean it in the sense that I could communicate with her. I meant that it was from the lips of Mr. Fletcher that I learned for the first time the glorious truth of the actual presence of the dead here with us. I did not mean that wholly in the sense of being able to communicate with them, but partly in that sense.

In what other sense? — That, under certain conditions, they

may have the power of communicating with living persons.
I was a neophyte at that time, and knew very little about
the matter.

Do you at this moment conscientiously believe that the
spirits of the departed have the power of communicating with
mortals?—Under certain circumstances.

Do you believe that the spirit of your departed mother has
the power of communicating with you?—Under certain circumstances she may. I do not know whether all spirits have
the power.

Do you believe that your departed mother has communicated
with you?—Yes; modified.

What do you mean by modified?—Because, since the first
communications of my mother, I have learned to consult my
common sense.

When did you first learn that?—My eyes were opened on
my way to America.

Has your common sense increased since the 21st of last
month, when you were examined here?—I hope it may
always increase.

By the way, what is your age?—Thirty-eight.

Is the state of your belief in the same state as it was on
Dec. 21?—It is *in statu quo.*

Did you on Dec. 21 avow that you knew your mother had
been present with you?—To the best of my belief she had
been. I did not say Fletcher was in a state of clairvoyance.
Trance was the word I used. I spoke of my mother and the
veneration I had for her. There is a difference between clairvoyance and trance. In a trance one is unconscious, but
clairvoyance is merely second sight. I believe in clairvoyance.
I did say I believed Fletcher had derived his information about
me by clairvoyance. That belief is very much modified. I
made the case in my evidence as mild as I possibly could.

Have you altered your determination to make it as mild as you can? — That depends upon the cross-examination. [Laughter.]

MR. LEWIS. — You will not deter me from doing my duty. I know the weapons I have in my hand. A number of letters were read yesterday: are those the only ones you received from Mr. and Mrs. Fletcher? — They are all that I can find. Possibly I received others. I was surprised at so many being preserved. According to the best of my belief, the letter of June 30, 1879, was the first I received from Mr. or Mrs. Fletcher. I certainly did not receive over two hundred letters from them. One or two letters were destroyed by the orders of Mrs. Fletcher, which I obeyed as I would have obeyed a sister's orders. When I visited Mrs. Fletcher's house in Gordon Street I swear I did not remove a single letter that I had written to her.

Mr. Lewis handed the witness a number of letters, which were identified by her as being in her handwriting.

Cross-Examination continued. — I was not a believer in Spiritualism as taught by Spiritualists until I met the Fletchers. I was unconsciously a Spiritualist. I seem to have been standing at the gates all my life. I accept Spiritualism in its higher phases. I believe in the immortality of souls, and the presence of the departed amongst us, and in progress in our after-life.

Is that Spiritualism? — It is, in the higher phases.

On how many occasions do you claim your mother held converse with you? — Claim! I make no claim. I remember. She held converse with me on three successive nights.

Did you communicate that fact to Mr. and Mrs. Fletcher? — No doubt, at some time or other. These apparitions of my mother occurred about the year 1876. I saw the spirit, but did

not speak to it. It appeared to me as a vision, and spoke to
me. Such an occurrence may have come to me subsequently,
as it does to other people, in dreams.

Do you mean these were dreams?—I don't know. They
may have been. I was in my bed. I don't remember whether
such a thing has occurred when I have been up and about. I
will undertake to swear I have not written to Mrs. Fletcher
giving her a message I had received from my mother. I am
not a medium. I have not received such messages. Since
1876 I have had what appeared to be a vision of my mother.
When I was ill in Tours, she seemed to come to take me away
or comfort me. I was alone, abroad, and ill. It is possible I
may have asserted that my mother appeared to me in a vision
in 1879. I have always asserted it was in a vision or a dream.
I do not remember whether I have ever stated that my mother
appeared to me while I was awake and in the act of writing.
I do not remember the fact. (A letter dated Sept. 3, 1879,
was then handed to witness.) I remember that letter. I was
staying with my aunt at Sandgate. I remember the whole
thing now. My mother's presence seemed to be around me as
a breath of air. I believed that then. I felt a sort of happiness.

Mr. Flowers. — Half the poets in the world have felt that
sort of thing. [Laughter.]

Mr. Lewis then read the letter, which referred to witness's
cool reception by her aunt and the company in the house at
Sandgate, and stated how, not listening to the conversation,
she held silent and unsuspected communion with her mother,
whose soft, familiar breath she felt upon her hands. It also
spoke of the dear brother and sister who had led her back to
her mother.

Mr. Flowers thought that a letter that might very well have

been read by the prosecution. He hoped Mr. Lewis would not unnecessarily prolong the case.

Mr. Lewis said he must make a foundation for a perfectly serious cross-examination upon the facts. He suggested this as a convenient time for an adjournment.

Mr. Flowers said there was other business before the Court, and consented to the adjournment."

It was Mr. Lewis's object to show that Mrs. Hart-Davies had been a Spiritualist, and believed herself to be a medium, long before she had become acquainted with us ; that we had not led her into this belief. Mr. Harrison has, since the trial, published a letter from Mrs. Davies, giving some of her spiritual experiences at a date anterior to our acquaintance.

It was evident from the beginning, that Mr. Flowers had made up his mind to send the case to the Criminal Court for trial. The fact that the government had adopted the prosecution probably had its influence : therefore he hoped that Mr. Lewis would not unnecessarily prolong the case. But Mr. Lewis had a conscience in the matter, a professional conscience, which urged him to do his duty to his client ; and he also held in his hands documentary proofs of the true-character of the prosecutrix, which would have proved her to be among the lowest of even abandoned women, and which he thought necessary to my defence to lay before the public. It was an error of judgment on his part. He had no idea of the prejudice, the vindictive hatred, of a large portion of the public against Spiritualism: to them it did not matter what she was; my character alone being criticised.

To him it was a delusion: to a vast number, the feeling against it is the hereditary feeling that made the people of England and America hang or burn witches. The last witch was burned in Scotland in 1710. Sir Matthew Hale sentenced witches to death much later. Since I have been in England, a poor old man was driven into a pond and drowned by a mob of people who believed him to be a wizard.

An Act of Parliament passed in the reign of George III. makes the *pretence* of witchcraft, sorcery, etc., a misdemeanor punishable with a year's imprisonment; and the ninth count of the indictment found against me by an English grand jury — probably without reading, or hearing it read, but simply because it had been drawn up by the solicitor of the treasury — charged me with this terrible offence of pretending to be a sorceress. It is true that some newspapers ridiculed it; but the old anti-witchcraft feeling, which destroyed millions of probably innocent men, women, and even children, all over Europe, now active against Spiritualism, was the basis of my prosecution, and secured my conviction.

On Jan. 28 Mr. Lewis was too ill to attend at Bow

Street. His clerk asked for an adjournment; but Mr. Wontner, the government prosecutor, would not consent. Mr. James McGeary, *alias* Dr. Mack, gave his testimony at length, proving the surrender of all the property of Mrs. Hart-Davies in our possession in America, the prompt and cheerful surrender on our part, and the arrest of himself and Mrs. Davies for some portion of their proceedings. He testified, that, though under bonds of forty thousand dollars to answer for this in America, he came to London to see after the property here; that Mrs. Davies followed him; that he consulted with the officials at Scotland Yard, who were not then inclined to interfere in the matter. Then he went to Mr. Abrahams; and, acting under his advice, he went with him to 22 Gordon Street, Gordon Square, and was present while Mrs. Hart-Davies removed her property — as well as our letters, and many other things which never belonged to her.

The last witness this day was Mr. Shrives, who arrested me at Greenock, and escorted me to London.

Mr. Wontner here asked for an order from the magistrate to enable Mrs. Hart-Davies and the police to search the property now at the Pantechnicon. The managers of that place refused to allow such a search without an order from the magistrate.

Mr. Flowers expressed his willingness to grant the order.

Mr. Wontner said, that, subject to the cross-examination, that would be the case.

The further hearing was then adjourned for a fortnight to enable Mr. Lewis to attend.

CHAPTER XXII.

CROSS-EXAMINATION CONTINUED.

THE case of the government had been completed. Mrs. Hart-Davies, the only witness of the least importance, had given her testimony, and been bound over, in her own recognizances of a thousand pounds, to appear at the Criminal Court as a witness; and I had been formally remanded to allow Mr. Lewis to cross-examine this witness.

The course now decided upon by Mr. Lewis, as absolutely necessary to my defence, was a very painful one to all concerned. I had received this woman as a sister: I had loved her and trusted her. I knew something of her past life and of her peculiar temperament, and what I regarded as a diseased condition. It was not for me to condemn her, but to do my best to save her. I pitied her deeply before she had so utterly debased herself in every one's eyes. I thought that if I, and a few devoted women whom I knew, could put strong and loving arms around her, she might be saved from evil impulses, and become, with her bright intelligence, a blessing to the world.

After she had turned against us, by a strange chance a packet of papers belonging to a gentleman with whom she had been criminally intimate came into the possession of my solicitor.

These letters were used with the full knowledge of their former owner, as he believed that he had been one of the unwitting causes of my misfortune. It was her jealousy, her foolish, groundless, wicked jealousy of him, he believed, that had made her turn against me, and filled her with a desire to be revenged.

Who that has read my story carefully will feel inclined to believe that any *good* motive caused her, or would induce any one possessed of the fine, modest, delicate feelings for which women are especially beloved, to betray the family with whom they have lived and professed to love; to appear for days and weeks in the loathsome precincts of a police-court, and to be the means of condemning one of her own sex to the greatest misery the law can inflict?

It is frequently alleged against women, that they are lamentably bitter against each other; and, with examples like Mrs. Davies, who can reasonably deny the charge?

Mrs. Davies did not love her husband, from whom she was soon divorced; and her letters were full of love — a sort of love, at least — for the courteous young Swede. They were illustrated with drawings not without artistic merit, but not more modest than her words.

I was at first inclined to put all these letters and drawings in the fire; they were really not fit for any thing else: and, had it been me only that this woman was attacking, I think I should have followed my first impulse. But through me she was injuring Spiritualism, the cause I love more than life; and my sense of justice to others, which was very strong, induced me to let the Court know the character of their only witness.

The cross-examination of Mrs. Hart-Davies revealed enough of her life and character to show her an utterly untrustworthy person, and to suggest explanations for her extraordinary conduct towards me. Being pressed to answer, she admitted that her first husband, Francis Rickard, was still living, and that "he and her family" procured the divorce. That the ground for divorce was adultery on her part there could be no manner of doubt; for after many evasions she said, in answer to the repeated question, "I refuse to answer it." The magistrate protected her, and she avoided an open confession. Mr. Lewis then showed her a letter (one of the series which so entirely compromised her), and, having secured the admission that she wrote it, was proceeding to question her upon the terms of affection employed, when the prosecutor objected that the question and the proposed line of defence were inadmissible. Mr. Lewis urged that the antecedents of the prosecutrix were of vital importance to the defence. He assured the magistrate that it could be shown that Mrs. Hart-Davies was wholly out of the pale of good society, alone, and without a friend in the world; that she had obtained an introduction to the Fletchers by stratagem; that the Fletchers were visited by people of the highest position, and that the prosecutrix desired above all things to insinuate herself into such society; that the deed of gift was prepared without the knowledge of the defendant, and the acceptance of the property was forced upon her and her husband; and that it was only ultimately, upon the express understanding and bargain that Mrs. Hart-Davies should be received into the house of the Fletchers free of expense, that the property was handed over. He believed the questions which he proposed to put were relevant and admissible, but confessed that they were at the same time within the discretion of the magistrate. Mr. Flowers decided against the questions, and would not allow the letters in evidence.

Mr. Lewis thereupon, being unable to present the facts under the ruling of the magistrate, said that there would be nothing to be gained by the cross-examination of other witnesses, nor by calling any for the defence.

I was then formally committed for trial at the next sessions of the Central Criminal Court, and was allowed out on the same bail as before for my appearance.

The cross-examination, and the arguments and proceedings following, will be found in the Appendix.

CHAPTER XXIII.

INFLUENCE OF THE PRESS.

IT is a rule of the English press, generally and properly observed, to make no comments on a case while it is *sub judice*. Certainly it would be wrong to influence judge or jury. But a whole community is often intensely excited and deeply prejudiced by the first, often erroneous and generally exaggerated, account of a crime supposed to have been committed. All the mischief may be done before a suspected criminal is arrested. The report of a coroner's inquest has in many instances settled the fate of a supposed murderer. A sensational police-report, or mere description of a crime, has prevented the possibility of an impartial trial.

In my own case the wild statements of Mr. Abrahams (even those afterwards withdrawn), read in millions of newspapers, were generally believed. There was no doubt that I professed to be a Spiritualist and a medium. That alone was sufficient with a large majority to convict me of being an impostor. If I

would deceive people by pretending to get messages
from their departed friends, why not get money by
other false pretences? If I were in the practice of
getting guineas by such frauds, why not thousands
of pounds if I found the opportunity? And, if I were
so base as to take such advantage of ignorance and
credulity, was it likely that I would stop at murder
if it became necessary? Mr. Abrahams knew very
well what he was about. But perhaps this is a good
place to say that I at no time gave professional *séances*
in London.

There were at this time three Spiritualist papers
in London. The oldest of these, the "Medium and
Daybreak," edited by Mr. James Burns, was consistently silent. So far as it had taken sides, it was the
side of Dr. Mack (McGeary).

The "Spiritualist," Mr. Harrison's paper, since
defunct, took up the cause of Mrs. Hart-Davies with
peculiar malignity. Events have since revealed the
editor's professed affection for Mrs. Davies; and now
my intelligent readers will readily perceive the cause
of this partisanship.

The new paper, "Light," was held in a neutral
position by a divided opinion or feeling among its
shareholders. Some were warmly for us, and some
bitterly against. I have no better friends than some
of its contributors, and no more bitter or mischievous

enemies than others. Thus there was little of aid or comfort to be expected from Spiritualist papers in England. In America I was persistently and consistently denounced by the "Chicago Spiritualist Journal," which is noted for its denunciations of suspected mediums, while I have had the generous support of, I believe, every other, especially the "Banner of Light" (Boston), "Mind and Matter" (Philadelphia), "Miller's Psychometric Journal" (New York).

The first notice of my prosecution in England which was sent to America, so far as I know, was in a letter from Dr. Nichols to the "Banner of Light," which will be found in the Appendix. It is printed to show how my case seemed to a personal friend, and a Spiritualist who had for twenty-five years given the phenomena of Spiritualism a careful investigation.

The letter begins by referring to the proceedings against Home and Slade, and relates the history of Mrs. Hart-Davies's acquaintance with Mr. Fletcher and myself, and of the unusual intimacy that followed. Dr. Nichols expressly acquits me of blame, but thinks I was not prudent or worldly-wise, because I should have foreseen what might happen on the part of such an unstable friend. He praises my intrepidity in going to meet my accusers, and gives an account of my examination, with which the reader is already acquainted. He hopes there will be a full and fair trial, and declares that the facts of Spiritualism can be established by hundreds of witnesses of the highest credibility.

My friend has rightly understood my motives in coming to England to meet my trial, and endure my punishment. I did what I felt impelled to do. I did what my spirit-friends wished me to do. Spirits are not infallible. Some spirits are neither wise nor good. But those who are good and wise see much farther into the future than we can see, and I believe it is safest and best to follow their guidance.

CHAPTER XXIV.

The indictment drawn by the well-paid solicitors of the treasury was an enormous document. As a rule, government officials are not troubled with ideas of economy. The wealth of a great empire was at their disposal; and they managed to cover sixty sheets of parchment, making a roll one hundred and twenty feet long, filled with my offences against "Our Sovereign Lady the Queen, her Crown and Dignity."

When this great and costly parchment — nothing so cheap as paper would answer — was unrolled in court, and ran all about, like an immense boa-constrictor, among the barristers, it made a great impression on the jury, as well as upon the spectators. Well it might, for they all had to pay their share of its cost.

In the first count, it is charged that the three defendants conspired to get possession of the jewelry of Mrs. Hart-Davies, by means of the false pretence that her deceased mother had made communications through Mr. Fletcher, in which she, the daughter, was advised

174

and requested to bestow the articles upon Mrs. Fletcher. A very long list of articles is subjoined.

In the second count the charge is conspiracy to cheat and defraud Mrs. Hart-Davies of certain laces and articles of clothing by means of the same false pretence as alleged in the first count (with some additions concerning " magnetic influences ").

The third count is a variation upon the same theme, alleging similar pretences to obtain from Mrs. Hart-Davies the deed of gift. In each of the counts in which the false pretences are charged, the negation is in similar words ; viz., " Whereas, in truth and in fact, the said " defendants " *had not then the power to communicate with or to receive communications from the said spirit of the said A. Heurtley, then deceased; and whereas the said* " defendants " *had not lately before then had any communications with, or received any messages from, the said A. Heurtley, then dead; and whereas the said A. Heurtley, then dead, had not lately before then, and after her said death, through the medium of the said S. W. Fletcher, sent a message to the said* " Mrs. Hart-Davies, " *directing her to share her property,*" etc.

The fourth count charges the defendants generally with conspiracy, by false pretences and by " artful and subtle stratagems and devices," to obtain possession of the property of Mrs. Hart-Davies, and to cheat and defraud her of the same.

The fifth count is almost a repetition of the fourth.

The sixth count charges the defendants with conspiring to steal the same property.

The seventh count alleges a conspiracy in regard to the deed of gift, and varies but little from the third count, omitting only the alleged message from Mrs. A. Heurtley.

The eighth count alleges a conspiracy to induce Mrs. Hart-Davies to execute a will in favor of defendants (the Fletchers) with intent to defraud the legal heirs of their just expectations.

The ninth count I copy in full:—

"And the jurors aforesaid, upon their oath aforesaid, do further present that the said Susan Willis Fletcher, John William Fletcher, and Francis Morton, on the day first aforesaid, and on divers other days thereafter, in the county aforesaid, and within the jurisdiction of the said court, unlawfully did pretend (to wit, to the said Juliet Anne Theodora Heurtley Hart-Davies) to exercise and use divers kinds of *witchcraft, sorcery, enchantment, and conjuration*, against the form of the statute in such case made and provided, against the peace of our said lady the Queen, her Crown and Dignity."

Some careless readers of this count may have supposed that the ancient laws against witchcraft and sorcery had been revived for my benefit; but the offence charged is *pretending to the possession of powers which every spiritual medium is known to possess*.

The reader will see that the real charge against me

was that I professed to be a Spiritualist, and that I falsely pretended to have received, or to have been the medium of, communications and messages from a mother in the spirit-world to her child.

It is evident that my only defence was to prove to the jury that such messages and communications from the so-called dead to the living are a reality. I could have called a hundred witnesses to prove this fact, — noblemen, noble ladies, men of science, intelligent and in every way unimpeachable witnesses, whose testimony would have been received in any court of justice in the world. From all of these witnesses I was not allowed to call one. *I was condemned without a hearing. No defence was made; no witness was heard.*

CHAPTER XXV.

THE OLD BAILEY.

THE sessions of the Central Criminal Court opened on the 1st of April with the usual address to the grand jury. The indictments were prepared and the witnesses ready. So short work was made of this grand preliminary investigation, that my trial was set down for the 5th of April. The grand jury went through the form of finding, perhaps, fifty indictments.

A day or two before my trial was to begin, I was taken with a strong desire to see the place where I was to be tried, and something of the procedure in criminal cases: so I asked Dr. Nichols to take me to the court. The Old Bailey runs north from Ludgate Hill to Newgate, under the morning shadow of St. Paul's. The courts, a cluster of them, are close beside the prison where so many men and women have been hanged and scourged and burned in the bad old times.

On applying to an officer, we were politely shown to seats in one of the courts where a trial was going on. On one side, on an elevated platform, under the royal emblems of the lion and unicorn, sat a judge in wig and robes, supported by two city aldermen without wigs, but wearing their robes of office. Opposite them was the prisoner's dock; and across the court from where we sat were twelve city jurymen packed in a box, which just held them in two rows. In the space below us were the barristers in wigs and gowns of stuff or silk, the latter worn by the higher grade of queen's counsel, from whom are selected attorneys and solicitors-general, judges, and, highest of all, lord-chancellors, whose office it is to keep the great seal and the monarch's conscience, and preside over the deliberations of the House of Lords, with a salary of ten thousand pounds a year, and then, after perhaps six months of service, a pension of five thousand a year for life.

The case on trial was that of a young Jew peddler accused of "ringing the changes." Several witnesses swore that he went into a public-house, called for a glass of beer, laid down a sovereign to pay for it, and then, by some sleight of hand, disputed the change, and got sixpence more than was his due. It seemed a clear case of getting money by false pretences. The pleadings were brief, and the only witnesses called were two as to character. Two Jewish tradesmen, in neat black coats and well-brushed silk hats, entered the witness-box. The clerk handed them a copy of the Old Testament, and they solemnly put on their hats, and were sworn. This bit of ritualism, or relic of old Hebrew ceremony, made an evident impression on the jury; and when these two sleek, comfortable-looking men swore that they had known the prisoner since he was a little boy, and that he had always borne a good character, the jury acquitted him at once, and he went out of court without a stain on his character.

The next case was that of a poor, dark, forlorn-looking little woman, indicted also for getting property under false pretences. There never was a clearer case. It was proved that she had been about buying sewing-machines and many other articles, under the pretence of acting for a house of business, with false cards, bill-heads, etc. The young barrister, who did his best to defend her, had really but one plea. It was that she had at some time been with a man who might be supposed to be her husband. The judge may have occupied ten minutes in his charge, and the jury put their heads together. Then came a curious contest. We could not hear a word they said, but they were arguing in groups. At last only one tall, good-looking juror held out against the eleven. There he stood with his back to the wall, all the rest assailing him.

" I think perhaps you had better retire," said the judge.

"We are eleven to one," said the foreman. "I think we shall soon bring him over."

Of course we thought the tall juryman was for acquittal; and, for the forlorn little woman's sake, we hoped he would persevere. He did a little longer, and then suddenly collapsed. The contest was over; and we waited for the "Guilty," that would send her for months or years to prison.

The verdict was "NOT GUILTY." Our philanthropist had stood out for a conviction. No one doubted the woman's guilt; but she was a woman, and the man she had been with *might* have been her husband.

When she heard the verdict she did not faint, she was not overcome with emotion: she simply turned round, and "scuttled" out of the dock without a word or gesture of thanks for her great deliverance.

The young Jew peddler, spite of his "subtle devices," was cleared because two men in shining hats swore to his good character. The poor little woman, though admitted by her counsel to be guilty of a whole series of impudent robberies, was cleared because her male confederate might or should have been her husband.

There really seemed some hope in such precedents. But I considered that neither of these cases had made the least sensation in the newspapers, and that neither of these prisoners was known to be a Spiritualist.

Their trials may have lasted an hour each. The judge's charges may have occupied ten minutes. The reports of the two cases, if reported at all, may have occupied a dozen lines. Had the verdicts gone against them, there would have been no leading articles next day, a column long, triumphing over their conviction.

The patient reader will see that my trial, so close at hand, was a different affair altogether. I had taken charge of property forced upon me; I had done my best to save and protect a very troublesome woman; I had returned her her property as soon as it was demanded. There was no doubt of my marriage, and I had plenty of friends to testify to my good character. But I was a Spiritualist, — confessedly and professedly a medium: so my indictment covered forty feet of parchment, my trial lasted many days. The judge took five hours to sum up the case, and charge the jury against me. The jury required three hours and a half to make up their minds. I was sentenced to twelve months' imprisonment, with a torrent of invective from Sir Henry Hawkins, in addition, such as is seldom heard, I trust, in any court of *justice;* and there were leading articles, triumphing in my conviction and punishment, in a hundred newspapers.

Why this difference between me and the other poor little woman, who went about deliberately defrauding small tradesmen? Guilty as she was admitted to be by her own counsel, only one juryman tried to convict her. The only plea for her was that of a rather violent presumption of marital coercion.

The real difference was, that I was a Spiritualist; while she got clear because she was only a common swindler, and because Englishmen — who formerly burned women alive here in this very street by Newgate for having counterfeit money, or whipped them horribly at the cart's-tail — are now tender and merciful to women, whether they be thieves or murderers, or whatever they may be, provided that they are not Spiritualists.

But I am getting a little, only a very little, before my story. I mean to give the facts of my case, and I do not mean to talk very much about them.

CHAPTER XXVI.

THE OPENING OF THE CASE.

DURING the time that elapsed between my commitment at Bow Street and my trial at the Old Bailey, preparation was made for my defence. Had it been a civil suit, I could have been put into the witness-box, and it would have been the oath of one woman against the oath of another. The jury would have heard the story of each, and been able to judge which was the true statement of the case. As I was accused of a crime, no such justice could be allowed to me. A few years ago, in this free England, no one charged with a felony was permitted to have counsel to assist him in his defence. No trial, even for high-treason, ever outlasted one day; and the felon convicted on Saturday night, if only of a petty theft or a constructive murder, was dragged on a hurdle to Tyburn, and hanged on Monday morning.

Things are not now so savagely bad, but in some ways they are equally unjust. On this trial, where the whole evidence against me, by the admission of the

184

judge, was the word of one woman, I insist that I, the woman accused of crime, ought in common justice to have been heard. Had it been murder, I should have been heard — *after the verdict*. *Then* the question would have been asked, —

" Prisoner at the bar, have you any thing to say why sentence of death should not be pronounced upon you?"

And then, with the gallows staring me in the face, if I had so told my story that judge and jury, and all who heard me, knew me to be innocent, all the same the judge would have put on the little black cap, over his great white wig, and sentenced me to death.

Since my trial, the judges of England have in this matter reformed their mode of procedure. They had ruled that an accused person who had engaged counsel should not speak for himself. There was no law for it. It was only the convenience of the judges. It saved them a little trouble. But as several failures of justice had come of bad defences, and as some innocent men had been hanged, and others sent to penal servitude who were afterwards known to be innocent, the judges, a year after my conviction, mercifully decided that thenceforth every accused person might exercise the right to tell his own story, even if he had counsel, if dissatisfied with the manner in which his story had been told. Of course this was always the *right* of a prisoner, only the judges had not recognized it, or had trampled it under their feet.

In the preparation of my defence, Mr. Lewis had taken down the evidence of several persons who had received, through my husband or myself, messages from their departed friends, or satisfactory proofs of their existence, and their power to communicate with them under favoring conditions. He had also the testimony of many men and women of the highest character and intelligence as to the reality of such manifestations. This testimony he considered, as I did, of the highest importance; since the indictment, as I have shown, again and again asserted the absolute falsity and impossibility of such communications, and also that I knew them to be false. The fact of Spiritualism itself was on trial; and it was that stupendous fact, and not my own liberty, which I wished to defend. What to me was the risk of five years' penal servitude, if I could in open court, by the sworn evidence of unimpeachable witnesses, prove the consoling truth and the sublime reality of Spiritualism?

I knew that I could put in the witness-box peers of the realm, members of the Royal Society and other learned societies, distinguished clergymen, lawyers and physicians, scientific and literary men of the highest reputation, who would prove the fact, which the indictment denied, THAT A MOTHER, " then being dead,"

COULD STILL SPEAK TO HER CHILD. I knew that three earls could testify to that, and some personages of higher titles, if I chose to call them. I knew that many men and women commanding a higher respect than any title can bestow could give such testimony, and that all the newspapers would be compelled to spread it before the world.

My friends wondered how I could be so foolish as to cross the Atlantic to meet my trial. My answer was and is, "*I did it for Spiritualism.*" If they ask, " Why did not your spirits protect you?" all I can say is, that spirits out of the body, as in it, are not infallible, and they are not omnipotent. They do what they can, as we do. If good spirits could do all they wish to do, this world would be much better than it is. God himself *does* not compel man to be just: he leaves us to " work out our own salvation." But I believe my spirit-guides could have done me no grander service than to allow me to be imprisoned for the truth.

No English solicitor, however learned in the law, however eloquent, can speak in any English court above the grade of a police-court, save in a whisper. My solicitor, Mr. E. D. Lewis, is learned in the law, and has written valuable treatises. He is a sympathetic and eloquent pleader, as I saw at Bow Street; but he could not speak for me at the Old Bailey. It was necessary to engage a barrister, and highly impor-

tant to have one of the highest position, and of course
to pay his price.   Queen's counsel are not now content, as in Erskine's days, to have a brief marked with
an honorarium of one guinea : they expect hundreds.
They are no longer knights-templars with lance in rest,
ever ready to defend the innocent without fee or
reward.   In our days all the learned professions seem
demoralized.   Clergymen buy good livings ; doctors
refuse to see patients until they are sure of their fees ;
and lawyers — well, they expect to be well paid, and
are engaged on one side unless they can receive more
on the other.

Mr. Lewis engaged for me as leader Mr. Addison,
Q. C., an able advocate at the English bar, and with
him Mr. Besley, a barrister of large experience in
criminal procedure.   Against me were Mr. Montagu
Williams, a favorite of the government, who is engaged
on one side or the other in nearly every important criminal trial, Mr. Snaggi, and Mr. Cavendish-Bentinck,
instructed by the treasury solicitor who appeared
against me at Bow Street.   How much, with this array
of legal luminaries against me, I have added to the
burdens of the British tax-payers, I have no means of
knowing.   But the government had determined to
crush out the heresy of Spiritualism, and did not count
the cost.   I was at the moment their Arabi Pacha,
and these were the great guns to blow down my
fortress.

Of course the money used was entirely wasted. That was not the fault of Mr. Lewis. But the simple fact is, that had I refused to expend one shilling, and had I gone into the prisoner's dock utterly undefended, or if I had made my own defence, I should not have been in any worse position, and I might have had the comforting advantage of telling my own story, and thus might have possibly secured my acquittal.

On the other hand, the utter failure of my counsel to make a proper defence has compelled me to make one here and now, before a higher court and a larger public; and I do it in the hope that a greater good may come of my conviction than could have come from such failure to convict as might have been caused by one firm, disagreeing juryman. I may not be able to see, but none the less do I believe, that it was all ordered by the highest wisdom, and that my triumph, or rather, much rather, the triumph of the cause I serve "through evil report and good report," was to come out of much suffering and much reproach.

The cause I serve is the hope of immortality — more than the hope, the CERTAINTY of the life beyond the grave. It was my sense of the value of this evidence that sustained me in the prisoner's dock for eight weary days, and for twelve months in a prisoner's cell, — not only calm, but happy to be a witness for the truth.

It was on the morning of the 5th of April, 1881,

that I drove past the Newgate Prison into the court-yard where judges and prisoners alight, and was escorted to the prisoners' dock, where I sat with the governor of Newgate and two female warders. The largest court-room in the building was crowded, — the bench and seats with ladies and gentlemen, the galleries with as many as could get into them. All rose as Mr. Justice Hawkins and two city aldermen came in and took their seats.

I have described the indictment. When its forty yards were unrolled, and ran about the floor, it made a visible sensation. It was a monster ready to strangle me in its coils. When called upon to plead to this indictment, which charged me with the most base, de-testable, and horrible crimes, I rose and spoke the only words heard from me during my trial, — "Not GUILTY, MY LORD!"

Mr. Montagu Williams, undoubtedly an able lawyer, with considerable facial expression and some dramatic ability, succeeds better as a prosecutor than a defender. In the cases of Lefroy and Lamson whom he defended, he melted the jurymen to tears; but they convicted, nevertheless.

Mr. Montagu Williams opened the case for the prosecution, saying that he had to lay before the jury "a story of fraud and chicanery seldom equalled, and never surpassed, in the history of the criminal courts." [1]

---

[1] The full report will be found in the Appendix.

He described the prosecutrix, Mrs. Hart-Davies, enlarged upon her wealth and possessions, and touched lightly upon her personal history, dexterously avoiding the stains upon her character. Still, he had to admit the fact of the divorce and the former intimacy with Lindmark. He sketched the beginning of her acquaintance with our family, and detailed the supposed arts by which he alleged Mr. Fletcher had acquired his influence over this confiding woman with a view of stripping her of her fortune. The means of influence being assumed to be false and fraudulent, the motive and the action were tainted with crime. He described the trip to America and the circumstances of the deed of gift. Then he read long spiritual communications taken from the note-book of Mrs. Hart-Davies. He again referred to Lindmark, claiming that there was a close intimacy between him and myself, and gave the jury to understand, that on our voyage to the United States my numerous trunks contained the bulk of Mrs. Hart-Davies's personal effects. He alleged that a good portion of the property was recovered by legal process, and that more was found at our house in Gordon Street after her return to London. He thought the jury would have no difficulty in coming to the conclusion that the defendants — myself and husband, and Mr. Morton who drew up the deed of gift — were swindlers, confederated together for the purpose of obtaining the property.

This was the opening of the case. I have already spoken of my relations to Capt. Lindmark. They were honorable to him and creditable to myself. I have nothing to regret in them, but the fact that I have been made by Mrs. Hart-Davies the means of giving a needless publicity to the scandal of their intimacy when they were unfortunately thrown together, so long ago, in South America. I very much regret that I must also, later on, give Capt. Lindmark's own sworn statement, which should properly have been given in the witness-box, in the course of my trial, and which would have been given had I managed my own defence.

The reader will see from the opening, as well as in the indictment, that the single point upon which the whole case turned was *the reality of spiritual manifestations.* The deed of gift and the transfer of property were perfectly legal, unless it could be shown that they were induced by false and fraudulent pretences ; namely, the pretence of having received communications from departed spirits.

A forged draft must be proved to be a forgery : its falsity cannot be assumed. The drawer or indorser must come into court, and deny his signature. In this case falsity was assumed when it should have been proved. The indictment charged that "dead men tell no tales," and that the mother of Mrs. Hart-Davies, being dead, could not advise her daughter.

It was not proved that the spirit of Mrs. Heurtley did not exist, or, existing, could not communicate with her daughter, but, so far as the daughter's testimony went, quite the contrary. Where, then, is the *proof* of false pretences?

On the other hand, Mr. Morton, who had come from America, and was ready to testify at my trial had he been allowed to do so, would have sworn in the witness-box, as he has done in his affidavit, that Mrs. Hart-Davies, before making the deed and the will, solemnly declared that *she had not been influenced, either by mortals or spirits.*

And there is no proof aside from her own testimony that she ever received the communications. Nor was there any evidence offered to establish the validity of the letters beyond Mrs. Davies's testimony.

The testimony, cross-examination, and speeches, being mainly a repetition of the case at Bow Street, are in the Appendix. That the reader may have a knowledge of my defence, I give the testimony as to character, and the substance of my counsel's speech.

CHAPTER XXVII.

THE TESTIMONY AND CROSS-EXAMINATION.

THE first witness called to support this opening statement was the friendly detective who arrested me at Greenock. He said, —

"The prisoner laughed at the charge which mentioned a string of pearls, remarking, 'I am rather amused at those pearls. I was charged with stealing them in America, and now I am accused of obtaining them by false pretences.' She added, 'I suppose they have them now; as they have been to my house in Gordon Street, and taken away what they thought proper. I left them in London when I went away.' At Bow Street, after the first examination before the magistrate, prisoner said to witness, 'If you go to the Pantechnicon, and search a small chest of drawers, you will most likely find the pearls; as I left them there when I went away.' He found the pearls in the place described."

Mrs. Hart-Davies gave about the same testimony as at the police-court, relating the messages which she said she believed came from her mother, and describing the movement of a small table across the room when it was not touched by any person present.

194

The day was consumed in hearing a part of her story, and in reading letters supposed to confirm it. On the second day, April 6, she said, —

"Before I left Farquhar Lodge I became acquainted with Col. Morton. He was introduced to me by the Fletchers, I believe, at their house in Gordon Street; and they told me subsequently that he was their lawyer."

The story, spun out by questions and answers, was, that at my suggestion she applied to Mr. Morton to draw up the deed of gift; that, before signing it, she became very ill; that Mr. Morton magnetized her, but she became fainter and fainter.

Did he write out the document before the pawing, or after? WITNESS. — He wrote it out before, and then came the mesmerizing.

Did you understand him when he read the document? WITNESS. — No. His voice sounded to me like a distant whisper. I could hardly understand the document, because I was so faint. He said he had complied with my instructions in regard to protection. When I had signed the document, I rested a little while, and then, later on, went home, feeling very bad. A few days after, I had another interview with Morton; but before that I had seen Mrs. Fletcher, and she had delivered to me another message from my mother, urging me to write a letter to her making things more binding. When I saw Morton I told him that Mrs. Fletcher wanted a letter which would make the protection more binding to her, so that she could keep it privately in case any thing should occur to me.

Was there any mesmerism on this occasion? WITNESS. — No. He made out a draught-letter, and proposed that I should put a head and tail to it in my own style, and copy it on my own crested paper. I took the draught home, and copied it, and sent the copy to Mrs. Fletcher; and I subsequently took the draught to Col. Morton, who said he wished to destroy it.

This letter was then read, and stated that the prosecutrix handed the property over to the prisoner as a free gift.

Examination continued.—Subsequently I made a will, about which I had several conversations with the Fletchers. Morton suggested that I should make the will. He said that I should take into consideration the delicate state of my health and the uncertainty of human life, and that I ought to make a will before my departure for France, suggesting that I should leave the money where it would be most wanted and useful.

Yes: what next? WITNESS. — I suggested that I should like to leave the bulk of it to the propagation of the cause of Spiritualism in its higher phases, teaching the truths of the life to come and immortality.

What did Morton say? WITNESS. — He said, legally speaking, that could not be done. It must be done through individuals; as the outside world might say I was mad [laughter], they having no sympathy with the cause. He suggested that it would be better to leave the money to my adopted brother and sister (the Fletchers).

Before you executed this will, did you have any conversation with the prisoner about the will? WITNESS. — About the will, but not about its execution. On several occasions we had conversations about the matter. On one occasion, when I was alone with the prisoner, I spoke to her, as my mother, about the proposition which Morton had made to me. She then went into a trance.

How did she go into the trance? WITNESS. — Oh! she went into it very quietly, — put her hands round me, and shut her eyes. [Laughter.]

MR. ADDISON. — I should like to know what this trance was like. The others we have heard of were attended with shivering. [Laughter.]

THE JUDGE. — They are not always alike, Mr. Addison. [Laughter.]

MR. MONTAGU WILLIAMS. — That was a male trance: this is a female trance. [Loud laughter.]

Examination continued. — In the trance the prisoner commenced speaking about the will. She told me to go to Col. Morton, as he would find a good solicitor for me. Subsequently I saw Col. Morton, and I asked him if he knew a good solicitor to make this will valid and draw it out for me. At first he mentioned a firm of solicitors, — Murray & Miller. I went to their office with him; and, having made some preliminary remarks, he left some papers of mine there. A short time after, I received a letter from the prisoner purporting to come from my mother. The communication said, the sooner I took the papers away from Miller, the better. I informed Col. Morton of the contents of the letter; and, having got the papers from Miller, I met Morton, and we then went to the firm of Field, Roscoe, & Francis, solicitors. We there saw Mr. Francis, and I was introduced as a friend of Fletcher. It was proposed that Mr. Francis should manage the matter for me. A will had been prepared by Mr. Morton, and was handed by him to Mr. Francis, who thought it necessary that a codicil should be added. A codicil was subsequently sent to me, and I signed it. I also signed the will drawn up by Morton.

THE JUDGE. — I do not observe any thing in the will or in the codicil about Spiritualism in its higher phases. Was any thing said about that to Mr. Francis? WITNESS. — No, my lord.

MR. MONTAGU WILLIAMS. — I think it fair to Mr. Francis that I should call him.

MR. ADDISON. — I should be glad if Mr. Francis could be called.

THE JUDGE. — Nothing has been said against Mr. Francis in any way.

MR. MONTAGU WILLIAMS. — No, my lord. Only it is not agreeable to be mixed up in such a matter as this.

THE JUDGE. — I only wanted to know whether any thing was said in the will about Spiritualism. WITNESS. — No, my lord. Col. Morton said it was not necessary.

The will was read by Mr. Read (deputy-clerk).

MR. MONTAGU WILLIAMS. — What induced you to make this will?

MR. ADDISON. — You have got that. She said she made the will with the view of propagating the cause of Spiritualism.

MR. MONTAGU WILLIAMS. — I will put the question in this form (to witness): Did you believe that the directions about the will really came from your mother? WITNESS. — Certainly I did, or else I never should have thought of making it. I believed the prisoner, and it was in consequence of what she said that I made the will.

The reason why Mr. Morton was included in the indictment, and so prevented testifying, is obvious; because he would have contradicted nearly every word of this statement, as he has done in his affidavit, which I will give among the suppressed evidence. He was at hand for the purpose of surrendering himself for

trial to meet the charges, and ready at any risk to
testify, but was assured that any effort to do so would
be perfectly useless to me, as it would have placed
him, silenced and helpless, in the prisoner's dock by
my side, and in all probability have consigned him to
penal servitude.

Among the letters read — all on one side, for the
·others had disappeared since the search was made in
Gordon Street — was one in which Mr. Fletcher had
written, —   .

I do not like your dream, because it showed to me how
weak you were.

Mr. WILLIAMS (to witness). — What were the dreams?

WITNESS. — Oh! something pretty. It seemed as if I were
walking in a beautiful garden, with the perfume of orange-
blossoms in the air. I thought I was walking with Fletcher.

THE JUDGE. — Where were the gardens? — I don't know.
I say I simply dreamed it.

THE JUDGE. — I suppose it could have been at Vernon
Place or Gordon Square. [Laughter.]

Mr. WILLIAMS (to witness). — You had written to Fletcher
to tell him what the dream was? — Yes. I told him that I
had been in his company and the company of sundry other
friends.

Can you tell us more definitely about this dream? — I
have told you. I dreamed that I was walking in a garden per-
fumed with orange-blossoms, jessamine, and other flowers.

THE JUDGE. — Stop a minute. I will just put in the jessamine. We hadn't that before. [Laughter.]

WITNESS (continuing). — I seemed to be walking and conversing with Fletcher, with the prisoner at the bar, and with many others.

THE JUDGE. — What were you conversing with Fletcher about ? — I was conversing with him about spiritualistic truths, about immortality, and about other subjects. It seemed a beautiful dream to me.

Who were the others there ? — It is impossible for me to remember now.

Was Morton or the handsome captain on the scene? [Laughter.] — I did not trouble my head about either of them.

They did not appear in the dream ? — Not at all.

Near the close of the second day, the judge, being tired of the monotony, interposed, wishing to know if it were necessary to read any more letters. They all contained the same sort of — well, he was going to say rubbish, but he would call it language.

MR. ADDISON. — Yes, my lord, the language of affection. I think it is important to the defence that the letters should be read, as showing how far they corroborate the charge of false pretences.

MR. WILLIAMS. — And the letters might be important in reference to the conspiracy counts.

MR. ADDISON. — There was a belief in Spiritualism among some of these people, who mixed up the subject with a great deal of affection; and what I want to show is, how far the false pretence alleged is unsupported by these letters. The letters are important to me as exhibiting the real motives of the prosecutrix in placing her property in the custody of the Fletchers. They show the march of events up to the point of "work and love and wisdom," when love and wisdom got jealous, and fell out.

MRS. HART-DAVIES.—That is untrue.

On the following day Mrs. Hart-Davies's examination was continued, when Mr. Williams proceeded to read additional letters of the same character as those already read.

Mr. Addison called attention to the fact that a portion of one of those letters had been torn away.

Witness, in answer to Mr. Williams, said, That was torn off because Mr. Fletcher considered that I thought otherwise of him than as a brother. My indignation was so intense, that I wrote to him to that effect; and I had a severe illness in consequence. Mrs. Fletcher ordered me to destroy all correspondence on that subject. There is not the slightest foundation for saying that there has ever been any improper conduct between myself and Mr. Fletcher. I wrote a number of letters to the Fletchers. I have never received any of them back, nor have I seen them since I sent them. When I returned from Tours, on the 1st of May, Mrs. Fletcher and I went to Gordon Street, where I found a room prepared for me. I remained in the house for twelve weeks.

Did you pay for your board?—I did not. I gave them my whole income, which was three hundred pounds a year. Capt. Lindmark frequently visited at the house while I was there. In early days the prisoner told me that my mother had desired that we should form a "trinity,"—love, wisdom, and work. Fletcher was to represent wisdom; the defendant, work; and I, the affection of the family to bind them all together.

Was the "trinity" ever formed?—I do not know. It was all a mystery to me.

MR. JUSTICE HAWKINS.—It is a mystery to me too. [Laughter.]

The story of the trip to America, the meeting with Dr. Mack and the Hornes, the search-warrants and arrests all round, and the escape of Dr. Mack and Mrs. Hart-Davies to England, were then tediously gone through with.

The cross-examination of the witness by Mr. Addison was more lively and interesting, and took up points of the evidence which in the direct examination I have omitted, because it did not seem desirable to tire the reader.

Mr. Addison, Q.C., is, as I have said, a man of eminence in the profession; but his idea of a proper method of defence was not mine nor my solicitor's. I wished to have the case seriously treated, and to call witnesses who would testify to the reality of spiritual manifestations, which the whole effort of the prosecution was to deny. The result of the trial did not trouble me. Whether the jury believed the evidence, or not, I wanted it put on record, and published to the world.

Mr. Addison thought it was enough to show the character of the only important witness, and so relied upon his cross-examination. Also he knew, apparently, that Mr. Justice Hawkins would rule out all the evidence I wished to offer. So he proceeded with his cross-examination, which I give as I find it reported in the newspapers.

I hope my readers will have patience to read this summary of Mrs. Hart-Davies's evidence. It will require but little imagination to reproduce the scene, and to appreciate the parts played by the different actors. The plausible, mendacious, and generally shameless part of the prosecutrix is sufficiently evident. Mr. Addison is seen goading the wretched woman, to force her to display her qualities before the Court; meanwhile he responds occasionally to the banter of the presiding judge as if they two had parts in a farce, or more as if they were the "end-men" in a minstrel show. This trifling, punning, and leering between comfortable, well-fed officials, while the liberty and honor of an unoffending woman were at stake, were unspeakably heartless and repulsive. We don't appreciate jokes and chaff from hangmen and undertakers.

Mrs. Hart-Davies was then cross-examined by Mr. Addison. She said, I wrote out the inventory of the property delivered to the prisoners in America. I had made out an inventory before, but the inventory I made in America was done from memory. The box of lace is not mentioned in the inventory, because I directed my attention chiefly to the jewelry; but the box of lace is mentioned in other inventories. My mother died in the year 1876.

Mr. Addison. — Does your trustee know any thing about the lace ? — I don't know.

Mr. Addison. — Is your husband in court? — I don't know. If you want to know the value of the lace, you had better go and ask my mother's spirit. [Laughter.]

Mr. Addison. — Oh, no! I cannot do that. [Laughter.]

Cross-examination. — I swear that I do not know whether my mother left a will, or not. I know that she wished me to have all her jewelry and other property; and I know that there ought to be a will, but that has to be investigated. I am supposed to be her administrator.

Mr. Addison. — You went to swear to the value of her property? — Well, yes.

And you swore that her effects were worth under a hundred pounds? — I did, on the advice of a lawyer.

Mr. Justice Hawkins. — Who was the lawyer? — Am I compelled to disclose my private affairs?

Mr. Addison said he did not care to have the name of the lawyer; and the learned judge said, as this was the case, he would not insist upon an answer being given.

Cross-examination continued. — Before my mother died, she had all the property locked up in boxes, and labelled with my name. I was in Paris when my mother died, and the property was handed over to me. I did not see my mother for two or three years before she died.

Mr. Addison. — Has anybody ever seen this mysterious box of lace? — I won't tell you.

Mr. Justice Hawkins. — But you must tell us.

Witness. — I believe Madame Michaud saw it.

Where does she live? — I don't know. In London somewhere. I don't know her address.

Cross-examination continued. — I believe Mrs. Weldon also saw the lace, and I think Madame Michaud saw it at Gordon Street. Before I came into connection with Mr. Fletcher, I had

never seen my deceased mother except in visions or dreams,
whichever you like to call them. Whenever I saw her, it appeared to me like a dream; but I have seen her when I was
wide awake.

MR. ADDISON/—In white robes ? [Laughter.]

WITNESS. —In something beautiful and bright which I cannot explain. In other respects she looked to me as she did
when she was alive. It is possible that I may have only seen
my mother, as other people do, in dreams. I was an "unconscious" Spiritualist before I saw Dr. Fletcher; and I believe
in immortality, and in the sympathy of those who have gone
before us. In the course of the conversations I had with Mr.
Fletcher, I said that either in dreams or in a vision I had seen
the spirit of my departed mother, and that it seemed to me that
she had conversed with me in a vision. In my dreams it appeared to me that my mother told me that there was no such
thing as death, but it was only a change; and she appeared to
me to say those words. I understood that she meant merely a
spiritualist change, and that this was how she was permitted
to come and speak to me. These visions occurred in 1876.
My husband first sent for Dr. Fletcher. By my husband I
mean Mr. Hart-Davies. I was perfectly aware that Dr. Fletcher
was what is called a "magnetic" doctor. I failed to feel any
magnetic influence when I first saw him: and he told me that
this was not his *forte*, and that his vocation was that of a
trance medium; and he went off into a trance.

MR. ADDISON.—Straight away ? [Laughter.] He took hold
of your hand, shivered, and went to sleep ? [Laughter.]

Cross-examined. —He told me not to be alarmed if he went
into a trance; and shortly afterwards he shut his eyes, shivered,
and then went off. My hand was in his all the time; and he
told me not to take my hand away, as it might bring on serious

consequences, and affect his system seriously. [A roar of laughter.] He shivered so much, that I had to hold on tightly to keep hold of his hand.

MR. ADDISON. — Then, you "shivered" together? [Laughter.]

WITNESS. — It was while he was shivering he began to talk about my mother. He began to get quiet while he was delivering the message from my mother. I was filled with awe while he was delivering the message. He spoke with his eyes shut; and I remembered all he said, and wrote it down immediately afterwards. All the time he was speaking, he said that he was under control, and that he was delivering a message to me from my mother. He knew that I had suffered persecution from a variety of causes. My first marriage was an unsuitable match, and I was also not happy in my second marriage. My sufferings were alluded to in the first message the prisoner's husband delivered to me from my mother. I was not in the habit of complaining of the persecutions that I had experienced. I have been present at spiritual manifestations at which the Fletchers were not present, and it seemed to me that the table has moved round when I and the others placed our hands on it. Certain questions were asked of the spirits, and vigorous raps were given in reply. [Laughter.] I would not swear that all this actually occurred, but it seemed to me as though it did.

The Court then adjourned for luncheon, and after a brief interval the proceedings were resumed.

Mrs. Hart-Davies was then further cross-examined. She said, I was never myself a "medium," but I have very often seen visions of my mother; and I communicated to the prisoner that I had had a most beautiful vision of my mother. This referred to my dream when I was in the garden with Mr. Fletcher.

Mr. Addison. — Are you quite sure that your mother was with you on this occasion ?

Witness. — Oh, yes !

Mr. Addison. — Was "J.," whom you speak of in your diary, your husband ? Was it "Jemmy" ? [Laughter.]

Witness. — I wish you would speak of my husband respectfully. [Laughter.]

Cross-examination continued. — I cannot tell who were mediums, and who were not. Perhaps the whole of us are mediums: I cannot tell. The matters I entered in my diary were all intended to be a truthful description of what occurred, so far as I could understand it. I put down what I seemed to see and hear. I could not tell whether it was true, or not.

Mr. Addison. — You understand the meaning of a medium?

Witness. — There are many kinds of mediums, — a medium of getting a dinner and other things.

Mr. Addison. — And I suppose there is a medium of love. Where was poor Mr. Hart-Davies during all the time you were having the private interviews with Mr. Fletcher ?

Witness. — Sir !

Mr. Addison. — Oh! don't be emphatic. I only want to know where your husband was all the time these things happened.

Witness. — He was in the house, and he objected to the *séance* with Mr. Fletcher.

Mr. Addison. — Did Mr. Fletcher say that it was better for your husband not to be present ? — Yes. He said it was better no one else should be present. He knew all that was taking place.

Mr. Addison. — Was he aware of the taking by the hand, and the shivering, and all that ? [Laughter.]

WITNESS. — Yes.

MR. ADDISON. — Perhaps he was glad to get his mother-in-law back again ?

WITNESS. — I don't know.   My husband had been a soldier and a sailor.   When the first interview took place, he sat in an arm-chair, and watched us.

MR. ADDISON. — He did not shiver, did he ?   [Laughter.].

WITNESS. — No.

MR. ADDISON. — Did he say any thing ? — No.

MR. ADDISON. — Not even "Shiver my timbers" ?   [A roar of laughter.]

Cross-examination continued. — I parted with Mr. Hart-Davies partly for private and partly for business reasons, but the Fletchers hastened the separation.   We considered it advisable to live apart, and that each of us should find our way to heaven in the best way we could.   My husband did not express any astonishment when he heard the first message came from my mother in heaven.   Dr. McGeary is now my spiritual adviser and brother.

The witness, in answer to another question put by the learned counsel, said it was a lie.

Mr. Justice Hawkins severely reproved the witness for this, and said she desired to be treated with respect, and he must insist that she should treat other persons with respect.

Mrs. Hart-Davies burst into tears, and some minutes elapsed before the case proceeded.

In further cross-examination she said, My husband was not present at the trances that afterwards took place, and Mr. Fletcher desired that he should not be present.   I am quite sure that I never told Mrs. Fletcher that I had been a medium from my childhood, and that I had heard voices.   I am sure that I never told Mrs. Fletcher that I was getting rapidly well under her husband's treatment.

MR. ADDISON. — Did you ever tell her that you could not live without her husband? [Laughter.]

WITNESS. — Never.

MR. ADDISON. — Could you have lived without him? [Laughter.]

WITNESS. — Certainly. I loved the defendant and her husband as saints, and I looked upon them as saints.

MR. ADDISON. — Which saint did you love best?

WITNESS. — I loved one as well as the other.

Cross-examination continued. — I have complained of my husband intending to poison me, but this was only in consequence of what other people told me. I never accused my husband of attempting to poison me. I did not ever say that he had deceived me as to his social position, and that he had represented himself as being related to a noble duke, when in reality he was only a common sailor. I never complained to the Fletchers that my husband had pawned some of the jewelry.

MR. ADDISON. — Did you never tell the Fletchers that you wished them to take care of your jewelry for fear your husband should get hold of it, and pawn it?

WITNESS. — I never said so, but I may have said that some of the jewels had been made away with in order to supply the necessities of my husband. I never complained to them that my husband had put arsenic in my wine.

MR. ADDISON. — Did you never say to them that you believed in the affinity of spirits, and that you considered Mr. Fletcher the counterpart of yourself?

WITNESS. — No. I believed in the affinity of spirits on this earth, but I did not say any thing about Mr. Fletcher. I followed them like a sheep. [Laughter.]

MR. ADDISON. — Was it not you who proposed to form a

triangle, or trinity, and that it was to be composed of the Fletchers and yourself ?

WITNESS. — No. It was they who suggested it to me.

MR. ADDISON. — And did you not say, in reply to the observation, that if the triangle were formed, and you went to live in the same house with the Fletchers, your position would be rather ambiguous, — that you would only be in the same position as five hundred other sisters were ?

WITNESS. — No.

MR. ADDISON. — And was not it said by some one, that, if the arrangement was carried out, the house would be full of "troubles" ?   [Laughter.]

WITNESS. — I never heard another thing said.

Cross-examination continued. — I do not remember any other persons than the Fletchers defrauding me of my property. My husband was not aware that I had placed the jewelry in the possession of the Fletchers. I did not dare to tell him that I had placed my jewelry in the hands of the Fletchers to take care of. They both insisted that I should not tell my husband that I had given them the jewelry. A great cart-load of boxes was taken from my house in Vernon Street to Gordon Street; and my husband wanted to know where they were going to, and I told him they were going to the Fletchers to be taken care of. I did not say any thing to my husband about the magnetism that was in the jewels. I did not talk to him about such nonsense.

MR. ADDISON. — Oh! nonsense, was it ?

WITNESS. — Well, it was solemn nonsense. It all seemed a mysterious affair to me, and I could not understand it.

MR. ADDISON. — But your husband had been present when your mother was first introduced to you by Mr. Fletcher, while he was sitting in the arm-chair, and his own papa was introduced on this occasion, standing behind his chair. There was no reason to conceal the mysteries from him. [Laughter.]

The witness went on to state that it was always understood that she was to have her property back whenever she wished to have it. The defendants did not say this, but it was always understood that this was the arrangement between them. It was an understood thing between me and the Fletchers, that I should not make any allusions to my mother's messages in my correspondence with them. They advised me not to write any thing about these messages. I don't know what has become of the letters I wrote to Dr. Mack (McGeary) or the Fletchers, but the same rule applied to all my correspondence. I was told not to tell; and I promised I would not, and kept my word. Mrs. Fletcher told me of the visions she had seen of my mother, and her description of her appearance appeared to coincide with what I had seen myself. She was present when the table moved in the way I have described. Mr. Fletcher was not in the room, but he knew what the table was wanted for. The "moving" took place in a room called the "Séance Room." It came towards me, but stopped before it touched me. [Laughter.]

MR. ADDISON. — That was rather fortunate.

WITNESS. — I was rather amused by the occurrence. The table moved first one leg, and then the other.

JUSTICE HAWKINS. — Like a fashionable dancer. [Laughter.]

WITNESS. — I thought the affair was ridiculous, but I did not exactly laugh at it. While the table was dancing, there were loud raps, and the table moved rapidly.

MR. MONTAGU WILLIAMS. — A sort of double-shuffle. [Laughter.]

JUSTICE HAWKINS. — What sort of a table was this extraordinary table?

WITNESS. — A little coffee-table.

MR. ADDISON. — Did not you try to get hold of it, and stop its proceedings? — Oh, no! certainly not. I did not think it at all extraordinary when the defendant asked me to look into the crystal ball. I had heard of such things being done among the Egyptians for the purpose of diving into futurity.

Did you expect to see a man with a brown beard writing at a table in the crystal ball?

I did not know what I should see. But when I looked, and saw the man with the brown beard, it did not have the effect of amusing me as the table-moving had done. I never saw any table-moving, nor heard raps, except when Mrs. Fletcher was present.

MR. ADDISON. — You are tolerably sharp in all respects, except when you are dealing with mysteries, I believe, Mrs. Hart-Davies?

WITNESS. — I don't understand you. She went on to say, At the time the table moved, there were raps; and Mrs. Fletcher called out to the spirits, and asked what they wanted. I certainly loved Mrs. Fletcher very much, and she professed to love me.

MR. ADDISON. — Was it that love that induced her to give you the photograph you have spoken about? WITNESS. — I cannot say what induced her to give me this photograph. Mrs. Fletcher had previously told me that some of the photographs were "naughty." [A laugh.] In the letter that has been called "the mutilated letter," Mr. Fletcher appeared to attribute to me a feeling towards him which was totally contrary to the feeling that I really entertained with regard to him.

MR. ADDISON. — Have you ever been "scrunched" by Mr. Fletcher? [Laughter.]

WITNESS. — Oh, certainly! And Mrs. Fletcher encouraged him. [Laughter.]

Did he not say something about your desire to trespass on Mrs. Fletcher's ground? [Laughter.]

WITNESS. — I looked upon it as an insult. I did not know what he meant by Mrs. Fletcher's ground. There may have been five hundred Mrs. Fletchers, for all I know. [Laughter.] I was extremely displeased at his imputing to me a passion for him which I never entertained or dreamed of. I sent his letter and my reply to his wife.

MR. ADDISON. — You knew that he was suggesting something that was very wrong?

WITNESS. — Yes. I was angry, and thought that he was impertinent.

MR. ADDISON. — Did he not entertain this idea in consequence of your telling him your dream about walking in the garden with him?

WITNESS. — I think that had something to do with it.

MR. ADDISON. — I see, that, in one of the letters, there is a reference to your being in Paris with the defendant's husband for twenty-four hours. Did any "cuddling" take place at this time?

WITNESS. — I may have had my head on his breast while we were sitting by the fire, but that was all.

MR. ADDISON. — Did you kiss Fletcher while his head was on your breast?

WITNESS. — I cannot say how many times I have kissed him, but I always kissed him as a brother.

Did you kiss him hard? — I do not know what you mean. I have kissed him countless times.

You really do not know what kissing hard means ? — I do not.

Were you all night, or part of the night, in this position ? — No. It is an aggravation of the offence to impute such conduct to me.

Mrs. Hart-Davies was about to say something more, when Mr. Montagu Williams begged her to be quiet, and answer the questions put to her, and not make speeches.

MR. ADDISON. — Do let your witness alone, Mr. Williams. Let her tell her own story. [A laugh.]

Cross-examined. — I was not aware that the defendant or her husband treasured up the letters that I sent to them. I know nothing about them, or what became of them. Since my return from America, I have not taken any steps to find my husband, and I have not seen my trustee; but I have seen my son. I have seen Dr. Mack several times since my return, but not every day, because he has a very large practice.

MR. ADDISON. — Practice as what ?

MRS. HART-DAVIES. — Is your memory so short ? [Laughter.] I have told you before what he is. He is a mesmerizing doctor.

I believe he is now your spiritual brother.

WITNESS. — Yes, he is.

Does he mesmerize you ? — No.

What sort of a passion did you entertain for Capt. Lindmark ? — The affection of a trusting young heart, — nothing improper.

By MR. ADDISON. — I introduced Lindmark to the Fletchers while my husband was alive.

Mr. Justice Hawkins said he really could not see the relevancy of this line of examination; and it appeared to him that the matter had nothing whatever to do with the real question at issue, which was, whether the defendant and her husband had conspired to cheat Mrs. Hart-Davies of her jewels. Even assuming that the latter had acted immorally, of which he was far from saying there was the slightest proof apparent to him, this had nothing to do with the real question.

Mr. Addison assured his lordship that he considered it most material that the prosecutrix should be cross-examined upon these matters.

Cross-examination continued. — I have seen Capt. Lindmark in Mrs. Fletcher's room. I was divorced from my first husband in 1875, and I was in France when the divorce was pronounced. I did not defend the suit, because I was instructed to take that course by my friends to get rid of a bad husband. I was quite innocent of any charge of adultery which was alleged against me. I was charged with having committed adultery with a foreigner named Armenio. I had been living with my then husband at Buenos Ayres, and I was going to Rio to join my husband: and Armenio was introduced to me for the purpose of taking care of me during the voyage; but I swear positively over and over again that there was not any improper conduct between myself and Armenio on board the ship.

Mr. Montagu Williams again interposed, and submitted that an inquiry of this kind ought not to be proceeded with, as it clearly had nothing to do with the question before the Court.

Mr. Justice Hawkins said he really could not see what the conduct of Mrs. Hart-Davies had to do with this case. Supposing she had acted immorally, what then ?

Mr. Addison said the defendant had been charged with giving the prosecutrix indelicate photographs, and it appeared to him very important to show what kind of woman the prosecutrix really was.

Mr. Justice Hawkins said he had every confidence in the learned counsel, and he would say no more upon the subject.

The cross-examination of the prosecutrix was then proceeded with. She said, There was nothing wrong in my conduct, and I only submitted to this course for the reasons I have stated: that I can swear. The photographs I possess are likenesses of myself and Armenio. He was an Italian. I have written to him in Italian, but I did not write any thing in those letters that was improper.

Mr. Addison then proposed to read various passages in the witness's letters to Armenio; but it was objected to by Mr. Montagu Williams, and the learned judge ruled that such evidence was not admissible.

Some letters were here handed to the learned judge by Mr. Addison; and, after having read them, Mr. Justice Hawkins said it appeared to him that they were utterly worthless as regarded the present inquiry. He added, that, in his opinion, if the jury had the whole of the letters placed in their hands, and they read them from beginning to end, they would not in any way influence their minds upon the main question they had to decide.

The cross-examination of Mrs. Hart-Davies was then proceeded with. She said Capt. Lindmark accompanied them to America, but she was not angry at his paying attentions to Mrs. Fletcher.

Was he not at that time your lover?—I swear that he was not. [A sketch of the witness and Capt. Lindmark was handed to the witness, and she said that it was made by her two years ago.]

A long technical discussion took place upon the point whether this sketch could be legally put in evidence in the present case. In the result, Mr. Justice Hawkins ruled that the sketch was not receivable as evidence on the present charge.

Mr. Addison, upon this intimation from the Court, said he would withdraw the letters.

Mrs. Hart-Davies, in further cross-examination, said that it was a very common expression to call each other "darling," "love," and "sweet brother and sister," and similar terms. I do not recollect that I have pictured myself as a wild lioness and a tame lioness.

MR. ADDISON. — I believe you are very passionate when you are roused?

WITNESS. — I am not aware of it. [Laughter.]

Mr. Justice Hawkins (to whom the picture referred to had been handed) said, I see nothing particular in it. It represents a young lady with her arms folded, and in a desponding mood; and then the same young lady is represented with her fist clinched, and apparently striking at something that looks like a cocoanut. [Laughter.]

Cross-examination continued. — I attended the camp-meeting at Montague. These meetings were of a spiritual character, and the fathers and mothers of some of the party are represented to be present. There were some Shakers there. [Laughter.]

MR. JUSTICE HAWKINS. — There were no "shiverers," I suppose?

MR. ADDISON. — Shakers, Shiverers, and Spiritualists, I suppose, all fraternized at these meetings?. Was Dr. Mack a Shaker?

WITNESS. — You had better ask him what he is, for he certainly is not a Shaker. He and all my other Spiritualist friends thought that I had been humbugged by the Fletchers, and he told me so. I consider that Dr. Mack has acted in a

Christian manner to me. My eyes were opened when I got to America; and I knew that I had not seen my "mamma," and that I had been cheated by the Fletchers. I was satisfied that my mother had never addressed any such message as desiring me to give to the Fletchers all the property I possessed in the world. I cannot tell whether my mother had ever really been in communication with me; but from what I heard from Dr. Mack I was quite satisfied that all the pretended messages to me from my mother, enjoining me to give my jewelry to the Fletchers, were impositions.

Mrs. Hart-Davies, in answer to questions put by the learned judge, said, After my mother's death I continued, as I believed, to hold communication with her; and during her lifetime there had never been any cessation of the affectionate and friendly intercourse that had existed between us. We had several intimate friends; but the only person she wished me to apply to for advice and counsel, in case of emergency, was a gentleman named Sampson. He is dead. My mother during her lifetime often spoke to me about her jewelry and other property, and she wished me to inherit the whole of it.

Dr. Mack, *alias* McGeary, gave testimony similar to that given at Bow Street. It was to the effect, that as soon as, furnished with a power-of-attorney, he had demanded Mrs. Hart-Davies's property in America, it had been restored to her; Mr. Fletcher saying he was sorry she had not herself asked for it, instead of employing another person. In his cross-examination he stated that he took a solemn oath in America that he would not leave the country, and was held in recog-

nizances of forty thousand dollars.   Notwithstanding,
he came to England, breaking his oath, and forfeiting
his bond, to assist Mrs. Hart-Davies in getting her
property from 22 Gordon Street.

Mr. Francis of the firm of Field, Roscoe, & Co., a
London solicitor to whom Mr. Morton had brought
letters of introduction from Boston, and to whom he
had introduced Mrs. Hart-Davies when she wished to
make a will, testified that —

Mrs. Hart-Davies appeared to be a very shrewd woman of
business, and perfectly able to manage her affairs, and seemed
remarkably clear about her will.   She accounted for leaving all
her property to the Fletchers by saying she did not wish her
husband to have any of it, and the Fletchers had been very
kind to her, and they might as well have it as anybody else.
The witness said that Mr. Morton was a member of the Boston
bar, and of good standing.

In reply to a question put by Mr. Montagu Williams, the
witness said that Mr. Morton was at his office last Monday,
and he complained of having been mixed up in such an unpleasant business.   He said that he had come over from America in the expectation that he could have given evidence; and
he found he could not do so, because he was included in the
charge.

The marriage-settlement of the prosecutrix was then produced, and this closed the case for the prosecution.

Mr. Addison took exception to the eighth count, which
charged a conspiracy to cheat and defraud Mrs. Davies of
property which was for her sole and separate use, on the
ground that there was no evidence that such property was for

her sole and separate use. The false pretence charged in relation to the deed of gift was not, he argued, the false pretence contemplated by the statute, as the lady was well aware of the nature of the deed when she signed it; and, moreover, she had said that it was simply executed as a means of protection, and that it was never intended that it should operate. The sixth count of the indictment was a conspiracy to steal, of which there was no evidence. A second objection on the second count was, that there was a conspiracy to steal the goods of Mrs. Hart-Davies, whereas she was a married woman. The general objection he had to raise upon the conspiracy counts was, that Mr. and Mrs. Fletcher, being husband and wife, could not conspire together; and, that being so, they could not conspire with a third person. Supposing, however, a conspiracy could be made between them and Morton, there was no evidence whatever of Morton having combined with the husband and wife to obtain the goods. As to the first three counts, which alleged false pretences, the learned counsel argued that the spiritual manifestations under which it was said that the property was obtained could not be regarded as a false pretence. Indeed, it would be a most dangerous thing to say that the statements of people in connection with their religious belief were capable of being made false pretences. On the doctrine of coercion, he submitted that the husband was the person who had been the main mover in obtaining the property, and that the prisoner was introduced by him to Mrs. Hart-Davies in the first instance.

Mr. Montagu Williams replied at length; and in the course of his remarks he cited, in support of the case for the prosecution, the Queen *vs.* Giles, which was an indictment against a woman known as the Wise Woman of Newbury, who pretended to bring back runaway husbands " over hedges and ditches " to their wives. She received money for so doing. In that case the judges held that this was a false pretence within the meaning of the Act, and that the prisoner was properly convicted. He further urged, that the counts alleging the prisoner to have exercised acts of witchcraft, sorcery, enchantment, and conjuration, were supported by the evidence, and that these counts should not therefore be withdrawn from the consideration of the jury.

Mr. Addison said he wished to take his lordship's opinion as to whether he should call witnesses. He had a large body of evidence, which Mrs. Fletcher earnestly desired he should bring forward; and the witnesses were persons who had seen the manifestations by Mr. Fletcher at Steinway Hall at different times, and who said he possessed the powers claimed for him.

MR. MONTAGU WILLIAMS. — You objected to my evidence upon that matter yesterday.

THE JUDGE. — What do you think, Mr. Addison?

MR. ADDISON. — Really, my lord, I must stand upon my privilege. I don't think your lordship is entitled to ask what I think.

THE JUDGE. — It really comes to this, — there is no doubt that the prosecutrix herself says that she really did believe these things, and was under that impression for a long while; and, if you are to believe her evidence, there were a great many people at the Steinway Hall who also expressed their belief. But I do not see how that will affect this particular case we are dealing with, as to whether these pretences were made with a view to defraud the prosecutrix of her goods. A great number of persons may tell us that they believed the prisoner had power to converse with spirits; but how will that affect the case?

MR. ADDISON. — Well, my lord, I have a large body of evidence of gentlemen of position, magistrates, members of the Royal Society, and gentlemen of high literary and scientific attainments.

THE JUDGE. — Supposing you take the case of an ordinary conjurer, who represents that he can turn a bird into a mouse and back again, and then into a pinch of snuff [laughter], and people believed that he had the power of doing it, would that affect any such inquiry as this? Could any one prove that Fletcher had any communication with this lady's mother? You may call evidence as to character, Mr. Addison.

MR. ADDISON. — These gentlemen would come and say that Fletcher had these powers.

THE JUDGE. — You may take it for granted, without exhibiting members of the Royal Society here, that there are thousands of people who believe, not only that Mr. Fletcher possesses these powers, but that others also possess them. I do not see, however, how these people can support the proposition of direct communication.

MR. ADDISON. — Then I call no witnesses, my lord.

I looked, and still look, upon this as a fatal surrender of my rights, and of the duty of my counsel to defend me. It was my right that the facts should be given. The truth is, that Mr. Addison did not believe in the evidence which he, as a mere matter of form, proposed to give. In his mind and in his heart he appeared to be with the judge, with the prosecution, with a large majority of the spectators in court, and with the jury, who, being of the usual class of London tradesmen, had no knowledge of, and of course no faith in, Spiritualism. So Mr. Addison surrendered to the ruling of the Court, and decided to call witnesses as to character only. Of these, though they were solemnly sworn to tell "the truth, the whole truth, and nothing but the truth," regarding the case on trial, he could, according to English procedure, ask but one single question, — that as to the reputation of the prisoner at the bar.

CHAPTER XXVIII.

SPEECHES OF COUNSEL, WITNESSES TO CHARACTER, AND A FATAL SURRENDER.

By not calling witnesses, Mr. Addison obtained what he probably considered an advantage : he got the last word. But in that he reckoned without his host. He forgot that the *last* word to the jury would come from Mr. Justice Hawkins, whose *animus* had been all along sufficiently evident.

But Mr. Montagu Williams was not at all disposed to give up his own rights in the case. He said, —

I must stand upon my rights, and claim a reply, as you have read a letter in the course of your address.

MR. ADDISON. — This is a most unusual course to pursue on the part of a prosecutor. But, standing strictly on my right, I deny altogether that the letter was put in by me. It was produced by the policeman Shrives with the bundle of letters produced on behalf of the prosecution.

MR. JUSTICE HAWKINS. — It matters very little who has the last word when we have an intelligent jury.

Mr. Montagu Williams, in answer to an appeal from Mr. Addison, said, I must decline. I intend to stand strictly upon my rights.

MR. JUSTICE HAWKINS. — You are here on the part of the Crown, Mr. Williams; and if there has been a misunderstanding, do you not think, on the part of the Crown, that it would be better that you should waive your strict rights? It is not a question of civil rights. We are trying a criminal case.

Mr. Montagu Williams said, that, in deference to the expression of opinion by his lordship, he would waive his right of reply, and would proceed to address the jury upon the evidence he had adduced. He contended that it had been fully proved that the prisoner had obtained the property belonging to the prosecutrix by false and fraudulent pretences, and that she did conspire with her husband, or with her husband and Morton, to obtain the property by false and fraudulent pretences. If she did either, she was guilty upon the indictment. He did not think there could be a doubt that Mrs. Hart-Davies was a witness of truth, and that her evidence had been corroborated up to the hilt by the documents he had produced. The Fletchers had undoubtedly played upon the imagination of the prosecutrix, and the fly had been caught in the web. The prisoner had practised a sham; and, where weak women were concerned, such people as the Fletchers were dangerous. Attacks had been made upon the moral character of the prosecutrix; but what was there to support the insinuations, except the production — the disgraceful production — of the letters written by Mrs. Hart-Davies ten years ago to Capt. Lindmark? But, suppose that all that had been suggested was true, what did it come to? In what position did it place the prisoner? Why, in the position of a woman who was conniving at, if not planning, her husband's adultery, — a woman engaging in a most revolting intrigue. He maintained that the evidence proved the prisoner and her confederates to be most dangerous people. Like the quicksand, they ingulfed any wretched person who came within their reach. The defence, he supposed, would be that the goods were given to the Fletchers for safe custody; but, if so, why all that tomfoolery about "mamma"? Why, if it were an honest and a *bonâ fide* transfer, was it necessary to invent that ridiculous warning to the prosecutrix, that the magnetism in her was so strong that it would be dangerous to wear the jewels? The fact was, that the prisoner and her confederates were charlatans and jugglers, who tried to shelter themselves from the consequences of their acts under the profession of Spiritualism. How did Mrs. Fletcher take care of the jewelry? Why, by wearing it, and carting it off to America. If the property was placed with the Fletchers only for safe custody, what need of the deed of gift, or what had been called the "protection letter"? To Mr. Francis, who belonged to one of the most respectable firms of solicitors in London, and who would not have lent himself to any thing in the nature of a fraud, the pseudo-lawyer, Mr. Morton, represented that the codicil executed by Mrs. Hart-Davies was her voluntary act; and in that way the Fletchers managed to trick the woman out of every thing she had in the world. He could not conclude without saying, that he considered the production of the Lindmark letters the most disgraceful thing that had ever been attempted in a court of justice. These letters were written by prosecutrix in the early part of her life to a man for whom she was supposed to have a strong affection. And where did they come from? They must have come either from Lindmark, or the prisoner; and, if from the latter, how did they get into her possession? In the whole vocabulary there were not words sufficiently strong to characterize the conduct of a man who would give up a woman's love-letters for the purpose of crushing and degrading her. Such a man might be a captain, but to his mind he was neither "handsome" nor gallant. Thank God he was not an Englishman! In conclusion, Mr. Williams submitted that the evidence of Mrs. Hart-Davies, and the letters of the Fletchers, abundantly made out the indictment that the prosecutrix' property was obtained by false and fraudulent pretences, and that there was a deliberate confederation and combination to obtain that property. The law, which Mrs. Hart-Davies now invoked, was made for the protection of the weak against the dangerous; and, if the jury considered that the case for the prosecution had been made out, they would by their verdict give something like a death-blow to a system, unfortunately growing up in this country, which was disastrous in the extreme, and which, if not checked, would involve many in speedy and irretrievable ruin. [Applause in court.]

The case, so far as the prosecution was concerned, was concluded on Saturday; and on Monday morning, on Mr. Addison rising to address the jury for the defence, Mr. Justice Hawkins said that the learned counsel need not trouble himself about the last count of the indictment (that which had reference to a conspiracy to defraud by witchcraft). In the first place, there was no evidence to support it; and the count was absolutely bad in itself. As to the first count, he wished to know whether there was any desire on the part of the prosecution to amend.

MR. MONTAGU WILLIAMS. — I do not see any necessity to amend.

MR. JUSTICE HAWKINS. — Well, I shall direct the jury that there is no evidence that the goods were for defendant's sole and separate use.

MR. MONTAGU WILLIAMS. — Then, I propose to ask your lordship to strike out the words "which belonged to her for her sole and separate use, apart from the control of her husband."

Mr. Addison said, that, as the defendant was now alone upon her trial, he submitted that the Court-had no power to amend the indictment, in which other parties were included.

Mr. Justice Hawkins said, that, if the other parties came in and claimed to be tried, he would reserve the nice point that had been raised by Mr. Addison for the consideration of the Court of Criminal Appeal. [A laugh.]

His lordship, after hearing the arguments on both sides, amended the indictment as required.

Mr. Addison submitted that there was no evidence on the fourth count, which was the general conspiracy to defraud Mrs. Davies of her property.

MR. JUSTICE HAWKINS. — Unless that count be amended, I am inclined to think so.

MR. WILLIAMS. — I submit that the property was found in the possession of the prisoner.

MR. JUSTICE HAWKINS. — But Mrs. Davies is a married woman, and it was not her property.

MR. WILLIAMS. — Then, I shall propose to put in the name of the husband as the owner of the property.

Upwards of an hour was occupied in making other amendments in the wording of the many counts of the indictment.

Those who are familiar with criminal procedure in Massachusetts and in many other States will see that I could not have been convicted if I had been on trial at home. In the United States generally, the allegations in an indictment must be proved as stated; but in England, it appears, that, when the proof varies from the statement of the case in the indictment, the Court gives the prosecution liberty to amend. A judge in Massachusetts, at the point we have now reached in the trial, would have promptly directed a verdict of acquittal on the ground of variance. Borrowing a comparison from the fisherman, the British prosecutor has the liberty to use a gaff and landing-net, as well as hook, to secure his victim.

Mr. Addison then asked the permission of the Court to call some witnesses, who were anxious to get away, to speak to the character of the defendant, before he addressed the jury. This was granted; and the first witness called was Mr. Desmond Fitzgerald, who said, I am an electric-telegraph engineer, and I have known the defendant nearly five years, ever since she came to this country. I consider her a polished, disinterested, and high-principled gentlewoman.

The Very Rev. Maurice Davies, archdeacon of the Church of England, gave similar evidence. He had also known the defendant five years.

Mr. Dawson Rogers said he had known the defendant two years and a half, and he always considered her an honest, honorable woman.

Mrs. Col. Western said she had known the defendant since she had been in London, about five years; and she always bore the reputation of a high-minded woman.

Mrs. Mary Boole, a lady of scientific reputation, also spoke to the excellent character of the defendant. She said she considered her more than honest.

Mr. Justice Hawkins asked the witness what she meant by that expression.

The witness said, because defendant and her husband had many opportunities of making money, which they would not avail themselves of.

Mr. Frederic Webley and Dr. T. L. Nichols of South Kensington gave evidence of the same character. The last-mentioned gentleman was one of the defendant's bail for her appearance to answer the present charge.

Dr. Nichols, in reply to Mr. Montagu Williams, said he had not seen the defendant's husband lately. He had written several letters in the newspapers on the subject of this charge, one of which was headed " Witchcraft in 1881."

Mr. Hensleigh Wedgewood, formerly a police magistrate at the Southwark Court, who was another of the defendant's bail, spoke of the good character she had always enjoyed among those who knew her.

Several other gentlemen and ladies of position gave similar evidence.

Mr. Addison then proceeded to address the jury for the defendant. He said that at last they had arrived at the close of an inquiry, which, although interesting in some, was still in many respects one of a very painful character. He said he would not dispute that his learned friend had conducted the case for the prosecution very fairly; and, if the result had depended upon speeches, he should have gone away on Saturday night with feelings of very great apprehension, after the beautiful and eloquent speech made by him. The defendant was prejudiced by the fact that the prosecutrix was a fascinating woman, who told her own story, and who by her demeanor and appearance was most likely to have created a strong impression on the minds of the jury. They had, however, heard the character given of the defendant by the numerous persons of high position and respectability who had been examined; and he would tell them in the first instance, that Mrs. Fletcher had come from America solely for the purpose of meeting this charge, and of vindicating her character in the eyes of the numerous persons who loved and respected her, and who she knew considered her incapable of committing such an act as was imputed to her. The jury would not forget, either, that the whole of the property of which Mrs. Hart-Davies was alleged to have been defrauded had been restored to her. With regard to the husband of the defendant not having surrendered to meet the charge, the defendant had nothing to do with that. He might have his own reasons for not coming voluntarily to trial; but the jury had nothing to do with them; and the only question they had to decide was whether the defendant was guilty of the offences of which she was accused. He argued, that the husband and Mr. Morton had been included solely for the purpose of endeavoring to convict the defendant of conspiracy, and thus make her responsible for acts that perhaps could only be imputed to other parties. An endeavor had also been made to show that the defendant was a witch; but his learned friend who had tried his hand at making out that charge did not know how to do it, and the witchcraft counts were now decided to be hopelessly bad. He said, that, after all, the substantial charge against the defendant was, that she had obtained these jewels by false pretences, and that was the sole question upon which they would have to give their verdict; but he hoped in the result to satisfy them that the defendant had never made any false pretences, and that there was no ground for this charge. He was not going to enter into a discussion as to the truth or falsehood of Spiritualism. A great many witnesses had been in attendance, who would have testified their belief in it, and have stated what wonderful things they had seen; but he was not surprised that this kind of evidence had been rejected by his lordship. He would only observe this, that if the Spiritualists could raise the learned judge in his chair to the ceiling, or, what would be

a more difficult task, waft the worthy alderman who sat by
his side through the ceiling of the court to the top of St.
Paul's, people might think there was something in Spiritualism.
[Laughter.] As it was, however, whatever persons interested
in the cause of Spiritualism might say, the world generally
would certainly entertain grave doubts as to there being any
power in Spiritualism. He should therefore confine himself
merely to the facts that had been proved in evidence, and he
should contend with great confidence that there was nothing
to show that the defendant had in any way deceived or defrauded the prosecutrix. He remarked that Mrs. Hart-Davies,
who had now found a near spiritual brother in Dr. McGeary,
admitted that she fully believed in the truth of Spiritualism,
and was under the impression, long before she knew the defendant, that her mother had communicated with her from
the spirit-world. He put it to the jury that Mrs. Hart-Davies
was a very difficult person to deal with, and her mind was
evidently in a most extraordinary condition. Although he did
not for a moment desire to accuse her of immorality or
improper conduct, still he must ask the jury to consider the
account she had given of herself, the peculiar relations that
existed between her and her husband, and her admission that
she had consented to a decree of separation, and submitted
to a charge of adultery for which there was no foundation.
Under these circumstances, he left it to them to say whether
she was not a woman of a very extraordinary character. She
was described by a gentleman who had acted as her solicitor,
as being a remarkably shrewd, clever woman. He asked the
jury to look at the conduct of the prosecutrix all through the
transaction, and he submitted that there really was no proof
that she had been deceived in the slightest degree. With
regard to her supposed great love and affection for her mother,

they would not forget that she never saw her mother for three years before her death; and, from what they had seen of the prosecutrix and her peculiar ideas, the probability was that they would have quarrelled. She represented that she had seen her mother several times in a dream or a vision after her death, and she was evidently in a sickly, morbid state of mind; but he submitted that there was no evidence to show that she had been deceived by any representations that were made by the defendant. The learned counsel went on to comment at considerable length upon the conduct of Mrs. Hart-Davies, and he asked the jury whether it was not very remarkable that her husband had not been called to corroborate her statement as to what took place between the defendant's husband and the prosecutrix when they were first introduced to each other. He said it appeared to him that it was impossible to rely upon the testimony of such a woman as Mrs. Hart-Davies. He then proceeded to urge upon the jury that the prosecutrix had several relatives living, that she had trustees and various other persons who took an interest in her, and yet not one single person had been called as a witness to corroborate her story, or to tell them what sort of a woman she was. He said it could not be doubted that she had all along been living in a peculiar atmosphere of her own, and that she could not give her attention to the ordinary relations of life. They had heard the evidence given by Dr. McGeary with regard to Spiritualism, and the astounding miracles he represented he had performed; and he asked them what right any one had to come to the conclusion that the defendant was an impostor, when, according to all the facts of the case, she believed that every thing she said was true in reference to the visions she saw. The learned counsel then drew an amusing picture of what took place at the table-moving in Gordon Street, and he remarked that Mrs.

Hart-Davies believed in the truth of every thing she saw on this occasion. Mrs. Fletcher, the defendant, was not present, and could not have been connected with an imposture of any kind, if such imposture had actually been practised. As to the crystal ball, he contended that what was done by the defendant was nothing more than the exhibition of a toy of some kind, and that it had no serious signification whatever; and the prosecutrix was not deceived in any way by what occurred with regard to this crystal ball. He next proceeded to call the attention of the jury to the extraordinary state of things that existed between the parties; and he submitted to the jury, that, having regard to this peculiar condition of affairs, it would be idle to suppose that the prosecutrix had been induced to part with her property by any false pretences made to her by the defendant. He did not mean to accuse the prosecutrix of wilfully stating what was not true; but what he desired to impress upon the jury was, that she was an hysterical, nervous woman, who was under a variety of delusions upon this particular question, and whose evidence in regard to such transactions was unworthy of credit. The learned counsel next gave an amusing description of the camp at Lake Pleasant, and said they could hardly imagine what extraordinary scenes must take place where hundreds of Fletchers and Davieses assembled, enlivened by Shakers and Shiverers. [Laughter.] He then reminded the jury, that, during the whole of the voluminous correspondence that had been produced, not one single word was said about Spiritualism, and that the real understanding between the parties was, that the jewels should be placed in Mrs. Fletcher's hands for safe custody, to be restored when they were wanted; and he said it appeared to him that this arrangement had been fully and honorably carried out by the defendant, and that there was not the least pretence for the charge made against her, of having obtained the jewels by false pretences. It was also pretty clear, that the defendant and her husband did not like to incur the responsibility of having such valuable property in their possession without having some document or other for their protection; and this was the explanation of the application that was made to Mr. Morton, who was a member of the American bar, and capable of giving advice in such a matter. He then observed, that it appeared to him to be a most extraordinary thing that they did not appear to have ever had any authentic statement of the actual value of these jewels and the other property, and that the prosecutrix herself swore that her mother's property was under the value of a hundred pounds when she administered to her effects. He also called their attention to the fact that neither the defendant nor her husband had ever pawned or misappropriated one single item of the property intrusted to them. He said that the prosecutrix appeared to be perfectly satisfied with the Fletchers retaining possession of the jewels until she met Dr. Mack at Lake Pleasant, and immediately after that event a new light seemed to have opened upon her; but, the moment the defendant was asked to give up the property, she did so at once. The learned counsel then referred at considerable length to the alleged loss of the box of valuable lace, and he argued that there was not the slightest evidence that any property of this description was ever in the possession of the prosecutrix. In conclusion, he dwelt upon the doctrine of coercion, and said that whatever had been done by the defendant, even if they should take an adverse opinion of her conduct, was done under the control and coercion of her husband, and that consequently she could not be held to be criminally responsible.

For the defence I do not wish to make any further comment. From his stand-point he doubtless did the best he could. Had he known more of his case, he would undoubtedly have done much better. When I had heard it, I determined then and there, that, if ever my liberty were again imperilled, I would save my money, and possibly some lawyer's reputation, by conducting my own defence. It may be that no English counsel or barrister could have done more. What I could, and I now see should, have done, was to avail myself of the only opportunity I could have, at that time, to tell my own story, and put my declaration from the prisoner's dock against the oath of Mrs. Hart-Davies in the witness-box.

CHAPTER XXIX.

ON the 12th of April, 1881, I took my seat for the last time in the prisoner's dock of the Central Criminal Court, and saw and heard the last of Mr. Justice Hawkins.

The summing-up, or charge to the jury, lasted five hours. Of course no newspaper could give it entire; and I can only give the fullest and most accurate report I can find, which in this case seems to be that of the "Daily News." On account of its length, the report of the charge is placed in the Appendix. The presiding justice laid down the law in regard to the indictment and the proof, and pointed out which counts were to be regarded in coming to a verdict. He commented upon the testimony as it affected the character and credibility of the prosecutrix, and as to the value of the property under consideration. He declared that the evidence fixed no culpability upon the defendant Morton. He sketched the beginning of the acquaint-

237

ance between Mrs. Hart-Davies and Mr. Fletcher, and referred pityingly or contemptuously to the delusion of spiritual communications, in which both parties shared, and then instanced the messages purporting to come from the mother of Mrs. Hart-Davies as having been continued for the purpose of deceiving the prosecutrix, and inducing her to part with her jewels, etc. He argued at length upon the deed of gift, regarding it as fraudulent, and as having been brought about by a combination or conspiracy. On this point he expended most of his force, really making the "charge" an argument for the prosecution, instead of the fair summing-up of an impartial judge. It was far more searching and more malignant than the speech of Mr. Montagu Williams.

I have taken the liberty to mark a few sentences of this charge with Italics. The reader will see how the whole case rested, first, upon the belief of the jury in the absolute truthfulness of Mrs. Hart-Davies, and, secondly, upon their disbelief of any truth whatever in spiritual manifestations. It was necessary, therefore, that the character of this witness should be known, and that witnesses should be called who could testify to the reality, the genuineness, and the nature of spiritual manifestations. All this was shut out. I could not call Mr. Morton, because the government prosecutors had included him in the indictment; and when

I proposed to call witnesses of the highest position and character to prove that spirits could and often did speak to their friends, and give them advice as to their affairs, the judge *absolutely refused to receive such evidence.* I continue to quote the newspaper report.

"His lordship's summing-up occupied *five hours*, and at its conclusion the jury retired to consider their decision. After an absence of little more than *three hours and a half*, they returned into court with a verdict of guilty on the counts charging the obtaining of the goods by false pretences. Upon the counts charging conspiracy, they found the prisoner guilty of having conspired with her husband, but not with Morton, to obtain the goods; and, upon the count charging conspiracy to obtain the execution of the deed of gift by fraudulent pretences, they found the prisoner guilty of having conspired with her husband and Morton. The jury further found that the prisoner had not acted under the coercion of her husband.

"Mr. Justice Hawkins, addressing the prisoner, said, 'Susan Willis Fletcher, you have been convicted, after a very long and patient trial, of having obtained a large quantity of property from Mrs. Hart-Davies by false pretences, in company with your husband; and the jury have also found that you have been guilty of conspiring with your husband and a person named Morton to procure the execution of a deed of gift. They have further found you guilty of conspiring with your husband, without Morton, of obtaining those goods by false pretences. Although a great many counts have been inserted in this indictment, yet, considering the whole of the evidence, I look upon it in substance as but one offence; and I cannot help saying that I think the verdict of the jury is perfectly satisfactory. Indeed, believing, as it is evident they do, the testimony of Mrs. Hart-Davies, and looking at the correspondence before me, I do not see that the jury could have come to any other conclusion. And, moreover, I think the jury have come to a right conclusion in considering that you were not acting under the coercion of your husband to such an extent as to make you irresponsible to the criminal law. It becomes unnecessary for me, in considering the findings of the jury, to reserve any question of law for the consideration of the Criminal Court of Appeal; and I therefore decline to do so. I have now only to consider what sentence I am to pass upon you for the offence of which you have been found guilty. You are standing here, and since the commencement of this trial you have stood here alone, unsupported by your husband. If he were here, I should have a great deal more to say upon the subject than I have to say to you; because, although the jury have rightly found that you were not acting under the coercion of your husband in a sense which would have rendered you irresponsible for your acts, yet I cannot help thinking that it was through him, and through his professions and his pretences, that you were first of all yourself induced to embark upon a fraudulent conspiracy upon which you unquestionably did embark. I cannot help thinking, that but for his designs, his counsels, and evil influence, you might yourself have abstained from attempting these frauds, and making those false and fraudulent pretences which you did. I take that into consideration in passing sentence upon you. In the result it comes to this, that you found a very weak, credulous, foolish woman, who was open to all the flattery which you thought fit to bestow upon her. You knew very well that she professed to have a great attachment for her dead mother, and you worked upon those affections; and you were tempted by the sight of her jewelry and valuable property to work upon her by pretending, falsely pretending, that her dead mother had sent messages to her, begging her to put her jewels and clothes into your possession, or that otherwise she would be speedily sent into spirit-life, because of the magnetism that was in them. It was a miserable, mean, paltry trick which you resorted to for the purpose of getting possession of her property. Fortunately, very fortunately, she has succeeded in obtaining possession of the greater part of it. There is another part which has yet to be recovered; and I do not know how much of that which you have obtained is still in the hands of those who are in a condition to give it up. I take all the circumstances into consideration; and I look upon your case as one in which you most unquestionably were guilty of the false pretence which is proved against you, and unquestionably guilty of having acted without that coercion which would have protected you in point of law.

"'I am not going to pass sentence upon you for any thing except that of which you have been found guilty. I myself feel that there is a great deal in these letters which shows to my mind that both you and your husband had entered into — I do not like to call it a conspiracy, in one sense, but into a filthy league to throw this wretched woman into the hands of your husband. That is not a matter for which I am going to punish you, because it is a matter of immorality, which the criminal law does not punish; and, if the criminal law does not punish it, I have no right to take it into consideration. At the same time it shows how little you deserve the character which a great number of witnesses thought fit to go into the witness-box to give you, one of them stating you to be almost a model of purity, honor, and honesty.

"'I, nevertheless, take into consideration this circumstance, that, but for your husband, you never would have embarked in such a fraud as this, or have been guilty of thóse false pretences which have brought you within the pale of the criminal law.   Under these circumstances I shall not pass upon you the sentence which the law would authorize me to do.   The law would authorize me to send you into penal servitude; but the sentence which I pass is, that you be imprisoned, and kept to hard labor, for the term of twelve calendar months.'

"The prisoner, who throughout the hearing of the case had maintained a calm demeanor, was but slightly affected by the sentence.   She was at once removed to the cells."

CHAPTER XXX.

SOME COMMENTS ON THE CASE.

I CAN well believe that I did not appear to be much affected by the sentence. I was fully prepared for it. Sir Henry Hawkins had his jury well in hand. The government expected him to do his work, and I have no doubt that the sentence had been discussed and settled beforehand. Seven or eight of the jurors, including a peculiarly active and hard-headed secularist-looking foreman, had early, I fear very early, made up what they called their minds to do their part to "crush out Spiritualism." That some were in doubt, and one or two even disposed to be friendly to me, is evident from the fact that they kept me in what might have seemed a dreadful suspense for more than three hours and a half. I was in no suspense whatever. I knew, rather I felt, and had felt for days, what would be the verdict. I knew that I should be condemned *without a hearing.*

Not one word from me, from first to last, had the jury that tried me heard me speak, save the two formal

243

words, "Not guilty." In justice to Mr. Addison I have given the best report I could find of his argument. My own, had I been allowed to make one, would have been very different. The jury, if at all fair-minded men, must have wished to know what I would say about it. I am glad, since my silent conviction, and so many other failures of justice, — a few of which have come to light, where persons, after enduring years of penal servitude, have been found to be perfectly innocent of the crimes of which they were accused, — that prisoners are to be heard; glad that the very judge that sentenced me has given his sanction to a more humane procedure. I predicted at my conviction that I should be among the last to be in that court convicted unheard.

The sentence itself was unexpectedly light. Five years of penal servitude was the least I had looked for. Certainly, if I had been guilty, I had deserved that, and more. A post-office letter sorter or carrier who steals a shilling's worth of postage-stamps from a letter, yielding to the momentary temptation, perhaps purposely placed in his way, gets five years of penal servitude; and I, who, according to Mr. Justice Hawkins, had deliberately conspired to deceive a poor woman in the most detestable way, taking advantage of her faith and affection to rob her of thousands, of all she had, — I, whose crime, had I been guilty, was

a thousand times blacker than that of any highway robber or burglar, or perpetrator of an ordinary commer-
cial forgery, was sentenced to a year's imprisonment!

And the reason for this extraordinary lenity was,
that, after all, I might have acted under the influence
of my husband. But I had just seen a woman confessedly guilty of a series of robberies *acquitted* because the jury thought *she might have had* a husband,
and have acted under his influence. If my husband
had made me join him in deceiving and plundering Mrs.
Hart-Davies, the judge should have instructed the jury
to bring in a verdict of not guilty. But if I was, as
he charged, the originator of the foul conspiracy, then
I deserved the severest punishment he could legally
inflict. And if I had been guilty of the immorality of
which he accused me by his summary, surely I was
unworthy of his mercy.

I cared too little for the terms of the sentence to
feel any indignation. It was enough to know that it
was unjust, and to have an entire faith that judge and
jury, my prosecutors and the public, would some day
know its injustice, and regret it more than I did.

There was one point I thought Mr. Justice Hawkins
might have alluded to. I think it was worth a passing
notice. Perhaps it escaped his mind. Had I been on
the bench in gown and wig, and he in the prisoner's
dock, I should certainly have mentioned it. It was,

that as soon as I heard, in America, of the accusation against me, I came to England to meet it. I had no other reason or motive but to meet my accusers face to face.

From the 7th of December to the day of my sentence, on the 13th of April, I had been at perfect liberty on bail. This bail was renewed from day to day during my trial. On the night of my conviction, when I knew my fate as well as I know it now, I could have gone by the night mail to Paris. Does any reader of these pages believe, had I been the mean and odious swindler, the sacrilegious deceiver and robber, I was accused of being, that I would have left husband, child, parents, and friends, and come alone to England, and staid here all through, to be tried, convicted, and imprisoned? Was such a thing ever known of any criminal in the world?

Mr. Justice Hawkins was careful not to even allude to it. Did the "gentlemen of the jury" give this matter a thought? When a martyr goes to a prison or the scaffold for his religion, it does not prove that his religion is true, for there are martyrs to all sorts of creeds; but it is a proof of the sincerity of his belief. Was it no proof of the sincerity of my belief in Spiritualism, that I came to England, and risked penal servitude for it, and endured Sir Henry Hawkins's insults, and the much lighter suffering of twelve months' hard labor in an English prison?

I was not alone in my opinion of the sentence of Sir Henry Hawkins. I find the following criticism in a legal periodical in England, — the "Law Times" of April 16, 1881 : —

"The long lecture delivered by Mr. Justice Hawkins to Mrs. Fletcher, when passing sentence in what is known as the Spiritualist Case, may have had a salutary effect upon public morality: we, however, are disposed to doubt it, and we heartily deprecate discourses of this nature. Such discourses are the more to be deprecated where jocularity has been the prevailing characteristic of the trial, the jokes not being by any means monopolized by the bar or the witnesses. A prisoner incurs a well-defined punishment by committing specific crimes. This is all that the law ever contemplates. To be scolded and discoursed upon by the judge may, in some cases, be a severe addition to the statutory punishment; and, where the prisoner is a woman, the severity of this additional punishment may be very great."

Others, by no means friendly to Spiritualism or " the Fletchers," wrote something besides pæans of praise about the trial and the presiding judge.

The correspondent of the "Western Morning News," writing at the close of the trial at the Old Bailey, said, —

"Mr. Justice Hawkins is, perhaps, the worst judge on the bench, from Mrs. Fletcher's point of view, that could have been appointed to try a Spiritualist case. He has no toleration for views of her kind; and he takes a cynical view of life, founded upon a not very favorable experience of it, which does

not include belief in mesmeric trances, or the devotion of **Mr.**
Fletcher to the high spiritual good of his devotees. Rarely has
a judge spent a more enjoyable week than that which his lordship has just passed. He has revelled in the equivocal and in
double entendre. He has hardly spoken without that curious
twist of the lips which has been more eloquent of laughter
than laughter itself. To-day his summing-up was mildly ironi-
cal in parts, but very much against the prisoner. The Spiritualists talk of instituting actions for perjury against the witnesses, and especially against the plaintiff. They hardly expect
to win in such an attempt. But Mrs. Fletcher wants to tell her
own tale, 'to set herself right with the Spiritualists of England,'
and to bring back sympathy to her side. Her mouth is, of
course, closed at present. By including other persons in the
indictment, her friends were also prevented from giving evidence; and she proclaims that she will not rest day or night
until she has forced the judges of England to listen to her
explanations."

How this writer could know what I was proclaiming
in my solitary cell, in which I was locked in Tothill
Fields, Westminster, is one of the mysteries of clairvoyance or clairaudience known to newspaper corre-
spondents.

The editor of "Light," the leading Spiritualist
paper in England, though careful not to defend me
himself, as he could not prudently have done, had the
fairness to publish the following letter: —

To THE EDITOR OF "LIGHT." *Sir,* —I think you will grant
me a little space for the expression of some individual opinions

for which no one need hold you responsible. It is right that allowance be made for my personal interest in the case, but I think I have a right to be heard.

My personal interest is this. I am an American, though now for twenty years resident in England; and Mrs. Fletcher is my countrywoman, severed from country, friends, parents, husband, child. She is also my friend, whom I greatly esteem for many talents and virtues, — eloquence, wit, great kindness and generosity, heroic courage, and unfaltering fidelity. Believing in her thoroughly, I have stood by her side during this trial. It was a small matter to become one of her bail, a trifling inconvenience, with no risk; because a woman who came across the Atlantic in mid-winter to meet an accusation against her, who left home, country, and safety, and risked penal servitude, simply and only to meet and repel an accusation which she alleged to be false, was not likely to run away. This heroic action was not so much as mentioned by Mr. Justice Hawkins in his charge to the jury; nor has it been even hinted at in the leaders of the press which have followed the conviction, — torrents of abuse which take the place of the dead cats, rotten eggs and worse, of the times of the pillory.

In many ways there has been a failure of justice. The whole case of the prosecution rested, as Mr. Justice Hawkins admitted, upon the credibility of one witness, and that was in no way tested. Her two husbands, relations, trustees, friends, were absent. Mr. Morton, who might have given important evidence, and who came from America to do so, was included in the indictment, so that his testimony was shut out.

The prisoner was not examined. Her story is yet untold. This is, in my opinion, a horrible feature of English criminal procedure. In other countries a person accused of crime can make his own explanations. I have seen a man convicted of murder in England, and then asked, *after* the verdict, what he had to say. His simple story convinced every one who heard it of his innocence. Had the jury heard it, they would never have found him guilty. The judge went through the ceremony of putting on the black cap, and sentencing him to be hanged, and then wrote to the home secretary to get the other farce enacted, of sending her Majesty's pardon to a man as innocent as herself of the crime of which he had been convicted.

In the case of Mrs Fletcher no defence has been made. She has been condemned unheard. I see it stated that some hundreds of pounds were expended for the defence. For what? To examine a hundred and twenty feet of parchment, every line of which I am taxed to pay for; for a cross-examination which had no effect; for calling a dozen witnesses to character whose testimony did not weigh a pin's head with judge or jury or the public.

Testimony was offered to prove the reality of spiritual manifestations, and that the prisoner at the bar might, and probably did, act in good faith. She was charged with making false pretences, "well knowing them to be false." All testimony to show that the facts of Spiritualism are genuine was ruled out of court. It was assumed that every medium is an impostor, and every believer in Spiritualism a dupe. The logic of the trial, — and the case put to the jury, — was this, Every person professing to be a Spiritualist is either a knave or a fool. The accused are not fools, *ergo* they are knaves.

The efforts to injure the character of Mrs. Fletcher in respect to matters not within the jurisdiction of the Court seem to me very cowardly. What had a photograph of a lady in a fashionable dress *not more objectionable than every one may see at any ball or dinner* — such a photograph as may be seen in a hundred shop-windows — to do with her guilt or innocence ? How could a photograph handed to the jury affect the question of obtaining property by false pretences ? So of the cruel insinuation that Mrs. Fletcher had promoted a criminal intimacy between her husband and the prosecutrix, for which there was no foundation, and with which the Court had nothing to do, but which was charged, by the judge in his sentence, against the silent and helpless victim, who sat there bound and gagged, and who could neither answer nor resist. With some men the days of chivalry are ended, or have never begun.

It is said that Spiritualism was not on trial in this case. No, not on trial; nor was Mrs. Fletcher. She and Spiritualism were alike condemned without a hearing. I see now that it would have been infinitely better, had she defended herself, and told her own story to the jury. It is a favorite saying of the lawyers, that a man who pleads his own case has a fool for his client. But in this case Mrs. Fletcher could not have done less, or done worse, and might have done much better. She would have had the satisfaction of telling her own story. As it was, the only words heard from her lips were, " Not guilty, my lord." They were said fervently and sincerely.

As a witness I have something to complain of. I fear that I committed perjury. I feel myself forsworn. I took a solemn oath to tell "the truth, the whole truth, and nothing but the truth;" and I was allowed only to answer one question, which was not considered of. the least importance. I could have given testimony which I think of some value as to the character of communications from departed spirits, and how they are affected by the characters of those to whom they are given and through whom they are received; but, after all my solemn swearing as to what I would do, I was only permitted to say that I had known Mrs. Fletcher for three years; that I had known her American friends; that I had in my possession her letters of introduction from high official persons in America to the Hon. James Russell Lowell, American minister, giving her the highest character for integrity and honor; and that I had formed the same opinion from intimate acquaintance. But my mouth was stopped, and I was not allowed to give much other testimony which I think ought to have been given.

For had the jury believed that messages were, or even could have been, received by the prosecutrix from her mother, through the Fletchers, they would have been bound to acquit the prisoner. If such messages are ever received, they may have been in this case. If Mrs. Heurtley could communicate with her daughter, she may have wished her to live with the Fletchers, and divide her property with them, or leave it to them "for the propagation of Spiritualism in its higher phases." It is a rule of law that an accused person must be considered innocent until proven guilty, and that, if a juryman sees any reason to doubt, the benefit of such doubt must be given to the accused.

The fact that the jury took more than three hours and a half to find a verdict shows that there was much doubt and hesitation, probably energetic bullying on one side, and weak surrender on the other. Few men have the firmness to stand by their convictions against a majority. We have read that "wretches hang, that jurymen may dine."

This trial and its result carry us back to worse times, when witches were burned or hanged, and Quakers were imprisoned and whipped. Tender Quaker women were whipped from town to town, chained to a cart's-tail, in Massachusetts, stripped to the waist, and the lash cutting into their naked bosoms. For very light offences, or for none, women have been burned at Smithfield, at Tyburn, and at Newgate. We may be thankful for so much of progress as that which gives to Spiritualists milder punishments.

That Mrs. Fletcher is a martyr to Spiritualism no Spiritualist now doubts. Had Mr. and Mrs. Fletcher been members of any other religious body, there would have been no criminal prosecution. The question as to property would have been settled in a court of equity. Questions often arise as to undue influence, wills are contested ; but we do not hear of criminal prosecutions of either Catholic priests or Protestant pastors. Mr. Fletcher, Mrs. Fletcher, and Mr. Morton have been convicted because they are Spiritualists.

T. L. NICHOLS, M.D.

APRIL 14, 1881.

CHAPTER XXXI.

BEFORE the establishment of the free and enlightened newspaper with its present enormous " world-wide " circulation, convicted criminals were sentenced to stand a certain number of hours, fastened upon a platform, in some public place, to be gazed at, jeered, execrated, and pelted with mud, rotten eggs, dead cats, and other male-odorous missiles, by the London mob. Some were nailed by the ear to the post in the pillory; some, especially libellers, had their ears cut off. In rare cases, prisoners exposed in the pillory were pelted to death. The author of " Robinson Crusoe " was put in the pillory. The Rev. Titus Oates was whipped through the streets, and exposed in the pillory, many times.

In more intelligent and humane times the pillory was abolished. It was not only a cruel and brutalizing spectacle, like bull-baiting or pigeon-shooting, but it left the punishment of criminals to the caprices or prejudices of the public.

254

My pillory, as one of my friends has happily said, was first the gratuitous, superfluous, and, as the " Law Times" holds, quite impertinent, tirade of the judge who sentenced me, and, next morning, the similarly cruel and very unusual abusive articles in the newspapers all over England, — cruel, in that they wounded many innocent persons (for I had parents, a son, and many friends), — cruel and unjust, because false, libellous, and in excess of my legal punishment. I had been condemned to twelve months' imprisonment with hard labor. Sir Henry Hawkins added some sentences of very bitter abuse on his own account, and set the newspapers a very bad example, which they were quick to follow.

Had I been a common thief or a common swindler, all these tirades would have been spared me. Nay, taking the case just as it was, and considering the restoration of the property, and my coming to England to meet the charge against me, can any one believe that I would have been convicted at all, had I not been a Spiritualist? and, had I been, would the case have been a subject of newspaper leaders all over the kingdom?

No doubt these articles are the mere echoes of the judge's charge and sentence, and the expression of popular prejudice and ignorance. They are not the less cruel libels, and aggravations of the punishment which a prejudiced verdict enabled the Court to inflict. I have not space to give them all: I have not seen them all. For a whole year I was not allowed to see a newspaper: so they were quite lost to me until they had been forgotten by everybody else. From the few that were saved for me, I must, however, as a matter of history, give a few extracts.

First let me observe, that it is quite safe to say that there are confirmed Spiritualists upon the staff of every important London newspaper. On several there are writers who have personal knowledge of my husband's mediumship and of my own. That makes no sort of difference: a newspaper supplies what the public is supposed to demand.

"The whole miserable story |says the "Times"] is as gross a case of vulgar chicane and imposture as can readily be imagined. We are not concerned, any more than the judge who tried the case, to consider in reference to it how many persons believe in what they are pleased to call Spiritualism. Its so-called phenomena may, for all *we know or care*, be a legitimate subject for scientific investigation; but, when its agency is employed for the purposes of direct extortion, it is quite impossible to regard it as any thing else than a very clumsy form of imposture, which the law does well to punish whenever it gets the chance. . . . The story of Mrs. Hart-Davies recalls in many of its features the memorable suit of 'Lyon *vs.* Home,' tried before Vice-Chancellor Giffard in 1868. Take an adroit 'medium' and a weak, foolish, fanciful woman with property in her own control, and bring them into communication, and the inevitable result seems to be, that a good deal of the property of the woman gets transferred to the medium. The medium, as Mr. Home explained in the case to which we have referred, is a mere vehicle of spirit communication: he cannot control the utterances of the spirits; he cannot summon them at will; he cannot even distinguish good spirits from bad, lying spirits from truthful ones. . . . Now, all this kind of thing may, as we have said, be a matter worthy of strict and patient scientific investigation; but to ordinary common sense, and still more to the eye of justice, dealing with accepted rules of evidence and with incontestable principles of human nature, it is nothing more than imposture, gross, palpable, and revolting. If, moreover, a medium is an impostor, he is a very clumsy impostor. A tenth-rate conjurer can beat him on his own ground. . . . No medium has ever yet revealed any thing that was at once true, worth knowing, and knowable only by means not accessible to the rest of mankind. Their levitations, table-movings, floatings in the air, and the like, are clumsy tricks at the best, easily wrought by a conjurer, and, even if due to undetected natural agencies, they throw no light whatever on the alleged communications of spirits; while as to their actual spirit-messages, they are so vulgar, fatuous, and puerile, that, if they could be believed by any rational being, they would add a new terror to death, and furnish, as Professor Huxley said, a new argument against suicide.

"The delusion of Spiritualism is no new one, but, happily, it is now a waning one. The Fletchers are now dismissed to join the Homes, the Slades, and other mediums whose vogue is past. It is certainly a very good thing that the machinations of mediums, magnetic doctors, and the like, should occasionally come within the reach of the criminal law. Not merely is their conviction a warning to the public at large to have nothing to do with people professing mysterious arts, who come from no one knows where, and live no one knows how; but the glimpses we get in evidence of their daily life and habits are sufficient to disgust all decent persons with the very name of medium, and with every thing associated with Spiritualism. . . . It would be well if the law were less tolerant than it is of such offences against public morals and public decency. Overt acts of imposture and fraud necessarily and very properly come within reach of the criminal law. But are the *séances* in which these things begin really less offensive to the public welfare? We punish and prohibit fortune-telling and other practices of the kind. But fortune-telling is nowadays a sorry and unprofitable kind of imposture, not to be compared with Spiritualism as a means of gaining a livelihood out of the public credulity. Spiritualism practised for gain is as false as fortune-telling, and far more mischievous. Why should we prohibit the old imposture, and leave the field open for the new ?"

Parliament has not yet seen its way to pass an act making it a penal offence to witness spiritual manifestations, nor to punish a belief in the existence of spirits by fines or imprisonment; and, as there are Spiritualists in both Houses, it might be difficult to put such a law in operation.

"In the old days [says the "Daily Telegraph"] Mrs. Fletcher might have been burned alive, or drowned in the nearest horse-pond, for her necromantic proclivities. Even so recently as forty years ago, a person convicted of 'pretending to exercise or use any kind of witchcraft, sorcery, enchant-

ment, or conjuration,' would have been locked up for one
year, and besides would have had to stand once every quarter
in the pillory, 'in the market-town of the county, on the day
when the market is held.' Mrs. Fletcher will not have to
endure the penalties of this particular offence, but she will
reap a richly deserved reward for her nefarious actions in the
sentence which Mr. Justice Hawkins has pronounced."

After a *résumé* of the case, evidently based upon
the summing-up of the judge, the "Telegraph" con-
cludes : —

"This case shows pretty plainly the danger of dealing with
professional Spiritualists. Mr. Fletcher seems to have been
gifted with all those peculiar powers which make a person
what is called a good 'medium.' His 'trances,' however,
were gross, and ought to have seemed, to any one of the least
perception, palpable shams. There are too many of these infamous impostors about, and it is to be hoped that this trial
will open the eyes of their dupes. Unfortunately the female
conspirator alone has been punished; while the worst offender,
Fletcher himself, remains at large. Probably he and Mr. Morton are enjoying themselves somewhere in America, but at
present the fact remains that justice has only been half satisfied by the verdict which the jury yesterday pronounced."

"'Spiritualism,' as it is termed [the "Standard" says], is
a matter with regard to which various shades of opinion are
known to exist. There can be no doubt, however, as to the
justice of the verdict delivered last evening at the Old Bailey."

Giving its version of the details of the case, the
"Standard" goes on to say, —

"There is, no doubt, a good deal in the case which has not been brought out. Mrs. Hart-Davies is clearly a very silly woman, capable of almost any folly; but there is no need for us to consider either the truth or falsehood of Spiritualism, or to take into account the precise degree of folly of which the prosecutrix was capable. After the whole pitiful story had been sifted out, the issues left to the jury were very considerably narrowed down. Had Mrs. Fletcher obtained valuable property from the prosecutrix? As to this there was no possible doubt. Had she done so by representing to the prosecutrix that such gift or disposition was at the instance, and, indeed, at the express wish, of the late Mrs. Heurtley? As to this, again, there was literally no question. It only remained, then, to ask whether Mrs. Fletcher herself believed in the truth of these messages from spirit-land; for, if she did not believe in them, she was clearly guilty of a fraudulent pretence. Such was the issue which Mr. Justice Hawkins left to the jury, and upon it the jurors have convicted Mrs. Fletcher.

"With the more enthusiastic adherents of Spiritualism it is idle to attempt to argue. No exposure is sufficient to shake their faith. But there are certain broad facts in the present case which those who are not too deeply pledged to the follies, and, we may add, to the something worse than folly, of this new philosophy, will do well to consider. In the first place, it is clear that professional mediums are, as a rule, persons of somewhat questionable antecedents. There is always an atmosphere of doubt about them. Spiritualism, in short, is disreputable; and its surroundings are disreputable, or even worse. No man who respects himself would allow his wife or his daughters to attend professional *séances*, or to habitually associate with professional mediums. Beneath all the rubbish that is talked about 'spheres of spiritual existence' and 'odic power,' there lies an ugly under-current, the nature of which any man of the world can at once determine for himself. Nor is it a fact without significance, that whenever a professional Spiritualist appears in court, it is to answer some such charge of fraud as the present."

The provincial press no doubt followed its leaders. I have seen but one example from a remarkably good newspaper, the " Leicester Free Press," which says, —

"The rogues and impostors who practise certain arts and tricks included under the heading of 'Modern Spiritualism' have received another warning. The news that Mrs. Fletcher, a 'Spiritualist,' has been sentenced to twelve months' imprisonment with hard labor, for obtaining property by fraud and false pretences, will, it is to be hoped, act not only as a deterrent to unscrupulous knaves, but as a caution to all credulous fools."

I have not given the most abusive passages of these articles. When a woman is once locked up in prison, it is quite safe, and I presume it is considered manly and honorable, to libel her, and " say all manner of evil against her, falsely." Whether it is considered manly and honorable, and worthy of the character of English gentlemen, to strike, or kick, or cover with torrents of abuse and lies, an utterly unprotected, imprisoned woman, I have no means of knowing. I think, however, that it is not usual, even in the case of criminals who are unquestionably guilty. Had I been simply a thief, a robber, a murderess, the prison or the gallows would have been thought punishment enough. Why, then, did the English press depart from its usual custom? I believe there is but one answer. It was because I was a *Spiritualist*. Had we all of us been members of any religious denomination, — Irvingites, Plymouth Brethren, or members of the Salvation Army, — the property question would have been settled in a civil court, and I should neither have been sentenced to Tothill Fields Prison, nor libelled in leading articles.

The best answer I can give to this ignorant and contemptuous, and, as it seems to me, contemptible, abuse of Spiritualists, is to call a moment's attention to the names and positions of a few of those who have given the matter a careful investigation, and avowed their belief in what are called " spiritual manifestations."

Americans are not considered less clever or less intelligent than Englishmen ; and in America, Spiritualists are counted by millions, including presidents, governors of States, professors of universities, clergymen, physicians, judges, lawyers, and men of every class and profession.

Among the more distinguished persons, living or dead, who have become satisfied with the reality of more or less of the phenomena called " psychic " or " spiritual," are the Earl of Crawford and Balcarres, F.R.S., president R.A.S ; W. Crookes, fellow and gold medallist of the Royal Society; C. Varley, F.R.S., C.E.; A. R. Wallace, the eminent naturalist; W. F. Barrett, F.R.S.E., professor of physics in the Royal College of Science, Dublin; Dr. Lockhart Robertson; Dr. J. Elliotson, F.R,S., sometime president of the Royal Medical and Chirurgical Society of London; Professor de Morgan, sometime president of the Mathematical Society of London; Dr. William Gregory, F.R.S.E., sometime professor of chemistry in the University of Edinburgh; Dr. Ashburner, Mr. Rutter, Dr. Herbert Mayo, F.R.S.; Professor F. Zöllner of Leipzig, author of "Transcendental Physics," etc.; Professors G. T. Fechner, Scheibner, and J. H. Fichte, of Leipzig; Professor W. E. Weber of Göttingen; Professor Hoffman of Würzburg; Professor Perty of Berne; Professors Wagner and Butleroff of Petersburg; Professors Hare and Mapes of U.S.A.; Dr. Robert Friese of Breslau; Mons. Camille Flammarion, astronomer; the late and present Earls of Dunraven; T. A. Trollope; S. C. Hall; Gerald Massey; Capt. R. Burton; Professor Cassal, LL.D.; Lord Brougham; Lord Lytton; Lord Lyndhurst; Archbishop Whately; Dr. Robert Chambers, F.R.S.E.; W. M. Thackeray; Nassau Senior; George Thompson; W. Howitt; Sergeant Cox; Mrs. Browning; Bishop Clarke, Rhode Island, U.S.A.; Darius Lyman, U.S.A.; Professor W. Denton; Professor Alexander Wilder; Professor Hiram

Corson; Professor George Bush; twenty-four judges
and ex-judges of the United States courts; Victor
Hugo; Baron and Baroness von Vay; W. Lloyd Garrison, U.S.A.; Hon. R. Dale Owen, U.S.A.; Hon.
J. W. Edmonds, U.S.A.; Epes Sargent; Baron du
Potet; Count A. de Gasparin; Baron L. de Gulden-
stübbe; H. I. H. Nicholas, Duke of Leuchtenberg;
H. S. H. the Prince of Solms: H. S. H. Prince Emile
of Sayn Wittgenstein; Hon. Alexander Aksakof, im-
perial councillor of Russia; the Hon. J. L. O'Sullivan,
sometime minister of U.S.A. at the court of Lisbon;
M. Favre Clavairoz, late consul-general of France at
Trieste; the late Emperors of Russia and France;
Presidents Thiers and Lincoln, etc.

This list might be greatly extended. Some of these
men are among the brightest lights of science, who
have given much time to these investigations; yet the
writers of newspaper leaders have no hesitation in setting them all down as knaves or fools, charlatans or
dupes.

Two centuries ago Spiritualism, in the sense of a
belief in the supernatural, was all but universal. The
present fashion is materialism. A century ago people
were hanged for witchcraft: now any person pretending to be a witch or sorcerer may be sent to prison
as a rogue and vagabond. When Mr. Slade was convicted in England, and escaped prison by an infor-

mality, he went to Germany, where his manifestations were thoroughly examined by the late Professor Zöllner of the University of Leipzig, who published the result, with photographic illustrations, in his "Transcendental Physics." He afterwards, with his brother-professors, made a similar series of investigations of the phenomena produced in the presence of my friend, Mr. W. Eglinton.

I give these facts, partly to show that the ignorance of some leader-writers for English newspapers is nearly as great as their — I leave the reader to supply the proper expression. I can think of no word but brutality, and my love for the poor brutes hinders me from instituting a comparison. They seem, in my case, to have been given over to "hardness of heart, and blindness of mind."

A London correspondent of the "Banner of Light" says of this curious outburst of intolerance, —

"The man who strikes at this helpless woman in prison commits an outrage against every Spiritualist. Her cause is our cause. Every medium, and every aider and abettor of a medium, can be imprisoned by English law, as well as Mrs. Fletcher. It seems to me mean and cowardly in the last and lowest degree to attack a woman in prison in any case, though almost the entire English press did so the day after Mrs. Fletcher was sentenced. But it is not their custom. They would not have done to a murderer what they did to a Spiritualist.

"The fact of Mrs. Fletcher being a Spiritualist was the only proof of her guilt; and that, in English law, is sufficient. It made Slade a rogue and a vagabond: it convicted Mrs. Fletcher of false pretences. The only false pretence alleged was that Mrs. Fletcher pretended to receive messages from the spirit of Mrs. Heurtley. Not a shadow of proof was offered that she did *not* receive such messages. It was assumed by judge and jury that she *could not* have received them. The verdict was based solely upon this assumption. It was preconceived opinion, and the assumption of English law, upon which Mrs. Fletcher was made a martyr for Spiritualism. It has been the same in every religious persecution. When Roman Christians were brought before Nero, there was no proof of guilt. It was not shown that Christianity was a pestilent imposture: that was assumed. 'My religion, the religion of the state, is true: your religion contradicts that; *ergo*, it is false. Take these Christians to the Flavian amphitheatre, and throw them to the lions. It will amuse the populace.' Spanish inquisitors, Calvin at Geneva, Henry VIII., who with perfect impartiality burned Catholics who denied his supremacy, and Protestants who denied the Real Presence, had the same convenient method of procedure. In the same fashion, Elizabeth filled the prisons of England with nonconformists, and Charles II. and James II. imprisoned Quakers and other dissenters; and women were whipped from town to town, tied to the cart's-tail, in old Massachusetts; while the parsons of the period, like some Spiritualist editors now, stood by, and encouraged the executioners to lay on harder, and make their lashes cut deeper into the naked flesh of their victims."

CHAPTER XXXII.

THE OTHER SIDE.

ALL this time the other side of the story had not been heard. The ancient maxim, "*audi alteram partem*," had not been so much as whispered. Evidently it did not occur to the writers for the press that there was any other side than the one which had been presented to the jury. In my case, which was a type of many more, there was a clamorous multitude and a silent prisoner.

I think, before giving an account of my twelve months in prison, I should give in this place some of the testimony that should have been given at the trial, not only in justice to myself, but for the sake of the honest people all over the world who were made to detest me by my conviction. It was a wrong to me, but the wrong to the millions who were deceived by such a "trial" was far greater.

I have given in the preceding chapter a list of men, who, after a thorough examination, have testified to the objective reality of the facts which constitute what is called " Spiritualism." All these men and women, and a multitude of others, as intelligent and as honest as there are in the world, would have testified to the fact of communications with departed spirits.

No doubt eminent men could have been called who would have said they did not believe these facts. Such negative testimony is, of course, worthless. We do not want the testimony of those who shut their eyes, and then tell us they cannot see. Those who have seen and heard and felt are the proper witnesses.

If permitted to do so, I could have abundantly proved that there are spirits who can make themselves heard, seen, and felt, so as to be recognized, as far as identity can be proven. These spirits are not necessarily wise or good, any more than those of living men and women. A foolish man or a silly woman does not become wise at once by getting out of an earthly embodiment. Having proved the facts of spirit-existence and of spirit-communication, why should not the departed Mrs. Heurtley, with her mysterious relations, communicate with her peculiar daughter? — why not wish her to be under her own care and guidance, by being with those through whom she might give her messages of such wisdom as she had learned?

There are American judges, like the late Judge Edmunds of the New-York Court of Appeals, who are intelligent and devoted Spiritualists. Had it been my fortune to be tried before such a judge, any reader can see that it might have made a difference.

Next to the witnesses that should have been called to prove the facts of Spiritualism, the most important witness was Mr. Morton, who was excluded from the witness-box by being included in the indictment. There is no doubt of Mr. Morton's legal position as a member of the Massachusetts bar, and also as a member of the bar of the Circuit Court of the United States; and his high and honorable position, professional and social, is thoroughly and strongly indorsed by gentlemen of high standing at the bar, as well as by those holding prominent positions in the affairs of state, and by letters from an eminent Boston lawyer to Mr. Francis, the London solicitor to whom he introduced Mrs. Hart-Davies.

We had known Mr. Morton in Boston as a Spiritualist. When he came to London, he called to see us; and subsequently, having more rooms than we required, we were able to offer him one. He was never our lawyer, or secretary, or any thing but an old acquaintance and respected friend.

Mr. Morton, writing from Boston on March 10, 1881, after the examination at Bow Street, and before the Old Bailey trial, said, —

"I believe it was not until Mrs. Hart-Davies came under the personal influence of James McGeary (otherwise called Dr.

Mack) that she ever *dreamed* of assailing the Fletchers; nor does her position at the beginning indicate that she intended to bring suit. But, once under the sway of a man who has been an openly avowed enemy of the Fletchers, it was impossible for her to stop. And thus she wandered on in her evidence, without fear of contradiction, assailing everybody else in order to protect herself; and her attack upon me is only another of the inexplicable turns of this extraordinary case. The giving a home to Madam Hart-Davies may have been an error of judgment; and, if so, let Mr. and Mrs. Fletcher be held responsible for it as an error, and not as a crime."

In his testimony in regard to his acquaintance with us, and his connection with this case, Mr. Morton says, —

"I had known Mr. and Mrs. Fletcher publicly and privately for many years in America, where they occupied prominent positions as mediums and lecturers of acknowledged ability.

"I was consulted by Madam Hart-Davies, as to the proper way to dispose of certain property so as to protect it from her husband, and which she desired to give and intrust to the Fletchers. I gave the desired legal advice, asking at the same time under what influence she had been led to bestow these things upon them. Her reply was, that *no persons, spirits or mortals, had influenced her in any manner.* Under her instructions a deed of gift was made and taken home, and copied by her. This done, Mrs. Fletcher was apprised of the fact, and the paper read to her. Subsequently Madam Hart-Davies made a will in her own handwriting, in order, as she said, that there should be 'no question as to her intentions,' and 'to prevent the possibility of future litigation.' The existence and contents of this will were not mentioned by me until the following year, September, 1880, after the suits brought in America, when I stated the fact to the Fletchers. Madam Hart-Davies went to France near the end of 1879, and returned to England in the spring, when she resided with the Fletchers, and in the summer came with them to America; and under the influence of others, whose enmity to the Fletchers has been acknowledged, she instituted legal proceedings against them, which were discontinued, and the Fletchers honorably discharged. A cross-suit had been instituted against Mrs. Hart-Davies and James McGeary, which was postponed for a settlement, when both defendants fled the country, and swore out a warrant against the Fletchers in England. On learning this, Mrs. Fletcher left for England, and, as she expected, was arrested on the steamer on which she took passage to Greenock, and subsequently tried upon an indictment in which I was included, apparently for no other reason than to deprive her of my testimony as a witness.

"I state from my absolute knowledge, that the evidence given by Mrs. Hart-Davies, the sole witness on whom the whole case rested, was a tissue of false statements. Had her evidence been investigated, and her true character known, her words would not have had the slightest weight with judge or jury.

"The clever device, or drag-net indictment, which closed my mouth, though I was in England at the time, only shows the weakness of her position. The ignoring of the testimony as to character, of the fact of Mrs. Fletcher's coming across the ocean to meet her trial, and the ruling-out of all evidence of the truth of Spiritualism, show that the Court was prejudiced against the prisoner. Could I have spoken at the time, I could have convinced any fair-minded man that Mrs. Hart-Davies was inspired by an insane jealousy on the one hand, and on the other influenced by enemies of the Fletchers.

"I am ready at all times to testify that Madam Hart-Davies sought the assistance and protection of the Fletchers; that she forced her gifts upon them on the pretext that she was friendless, but with an ulterior purpose; that, when defeated in this, she sought to be revenged."

I give this letter of Mr. Morton, which he has solemnly confirmed in the following sworn and legally certified affidavits, containing some of the testimony which should have been given in court, but which the government, the "crown" of a clement and merciful queen, was made, by her officers acting in her name, — "*Regina versus Fletchers and Morton*," — to unjustly and tyrannously exclude.

In the matter of Mrs. JULIET ANNE THEODORA HART-DAVIES *versus* Mr. J. W. FLETCHER *and* Mrs. SUSAN WILLIS FLETCHER, *now pending in Bow Street Police-Court, London, Eng.*

I, Francis T. Morton of Boston, Mass., U.S.A., hereby depose and say, That the statement made by Mr. S. B. Abrahams on the 3d of December, A.D. 1880, at Bow Street Police-Court, to wit, That I influenced Mrs. Hart-Davies in the making of a certain will dated Oct. 23, 1879, either by word, action, or in any other manner whatsoever, is absolutely untrue in each and every particular.

That the statement that I have ever at any time been or acted as "private secretary to J. W. Fletcher" is devoid of truth.

That the statement, that in coming over to America Mr. Fletcher, Mrs. Hart-Davies, and a lady went one way, and Mrs. Fletcher and Mr. Morton another way, is equally untrue.

I further depose and say, That Mrs. Fletcher was not a passenger on the steamer which brought me to America in September, 1880, and that Mrs. Fletcher was not in England when I left there, but was in America.

I further depose and say, That I have good reason to believe that Mr. S. B. Abrahams and his client, in making the above statements, and in saying that I was in the abode of free-lovers, and that I was a disciple of free-love, did so for the sole purpose of maliciously assailing my character and good name and that of others, both in open court and through the press, and that of my family and friends, not only here, but in England as well. And I regard it as a duty that some correcting statement should be made, not only on my own account, but that these public slanderers be prevented from doing further injury in future, and this high-handed injustice be hunted down.

I further depose and say, That upon my return to London from the seashore, in the month of August, A.D. 1879, Mrs. Hart-Davies requested and obtained an interview with me in my study, at No. 22 Gordon Street, Gordon Square, where I was then living; and after alluding to the relations existing between herself and husband, of his and her solicitors, of her trustees, and of her aunt, from whom she derived her only income of three hundred pounds per annum, she said substantially these words, "I have not one friend in this world whom I can trust, and to whom I can go for advice and assistance. Will you give me counsel and advice?" I answered that I was not conversant with English practice, and could not in any way be mixed up in her affairs, and thereupon advised her to go to some responsible firm of solicitors, who would see that she was protected in her rights if they had been in any manner infringed upon. She replied, that she knew of no solicitors, and had no friends who could or would give her such introduction, and again asked for my assistance and advice, and thereupon declared her purpose to make a conveyance of certain property, and stated in most unmistakable language the subject-matter contained in a certain deed of gift dated Aug. 25, 1870, and which after signing, she requested me to sign my name as a witness thereto, and which I accordingly did. The schedule of certain property therein referred to was never given nor annexed to the said deed of gift, although so intended by Mrs. Hart-Davies on Aug. 26, 1870. Before subscribing my name as a witness to this deed of gift, I asked Mrs. Hart-Davies why she had made this conveyance to Mrs. Fletcher, and if she had given the matter careful consideration, and whether she had been influenced by any one in making this conveyance. To which she replied, that no persons, either spirits or mortals, had at any time, or in any manner whatever, influenced her in making this conveyance. That Mrs. Fletcher was the best and truest friend she had in the world; that she had by her kindness saved her life when she was friendless, and knew not which way to turn; that she had no relatives other than a brother, who was living in South America, and could take care of himself; and that she wished to leave this property to Mrs. Fletcher, and was determined the property should go to no one else. I said I doubted very much if Mrs. Fletcher would allow her to do so. Mrs. Hart-Davies replied, that she did not expect to live a great while longer, and that there was no one else to whom she wished to leave her property. The statement of Mrs. Hart-Davies, or that of her counsel, that I at any time, or in any manner whatsoever, influenced her, either directly or indirectly, to make the said conveyance above referred to, is a base and malicious falsehood, and as outrageous and villanous as it is false.

I further depose and say, That in the following month of October Mrs. Hart-Davies came to me and declared her purpose of making a will, and not only asked, but *begged*, my assistance in so doing. I replied, that, while I would cheerfully assist as far as I could, I was not familiar with the requirements of the English practice in such matters; that in a matter of this nature she ought to go to a good solicitor, who would see that whatever she did would be rightly and properly done, and suggested that the trustees would probably know of some reliable solicitors. She said, "No, I don't wish to ask my trustees for any thing;" and then asked me if I would take the responsibility of introducing her to some solicitors whom I might know; that she would be under lasting obligations.

I further depose and say, That I did subsequently introduce Mrs. Hart-Davies to one of the most respectable firms of solicitors I knew of in London (and this upon her urgent solicitation, and from no desire of my own), to whom she stated her case in terms and language that admitted of no doubt as to her motives, intentions, and purposes; that she subsequently gave or sent to the said solicitors a "will," written in her own handwriting, in order (as she said) that there might be no question as to her intentions, and to prevent the possibility of future litigation, the original draught of which, I presume and trust, is still in existence. The solicitors in question declined at first to have any thing to do with her matters, in view of her having previously employed other solicitors, and the uncertain condition of her affairs, but subsequently were kind enough to act as her solicitors. The introduction was made by me in good faith; which good faith, on her part, has been most shamefully violated. It was made at great personal inconvenience, and with intent to wrong no one, but to help this woman, Mrs. Hart-Davies, who came to me representing that she was persecuted and wronged. And the statement made by her or her counsel, that I either influenced her in the making of any will, or conspired with any person or persons whatsoever in so doing, is a most infamous falsehood, and without a semblance or shadow of truth, calculated to deceive the Court, and poison the mind of the public before a reply thereto could be made, and its falsity be proved.

I further depose and say, That I have always regarded Mrs. Hart-Davies's interviews as a professional matter, and until September, 1880 (after Mrs. Hart-Davies had brought her suit in this country [America]), have never spoken of the will to any person or persons whatsoever, in England or elsewhere (other than to her solicitors), either directly or indirectly. And furthermore, to be more explicit, I never had a word of conversation with J. W. Fletcher, or Susie Willis Fletcher, about the subject-matter of this or any other will, until September, 1880. Nor did Mr. and Mrs. Fletcher ever consult with me as to the making of the said will, or of any codicil, or of any solicitors in connection therewith, in behalf of Mrs. Hart-Davies, or any other person or persons. And, furthermore, Mrs. Hart-Davies stated to me in the most positive terms, that she had *not* been influenced by any one, either spirits or mortals, in the making of, or in her purpose of making, the said will, or in the making of any will whatsoever. And the statement of Mrs. Hart-Davies or her solicitors, that J. W. Fletcher or Susie Willis Fletcher conspired with me, or I with them, to influence in any manner whatsoever, or to induce Mrs. Hart-Davies to make this or any other will, is a most contemptible and outrageous falsehood, —

a statement which she failed to make, and dared not make, in the suit she brought in this country in August, A.D. 1880 (and quite similar to that now pending in London), and in which she was non-suited, having fled the country before it was tried, and without the knowledge of her counsel, as the records of the court will show.

I further depose and say, That between the first and twelfth day of June, A D. 1880, and on two different occasions, Mrs. Hart-Davies, after stating that she was about to visit America, asked me to draw up a paper which she might take with her to America, the better to protect herself and Mrs. Fletcher in the property she intended to take over with her. I told her she should consult her solicitor in London, or her lawyer in New York on her arrival there, and did not draw up the paper as requested.

I further depose and say, That from the first Mrs. Hart-Davies came to me, not only of her own accord, but quite unsolicited; that I gave her the best advice, counsel, and assistance in my power; that I have never asked nor received one farthing from her for any services rendered her; and that, up to within two days of her leaving London for America, she expressed her gratitude to me for such kindness in terms of confidence and respect.

I further depose and say, That the attempt of Mrs. Hart-Davies and her advisers to injure my character and standing in the courts and through the press, both socially and at the bar, not only in this country, but in England and on the Continent, whether to serve her own purposes, or for any other reason, is without cause or justification.

The purpose of this statement is to hunt down and punish injustice whenever and wherever found. And, the better to serve this purpose, I forward herewith certified certificates as to my standing in the courts of this State, and other papers as to my character in this community.

FRANCIS T. MORTON.

Counsellor-at-Law.

40 SIMMONS BUILDINGS, BOSTON, MASS., U.S.A.,
Dec. 27, A.D. 1880.

This affidavit was duly certified by a notary-public and the British vice-consul.

These are the facts known to Mr. Morton, which should have been placed before the jury, strengthened and confirmed by ever so rigorous a cross-examination.

My next witness should have been Capt. Canute Lindmark, my Swedish friend, who had been, long before he knew me, an intimate acquaintance of the prosecutrix, on whose testimony, as Mr. Justice Hawkins told the jury, the whole fabric of the prosecution rested. It was therefore of great importance that there should be some witness who knew the character of this woman, and who could testify as to her relations to us. Capt. Lindmark had been introduced to us by Mrs. Hart-Davies as her friend. He visited us often in London : he accompanied us on our visit to America, having also business of his own ; and, next to Mr. Morton, he knew more of the facts than any other person. Moreover, *he was not and is not a*

Spiritualist: so that in every way he was a most important witness.

I do not know why he was not called. I know that my solicitor, Mr. Lewis, who prepared my defence, wished to call him and many other witnesses, and that not one, except witnesses as to character, was called by Mr. Addison, and that this action was without my knowledge or desire.

I copy the following affidavit of Capt. Lindmark from a memorial to the home secretary, by T. L. Nichols, M.D.

The Declaration of Capt. CANUTE LINDMARK *in matters concerning* Mrs. SUSAN WILLIS FLETCHER, *a prisoner in London.* ·

I am late captain of the Royal Swedish Engineers, and at present engaged as consulting engineer and shareholder in various industrial undertakings.

I made the acquaintance of Mrs. Hart-Davies in Buenos Ayres, about the year 1872. She was then married to a gentleman named Rickard, who for some time was employed by the Argentine Government as inspector of mines. I was at the time vice-director of the engineering department of the Argentine Republic, and chief engineer of the public works. I also know Mrs. Davies's brother (who, married to an Argentine lady, is living in Buenos Ayres), her second husband, and her pretended aunt, Mrs. Sampson; and I was personally acquainted with Mr. Sampson, the late editor of the "Times," whom she always represented to me as her mother's brother.

Her mother, Mrs. Heurtley, I saw only once, when living at Hampton Court with Mr. Sampson. As regards her father, I understand that it is not known whether he is living or dead. He was a quack-doctor, who, leaving his wife, went to America years ago.

Soon after I had made Mrs. Rickard's acquaintance, she made me her confidant, describing how much she had suffered, and how badly she now was treated, not only by her husband (who needed to go away travelling) leaving her alone in Buenos Ayres without protection, and sometimes without sufficient money to subsist on, but also by her own mother, who had forced her to marry Mr. Rickard, whom she never loved, and now would not allow her to return to London. Believing her statements to be true, I felt pity for her, and gave her what assistance I could afford. On several occasions I advanced her money; and in 1873, when her husband was away in Europe, and her health was very bad, I took her to the mountains, distant four hundred miles from Buenos Ayres, in order that she might improve by the change of air. This step, however, I afterwards regretted; because, instead of getting strong, she rather grew weaker. Nevertheless, and in spite of my earnest protestations to the contrary, Mrs. Rickard from that time always used to speak of me as the savior of her life.

In 1874 Mr. Rickard came back to River Plate to take his wife and son over to England, where he had determined to settle. They all landed at Liverpool about the month of June of the same year. There Mr. Rickard left his wife, and together with his son went to London, where he immediately instituted proceedings against her for adultery, committed on board the steamer, with an Italian named Amadeo. The proofs being convincing, her mother, Mrs. Heurtley, in order to avoid scandal, suggested to her not to dispute the charge; and thus the divorce was granted. When Mrs. Rickard came to London, neither Mrs. Heurtley nor Mr. Sampson would see her; and she was obliged to go and live with strangers. But Mrs. Heurtley would not even allow her daughter to live in the same country where she lived; and thus Mrs. Rickard was obliged, after some months, to leave England, and settle in Tours in France.

When these events took place, I was in London, having been commissioned by the Argentine Government to inspect some railway materials; and during that time, and also afterwards, Mrs. Rickard used to write to me about her private affairs. Soon after, I returned to River Plate, which country I left in 1876 to settle in Sweden. On my way home I visited Mrs. Rickard in Tours, and found her occupying a small bedroom in one of the hotels, evidently in a very poor condition. She complained to me bitterly, that her mother not only kept her in exile, but refused to give her sufficient to live on, her yearly allowance being only one hundred and fifty pounds. Moreover, this allowance was paid only to herself in person at Tours in small instalments, so that she could not go and live anywhere else.

The following year Mrs. Heurtley and Mr. Sampson both died, and then Mrs. Rickard was not prevented from returning to England.

Mrs. Rickard had often stated to me that her mother was very rich, having a yearly income of from nine thousand to twelve thousand pounds; and on the death of her mother and uncle she wrote to me from France, stating that she and her brother had inherited all their property. She also informed me that she already had had three offers of marriage, but refused them all. In reply, I wrote to her, that, in my opinion, the best thing she could do, under the present circumstances, was to marry again; and some time after she engaged herself to Mr. Hart-Davies.

Returning from France, Mrs. Rickard went to live with Mrs. Sampson at Hampton Court. There I visited her twice, — once before her marriage with Mr. Hart-Davies, and once after. She told me that she had married Mr. Davies, not because she loved him, but out of pity, seeing how deeply attached he was to her. She meant to use her influence over him to improve his mind, and raise him from the low position he had formerly occupied. Speaking of her trustees, she said that they would not give her any money, and insinuated that they systematically robbed her.

Again, in the autumn of 1879, I came to London on business, and went to see Mrs. Hart-Davies, who was then living with her husband at Vernon Place. I found her in a state of great excitement. She told me that she was most unhappy. Her husband was a drunkard, who would do no work, and only wanted to live on her money. She had been obliged to move from Farquhar Lodge, where they lived before, to London; because she had noticed that her husband intentionally left her without medical assistance when she was very ill, thus endangering her life. While I was sitting in the drawing-room with Mrs. Davies, her husband came home, and, without entering the drawing-room, passed up stairs to his own private apartments. I then saw Mrs. Davies on his approach become very agitated, seemingly trembling with fear. Upon that she began to speak of her new friends, the Fletchers, who had been very good to her during this time of unhappiness, and asked if I would not allow her to introduce me to them. I replied that it was hardly possible, as I was going to Sweden in a couple of days, and my time was very much engaged. But finally, on her insisting, I consented; and on the following evening I accompanied her to their house at 22 Gordon Street.

On our way home, Mrs. Hart-Davies said that her hope was to come and live with the Fletchers, and that she would do every thing in her power to become a member of their family. I got rather surprised at this statement, and did my best to show her the imprudence of such a step. "The Fletchers," I said, "have both of them impressed me very favorably; but they are North-Americans and Spiritualists, and as such it would not be advisable to place your future in their hands." She replied, that she was sorry to see that I shared the common prejudice of the English people; that the Fletchers' house was frequented by the very best people in London, and that she herself had seen the Princess of Wales come and pay them a visit. In fact, she would not at all listen to my advice, but continued to speak of the Fletchers in the most enthusiastic terms. Soon, however, I found that Mr. Fletcher was the principal, if not the sole, object of her admiration. Indeed, neither on this occasion nor afterwards, did Mrs. Davies, speaking of Mrs. Fletcher alone, represent her friend in a favorable light: on the contrary, she described Mrs. Fletcher to me as a cold-natured woman, devoid of the natural feelings of her sex.

I returned to Sweden the following day or the next. After my arrival in Sweden, I received a letter from Mrs. Davies requesting me to lend her five hundred pounds in order to defray the expenses of her intended voyage to France. This money, however, I declined to advance her.

In the beginning of last year I returned to England; and, six or seven weeks after my arrival in London, I went to see the Fletchers. They informed me that Mrs. Hart-Davies was going to live with them after her return from France, and that they expected her in a month's time. Mrs. Davies had solicited their protection, because she found it impossible to stay any longer with her husband, and because her aunt, Mrs. Sampson, would not receive her in her house.

In May Mrs. Davies arrived from France, taking up her abode with the Fletchers. I now visited their house frequently; and, being an old friend of Mrs. Davies, I also became intimate with Mr. and Mrs. Fletcher. Mrs. Hart-Davies availed herself of the first opportunity to explain to me more fully the reasons why she had left her husband. Mr. Davies, she said, had after their marriage endeavored to impress upon her the necessity of making a will, and one day, while they were living at Farquhar Lodge, he brought with him from London two men whom she did not know, but who were introduced to her as solicitors. They laid before her a document, which she found to be a will in favor of her husband, and which they forced her to sign. After this she began to suspect her husband of entertaining plans against her life, and said she had once discovered him bringing a glass of port wine that was poisoned; and that, not succeeding in poisoning her, Mr. Davies had taken measures to have her shut up in a lunatic-asylum, and for several days she saw men of suspicious appearance strolling about her house at Vernon Place. It was then she secretly left her husband, and went to France without letting him know her address.

All these incidents Mrs. Davies related to me in full details, and with such an air of conviction that for some time I believed her. Afterwards, however, I found, from what her husband, and her trustee Mr. Burrows, told me, that her story was false from beginning to end. At Farquhar Lodge she had really made a will in favor of her husband; but it was made entirely of her own accord, and without her husband interfering at all. This will she soon after cancelled. The Rev. Mr. Burrows, a trustee of Mrs. Davies, was under the impression that she never gave her husband any money. "Mr. Davies [he said] possessed before marrying a little capital of his own; and that capital, together with a considerable sum which his brother had advanced him, was spent in sustaining the house." When Mr. Davies could not procure any more money, his wife left him.

I asked Mrs. Hart-Davies if her husband, knowing that she lived with the Fletchers, could not compel her to come back to his house. She answered, that he would not dare to do such a thing; because he knew, that, the moment he evinced such an intention, she would petition for a divorce on the ground of his physical failing. In fact, he never made the slightest attempt to induce his wife to return.

With regard to her trustees, Mrs. Davies used still more abusive language than before; declaring it was her intention to bring them up before the Court of Chancery as soon as she could procure sufficient money to pay the law-expenses.

Mrs. Davies had not been a fortnight with the Fletchers before she commenced to reveal her true character. Finding her intentions frustrated with regard to Mr. Fletcher, who, she saw, loved and respected his wife too much to be more than a friend and brother to her, she suddenly changed, from the pure and suffering victim she had artfully represented herself to be to the Fletchers, to a jealous and capricious woman.

When I saw how disagreeable she made herself to her hosts, and that neither of them was capable of pacifying her bad temper, I one day, in a private conversation, expressed to her my surprise at her strange conduct, which appeared to me the more inexplicable as she was treated with the greatest kindness. She interrupted me, saying, "They ought to be kind to me. I have shared with them my worldly goods, and even made a will in their favor. But that, of course, I can all cancel to-morrow if I like," she added; and with these words she left me. When I next saw Mrs. Fletcher, I asked her if Mrs. Davies had made a will in her favor; to which she answered, "No." — "But she herself told me so," I said. "Then, she has done so without our knowledge," Mrs. Fletcher replied. "The only document I know of is a deed of gift, by which she made over to us the things she brought to the house, so as to prevent her husband from claiming them." Thinking that Mrs. Davies, using the word "will," had really meant the deed of gift, I did not inquire any further into the matter.

Mrs. Fletcher, although she occasionally wore Mrs. Hart-Davies's jewelry, and had some old china and crystals belonging to Mrs. Davies in her drawing-room, did never, to my knowledge, pretend that these things were her own. In fact, one day, when Mrs. Fletcher, Mrs. Hart-Davies, and myself were sitting in the back drawing-room, Mrs. Fletcher, pointing at various things, said to me, "Nearly all these dainty things you see in this room belong to Juliet."

Mrs. Davies's extraordinary conduct, as also the fact that none of the many old friends she pretended to have in London came to visit her after her return from France, greatly astonished Mr. Fletcher, and caused him to make inquiries about her former life, of which she evidently had given him quite an erroneous idea. One afternoon, when I happened to be alone in the drawing-room, Mrs. Davies entered in a very agitated state. Throwing herself on the sofa, she began to cry hysterically. "Willie has made me confess," she said; "and now he despises me."

Indeed, after this it seems to have become clear to the Fletchers that Mrs. Davies could not continue to be an inmate of their house, but that she must sooner or later leave them. On one occasion I was present when Mrs. Davies began to complain, as she often used to do, to Mrs. Fletcher of the coldness of her husband. "He is my brother," she said; "and as such he ought to be more kind to me than he is: now he scarcely notices me." And so she went on, till at last Mrs. Fletcher, growing angry, told her plainly, that, if she was not satisfied with her husband, she had better take her things, and leave the house at once; upon which Mrs. Davies had a hysterical attack, and then asked Mrs. Fletcher's pardon.

In the mean time I returned to Sweden, having previously agreed to accompany Mr. and Mrs. Fletcher on their voyage to America, which country I intended to visit for the purpose of inspecting certain manufacturing establishments. Consequently, I returned to England towards the end of July, when we all left for America, Mrs. Davies and Miss Spencer being also of the party.

On board the steamer, Mrs. Davies became so conspicuous for her imprudent behavior, remaining on deck till late in the night, after all the other lady-passengers had retired, that I felt bound to signify to Mr. Fletcher, that, for the decorum of the party, he should compel Mrs. Davies to conduct herself properly. In this he succeeded, but only after threatening to separate her from the party, and send her back by the returning steamer to England.

We disembarked at New York, and went from there to a Spiritualistic camp-meeting at a place called Lake Pleasant, not far from Boston. At this meeting were also two men, both Spiritualists, of whom Mrs. Fletcher had on several occasions spoken to me as her bitterest enemies: they had come over from England only a few days before us. One of them calls himself Dr. Mack, and the name of the other is Rondi. The latter is an Italian artist.

With these men, whom Mrs. Fletcher did not even recognize
at the camp, and of whom at least Dr. Mack was entirely
unknown to Mrs. Davies, she immediately formed intimate
relations; and, in concert with them, the plan to defame the
Fletchers was conceived, which afterwards was so successfully
carried out. About a week after our arrival at the camp-
meeting, Mrs. Davies told me that she was going to spend a
few days at the watering-place, Saratoga, with an American
family whose acquaintance she had just made, but that she
would be back soon. She then left the camp, taking scarcely
any luggage with her. But, instead of going to Saratoga, she
went with her two friends, Dr. Mack and Rondi, to a village
in the neighborhood. There they got a search-warrant; and
provided with this, and a power-of-attorney from Mrs. Davies,
Dr. Mack presented himself at Lake Pleasant to recover Mrs.
Davies's stolen property from the Fletchers. I did not then
know that there had been any difficulties whatever between
the Fletchers and Mrs. Hart-Davies with regard to her property, nor do I believe that there ever existed any. I had heard
Mrs. Fletcher say to her husband, shortly after Mrs. Davies
had left the camp, "I asked her to take her things with her;
but she would not, saying that she intended to come back in a
few days." Consequently, I thought Mrs. Davies's behavior
atrocious, and advised the Fletchers not to give up the property to Dr. Mack. However, they did not follow my advice:
so he got the things. It seems natural, if there had actually
been any dispute about her jewelry and other things, that Mrs.
Davies should have addressed herself to me, her old friend,
who on various occasions before had assisted her, instead of
having recourse to two strangers, whom she, moreover, knew
to be enemies of the Fletchers; but on that subject she never
said a word to me.

From Lake Pleasant, Mr. and Mrs. Fletcher, Miss Spencer, and I went to Boston. Dr. Mack, Mr. Rondi, and Mrs. Davies also went there. There they got a new search-warrant, claiming part of Mrs. Davies's property that was left in the Fletchers' house in London, such as a string of Oriental pearls, etc., mentioned during the trial. Dr. Mack and Mrs. Davies, accompanied by detectives, came to the house where we lived between three and four in the afternoon, and had the house ransacked. Some linen clothes belonging to Mrs. Davies being found in Mrs. Fletcher's trunk, they on that account arrested Mrs. Fletcher; and as they had fixed the bail at the enormous sum of ten thousand pounds, which of course could not be procured in the afternoon, she was obliged to go to prison. The following morning the judge released her on a bail of only three hundred pounds. Mr. Fletcher was out of Boston at the time, and was not imprisoned. Mrs. Davies also caused my trunks to be searched, evidently in hopes of finding some of her things amongst mine, which would have given her an opportunity of implicating me in the affair.

The reporters of the newspapers being now invited to interview Mrs. Davies, she told them the most extraordinary stories about herself and the Fletchers, which afterwards circulated through the whole American press; numerous copies being also sent by Mrs. Davies and her associates to Mr. and Mrs. Fletcher's friends in England. She there represented herself to be a high-born young lady, and very rich, and stated that the property alone which she had recovered from the Fletchers at Lake Pleasant was worth sixteen thousand pounds. As for the Fletchers, there is not an infamy with which she did not charge them.

When the case was brought before the Police-Court in Boston, it was at first postponed in order to allow the Fletchers to

get over from London certain documents referring to the transfer of Mrs. Davies's property. Before they arrived, I asked Mr.
Fletcher about their contents. "I cannot tell you," he answered. "I never saw them, and I do not know whether there
are two, or only one." I then put the same question to Mrs.
Fletcher, and her lawyer also asked her; but neither could she
tell. "There is a deed of gift," she said, "which Mrs. Davies
made in our favor before she went to France; but I cannot
remember what it contains. It was read to me only once; and
then I remember to have remarked that a clause must be put
in explaining that she made it entirely of her own accord, and
free from any influence of others."

After the arrival of the documents, the case was again postponed for about six weeks; because a settlement had been
offered and accepted, by which Mrs. Davies was to pay the
Fletchers compensation for all their trouble. Mrs. Davies,
however, instead of carrying the agreement into effect, escaped
with Dr. Mack to England, while the Fletchers were detained
in Boston to answer the charge at the next hearing before the
Police-Court.

In October I returned to Europe. Before leaving Boston,
Mrs. Fletcher asked me, when I arrived in London, to go to
their house, and have all their letters from Mrs. Davies collected and secured. "These letters," she added, "are of the
greatest importance in case of any future complications; as
they show how Mrs. Davies came to live with us, and make
out the deed of gift." Accordingly, the very day I arrived in
London, I went to 22 Gordon Street, where I was received by
Mrs. and Miss Maltby and Miss Gay, who were taking care of
the house during the Fletchers' absence. On inquiring about
the letters, I was told that Mrs. Davies and Dr. Mack, accompanied by Mr. Abrahams and a detective, had, eight days

before my arrival, forced themselves into the house, and ransacked it from the top down to the cellar. Mrs. Davies had taken away, not only what belonged to her, but also a quantity of things which they knew belonged to the Fletchers, as well as their private letters and other papers. "Then," I said, "there is no use for me to look for Mrs. Davies's letters." To which Miss Gay replied, "After they had gone, there was not a letter of hers left in the house, except one, which I found in one of the bedrooms, and which I afterwards sent to Mrs. Fletcher." I was also told that Mrs. Davies, after coming back from America, had been calling on numbers of people whose acquaintance she had made in the Fletchers' house, calumniating them in every imaginable way. Amongst other stories she told was, that the Fletchers had tried to poison her both in London and America. In this laudable occupation she seems to have been faithfully assisted by her two associates.

I now went to call on Mrs. Davies's trustee, the Rev. Mr. Burrows, at Hampton, to request him to see Mrs. Davies, and prevent her from creating any further scandal. He answered, that he had not seen Mrs. Davies since she had come home from America. She had written to him, asking him to visit her; but he would not go, because he considered her such a bad and "dangerous woman," who by her slander might damage his reputation as a clergyman. He considered the Fletchers respectable people, and believed them entirely innocent of the crimes charged in Mrs. Davies's vile accusations. "If anybody has been deceived in this affair," he said, "it is not Mrs. Davies. She is too shrewd and clever a woman to be duped in such a coarse manner as she pretends." Moreover, he told me he suspected that jealousy was at the bottom of the whole affair, and asked me if Mrs. Davies had not been Mr. Fletcher's mistress. With regard to me, he said that Mrs.

Hart-Davies had felt greatly disappointed because I did not make her an offer of marriage when I visited Hampton Court, soon after the death of her mother and Mr. Sampson.

Speaking of Mrs. Davies's property, he said that the only thing of value that she brought to the Fletchers' house did not belong to her, but to the trustees, and that her own property was worth nothing to speak of. I told him that he must be mistaken; as I myself had seen some jewelry of considerable value that formerly belonged to Mrs. Heurtley, and now was in her daughter's possession. Mr. Burrows looked rather surprised at this statement, and wondered how her possession of these things could have been kept a secret from him. I also visited Mrs. Sampson, who was living at Sandgate. She stated to me, that she delivered up to Mrs. Davies her mother's jewels and wardrobe when she came back to England, after Mrs. Heurtley's and Mr. Sampson's death.

When Mrs. Fletcher was brought up before the Police-Court in Bow Street, Mrs. Davies represented herself, through Mr. Abrahams, as a lady of great wealth and of high social position and moral character, while she charged Mrs. Fletcher with defrauding, stealing, attempts at poisoning, and keeping a free-love establishment. Knowing that all these vile accusations were utterly false, and that I myself, by my attentions to Mrs. Fletcher, had contributed to awaken Mrs. Davies's jealousy and hatred, and that Mrs. Fletcher, after having been robbed of all her letters and other papers, was left without any means of defence against an unscrupulous enemy, whose evidence, according to English law, would be valid before the Court, I thought it my duty, in order to save a person in my opinion unjustly accused, to deliver up to Mrs. Fletcher's solicitor certain letters, which, written by Mrs. Davies, and showing her true character, would to a great extent invalidate her testimony. These letters were not admitted as evidence before the Court, and consequently Mrs. Davies remained to the end of the trial, in the eyes of the judge and the jury, the pure and victimized woman she represented herself to be. And, as might be supposed from the nature of her character, she did not hesitate to make the gravest misstatements in her evidence before the Central Criminal Court, so as to get the object of her hatred convicted. To my knowledge she perjured herself when stating —

1st, About her relations to me.

2d, That she was not guilty of the adultery on account of which her first husband obtained a divorce.

3d, That she always lived on the best terms with her mother, — a statement sufficiently contradicted by the fact admitted at the trial; namely, that, during several years before her mother's death, she (Mrs. Hart-Davies) was not allowed to see her.

4th, That Mrs. Heurtley during her lifetime gave her the jewels and other things which Mrs. Davies herself values at ten thousand pounds, and which she accused the Fletchers of obtaining from her by false pretences. This statement Mrs. Sampson contradicted to me as above mentioned: she allowed Mrs. Hart-Davies to take possession of her mother's jewels and wardrobe after the death of Mrs. Heurtley and Mr. Sampson. Mrs. Davies, consequently, had already committed perjury before the Probate Court, when she stated that the property she took from Hampton Court was worth only a hundred pounds.

5th, That she never told anybody that her husband tried to poison her.

6th, That she never spoke of her trustees in abusive terms.

7th, That she never pretended to be a Spiritualistic medium. On several occasions she spoke to me of her mediumship, and

that she was in constant communication with her deceased
mother.

8th, That she did not take away any letters when she and
Dr. Mack, on their return from America, ransacked Mr.
Fletcher's house in Gordon Street.

9th, That she only loved Mr. Fletcher as a brother.

When I first made Mrs. Davies's acquaintance in Buenos
Ayres, she wanted me, too, to be her brother; yet her feelings
to me had nothing of a sister's. Mrs. Hart-Davies is naturally
a woman of great intelligence and penetrating mind, which
qualities are further enhanced by a good education, and travels
in foreign countries. She speaks French and Spanish tolerably
well, is clever at drawing, and writes both prose and poetry
beautifully. Unfortunately, these qualities are neutralized by
her sensual propensities, which, greatly developed during the
last few years, not only make her forget her own dignity and
her family's honor, but cause her to grow nearly insane. To
gratify her desires in this respect, she is capable of any thing.
Being infatuated with Mr. Fletcher, she makes him believe
that she is a fervent Spiritualist and an innocent victim of the
ill-treatment of her husband, her relations, and her trustees, so
as to awake his sympathy and pity. Upon that she asks him
to take care of her property in order to save it from her rapa-
cious husband and trustees, and thus succeeds in becoming a
member of his family and circle of friends. At last, seeing
that all her efforts with regard to Mr. Fletcher had been made
in vain, she addresses herself to me and others with similar
intentions.

Not gaining her object in any way, she naturally ascribes
her failure to Mrs. Fletcher, whom she sees admired by everybody visiting the house, while she herself is scarcely noticed.
Her jealousy of Mrs. Fletcher I discovered immediately after

her coming to live with them; and my conviction is, that she never loved Mrs. Fletcher, nor suffered herself to be influenced by her, as she stated before the Court. This became so obvious to me, that once or twice I warned Mrs. Fletcher, saying I believed that Mrs. Hart-Davies hated her. She, however, would not believe it.

With regard to Mrs. Fletcher, I entertain a high opinion both of her intellect and moral character, and believe her utterly incapable of committing a fraud such as that of which she has been convicted, and which has been justly stigmatized as one of the coarsest and most clumsy that ever were attempted. Indeed, I cannot believe that any woman having in view to defraud another of her jewels should, on the second time they meet, be so stupid as to reveal her intentions in the way Mrs. Davies testifies with regard to Mrs. Fletcher, nor that there is any woman that could possibly be deceived in such a coarse manner. Mrs. Fletcher is a sincere believer in Spiritualism, and among Spiritualists she is considered to be a powerful medium. However, of her mediumship I cannot myself judge; as I never was present at a *séance*, neither with her nor with Mr. Fletcher. But I could not fail to notice during the time I frequented her house, and during the voyage to America, how with the Fletchers, as with other Spiritualists whose acquaintance I made, spiritual communications interfered even with the most trivial occupations of daily life, at the same time that they furnished a constant subject of conversation. Mrs. Fletcher, though fully aware that my opinions in this respect entirely differed from hers, would often tell me that she had seen my deceased mother's spirit, and that it had spoken to her; and after I had parted from her in America, and gone home to Sweden, she wrote me several letters, in which visions of this kind were referred to.

Contrary to the jury's verdict, I therefore fully believe that Mrs. Fletcher, when writing to Mrs. Davies, while in France, about her deceased mother, really was convinced that Mrs. Heurtley's spirit communicated with her.

(Signed)

CANUTE LINDMARK.

The above affidavit, duly sworn and certified, was sent to the home secretary by the Swedish minister. It is not in the least probable, however, that he ever saw, much less read, it. If he had read a declaration so transparently honest, he could not have kept me one day longer in the prison I have yet to describe. I am sorry that Capt. Lindmark is not a Spiritualist; but a more simple-hearted, honest. and honorable gentleman, or a truer, more unselfish friend, I have never known. He has some of the faults of the heroic Scandinavian character; but he has its virtues as well, and one of them is simple, unwavering veracity. But the home secretary was too busy making political speeches to give any attention to Dr. Nichols's memorial, and its most important accompanying documents.

Among these documents were the statements of several persons most intimately acquainted with our life at Gordon Street and our. relations to Mrs. Hart-Davies. One of these, Miss E. S. Gay of Penzance House, Cornwall, happened to be at our house when Mrs. Hart-Davies, accompanied by Dr. Mack and Mr. Abrahams, came and removed whatever property the lady claimed to the Bedford Pantechnicon, including many articles which had never belonged to her, and her part of our correspondence, as has been already stated.

Miss Gay says, —

"I saw her search the private desk of Mr. Fletcher in the dining-room, and remove letters from it, the said desk having been previously arranged by me for the sake of convenience, in the presence of Miss Maltby, when we both noticed that the whole of the letters were addressed to Mr. and Mrs. Fletcher; and I also noticed that letters which were placed behind the mirror had disappeared, by which proceedings Mrs. Hart-Davies was enabled to deprive the Fletchers of an important part of their defence. On the trial she denied on oath that she had even seen any letters. The cellar-door was burst open forcibly, and the whole of the wine removed, and the house left in confusion. A few days subsequently we heard from a person sent from Mr. Abrahams's office, that Mrs. Hart-Davies threatened legal proceedings against the Fletchers. I telegraphed the occurrence of her visit to them, and also wrote to inform them of the threatened arrest ; which letter was received by them before Mrs. Fletcher left Boston to return to England, which she said she should do to vindicate her character; although we learned from Capt. Lindmark, on his return to London on Oct. 31, that she had been very ill from the anxiety and injustice she had already experienced. She requested me to secure bail, which I did; but before she could reach London, she was arrested at Greenock on Dec. 2, and her boxes were seized, and private papers, including the agreement; which papers have remained in the hands of the prose-

cution.   Mrs. Fletcher informed me that she had sent copies
of a Boston daily paper, a copy of which was also forwarded
to me, notifying her intention of sailing by the steamship
' Anchoria,' to both Mrs. Hart-Davies and James McGeary."

Miss Gay is a lady whose social position, character,
and talents add value to her firm and unvarying friendship ; and I owe much to her unwearied exertions to
set this matter before the public in its proper light,
especially for printing and circulating at her own expense an edition of Dr. Nichols's memorial.

Mrs. Frances Maltby, so well known for her fidelity
and zeal to all London Spiritualists, and who kindly
took charge of our house in our absence, makes the
following statement : —

" On Oct. 19, 1880, in my temporary absence from 22 Gordon Street, Mrs. Hart-Davies and James McGeary entered the
house, and on my return I found them and Mr. S. B. Abrahams in possession of it.   Mrs. Hart-Davies ransacked the
house, opening all drawers, boxes, and desks, and searched
a private desk belonging to Mr. Fletcher, and removed letters
from it.   The cellar-door was forcibly burst open, and the
house left in confusion, and the property was conveyed to
the Bedford Pantechnicon.   A few days subsequently we heard
from a person sent from Mr. Abrahams's office, that Mrs. Hart-
Davies threatened to arrest Mrs. Fletcher, to whom notice was
at once given."

Miss Agnes Maltby, testifying to the same facts of the invasion of the house and seizure of the property, says, —

"A few muslin curtains, etc., were found under the mattress in her own room, which had been placed there for convenience. I saw Mrs. Hart-Davies search the private desk of Mr. Fletcher, and remove letters from it. Miss Gay had arranged the desk in my presence, and all the letters were addressed to Mr. and Mrs. Fletcher. While Mrs. Hart-Davies was in Mrs. Fletcher's room, I overheard James McGeary ask her if she had looked for letters and papers, alluding to letters which she was selecting from boxes on the table. After she had left, I noticed letters had disappeared from behind the mirrors, etc., where they had been placed. On the trial I heard Mrs. Hart-Davies deny on oath that she had even seen any letters. The cellar-door was forcibly burst open, and the house completely ransacked. After this we heard that Mrs. Hart-Davies threatened to arrest Mrs. Fletcher, who was at once informed of her intention, and returned to London, as stated in letters received from her by us, with the hope of obtaining justice and a fair hearing of the case."

My faithful and intelligent servant, Ellen Partridge, says, —

"I, ELLEN PARTRIDGE, now residing at 22 Gordon Street, entered the service of Mrs. Fletcher in 1879. One day, so far as I can recollect in the month of August in that year, Mrs. Hart-Davies came to the house with only her hat on, and with her dress torn, in an excited and trembling condition. She begged to see Mrs. Fletcher; and I conducted her to the drawing-room, when she told me her husband had been threatening to put her into a lunatic-asylum, and had tried to poison her. [Denied on oath by Mrs. Hart-Davies on the trial.] Mrs. Fletcher saw her. I mentioned these statements to a fellow-servant, who can state that I did so at the time.

"I remember many letters arriving from France while Mrs. Hart-Davies was in Tours; and I placed some of them behind the mirrors in Mrs. Fletcher's bedroom, and in boxes on her table.

"Three or four days before Mr. and Mrs. Fletcher left for America, I saw Mrs. Fletcher with Mrs. Hart-Davies in her bedroom; and both were looking over the jewelry. I heard Mrs. Fletcher propose to Mrs. Hart-Davies that she [Mrs. Hart-Davies] should take charge of it herself; which she refused to do, saying, that, if she wanted any of it, she could have it, as Mrs. Fletcher would have the jewels with her."

The statements of these witnesses were carefully taken down by my solicitor, and the witnesses were in court ready to give testimony. I do not know why they were not called, as well as Mr. Bastian and Mr. Eglinton.

Mr. Bastian is, like myself, an American, and well known over Europe. Born in Alsace, he speaks German as well as English, and has spent much time in Germany and Austria, where he has introduced the subject of Spiritualism among the highest nobility.

Mr. Bastian says, —

To whom it may concern. — I, Harry Bastian of Chicago, Ill., at present residing at 32 Fopstone Road, South Kensington, make this declaration: —

In the month of October, 1880, Mrs. Juliet Anne Theodora Hart-Davies called upon me at my then lodgings, No. 2 Vernon Place, Bloomsbury, saying she had heard about me in America, and asked me if I was acquainted with Mr. and Mrs. J. W. Fletcher. I said I knew them by reputation. She asked if I had heard of the trouble she had had with them in America. I replied that I had read about it in the papers, and asked her how she came to give them her property. She said that Mr. and Mrs. Fletcher had been very kind to her, and that she had loved them, and gave them her clothes, lace, and jewels in consideration of having a home with them. She said, further, that her husband, Mr. Hart-Davies, was intemperate, and abusive to her; that he was pawning or selling her jewels, and had threatened to put her into a lunatic-asylum, and also to take her life. Therefore she had gone to live with the Fletchers, and given them her property.

Mrs. Hart-Davies further said, they (the Fletchers and her self) had lived amicably together until they went together to America, where she met with James McGeary, *alias* Dr. Mack, and other persons, who told her that the Fletchers were not what she supposed them to be, and advised her to get back her property, which was surrendered to her; she, in the settlement, giving to Mrs. Fletcher certain things to pay for her board, passage, and expenses in America. Then she returned to London, and went to 22 Gordon Street, and got the rest of her property. After this, Mr. W. H. Harrison and others advised her to prosecute the Fletchers on the ground that it would be a benefit to Spiritualism to get rid of them and have them punished; but she said that she did not wish to do them any harm, and did not know what to do about it. As I was about leaving England for the Continent, she asked me to call on my return upon her. I saw Mrs. Hart-Davies next when she appeared against Mrs. Fletcher at Bow Street; and she asked me to visit her at her lodgings in Upper Baker Street, which I did, when she said that those who were interested in the prosecution of Mrs. Fletcher, fearing she would drop the case, had got the public prosecutor to take it up.

(Signed)

HARRY BASTIAN.

Mr. W. Eglinton, an English Spiritualist medium, who is well known in the highest Spiritualist circles of England, Germany, Austria, America, the Cape of Good Hope, and India, and esteemed by those who know him as most truthful and honorable, makes the following declaration : —

I, William Eglinton, residing at 32 Fopstone Road, South Kensington, am ready to swear to the following facts; viz., that in the month of June, 1880, I called at the residence of Mr. J. W. Fletcher, 22 Gordon Street, Gordon Square, and was introduced to Mrs. Heurtley, whom I have since known as Mrs. Hart-Davies. In conversation with her she was enthusiastic in her praise of Mr. and Mrs. Fletcher for their kindness to her; and, though I was up to that time an entire stranger to her, she informed me, that, in gratitude to them, she had decided to permanently reside with them, and, to compensate them, was going to will them all her property, though she could never fully repay their kindness. She also spoke in the most affectionate manner of Capt. Lindmark, — with whose brother I had become acquainted in Stockholm, Sweden, — and

declared that he was the only man that she could ever love
and respect. This was my only interview with Mrs. Heurtley
alias Hart-Davies, until I saw her prosecuting Mrs. Fletcher
at the police-office in Bow Street.

(Signed)

WILLIAM EGLINTON.

People who hold that every Spiritualist must necessarily be either a knave or a fool may not place re-
liance on the testimony of witnesses who are avowed
Spiritualists ; but as the same might be said of persons
holding any religious doctrine, by its opponents, and
as we know that persons of every creed, and of no
creed, may be honest and truthful, I do not see any
good ground for rejecting the testimony of Spiritualists, more than that of, say, Swedenborgians, or San-
demanians.

I have given somewhat of " the other side," which
I think ought to have been heard in what was called
my trial. But surely that is not a trial in which
really but one witness was heard.

Above all, I think the testimony to the reality of
Spiritualism should have been given. The whole case
turned upon two facts, — the existence of spirits, and
their power to communicate with mortals. To prove
false pretences against me, it was necessary to prove,
either that the spirit of Mrs. Heurtley did not exist,
or that, if existing, she had no power to communicate

with her child, or that I could not be the medium of such a communication. No such proof was given. I was not convicted: I was simply outlawed, condemned without a hearing, sentenced to a year's imprisonment, and abused by Mr. Justice Hawkins and the whole pack of his echoes in the newspapers, for being a Spiritualist.

This state of things cannot last long. As one of my friends has said, —

"Spiritualists are too numerous to be outlawed; and there are among them so many persons of high ability and position, that their rights must be respected. In a recent will-case in Chicago, Judge Tuley, two of whose four colleagues on the bench were pronounced Spiritualists, ruled that belief in Spiritualism is no evidence of insanity.

"'Prominent men,' he said, 'in various professions, whose integrity, intellectual ability, and perfect sanity would not be questioned, had testified that they had seen spirits, had had communications with departed friends, and generally that they believed in the same spiritual phemomena as Col Cushman did. Such phenomena could not now be dismissed, as in the case of Lyon *vs.* Home, with the remark that they were "mischievous nonsense." It was a notorious fact, that men who stood high in science, judges who adorned the bench, attorneys and solicitors amongst the foremost at the bar, clergymen, physicians, literary men of the highest ability, and, in effect, persons of prominence in every walk and profession of life, honestly believed in the truth of such phenomena; and it would be the sheerest nonsense to hold that such belief was any evidence of an unsound mind.'

"Quite recently the Rev. J. Page Hopps, a well-known Unitarian clergyman of Leicester, taking the chair at a Spiritualist lecture, said, —

"'Hundreds of thousands of persons, one might safely say millions of persons, in all circles of society, — in America, in India, in Africa, in China, in Australia, in Russia, in France, in Germany, in Italy, in England, — solemnly and pertinaciously declare that spirit-communion is a reality. Professors of science in universities, and mechanics at the bench, clergymen and colliers, statesmen and shopkeepers, poets and porters, titled ladies and seamstresses, artists and hard matter-of-fact manufacturers, in all parts of the world, hold to the belief of spirit-communion. Horace Greeley was a believer in spirit-communion, so was Lloyd Garrison, so was Abraham Lincoln, so was John Pierpont, so was George Thompson, Robert Chambers, Archbishop Whately, and William Howitt. So, it is believed, were Lord Lytton and W. M. Thackeray. So, I believe, is the poet Longfellow. So are men like Professors Scheibner, Weber, Hoffman, Zöllner, and Fechner in the universities of Germany, Butleroff and Wagner in the university of St. Petersburg, and many men like our own Alfred Russell Wallace, William Crookes, C. S. Varley, S. C. Hall, T. L. Nichols, Professor Barrett, and Lord Lindsay.' But, after all, these more modern men only echo what has been affirmed from the days of Plutarch, Tertullian, and St. Augustine, to the days of Lord Bacon, Thomas More, and John Wesley. There is, besides, a varied, important, and cultured literature on the subject, with a mass of evidence that is positively overwhelming, whether from a scientific, personal, or religious point of view. It seems to me, therefore, that we shall do well to give a respectful hearing to any intelligent person who declares that he also has investigated, and is convinced that this thing is true.'"

Before leaving this part of my tiresome case, there is one point on which I think more evidence ought to be given. In her evidence Mrs. Hart-Davies declared her belief in Spiritualism; but later she "fenced" with the question, and allowed the prosecution to represent her as a new convert, innocent and deluded. Her most intimate friend, next to Dr. Mack, Mr. W. H. Harrison, editor of the late "Spiritualist" (newspaper), has given plenty of evidence that Mrs. Hart-

Davies was an old and advanced Spiritualist. In "Psyche," a magazine of which a few numbers were published as a monthly continuation of the defunct "Spiritualist," he published in May, 1882, some extracts from a private letter from "Mrs. Heurtley," as she then chose to call herself. She says, —

"Our father was reserved, and somewhat unapproachable by young, timid natures; but of our *mother!* — what shall I say to convey even a faint idea of the majestic beauty of her mind and character? She was much occupied in the duties involved by her influence over a brilliant and intellectual society. . . . Allowed no companions, I had full opportunities for cultivating my innate desire for sequestered meditation. The inner consciousness of being often surrounded by a particular 'presence,' as I called it, grew with my growth. In my ignorance I knew not what it was, but dared to venture *to believe for myself* that invisible and intelligent witnesses were around us, and I supposed they might be ethereal 'angel guardians.' . . . All this time I knew nothing of Spiritualistic teachings When my mother died, I was abroad. *Then* came to me *her visible* '*presence;*' and, although quite awake, yet I found myself by her side somehow, and in a lovely garden lighted neither by sun nor moon nor stars, and the light was softly bright, making the foliage and flowers to shine like gems. I *heard* her tell me, '*My child, they will tell you I am dead; but it is not so. I thought I had died, but found myself gazing on my own dead body, and still that I was more alive than ever. . . . Tell every one that there is no death — only change.*' Imagine the effect of these words upon one who had so long sought for an assurance, beyond that derived from mere tradition, of this all-

satisfying fact. And it was this incident that turned my attention to Cahaynet's works, and subsequently to hearken to the
trance-messages given through Fletcher's remarkable mediumship. . . . Thus you may, perhaps, be enabled to comprehend
easier the real, unselfish motive for my extreme eagerness at
catching hold of the first examples of *practical* 'Spiritualistic'
teachings presented to me. Amid a thousand other misconcep-
tions of my character, actions, and motives, which have been
industriously spread abroad, is that of my having 'suddenly
rushed into Spiritualism,' 'caught' by a few spirit-messages,
and a few fawning promises of encouraging aid in my re-
searches. . . . Personally I bear no resentful feeling against
the Fletchers, though *they only* know how deeply they have
sinned against her who desired only to have been their benefactress.''

This letter was written in March, 1882, *near the end
of my imprisonment.* It settles the question about her
having been a Spiritualist long before we ever saw
her, and her desire to be our '' benefactress.''

Jan. 27, 1882, Mr. Harrison, editor of the '' Spiritualist,'' in an article headed '' The Shadow of a Great
Crime,'' again implored Spiritualists to take up the
cause of Mrs. Hart-Davies. He says, —

'' A joyous and enthusiastic new convert, out of an all-
absorbing love for her departed mother, strove in an inexperi-
enced and ineffectual way to do material good beyond all
precedent to Spiritualism, and was then swindled, and treated
in the most abominable manner.''

This enthusiastic new convert, who had been, according to her own story, published in Mr. Harrison's own paper, a Spiritualist and medium from her childhood, wished " to do a material good beyond all precedent to Spiritualism " by joining us, and sharing with us her mother's wardrobe, while we, in return, were to give her a home for life.

> "The very head and front of my offending
> Hath this extent, no more."

The crime for which I was one year in prison, Mr. Justice Hawkins said, was consummated when the first jewel, the poor little amethyst brooch, was placed in my hand by this " joyous and enthusiastic new convert," who complained that her drunken husband had beaten her, was robbing her, had tried to poison her and put her in a lunatic-asylum, and urged that it be accepted as some liquidation of the debt due my husband. Under these circumstances if her story was true, or under these false pretences if not true, she sought our protection, and volunteered to aid us in our work. We were imprudent if you please ; unfortunate, as we saw too soon : but in what way were we criminals?

CHAPTER XXXIII.

SOME COMMENTS ON THE CASE.

I DO not wish to weary my readers; but, before beginning the story of my imprisonment, I wish to give a few comments on the case, such as I might have addressed to the jury, had the present mode of procedure been adopted a little earlier. The right of a prisoner to tell his own story to the jury had always existed, always been lawful; but the judges, who are first lawyers, and mindful of the interests of the craft, had set it aside. I am glad that they have at last restored the exercise of this right, so long desired — only it came, for me, a little too late.

First, of the accusation at Bow Street, when Mr. Abrahams had his opportunity to libel me, and by a series of utterly false statements, reproduced in the newspapers, so deeply prejudiced the public against me — as if a libel uttered in a police-court, and printed in a newspaper report, were not as great a wrong, and as deep an injury, as any other libel! A false witness may be prosecuted for perjury. A lawyer may tell a series of horrible falsehoods, and have them published all over the world, to the utter destruction of character, business, and prospects, with entire impunity. Surely this is a hideous wrong.

Mr. Abrahams said Mrs. Hart-Davies's separation from her husband had no reference to the case. The reader has seen that the conduct which she said was the cause of the separation induced her to seek our protection.

The falsity of the story about the mother's jewels being dangerous to Mrs. Hart-Davies is shown by the fact that she continued to wear them, and was never without them. Mr. Abrahams declared that I had broken open her boxes, and stolen valuable velvets and laces. The fact was, that she and I unpacked and repacked together, after the things had been forced upon me by the deed of gift. The " Oriental pearls " on which such stress was laid, and which I was charged with stealing, after they had been formally given to me, were found by Mr. Shrive the detective at the Pantechnicon, where Mrs. Hart-Davies had stored them.

Mrs. Hart-Davies was represented to be her mother's administratrix. But her mother left no will : she was not the sister of Mr. Sampson ; it was shown that her relation to that gentleman was of quite a different nature. Mrs. Hart-Davies swore that the property left her by her mother was under one hundred pounds :

after it was in my possession, she claimed that its value was fifty thousand dollars. This fraudulent under-valuation was sworn to for the purpose of avoiding the legacy or succession duty. In court she testified that the property had been given to her before her mother's death.

All the matter of the will, and the "deed after deed," in Mr. Abrahams's statement, is disposed of by the testimony of Mr. Morton, and the London solicitor, Mr. Francis, to whom Mr. Morton introduced Mrs. Hart-Davies when she wished to make her benefaction to "Spiritualism in its higher phases."

The charge of our attempting to poison Mrs. Hart-Davies, and that of some mysterious connection with "free-love" doctrines, made by Mr. Abrahams, were quietly dropped out of the case by the government prosecutors, and were evidently introduced to prejudice the magistrate and the public against us.

Mr. Morton was convicted of conspiring with us, or I with him and my husband. But let me ask in passing, if he had been engaged in a criminal attempt to rob this unprotected woman, would he have taken her to a firm of most respectable London solicitors, that she might be guided by their advice as to the disposition she should make of what Mr. Justice Hawkins ruled was her husband's property?

If Mrs. Hart-Davies, on coming to our house, was

" treated with indignity," and " almost starved," and
" felt very weak and ill after drinking her morning
coffee," why did she go with us to America? The
fact is, that she had five meals a day, and always
extra provisions in her own room.

I have said enough, perhaps, of Mr. Abrahams; but
I cannot doubt that the utterly false coloring he gave
to the case created a prejudice which made a fair trial
and a just verdict impossible.

The testimony of Mrs. Hart-Davies was full of what
Lord Sherborne calls " slatternly inaccuracies." Even
on trifling and unimportant matters she seemed to
choose the opposite of truth.

It was said that when we went to America we had
no intention of returning. What were the facts? We
left our house in charge of a friend and the servants,
with all the furniture, — that which had belonged to
Mrs. Hart-Davies, and our own. Mrs. Hart-Davies
swore that I took eight trunks; but there were only
six in all, of which two were hers, one Mr. Fletcher's,
one my son's, and two my own. We had engaged
Steinway Hall for the winter, and made all our arrangements to return in the autumn.

Mrs. Hart-Davies admitted, that, when she ransacked my house with Dr. Mack and Mr. Abrahams,
she " might have accidentally removed a few of my
things with her own." When I went to the Pantech-

nicon, with a clerk of the solicitors of the treasury, and looked over the things, I found so many articles of my own property, that the inventory covered several sheets, and among them private papers which she swore she had never taken. She made much of finding some of her things between the mattresses. The articles she found were a few cotton dresses and curtains, placed between the spring and mattress in her own bedroom, and placed there at her own suggestion.

But the letters read in court? — what have you to say to them?

I have to say, that, had the letters on both sides been read, one set would have fully explained the other. Mrs. Hart-Davies took very good care that her letters should not be produced in court.

What did these letters prove, beyond our friendly feelings, *when every letter produced was written after the deed of gift and her will had been made*, and all the property to which they related had been placed in our hands for safe keeping, with, as she stated, " the honorable understanding that it should be returned to her whenever she should demand it? "   And it was.

The transaction having been completed, what had the letters which passed between us subsequently to do with proof of fraud or false pretences?   It was the same as if they had been written ten years afterward.

And it is to be observed, that, when this property

was in our possession, it so remained. It was not shown that any jewel, or any article of any kind, was ever sold, or in any way disposed of. Is this the fashion of swindlers and thieves? In America the jewels were placed by Mr. Fletcher, with the concurrence of Mrs. Hart-Davies, in safe keeping. When she demanded them, he gave her an order to get them. I ask again, Are these the proceedings of swindlers and thieves?

If I complain of the introduction of private letters on one side, written after the acts indicted as fraudulent, what is to be said of my photograph, commented upon by the judge, and given to the jury? If it was as a study of physiognomy, they had me before them for six days, and had ample opportunity to see if I looked like a thief, a witch, or a sorceress. What proof could a photograph, taken either before or after a crime, be of the guilt of a prisoner? There was no question of identity. I had not denied my name or profession. Then how came my photograph to be given as evidence against me, and commented upon in a way to create more prejudice in the public mind, perhaps, than any fact or fiction during the trial? *As it was not shown,* it was assumed to be something very dreadful.

What was this terrible photograph? One day I went with my husband to one of the best London photographers, and was pictured in a low muslin waist. All ladies are required to wear low dresses at her Majesty's drawing-rooms; and, in their progress through St. James's Park to Buckingham Palace, they are exposed to the gaze of the public with very little covering, and many remarks. This photograph, taken for my husband, and kept by him, was stolen by Mrs. Hart-Davies, — it being among the papers she found in our house in Gordon Street during our absence in America. Mr. Abrahams thought proper to introduce it as evidence against me at Bow Street, where he passed it through the court-room; and Sir Henry Hawkins handed it to the jury at the Old Bailey.

There are always differences of taste and opinion as to fashions of dress. Quakeresses cannot be presented at court. Fastidious people do not like the low dresses worn at dinners, balls, and generally for what is called full or evening dress. I do not care to defend the fashions of society, or the taste of either my husband or the photographer; though the latter assured me that he had taken photographs of many very elegant and fashionable ladies, among whom were wives of aldermen who assisted at my trial, more *décolletées* than mine. I have only to say, that it was a private keepsake for my husband, not intended to be shown, not more scandalous than may be seen at dinners, balls, the opera, and the Queen's drawing-rooms, and that it had nothing to do with my guilt or innocence in any way whatever.

It was pretended that I was photographed in some of the jewels said to have been obtained by false pretences. There are no jewels in the photograph but a small pendant and ear-rings, and a single string of pearls, which I had long before I ever saw Mrs. Hart-Davies.

Showing a photograph, and talking about it, to prejudice the public against me, was of a piece with the whole trial. It was probably introduced to sustain the ninth count of that long indictment, which charged that I pretended to exercise witchcraft, sorcery, etc. Had I been on my trial for murder, or the attempt to murder, as at first charged by Mr. Abrahams, would my photograph in a low-necked dress have been given to the jury as a proof of guilt? Is every lady who wears on any occasion a low-necked dress a swindler, and a possible or probable murderess?

Hereafter I shall advise ladies to be photographed only in high-necked dresses, — as I intended to be on that occasion, — and to wear them, as I always do, wherever the customs of society will admit.

The indictment assumed the impossibility of spirit-communications. Mrs. Hart-Davies swore, on the trial, that they had been given ; though she solemnly assured Mr. Morton that she had not been influenced by any one, spirit or mortal, in giving us her property, but only wished to save it from being squandered by her drunken husband, and have it used for the promotion of Spiritualism.

The reader who has had the patience to read the trial, especially the charge of Mr. Justice Hawkins, will see that it was the assumption of the falsity of Spiritualism, and the truthfulness of the only witness against me, — the one " on whom the whole fabric of the prosecution rested," — that secured my conviction, and sent me to the prison which must be the scene of what remains of my story.

CHAPTER XXXIV.

HER MAJESTY'S PRISON, WESTMINSTER.

I HAD taken leave of my friends, and written to those I could not see ; because I knew, that, from the moment the verdict of guilty was pronounced, I could not speak or write. In saying good-by to Dr. Nichols, one of my bail, who had every day received me on my arrival at the court, as he had done at Bow Street, to give me his arm, and conduct me to the prisoner's dock and from it, as he would have taken me to my box or stall at the opera, I said to him, " I shall be convicted, and the next time you see me it will be in a prison. Do nothing for me. Do every thing you can to change the laws of England, so that in future there may be justice for Spiritualists."

When the blow fell — when, after waiting more than three hours and a half for the verdict that was not in the least doubtful to me, that I knew would come — I was quite prepared, and was only weary from waiting so long. I showed no emotion, for I felt none. There was no surprise, and I rose to receive my sentence. I

318

heard the beginning of that sentence, but not the end. There came over me a sort of paralysis, a partial trance, in which I heard the voice of the judge like a distant, indistinct murmur. The scolding and the insults, so far as I was concerned at the time, were quite thrown away.

Two female warders of Newgate stood ready to receive me; but the governor, who had been most kind and gentle to me, said to them, " You go away: let me take her." He took me into the prison, and gave me to a woman there, who placed me in the cell lately occupied by Mrs. Weldon, — a large double cell, very clean and comfortable. The female warders at Newgate seemed to me the best of their class.

I slept that night in Newgate, and was allowed to see one visitor. Miss Agnes Maltby, who brought flowers to me at Bow Street, and wished to go to prison in my place, walked into Newgate so determined to see me, that the governor did not see his way to refuse her. I was also allowed to write one letter, which was read by the inspector, and then posted to my husband.

While this passed I was in a kind of maze, much as if I had been sitting in a theatre, and seeing a play enacted on the stage. I was as a spectator of things done and endured by another.

At half-past twelve I was taken in a cab with one

of the warders, instead of going in the prison omnibus, the " Black Maria." This was, I believe, a very unusual favor, done to protect me from contact with other prisoners. A male officer of course went with me. I put out my hands for the handcuffs. He looked at them a moment, and put the implements into his pocket, with an emphatic " No!"

" Pray make no difference for me," I said.

" No. I will not put them on. Of course you will give your word to make no trouble."

" Only the trouble of seeing me to my destination," I said. And so I went, free of the shackles, on my parole.

I did not know then how much I had been spared by being sent in a cab at an unusual hour. It saved me from mingling with the poor unfortunates gathered from the police-courts; from the filthy horrors of the reception, when all wash from one tank, and wipe on one towel, and the poor women, wild with grief, or crazy with delirium-tremens, are screaming in the reception-cells.

In the office, my clothes were taken, neatly folded and put away, and my money, watch, and such jewels as I had, were registered, and safely deposited. The female warders, officers as they are called, treated me with every possible consideration. They gave me the best shoes that could be found, selected the best fitting brown serge prison-dress they had, with a not unbecoming white cap. If the prison-costume was not all that could be desired, my friendly officers did the best they could for me, and I had a clean suit at every fresh supply. The stockings are blue with a red stripe, and very coarse. The shoes are made low, with very thick soles, and fit as it may happen. There is one white flannel skirt, and a flannel under-vest if the prisoner is wearing one at the time of admission; but there are no drawers (and this slight addition would prevent much suffering), a brown serge petticoat, skirt, and jacket, a blue check handkerchief to wear under the jacket, and another for the pocket (very coarse and rough), and a white cotton cap.

At the reception-cell I was visited by the lady superintendent, the Protestant chaplain, and the physician.

They were all polite and kind. The lady superintendent expressed her regret that no difference could be made in the prison-diet. She could make no exceptions. I told her I did not expect to find every thing easy or agreeable.

The Protestant chaplain, finding that I was not to be placed with his fold or his branch, had very little to say to me.

The doctor inspected me, and asked about my health. He wished me to take off a ring I had not been able to give up at the office, it fitted so tightly. In a week it came off very easily.

After this ceremony of reception, I was sent to my final prison.

Her Majesty's Prison, Westminster, now set apart for female convicts not sentenced to penal servitude, is in what used to be called Tothill Fields, south of Victoria Street, between Westminster Abbey and the Houses of Parliament on the east and the Victoria Station on the west. A wall about thirty feet high encloses a large octagon. In its centre is an open space with grass and trees, around which are ranged the prisons and offices. A great double iron gate on the south side is the only entrance.

My cell, to be my home for twelve months, was very solidly made of stone, nine or ten feet long, seven feet wide, with walls seven feet high, and arched so as to make the roof nine feet high in the centre. The window is of thick yellow glass, shaded by *louvres*. On the light side of the prison these windows admit light enough to read by, but not on the dark side; so that half the cells are too dark for reading, and of course much too dark to be healthy. The ventilation is by means of perforated iron in the wall and an opening at the bottom of the cell.

My bed was a canvas hammock, six feet long and thirty inches wide, suspended across the cell, in which one has to lie quite straight, and be very careful not to tumble out. I had three blankets, two white and

one colored, which are supposed to be washed once a
year, and are inherited by a succession of short-term
prisoners; and I had also a pair of sheets and a case
for my sawdust pillow, which were washed once a
month. There was no mattress.

In winter these cells are very cold and damp, as
well as dark. The air is warm in the corridors; but its
moisture condenses on the walls of the cells, and runs
down upon the floor. Sleeping without a mattress,
and with insufficient covering, prisoners — especially
the feeble, the old, the rheumatic, and those debilitated, as most are, by intemperate habits — have dreadful suffering. The healthiest nearly perish of cold.

Of course they are sent there — some thousands of
women every year, an average of five or six hundred
at a time — to be punished, but not, I think, to have
their health destroyed by being kept twenty-three hours
out of every twenty-four in solitary confinement in
dark, cold, damp cells, like so many tombs. I cannot
believe that it is "her Majesty's pleasure," if it is
her home secretary's, that her Majesty's unfortunate,
or even guilty, female subjects should be so cruelly
treated.

"Unfortunate!" — yes, far more unfortunate, the
greater part, than guilty. Nine in ten, and I think a
larger proportion, owe their imprisonment solely to
drink sold to them by respectable men licensed by

government, and so employed to collect the revenue. The government tempts these poor women to drink, pockets a large part of the money they pay for their "liquid damnation," and then shuts them up in this dark, cold, and horrible prison to get sober, and then get drunk again ; and so on, until they sink into a cell a little darker and narrower, — the pauper's grave.

My little, dark, cold room was not encumbered by superfluous furniture. There was a table of unpainted wood about twenty inches by thirty, a box to sit on twelve inches by eighteen, and eighteen inches high, a two-quart tin can for gruel, a three-quart tin to hold my daily supply of water, a pint tin can to drink from, a tin plate, a wooden spoon, and a tin bucket for slops (without a cover), a coarse and fine comb, a tin wash-basin, a towel changed once a week, and the rules of the prison in French and English, headed in large type, "Convicted Prisoners," which words I was so tired of seeing, that I turned them to the wall.

Each cell has a Bible and a prayer-book. In the Bible I read, "I was in prison, and ye came unto me. . . . Inasmuch as ye have done it unto the least of these my brethren, ye have done it unto me." The rules provide that each well-behaved prisoner may receive a visit once in three months, in presence of a warder. After two months, if a prisoner has no bad marks against her, she can have a book from the library, — a volume of "The Leisure Hour," or some moral and religious book suitable for female prisoners. These rewards of merit can be changed once a week, and are a great comfort to those whose cells have light enough to read by.

The great bell of the prison wakes its five hundred sleepers at six A.M. ; and all must be dressed to receive their officers (warders), who unlock the cells at half-past six, when all pass out with their uncovered slop-buckets and water-cans, — to empty the former, and fill the latter. The water-tank and place for emptying slops are together ; and fifty women of one division are expected to get back to their cells in ten minutes.

At eight o'clock comes breakfast. For those sent for more than three months, there is a pint of oatmeal gruel, six ounces of bread, coarse and dark, varying in quality, and sometimes sour or mouldy. When complaints are made, it is better, and when well made, according to regulation, prison-bread, coarse and brown, is doubtless more healthful than the fine white bread of the common bakers.

At half-past nine A.M. we were let out to exercise in the yard for fifteen minutes, and then go to chapel — Protestant, or Catholic, as we are registered — for half an hour, and on coming out were marched in single file round the yard again for fifteen minutes. It was a curious sight to see this regiment of women, from eighty-five years old to twelve, all dressed alike, but looking so different,—a regiment composed almost entirely of drunkards, prostitutes, thieves. One aged prisoner had with her her daughter and grand-daughter, who, she proudly said, she believed were without exception the best thieves in London, because she had learned it " scientific " herself," and taught them the same way. Mrs. McCarty is a little thin, dried-up old woman, who had been to prison sixty times, and five times during that year. Women are often released on Thursday, and come back to their old cells again on Saturday.

Surely the " wisdom of Parliament " might contrive some better way than that. Of course the cause, in nearly all such cases, is drink; and while the wisest and best government keeps an open, ever-flowing fountain of intoxicating liquors at every corner, because it extracts an enormous revenue from those least able to pay it, it is necessary to have policemen to catch, and great prisons to confine, those who so vainly pray, " *Lead us not into temptation, but deliver us from evil.*"

Of course governments must have money; but is there not a better way than the encouragement of vice in order that it may be taxed to pay a revenue? And why not go a step farther, and tax a few other vices, that might be nearly as profitable? But I fear I am diverging into politics, with which women have no business — except to suffer whatever masculine legislation may inflict.

Pardon this digression. At twelve o'clock comes dinner, — a dreadfully unfashionable hour ; but Queen Elizabeth dined at eleven. On Monday each prisoner who is not on the bread-and-water fare of short-comers, or in the bad-conduct cells, gets three potatoes in a net, six ounces of badly-cooked beans, and generally vile bacon, and six ounces of bread. The only eating-utensil is a wooden spoon half an inch thick, with which she must peel her potatoes, and divide her meat. But I remembered with no little consolation that her Majesty's is the most aristocratic government under heaven.

On Tuesdays the Right Honorable the home secretary provided us with a pint of very bad soup, flavored with cabbage, looking very green, and smelling very badly, and bread, which is brought in great baskets, emptied upon the stones in the yard, counted, and broken, the prisoners meantime walking over it. This does not improve the appetite.

On Wednesdays we had six ounces of dark suet-pudding and three ounces of bread.

On Thursdays, the delightful soup again, and six ounces of bread.

On Fridays, we had the luxury of Australian meat, specially allotted on this day for the benefit of the

Roman-Catholic prisoners; the government following, in this matter, the edifying example of the late Rev. Dr. Cumming of Crown Court, who collected funds, and instituted one meat-dinner a week for the little ragamuffins of Clare Market and Drury Lane. As three-fourths of them are Papists, he gave his meat-dinners on Fridays. If the Papists in her Majesty's Prison, Westminster, are conscientious, or are not dispensed while in prison, this arrangement may be an economical one for her Majesty's government.

On Saturday, bread and soup again; and on Sunday, suet-pudding.

At one o'clock P.M. the dinner vessels in the cells are taken out and washed, and prisoners locked in their cells till five P.M., when supper of bread and gruel is brought them, after which they are locked in for the night.

"Are you all right?" asks the warder. "Good-night." These two sentences are all the words allowed to be spoken to a prisoner, unless they have to be scolded for some breach of the regulations, and these more to be assured of their occupant than from courtesy or kindness. Thus each prisoner is locked in her solitary cell for twenty-three hours out of every twenty-four; which is in itself a very dreadful punishment, bad for the health of the body, worse for the health of the mind — abnormal, inhuman, diseasing, demoralizing.

A saint might grow more saintly by such a discipline, perhaps; but even a saint's body could hardly get more healthy. Common men and women, social beings, with all their best instincts unsatisfied and blighted, must be made worse in every way by such unnatural conditions.

The treatment of a prisoner depends upon the character and disposition of the warder. The warders may be very kind or very cruel without breaking the prison rules. If well disposed, they can favor a prisoner in many ways; if ill disposed, jealous, harsh, or cruel, as some warders, even female warders, are, they can make a prisoner's life very uncomfortable.

They are directed to treat their prisoners as kindly as they can consistently with their duty to enforce the rules. They are not allowed to strike a prisoner. If a prisoner is so refractory as to be unmanageable, male officers, who are at hand, are sent for. The prisoner has, however, no possible remedy for any amount of ill usage. The word of a prisoner would never be believed against that of an officer. For the slightest offence, a prisoner may be reported to the lady superintendent for punishment, and consigned to a padded cell without bed or furniture, with no exercise or chapel, with bread and water, and loss of good-conduct marks and money. For the best possible conduct a prisoner may be allowed to come out of her cell, and scrub, or break stone. *This is called " occupying a position of trust."*

From November to March prisoners are allowed to light gas in their cells from five P.M. to eight. The corridors of the prison are warmed with hot-water pipes; but this begins late in the season, and is regulated, not by the thermometer, but the almanac and the number of royal marriages, which, of course, affect government appropriations.

We were expected to keep our cells clean, but were provided with no soap (except about half an ounce a week for our hands), no washing flannels, no stones for the floors, really no means of cleanliness. A prisoner is allowed a bath, hot or cold, of ten minutes, once a fortnight. I, who had been accustomed to bathe two or three times, a day found this scarcity of water a great deprivation. The bath, even at these long intervals, is not of obligation; and very few prisoners bathe at all, leaving them undesirable company for those who do.

Prisoners who are seriously ill are removed to the infirmary, where they have a better diet, beds to sleep on, and gas. The doctor can be summoned at any time, but he has a difficult position. Prisoners want to get into the infirmary cells for the better diet and other privileges. The cunning may deceive even a very clever physician; while the really sick and suffering may possibly, if under a hard warder, be neglected.

On the whole, the behavior of the prisoners, no longer exposed to the influence of drink, was remarkably good. There is a great difference between drunk and sober. A little alcohol converts an angel into a demon. The amount of whiskey on which the chancellor of the exchequer gets threepence may make all the difference between vice and virtue, innocence and crime. If these hundreds of poor women could only be sent to some country, possibly Pagan, where they could get no whiskey, they might be chaste wives, fond mothers, and good Christians.

The rule of this prison is a rule of solitude and silence. Prisoners must not make a noise in walking, must not sing, or talk with their warders or each other. But no home secretary can absolutely govern the tongues of five or six hundred women. They manage to talk with each other through the ventilators : during exercise there may be some furtive conversation between those who are thrown together, and still more during the singing in chapel.

Considering the sort of persons who would naturally seek for such an employment, even with the prospect of a retiring pension after many years of service, the warders were better than one would expect, and some very intelligent and very kind. There are, however, in all prisons, I fear, officers quite the reverse, — ignorant, low-bred, drunken, and innately, constitutionally cruel. The lady superintendent at Tothill Fields, a firm, capable woman, had been obliged, I heard, to rid herself of eight drunken warders and several thieves. I have myself seen warders reeling from drink. Prisoners who are often there, and come to know the officers, say of this or that one, " You'll get on all right with her when she isn't drunk."

One miserable drunken warder seemed to take a special spite at me: she would have liked to have me under her, and she took every opportunity to assail me with rough and brutal language. When I was very ill, so as to be scarcely able to walk, she said, if I only belonged to her, she would make me walk faster, or she would have me carried by my head and heels.

Of course female warders are jealous of each other. Singers and actresses, and many other women perhaps, are not quite free from such small frailties. Naturally they suspect and complain of favoritism. It is as much as the doctor's life is worth to show the slightest partiality to officer or prisoner. The lady superintendent better than any one else can tell you why.

CHAPTER XXXV

PRISONERS AND PRISON-LIFE.

Choosing to go upon the Catholic side, my chaplain, of course, was the Roman-Catholic priest appointed by the cardinal-archbishop for this arduous and responsible position. As the bulk of the Roman Catholics in London are the poor Irish, crowded by their poverty into the worst conditions, and subjected to all its temptations, there are many Catholic prisoners.

The Catholic chaplain was a Jesuit, and of course highly educated. Whatever else Jesuits may be, they must be *that*. They may hold that "the end sanctifies the means;" but some of their means seem to be a careful selection of candidates, a thorough educational course extending over fourteen years, and the polished manners which fit them to shine in the highest society, and to deal effectively with the lowest. For the rest, I presume a thoroughly educated, well-bred man may possibly also be a good one.

My chaplain selected me to take charge of the chapel, to keep it clean, and to dress the altar for the daily

333

mass. This was a great favor and a great happiness. On the first Saturday I was in prison, a friend of mine, a Catholic gentleman, brought an armful of beautiful flowers for the altar; and every Saturday for ten months, in storm or sunshine, through summer and winter, he came to the gate of the prison with the same beautiful offering to our friendship, which brightened the eyes, and gladdened the hearts, of the poor prisoners. I suppose it may seem to many a superstition to ornament a chapel with flowers, but it is at least a very pretty one. And why not flowers in a church, as well as in a drawing-room or on a lady's bonnet? The poor prisoners at least did not see any harm in it; and I, for one, found a great happiness, until, toward the end, I became so ill that I could no longer bear them.

There is a religious service at nine o'clock every morning at each chapel, and two services on Sunday. Every Protestant prisoner is obliged to attend. They go together, each prison forming a group, with the warders to keep them in order; but there are not enough to prevent them from talking, and sometimes using very bad language with each other. The Catholic chaplain can send for any of his prisoners to his room, or see the older ones in their cells, with the warder outside; but I believe the Protestant chaplain sees all prisoners in the presence of the warder, which is also the rule with the doctor.

There is a school for all prisoners who are not tolerably well educated. The warders teach, and the pupils are examined by the chaplains.

Five-sixths of the women at Tothill Fields are of the class of prostitutes. As there is no classification or separation of prisoners, they have many opportunities to corrupt those who are still innocent; and young girls are induced to join them when their terms of imprisonment have expired. It is said that women get sent for short terms for no other purpose than that of making such acquaintances.

I was surprised to find these women of ill fame so frank as to their mode of life, so determined to persevere in what they considered one of many modes of getting a living, so resolutely set against any idea of reform, or of giving up their unhappy relations. Those who were registered as Catholics, if they disliked their warders, would register next time as Protestants.

One of my fellow-prisoners was poor Mabel Wilberforce, who had been convicted of perjury, and sentenced to nine months' imprisonment, for doing about what is considered as the proper and honorable thing for men who are co-respondents in divorce-suits. She complained of being cold for want of sufficient clothing, especially at night, and was considered fault-finding and troublesome. Then she accused her warder of drinking; but, when she was summoned before the commissioners, it was shown that the warder had a good reputation in the prison, and Mabel was defeated, and placed under Miss Henschell, one of the severest and most inhuman warders in the place. For what were considered groundless complaints, she was kept about half the time in the solitary confinement of the padded cells, on bread and water, until she became thin, pale, desperate, and an utter wreck, — so weak that she could scarcely stand. One day when a kind officer had taken her down into the yard, and said to her, Poor child, try to keep up," she answered, "Oh, for God's sake, don't speak to me in that way! I have not had a kind word said to me in this prison, and I cannot bear it."

She tried to commit suicide by putting her handkerchief round her neck, and tying it to the gas-pipe, but was seen by her officer, and kept several days in a strait-jacket; that is, laced up in a sack night and day, and so kept, when very ill. Her bed was taken from her during the day ; and, bolt upright, she had to endure, with some management, this terrible torture. She afterward was admitted to the sick-cells, and given a better diet. She was young, pretty, and clever, but seemed also vain, frivolous, and ambitious ; but for this should she have been so punished?

I had been condemned to twelve months' imprisonment with hard labor. Had I been guilty of half that was charged against me, it would have been far too light a punishment. For much smaller offences, men and women are sent for from five to ten years to penal servitude. My inference is, that Mr. Justice Hawkins did not believe me guilty. He is not in the habit of giving people *less* than their deserts.

The " hard labor " at Tothill Fields is rather a myth. There is very little oakum-picking. The cell-work of assorting waste-paper is very light. The laundry, the working in the cook-house, and what are called the " places of trust," are the only hard labor. •I did a little knitting, because I liked it, and I took care of my chapel, but not an hour's hard labor during the twelve months.

Such a prison ought to be a reformatory school. But what can be done with short sentences constantly repeated? Women who get drunk and noisy are sent for from five to twenty-one days. They manage to make acquaintances ; and one who was sentenced for four months sent so many girls to her house of ill fame, that she said it was the best four months' work she had ever done.

What is needed is classification according to the sentences. Now a woman of forty, who has served two hundred and forty-six sentences, may be put in the next cell to a young girl sent for the first time. She gets next her at exercise, sits by her at chapel, talks during the singing. A sweetly pretty girl who had the misfortune to get tipsy on a bank holiday, and became riotous, and broke a window, was sent for three months. A procuress in the next cell got her to become an inmate of her house as soon as she was released. .

My own cell was between the cells of two noted thieves. One had served two, and the other three, terms of penal servitude. Some spend more time in the prison than out of it, and seem to prefer the freedom from care and the more orderly life. The warders think all prisoners ought to be equally contented.

My warder was very good to me. She looked at my hands, and said, "You don't look as if you could do hard work. Can you knit?" — "Yes." — "Can you sew?" — "Yes." — "Which can you do best?" — "Whichever you please; but, if it is all the same, I would prefer the knitting."

But I soon went to the chapel. There was some really hard work, — scrubbing, dusting, and making it as clean as it ought to be; but, this being done by another, I had only to oversee the work, and dress the altar with the .flowers that came every Saturday and the vigils of holidays of obligation. I also kept the priest's vestments in order, and was very happy to have such work to do and to be able to do it.

CHAPTER XXXVI.

I HAVE tried to give a general idea of my position as a prisoner before relating some of my special experiences as a Spiritualist. Doubtless the question comes into the mind of the reader, "Why did your guardian spirits, so wise and so powerful, allow you to go to prison at all? Surely they could have protected you from such a misfortune."

This opens up a very large question. Why are men made liable to physical and moral evils? Why are not all protected and saved from errors, vices, and crimes? What is the divine purpose of evil and sin and suffering?

I received Mrs. Hart-Davies as a friend and sister, because, at the time, it seemed to me to be my duty to do so. Spirits are not infallible: it may be that they see what will in the end be for the greatest good. When I was accused of crime in England, after being cleared of all such imputation in America, I felt it to be my duty to come and meet the accusation at what-

339

ever peril to myself. It seemed to me that it was a
duty to myself, to my friends, and to the cause of
Spiritualism. Therefore I came, not thinking about
its being heroic or quixotic.

I believed also that I had the protection of wise and
good spirits, who would help me to do what was best.
A few nights before I was sentenced, I was visiting
with some friends. Mr. H. Bastian, the medium, was
one of them, and we had what is called a *séance*.
Several spirits came and talked with us. One whom
I have often seen and heard and felt, and whom I
recognize as one of the sweetest and loveliest, wisest
and best, came in her beautiful form, and beckoned to
me to come near to her. I went forward and sat upon
a sofa, when she came and put the soft white veil
that covered her head also over mine, kissed me on
both eyelids, and gave me some words of comfort to
strengthen me for the coming trial. In her earthly
life she had experienced misfortunes, as we call them,
to which mine have been the merest trifles. She was
maligned, imprisoned for many years, and then judi-
cially murdered. I will not give her name; but I felt
greatly honored by her recognition and friendship, and
hoped I should suffer my small inconveniences in some
measure as she did her great martyrdom.

After my sentence I spent, as I have said, my first
night in Newgate. As I lay on the bed in my cell, a

little stunned and much wearied with what had been passing, — the eight consecutive days of the trial, and the five hours summing-up of the judge, — I heard "raps". all about me. I had thrown myself on the bed, too tired to undress. The sounds seemed to me a mockery. I did not feel like asking any questions.

Then I felt a small hand come into mine, and a sweet little voice I knew — oh, so well! — said, "Mamma, it will be better for you, dear, if you take off your clothes and go to bed."

Coming in my utter desolation, this little voice was the sweetest music I ever heard. There were only two voices in the world that had the right to call me "mamma," — one, that of my boy in America; the other, that of my boy in heaven.

"It doesn't matter about my clothes, darling," I said. "But I know you, baby dear, and it is so sweet of you to come to me! but I am afraid taking off my clothes will not bring me rest."

Then I felt two little rosebud lips on my forehead, like dew; then heard the little cheery voice, which said, "But you know, mamma dear, your clothes are tired, and you should give them rest."

I rose and took off my clothes, and carefully spread them out to rest. I felt that they might indeed be tired. And the voice I knew and loved said, "Poor mamma's clothes are having a rest; and now poor mamma's heart shall have a rest too."

Then I saw clairvoyantly my beautiful boy kneeling at my bedside, praying for his mother. After a few moments of silence, he kissed me again, and said, "I am going to papa and dear brother; and I will come back to-morrow, and tell you how they are."

The ice melted from about my heart, the great thick stone walls were gone, my imprisonment was ended. I did not sleep in Newgate; but I did sweetly rest — so rested in spirit as in body, that in the morning, when I said my prayers, I said one for the unhappy woman whose perjuries had brought me there. I said, "Forgive us our trespasses, as we forgive them that have trespassed against us."

Recording this experience reminds me of one I had at Clerkenwell Prison, where I was taken at my first remand at Bow Street, and before the magistrate had made up his mind to admit me to bail.

When the warder opened the door of the cell assigned me, I saw the radiantly beautiful form of a woman pass into the cell before me, and turn round, and stretch out her arms to receive me. She wore a long rosary and crucifix at her girdle. She held out the crucifix to me. I fell on my knees, took it in my fingers, and kissed it. It was as tangible as any I ever touched. Then she said, —

" You enter under the shadow of the cross : you will go out into the sunshine. Meditate well upon the passion of our Lord, for when next you celebrate it your hour will have come."

My next Easter Sunday was spent in prison.

She bent over me, and kissed and blessed me, and left the cell, seeming to pass through the closed door; and as she drew after her, fold upon fold, her white dress, it seemed as if she left wave upon wave of sweetness behind her, and my loneliness seemed peopled with love.

Thus it was that the two prisons of Newgate and Clerkenwell became holy places in my memory, and my life, hard and bitter as it seemed, was filled with ineffable consolations.

After the weary trial and my sweet night's rest in Newgate, I was taken by some special favor, as I have related, in a cab to Tothill Fields. When I had passed through the ordeal of the reception-room, and the female warder to whose custody I was committed had shown me my cell, and then shut and locked my door, the turning of the key sounded like a farewell to the universe. I had been interested by the novelty of my position and the strange persons and things about me; but now all my world — sea, sky, pictures, music — all was in my cold, dark, lonely cell.

In the first moments of isolation the shadow of all the coming year of loneliness fell over me. When the key turned, my heart sprang to my lips with a farewell to everybody and every thing, — home, husband, child, friends. It was like a living death of all I prized and loved. I threw myself upon my knees on the cold, hard stone, and put out my hands as if to feel for the touch of some human hand to comfort me; and there, again, I felt the little fingers touching mine; and the little voice I had heard at Newgate said to me, —

"Mamma, as, when I died, an angel came to tell you of your first work, and show you my resurrection, now at this second death a legion of angels comes to show you your second work and your own resurrection. Mamma dear, nobody has died, and nothing has died, but yourself."

I heard no more, but I think I realized the meaning of what I had heard. The feeling of vacillation, and the sense of being diffused throughout the world, left me; and I felt as if this death was a white angel, that had taken off all my black garments, and given me new white robes, and shown me the use, as well as the use-lessness, of the world. Just as all the bitterness of my trial came into the half-hour of parting with my friends, so were all the sufferings of my twelve months' imprisonment crowded into this first half-hour in my cell.

During that afternoon I thought of the length of my imprisonment. If two hours went so slowly, and seemed so long, how *could* I pass twelve months? The time seemed very long and very heavy. I took a pin, and marked each half-hour by the striking of the great prison-clock. I did this till midnight. But it was very cold, and at last I lay down upon my hammock. As I lay there, when an hour had passed I saw a little beam of light come, and mark off the hour upon the wall. And from this time there was no night in which the hours were not so checked upon the wall ; and when the great clock was out of order, as it often was, and ceased to strike, the ray of light still marked each passing hour.

I wondered, the first night I saw this marking ray, whether it would come again, and watched for it ; so that this employed my mind, and made the time pass more easily. Once, watching intently for the ray, and feeling as if the hour would never pass, there came letters of golden light upon the white wall, forming this inscription : "The gate which shuts out the world gives the angels entrance."

So passed the night, and so the shadows were lifted from my weary heart. I have often wondered if Mrs. Davies' was not more heavy than was mine.

The first time I went to the prison-chapel was on Maundy Thursday, the day before Good Friday. I fear I was not in a mood of resignation, or a religious mood of any kind. It seemed to me, that, if the good God had any power, among the many who had been unjust to me he might have found one soft, impressi-

ble heart. A new, strange, painful bitterness came
into my soul. I had pitied those who persecuted me:
I was beginning to hate them. But, as the service
continued, I felt that my proper attitude was one of
resignation ; and, as I raised my eyes to the altar, above
the crucifix there seemed to come a form of the living
Christ, and from it came a voice so loud and clear, that
I wondered every face was not upturned. It said, —

" *I to-day bear my share in the misery of the world:
can you not for my sake wash this bitterness out of your
heart?* "

I said " YES," not only with my lips, but it seemed
as if all my blood was in a revolution, and that even
if I had a whole army against me, in my feelings, my
prejudices, and this bitterness which seemed to me so
gigantic, — at this moment the Christ-love entered my
heart, and I hope my better soul became a victor over
my poorer self.

The prison did not seem so small after that, nor the
poor women about me so hideous ; for I felt that the
place where angels sweet and grand could come, was
not utterly unfit for me, nor the women there wholly
abandoned.

During the service the raps that came about me
were so loud and frequent, that my warder thought
some of the women were making them, and peered
about, and watched them. While she was doing this,

I mentally asked who was making the raps; and, calling over the letters of the alphabet, the letters marked by the raps spelled this message : —

" *This warder is my wife. Tell her that I am not dead, but here, and this place will seem to her less dreadful.*"

Weeks afterward, when I had come to know her, I told her of this message. It was my first lesson to my warder in Spiritualism.

Some days passed without any more direct communication from spirits; but my mind, and the whole place, seemed pervaded by their influence.

For several days after I came to the prison, I could not eat. The food was very different from that to which I had been accustomed : I had no appetite, and could not bring myself to taste it. After nearly a week of this fasting, when I was becoming exhausted, I was wakened one night from a feverish sleep by feeling something in my mouth. I felt, and then pressed and tasted it. It was a ripe, delicious grape. Another and another were given me, until I had eaten a considerable cluster. In the morning the stalks, skins, and seeds were found by my warder lying on my table. She asked me how I had got the grapes. I told her the spirits had brought them. As she could see no other way, she thought I must be going insane; but, not wishing to get into trouble, she was obliged to accept my explanation.

One night, when between three and four weeks had passed, I thought, "Oh, dear me! when a month has passed, what a time will still remain!" And then I heard the spirit "Joey" (known to so many people all over the world through Mr. Eglinton), saying in his very peculiar and most welcome voice, —

"Don't be down-hearted, Bertie! don't be down-hearted!"

The dear voice seemed to embrace and warm me. I said, —

"Joey dear, I have been here only three weeks and a half, and it seems like eternity. If it were only a month, it would be a twelfth part of the whole."

"You have been here more than a month," said Joey.

I thought he was joking, or that I had been crazy, and had lost my account of the time.

Evidently "Joey" could read my thoughts; for he said, —

"If you don't believe me, look on your card."

My card was a bit of pasteboard on the door of the cell, on which is inscribed the name of the prisoner, and her age, offence, and length of sentence. On looking at it next day, as directed by "Joey," I found, to my great surprise, that the term for which I had been sentenced began with the opening of the sessions, March 27, instead of April 13, the day of my conviction and sentence. The card stated that my term would end on March 27. Still feeling that there must be some mistake, I took the card to my warden, and she explained it. " Joey " was right; and I had got through six weeks, instead of three weeks and a half.

Some day I may have a fortune of a million pounds given to me, or I may become sovereign of some grand empire; but I shall never again feel so rich or so grand as I did over the unexpected gain of those three weeks of my term of imprisonment.

CHAPTER XXXVII.

WHEN I entered the prison, I was absorbed in my own sorrows and wrongs. I was very selfish, and had no time or space for the greater griefs and greater wrongs of so many others; but, when I began to look about me, I found a new world, and soon came to think of others as well as of myself. My fellow-prisoners were a new people to me, forming an entire new world, of which I had hitherto had no idea. I watched the faces of those I found, and of all new-comers. The coming of each new group of prisoners brought afresh the memory of my own conviction; and, as each group departed, I fear I suffered a new pang in being left behind.

One day there came into the prison a woman with a face so sad, so quiet in its depth of feeling, so unlike the faces of most of the prisoners, that I could not rid myself of the impression of deep grief it made upon me. As I knelt upon my stone floor that night, I saw on the other side of my hammock a human form so

350

real, seeming so tangible, so unlike a spirit, that I
thought it must be a living woman. She was dressed
in the poor, clean clothes of a respectable, neat work-
ing-woman, and was engaged in saying her rosary, the
beads passing through her thin fingers, and her lips
moving with the prayers.

I waited — I did not like to interrupt her — so I
watched her, steadily passing bead after bead, and not
seeming to see me at all. I heard her pronounce the
name of "Mary;" but, as that beautiful name occurs
continually in the rosary, I waited until she had finished. She rose and seemed about to leave me, when
I reached over and touched her dress and said, "Are
you a spirit?"

She started as if she had not before seen me, then
looked at me and at my prison-dress, and said, "Are
you one of them?"

"Yes," I answered: "I am one of them, and very
helpless. But, my good woman, you seem to be in
trouble. Can I do any thing to help you?"

She looked at me earnestly for a moment, and then
said, —

"Yes. Pray for her."

"Pray for whom?"

"Pray for Mary — for my child. She is innocent
as a babe unborn; yet they have put her into this
dreadful place, and taken her children away from her,

and sold her home, and she is going mad — mad — mad!"

These words seemed to ring through the prison: so I said, "Hush! somebody will hear you."

She reached over, and clutched my dress. "You look sweet and good," she said; "and I believe our Blessed Lady will hear you. Pray for her! Pray hard, pray hard!"

As she talked to me, the face that had so impressed me that day seemed to come to me again; and I said, "Are you speaking of the woman in No. ——?"

"Oh, yes!" she said. "She is my child — all the child I had in the world. When she was a baby in my arms, she was very ill, and I thought God was going to take her from me; and now I wish he had, I wish he had. I cannot bear to see her suffer."

This became dreadfully oppressive to me, it was so terribly sad. But soon a spirit-friend of mine came and put his arms about her, and the two soon disappeared.

I kept the sad story in my mind, and thought much of the poor prisoner in Number ——, but did not see her. She was in the tier of cells above mine, where we were never allowed to go.

One day at the end of the week when this "vision" had come to me, while I was out of my cell, I heard a bell ring violently in that tier, and my warder asked

me to go and see what was wanted. When I went up,
I intended to make use of the opportunity to peep into
Number —— ; but, when I reached the tier, I saw
that it was Number ——'s bell that had rung, for the
number had sprung out to show it.

Peeping through the inspection-hole, I saw the woman. She had been picking oakum, and had gathered
it into the skirt of her dress, and was walking about
the cell, talking wildly.

"Poor little Johnny!" she said, holding out a
wisp of the oakum, "he shall have this to play with."

I remembered what the spirit had said, and, looking
at the card, saw that the name was "Mary." I
reported what I had seen to the warder, and my impression that the poor woman was mad. The warder
went to see her, and on her return said, —

"I am afraid she is losing her mind, poor thing.
Her case is a very hard one. She has three little children, and when she was convicted they were sent to
the workhouse. She is here for nine months. Her
furniture was sold while she was in the prison at Clerkenwell. The separation from her children preys upon
her mind, and she spends her time making toys of the
oakum for them to play with.

"Her case was reported to the doctor; and she was
taken to the sick-cells, and pronounced insane. But
there seems to have been some difference of opinion

among the prison authorities; for in a few days she was sent to the paper-prison, and set to sorting the waste-paper, working till eight o'clock in her cell by the gaslight.''

One night the warder, making her rounds, smelt burning paper. Searching for the cause, she found that the poor mad woman had set her stock of paper on fire, so that her cell was in a blaze of light, and there she was sitting, throwing up the burning papers, and shouting, '' *Oh, the children will be delighted! The children will be delighted!* ''

Of course she was sent back to the infirmary.

CHAPTER XXXVIII.

A VISIT TO MY HUSBAND.

One day in midsummer I was taken with a great longing to see some friends, to escape from my monotonous environments. It was an uncontrollable, unappeasable hunger of the soul, so intense that I could not think or will myself out of it.

Suddenly, in the midst of this almost insane longing, there fell over me a great calm, a complete repose of emotion. I began to grow sleepy, but in this sleepiness there came violent palpitations of the heart. I was not surprised at this, it seemed the natural result of strong emotions. This state was soon followed by what seemed to me suspended circulation, so that I thought I was dying, and soon became unconscious.

I have no means of knowing how long I remained so; but when I found myself, my real self, as I thought or felt, I was in a room with two gentlemen. One of them was my husband; the other, a stranger to me. Of course my first impulse was to rush into my husband's arms, but I could not do so. I seemed to have no

355

power to control my movements, and began to be
doubtful of my condition. For a few moments the
desire to get near him, and the impossibility of doing
so, gave me a very painful sensation. It seemed like
being buried alive, and hearing one's friends moving
away from the grave.

But, as this sensation was growing unbearable, I saw
one of my spirit-friends whom we call "Dewdrop."
She cried out, "Now you see what kind of difficulties
we spirits get into sometimes, and you must find out
that when we can't do what we like we must do what
we can. Come, tottle along, and we will have a
séance."

In my "double," as this separation of the spirit
from the body is called, I seemed to myself as much a
spirit as she was. She took my hand, and led me to
a table at which the stranger was sitting. I sat in
one of the chairs, while "Dewdrop" reclined grace-
fully on the centre of the table, and began making
"passes," gently moving her hands, over the table
and me and the gentleman. These "passes" seemed
to etherealize, so to speak, every thing about her,
until she and the table seemed to grow light as air,
oscillating with the aerial movements. I found it difficult to stay in my chair. As the table moved, I heard
the gentleman say to my husband, —

"Oh! spirits here, Fletcher. Come and sit down,
and let us see what they have to say to us."

As my husband started to come to the table, I wished very much that he would come and sit by me. Instead of that, he sat by the gentleman who had called him. As he sat down, he put his hands upon the table, and immediately I saw a change in the color of the aura surrounding it; and, instead of its being like a filmy cloud, rays of light, which seemed as solid as metallic wires, came from his fingers, and spread across the table.

"Dewdrop," leaving her perch, came round to my side, and placed her fingers upon these points of light. As she did this, the oscillations of the table ceased, and she said, —

"Lines all ready. Would you like to send a message?" .

Though I knew my husband could not see me, I yet foolishly felt hurt that he did not speak to me; and I did not at all fancy the awkward, undignified, slow way of rapping out a message to him letter by letter, when he ought to have come round to me. It seemed impossible for me to go through the stupid process of telegraphing to him across a table. I felt as if I would rather go away.

"Quiet, quiet!" said my pretty "Dewdrop." "Don't you see the cross-lines? You are getting too positive."

I had put my hands unconsciously on the table;

and I now saw lines from my hands crossing those coming from my husband's.

"Oh! won't there be a row?" said "Dewdrop." "Bad conditions; no *séance!* Harry will be in such a temper!"

"Who is Harry?" I asked.

"*That's* Harry," said she, pointing to the stranger; "and he is our medium."

When she said this, the thought came to me, if I am interrupting conditions, I must go away; only I could not go.

After a few minutes of this suspense, the medium said to Mr. Fletcher, "I wonder what the trouble is. Ask some questions, Fletcher: let us see what's up."

What came next seemed very droll to me. Mr. Fletcher bent over the table, and said, "Dear spirits, are any of you present?"

No response.

After a moment's silence, he said, "I thought I heard raps."

"*No!*" said the medium, in a big, rough voice. "*My* raps *are* raps. When they come, you can't mistake them for the creaking of a table."

In my amusement at the recollection of *séances* I had attended, I forgot myself, and became less "positive;" and the lines from my fingers moved round, and became parallel with the others. As they did so,

"Dewdrop" reached over, and put her fingers on the lines, like a telegraph-operator; and loud, full, vigorous raps responded to her touch.

"Oh, they have come!" said my husband. "Is it any friend of mine?"

(Three raps for yes.)

"Who is it?"

(Five raps for alphabet), and my husband began to say his A B C's; and the raps marking the letters spelled out, "D-e-w-d-r-o-p." As the word was spelled out, she turned to me with, —

"Keep your ears open for the next question."

"O Dewdrop! have you seen Bertie?"

(Three raps.)

"Is she well?"

"I should like awfully to tell a crammer; but I can't," said "Dewdrop" in an aside to me. Then she rapped out, —

"Not very, but getting better fast," with a triumphant look on her little face at the idea of giving him comfort.

I had forgotten how he had neglected me just now, and wished only that he should be comforted: so I reached over, and tried to work the wires, so as to send him a message, but did not succeed.

"In Heaven's name, 'Dewdrop,'" I said, "can't you manage so that I can say a word to him?"

"Be patient a little minute, and I will see what I can do for you."

She disappeared, and instantly returned with one of the most beautiful men I ever saw. He went directly to the medium.

"Dewdrop" put up her finger. "Don't ask any questions," she said. "He is a mystic."

I neither spoke nor moved, and saw him take from under his loose robe, and place upon the table, something like a kernel of rice. Leaving it there for some moments, he picked it up, and seemed to insert it under the nail of the medium's forefinger. He then made five raps on the table; and, as the alphabet was called, he rapped out the word, —

"S-l-a-t-e."

The medium sprang to his feet, saying, "There is a most tremendous influence here. I must write."

He took a slate from the sideboard, and held it in his right hand, higher than his head, but over the head of Mr. Fletcher.

"Now is your chance," said "Dewdrop." "And don't waste time, for this influence don't last long."

"Why not put the slate upon the table?" I said. "I can't write on it up there."

"Can't have it down here," said she: "the atmosphere is too dense. You must climb up." And, as if in obedience to my desire, I began to float slowly

toward the slate. As I did so, the medium changed
the slate to his left hand. I put my hands upon his
head without knowing why I did so. I seemed suspended in mid-air, and liable to fall. I went to write,
but I had no pencil. "Dewey" had vanished. Then
the medium said, —

"This is apparently some spirit that does not know
how to write. — Dear spirit, if you will take my forefinger for a pencil, you can write."

I took his finger, and wrote, "Darling Willie, I am
not very ill, nor very unhappy; but I do want you
very, very much. Bertie."

The influence left me; and I came rapidly to the
ground, close to his feet. As the medium lowered the
slate, he said, —

"Fletcher, this is the spirit of some living person
who has written this message. I can always tell the
difference between the embodied and the disembodied
spirit."

My husband took the slate. He recognized the handwriting, and read the message. As he read it, he burst
into sobs, and cried, "O my Bertie, Bertie!" and,
pushing the slate toward the medium, he said, —

"This message is from my wife!"

I wrapped my arms around him. I tried to comfort
him. As I did this, the "mystic" came, and touched
me on the shoulder, and said, —

" Little woman, you must come back. If animation is any longer suspended, your body will die."

I went back. How, I cannot say ; how long it took me to return, I cannot say. It seemed that I must go, and I went.

I woke to find myself lying on the stone floor of my cell, where my body must have fallen when my spirit left it ; and I had the feeling that the few inches of clay, my body, was a very small world to live in, and that I now knew something of the difficulties the hosts of spirits who visit mediums encounter in trying to communicate with their friends. I thought I should never again sit in a *séance* without feeling a greater sympathy and a deeper charity for the sufferings of spirits and the so-called failures of mediums.

When I next heard from Mr. Fletcher, who had the privilege of writing to me at stated periods, I received from him a full and circumstantial confirmation of this experience.

CHAPTER XXXIX.

FLOWERS BROUGHT TO MY CELL. — A LOCK OF HAIR
AND A LETTER.

I KNOW very well that great numbers of persons seem incapable of believing such relations as I am compelled to give. Some have a natural, perhaps hereditary, incredulity; some are committed to forms of belief or unbelief which shut out all spirit-manifestations as impossible. Of course no materialist can believe in the existence of spirits, and a great many Christians hold that every thing supernatural ceased at the end of the apostolic age. The "greater things" that are to "follow them that believe" are to come in the millennium of a far future. But I have nothing to do with men's beliefs or unbeliefs, or even their capacity to believe. I have only to give a true account of my own experience, without reticence or exaggeration. My simple mission is to be a witness of the truth. I know that there are now some millions in the world who *can* believe me, and many who *will*.

One morning, before I woke, one of my spirit-friends came, and said to me, " Be very particular about your bathing this morning, and don't take any food to-day. It will be better that you do not."

I was accustomed to fasting. I did not eat for several days after I came into the prison, and several times fasted three or four days, taking only a little water.

All this day I felt very quiet, and stronger and better than usual, which made me think my friends were doing something for me which was of more substantial benefit than any food could be. ·

At about half-past five P.M. I felt impelled to go to the chapel and say my prayers, feeling that there, in that narrow compass, I was resting in the arms of some one who understood me ; and, as I knelt there in perfect peace, I felt something touch my face, and inhaled a strong odor of mignonette, but saw nothing. I was not surprised, for it seemed as if any sweet thing might come there.

When I had finished my devotions, I returned to my cell, and went early to bed. At about ten o'clock my cell seemed suddenly filled with light; and, standing in this light, I saw the spirit called " Ernest," holding in his hand a little bouquet of violets and heliotrope. Giving them to me, he said, —

" I have brought you these flowers from dear Mrs.

Nichols and Mrs. Western (of London) with their love. There was a spray of mignonette which we gave to Marie Thérèse, and which she has placed upon the altar. You caught its perfume to-day ; and to-morrow, if you search, you will find the flower."

I reached over to grasp his hand, and take the flowers ; and he bent down, and tenderly kissed me on my forehead. I kissed him twice upon his lips, and told him to take my kisses, my love, and my grateful thanks, to the dear friends who had sent me the flowers. I hid them in my bosom, and kept the dried leaves and petals in my cell as long as I remained in prison.

Next day I searched in the chapel for the spray of mignonette, and found it at the foot of the crucifix. I thought I could safely take this to my warder, and tell her where I had found it. Looking at me earnestly, she said, "Perhaps your angel brought it." I thought how much wiser the little woman was than she knew.

I heard a little later from Mrs. Nichols. She said, "Mrs. Western and I have prepared a little bouquet of flowers ; and 'Ernest' has taken them away, and promised to give them to you if possible. The spray of mignonette and the heliotrope were my contribution ; the violets, Mrs. Western's." What better corroboration could be had than this !

One night, between nine and ten o'clock, "Ernest" came to me in my cell, and said, "I want to give a test to a friend of yours who is very sceptical, and who wishes me to bring him something from you."

"Dear 'Ernest,'" I said, "I have nothing to send him but my clothes or my hair."

"It is a lock of your hair I want," he said; "but it may exhaust you a good deal for me to take it. Are you willing I should do so?"

"Certainly," I replied, having no idea how taking a lock of my hair could do me any harm.

He took from beneath his robe something like a poniard, and, lifting a little lock of my hair, quickly severed it, and disappeared. At the stroke it seemed as if my heart stopped beating.

Some time after, when I was relating this with other experiences to a friend, he said, "Did you know to whom that lock of hair was taken?" — "Not in the least," I answered. He took a lock of long hair from his pocket-book, and placed it beside mine, with which it perfectly corresponded in color and texture. There was no doubt of its identity; and he told me of a wonderful *séance* he had had with a medium, a friend of mine, when, in answer to a mental wish that something might be brought from me, this lock of hair was placed in his hand. He did not mention the fact to the other persons present at the *séance;* but, comparing the time with my account, he found that the transfer, at some miles distance, must have been almost instantaneous. It was pretty certain that "Ernest" did not travel by cab or rail.

I regret that I cannot give the names of persons in this case, as I do in most cases: but my friend occupies a position in which he might have some annoyance; and I have always, at whatever risk or loss, carefully refrained from bringing any trouble to others. Persons in high positions may be far from occupying independent positions. There are some whose influence, I have sometimes thought, might have saved me from some suffering; but, if so, it was theirs to offer, and not mine to claim. "*Noblesse oblige!* "

At about seven o'clock in the evening of one day when I had felt that I must fast, "Ernest" came to me in my cell, and said, —

"Dear friend, I wish you to be very quiet; as, owing to your not having taken food to-day, I find you in a good condition for manifestations."

"O 'Ernest!' " I said, " what do you want to do to-night? "

"Keep perfectly quiet and you will see."

He disappeared; and soon there came three spirits, bringing with them a crucible from which arose a flame. They set it on my table.

I spoke to them, and asked what they were doing; but they made no response. They seemed to be doing something with their fingers over the crucible. In a few minutes "Ernest" returned, and asked the other spirits, "Is every thing ready?" Receiving an affirmative answer, he said, "Every thing to-night seems favorable to our attempt at recreation."

My cell was one of the dark ones, and at five o'clock was dark enough for any manifestation. People quarrel with dark *séances*. They want every thing in the light. But they must darken rooms for photography, for the magic-lantern, for the solar-microscope; and chemists find that some gases can only be kept in darkness, because a ray of light causes an explosion. Spirit-lights can only be seen in a dark room. It seems best to allow the spirits to choose their own conditions for doing their own work.

The three spirits with the crucible vanished, and "Ernest" said, —

"I wish you to write a note that I can take to one who is present at our *séance* to-night at Dr. Nichols's. He is now a stranger to you, but in the future you will make his acquaintance."

I asked the name, and it was given to me.

"But, 'Ernest,'" I said, "how can I write a note? I have neither paper, pencil, nor light: how can I write?"

He pointed to a book on the table, and said, "Take a blank leaf from that, and I will return presently with a pencil."

He was gone perhaps a minute, and came bringing a common lead pencil and a light in the form of a luminous cross,—a soft pure light, like that of the planets. He gave me the pencil, and held the cross while I wrote on the fly-leaf of the book a brief message, which "Ernest" took, and quickly vanished. But before he went I said, "'Ernest' dear, where did you get this pencil?"

"Took it without leave," he answered; "and I shall leave it with you to return."

My first idea was to conceal it, as prisoners are not allowed to have such things; but, as we and our cells were thoroughly searched every week, I knew it would be found. So I left it on the table.

Next morning, when my warder entered the cell, she saw the pencil, and asked where I got it. I thought the best way was to tell her the truth : so I said, "One of my angels brought it."

She smiled incredulously and said, "Then we ought to detain your angel, for he has stolen my pencil." She looked at it. "That is my pencil," she said, "which I certainly locked up in my table-drawer when I left the prison last night. I don't know any thing about angels; but I *know* that that is my pencil, and I had better not find it in your possession again." [1]

<hr/>

[1] On the night of the 23d of September, 1881, there was a *séance* at my house, 32 Fopstone Road, South Kensington, which is about two miles "as the crow flies," from the Tothill Fields prison. The medium was Mr. William Eglinton; and one of the sitters was Mr. Sweeney, Esq., then residing at Paris, and staying with us, while making a business-visit to London.

After some manifestations, Mr. Eglinton, sitting next to Mr. Sweeney, asked him to put his hands together, palm to palm, so as to make an impervious casket. He did so, and Mr. Eglinton strengthened it by clasping his own hands over those of Mr. Sweeney. In a few moments, during which the hands of the medium seemed to clasp Mr. Sweeney's with convulsive energy, they were suddenly removed, and he said to Mr. Sweeney, "Open your hands." He did so, and lying on the palm of one of them was a folded paper about two inches square. It was passed across the table to me. I opened it out, a half of a leaf, which might have been torn from a book, on which was written in pencil, in the to me well-known hand of Susan Willis Fletcher, the following words : —

8 P.M., FRIDAY, Sept. 23, 1881.

MY STRANGER FRIEND, — Professor Hare and "Ernest" have told me of your kindly feeling and good wishes, and that you will be glad to receive a message through their agency.

Your sympathy is to my spirit what the dew is to parched flowers. God bless you!

SUSAN WILLIS FLETCHER.

On a corner of the reverse is written, —

Please, dear "Ernest," to carry this to Mr. Sweeney, who, you say, is at Mrs. Nichols's, and oblige

BERTIE.

I certify that I was a witness of the facts above recorded, and the paper is now in my possession.

T. L. NICHOLS, M.D.

AUG. 1, 1882.

CHAPTER XL.

ON the 26th of November, 1881, at six o'clock P.M., "Ernest" came to me in my cell, with his cross of light, and said, "Get ready to write. I want a long letter; and, as you must write rapidly, we shall help you to write it."

Of course I had to say, as before, that I had no writing-materials. "We have provided for that," he said, and produced a lead pencil and three sheets of thin foreign note-paper.

"To whom am I to write?" I asked.

"Look at the corner of the paper, and you will see."

I looked, and found the name of a friend of mine, also a pet name he had given to me, which was known to no other person ; and both names were written in his own handwriting, as familiar to me as my own.

I began to write. My hand was controlled, so that

371

I wrote almost as rapidly as I thought; yet it was my own handwriting. After I began to write, the cell seemed flooded with light; and in the very corner of the cell I distinctly saw the form of Mr. Eglinton, the medium.

I filled the three sheets in a little more than a quarter of an hour. There was one little interruption. When I had about half finished, the lead of the pencil broke; but instantly "Ernest," with a movement of his fingers in the air, produced a short piece of pencil with which I finished my letter.

When it was completed, "Ernest" took the paper in one hand, and placed the other on my head, holding it there for a moment, and said, in words I seem to perfectly remember, —

"Bertie dear, at present, in this world, there is no redress for your great wrongs; but Heaven has constituted itself a court of appeal, in which God sits as your judge, and the angels as your jurors; and, while you are suffering here, your mediumship shall be established, and, ere many years have passed, the verdict of Heaven on your character shall be adopted by the world. Love God, be faithful to us, be kind to every living creature, and victory shall be yours."

He vanished with the luminous cross, the cloud of light, the message I had written to my friend, and, what was sweeter than all, the warmth of his own dear presence, but leaving with me a stronger heart, a deeper faith, and an abiding courage.

Before sunrise on the morning of Nov. 28 I again saw the light which usually heralded the approach of my spirit-friends ; and I soon saw "Ernest," and the beautiful feminine spirit who calls herself "Violet." She came to my hammock, turned down the clothing, and placed a little square packet over my heart. "Read and be comforted," she said, and pressed her lips upon my forehead ; when both disappeared.

In the morning, as soon as it was light enough, I opened the packet, and read and was comforted. It was a letter from the friend to whom I had written the long letter on the evening of the 26th, acknowledging its reception, and replying to its contents.

My friend, Mr. I. E. Mengens, to whom I had written, was then at his home in Calcutta, India. Mr. Eglinton was then staying with him, being on a visit to India. The sheets of paper bore his stamp ; and the one on the corner of which he had written, Mr. Eglinton, as I have since learned, carried for two or three days in his pocket, and then placed in a book. The paper was removed from the book by my spirit-friend "Joey," who took two more sheets from a writing-desk, because one was not enough, and gave them to "Ernest," who brought them to me.

I have given the particulars of the letter of Nov.

26, because this was one of the most remarkable instances I know of the exercise of spirit-power in this direction. The carrying of articles for moderate distances and with immense rapidity is a common phenomenon. Space and time seem to be quite different to spirits from what they are to us. With them —

> "Stone walls do not a prison make,
> Nor iron bars a cage."

The passing of matter through matter is a common phenomenon. Books, masses of flowers, etc., are brought into perfectly closed rooms, in spite of locked doors and shuttered windows. Carrying letters and similar articles several thousand miles over land and sea in a few moments of time has not been so frequent.

The letter to Mr. Mengens of Nov. 26 was not the first. I had written to him, on the 13th of January, a letter to be sent by post. On the 20th, when it had been only a week on the way, it was brought to him in Calcutta. It bore the stamps and dates of the post-office, and must have been taken from one of her Majesty's letter-bags on the mail-steamer. Mr. Mengens was in bed, when he was told to turn down the clothes, and find the letter. His testimony, and that of his brother, Mr. Marc Mengens, and of Mr. Eglinton, to the facts respecting the instantaneous transmission of letters between London and Calcutta cannot be impeached.

I must now give what may seem to many readers a more extraordinary experience, which may have been in some way preparatory to those just related.

On the morning of the 20th of November "Ernest" came to me, and said, "Have something ready for us to-night at seven o'clock." He said he wished to give a test of spirit-power, and would try to take a letter from me to India. Now, I knew that Calcutta was more than five thousand miles distant, with between five and six hours difference of time between us. That a spirit could be where he willed to be in a moment, "in the twinkling of an eye," I could believe; but that a letter, or any material object, could be conveyed five or six thousand miles instantaneously, or like a flash of light, or with the rapidity of the electric-telegraph, was not easy to believe. After all I had experienced, I did not realize the power of spirit over matter. When "Ernest" came at night, I had not written, and I had to confess my doubt and my neglect.

He smiled very wisely, and said, "I knew you would not have it ready: so I have made other arrangements. Go to bed now, and try to go at once to sleep."

He vanished, and I went to bed as he desired; and,

which was very unusual, fell at once into a profound
slumber. I seldom got to sleep before three A.M.

I slept until about ten ·P.M., when I again saw
"Ernest," who began to make passes all down my
body, and I began to feel as I did before, when my
spirit went away from it. In a little time I lost all
consciousness. I do not know how long this uncon-
sciousness lasted; but the first thing I knew was, that I
was in a room quite strange to me, where five persons
were seated at a table. There may have been more,
for there were what seemed to me blank spaces.

"Ernest" was with me, and said, "As you would
not do your writing at home, perhaps you will do it
here. We who work only for results do not mind using
what may seem very undignified means: so perhaps
you will not object to getting under this table. We
have established our batteries there, and it is the only
place that will serve you for a writing-desk."

I did as I was directed, and went under what he
called the table; but it looked like a little workshop,
with batteries, crucibles, and other apparatus, two
books, and pencils. But in trying to enter this place
I found an impediment. "Ernest" smiled, and said,
"The strongest things are not visible. You will find
that true the world over; but, as these are only magnetic wires for the protection of our conditions, I think
we shall soon find an entrance."

As he ceased speaking, the impediment was removed. Once inside, I saw the barrier, like a thin plate of iron, dense and solid now, but from the outside invisible. "Ernest," who seemed to do easily whatever he willed, produced a light, and gave me pen and paper, and I wrote my letter. I supposed it was to be given to the person to whom it was addressed, who was one of the sitters at the table ; but no sooner was it finished than "Ernest" said most peremptorily, "You must come back at once : we have already kept you too long from your body."

While I had been there, manifestations had been going on around the table. I saw "Joey," and also two very exalted spirits, and could hear "Joey" talking, and at times he came into the little workshop. I could also very plainly hear the exclamations of the sitters.

In the midst of this my spirit-friend "Dewdrop" peeped in, and said, "Oh! I want you to know Mrs. Cheetham, she is such a nice little medium! and Mrs. Gordon, who will in the future be among your best friends."

I thought she referred to two ladies sitting at the table. Those whom I knew already were Mr. Eglinton the medium, and Mr. Mengens,* to whom I had written my letter, which I left under the table when "Ernest" took me away. Instantly, as it seemed to me, I was in my cell, and saw my body lying in my hammock. It seemed bad enough to re-enter my cell, so small, so cold and dismal; but the idea of re-entering my body was still more repugnant. It was doubly a prison, a prison in a prison; and I refused to go. No one can understand what I felt who has not had a similar experience, and known how imprisoned a free spirit can be in its " tenement of clay." It was so unpleasant to me, that when "Ernest" urgently appealed to me to exercise my will to re-enter and re-animate my body, I told him I had no such inclination, and could not will it.

" Ernest " seemed disturbed and agitated, and summoned six other spirits to his aid. I recognized one of them as my husband's "control," "Winona." These spirits seemed to magnetize my body. Probably only a few seconds elapsed, but it seemed an hour, when I began to feel that I should not be obliged to re-enter my body; and this feeling was accompanied by such an atmosphere of sweetness and exhilaration, and such a calm, placid happiness as I had not felt since I left my husband in America, and came to meet my trial in London. But as my happiness increased, so did the trouble of " Ernest;" and he held a little conference with " Winona," when she quickly disappeared.

Every instant I grew more light, more buoyant.

The prison-walls vanished, and I could see sky and moon and stars ; clouds did not impede my vision ; and beyond them were legions of angels, and I felt a strong desire to join them, which seemed very easy to do ; for I felt myself rising, rising, in an ecstasy of freedom, which no one can ever feel whose feet have not been raised from off the earth by this soul elevation. This earth, and all its conditions and relations, seemed annihilated, as if the whole quality of my mind had been changed. Even the memory of earthly experiences seemed fading out of my mind.

But as I rose in the air I saw myself still connected, by a line of light fine as a silken thread, to my poor body. It became finer and finer, lengthening as I rose.

While in this perfect entrancement of freedom, I saw " Winona," and with her my husband. He seemed to look at my body, and take it in his arms. He cried, " O Bertie, Bertie ! come back to me ! Are you really dead? Has that hideous woman become your murderess ? "

He held my poor body closer to his heart, and kissed my face, and I wondered how he could caress so poor a thing as my cast-off body. But, as he continued to implore me to come back, I felt the little line of light tighten, and then it seemed to be pulling at my heart. My inclination to reach him became stronger than my desire to go to the angels ; and so my spirit glided back into my body, and I found myself alone in my cell.

This was on the 20th of November. At Christmas, in accordance with prison-rules, I received a letter from my husband, in which he gave me an account of his lectures, and in which he wrote : —

"Sometimes I have thought that evil spirits were conspiring with our enemies to torture and destroy us. On the 20th of November, when I was reading a book you gave me, late at night, suddenly 'Winona' came to me, and said, 'Shut your eyes, Willie, and go to sleep. You have read long enough.' I put down my book, closed my eyes, and instantly I seemed to be in a little white stone cell, and you seemed to be there; but I thought you were dead. I folded you in my arms, and cried aloud to you to come back; but it seemed as if you would never come. At last I fell on my knees, and felt that that hideous woman had been your murderess; and I called out in despair, 'O God! why hast thou forsaken me?' At last I felt your breath upon my cheek; and, bursting into tears of joy at your restoration, I felt myself whirled through the air by 'Winona,' and then resting upon my bed. As she was passing from the room, she said, 'You have saved Bertie's life; but we were obliged to take you away from her, for she can bear no more.' What can it mean? Are you ill? or was it only a vision sent to torture me?"

CHAPTER XLI.

FURTHER EXPERIENCES.

On the night before Mr. Eglinton departed for India, "Ernest" came to me and said, "I want my last work in London before we go to be for Dr. and Mrs. Nichols; and I wish you to write a note to one of them to-day, and place it beneath the altar in the chapel. Write to the other also, as near noon to-morrow as circumstances will permit, and put it in the same place. I will take them when I can." I did as directed. At night I looked where I had concealed the little notes, and they had vanished, when and how, I had no means of knowing; but Dr. Nichols has since written to me : —

"Two little notes in your well-known handwriting were punctually delivered. Sitting in my study, Mr. Eglinton, 'under control,' took a slate, and held it horizontally above his head near the gaslight. Something fell upon it. On his lowering it, I found your little note addressed to Mrs. Nichols. A little after, Mr. Eglinton asked me to come with him near my writing-desk. He put his open hand into the obscurity under the desk for a moment; and on taking it out, there lay on it a welcome note from ' Bertie.' "

In the month of November " Ernest " came to me one day, seemingly in haste, and said, " A great trial awaits dear Mrs. Nichols. A calamity will befall her which we have no power to avert; but we wish to prepare her by placing every means of strength which we have at her disposal. I want you to send her a lock of your hair, dear; and I am sure it will comfort you to know that in her hour of greatest distress it will afford her comfort and relief."

Of course I was glad to do any thing possible for my dear friend who had so faithfully stood by me in all my trial; and " Ernest," instead of cutting off a lock, as before, with a poniard, seemed to remove it by imperceptible dematerialization.[1]

Letters were taken from me by my spirit-friends to Mr. Eglinton, to Capt. James (a retired army officer living in Gower Street, who has been for many years a most intelligent investigator of the phenomena of mesmerism and Spiritualism), and to Signor Rondi, whom I believe to have been sincerely sorry for what he was induced to do against me in America, overcome, as I believe he was, by Dr. Mack or other

---

[1] I found, upon inquiry, that Mrs. Nichols received this lock of hair, two miles distant, just after she had broken her thigh, and while the surgeon was setting it.

machinations. Signor Rondi wrote me a long letter, which was brought to me by "Ernest." My reply was taken to him in the same way, and received in the presence of Mr. Eglinton. I am sorry for his fault, and believe that he is sorry also.

The manner in which Mr. Eglinton received one of my missives was curious. He was going along the Holborn Viaduct in an omnibus, when a spirit-voice directed him to alight, and go to some quiet room. He stopped the omnibus, and went into the great hotel of Spiers and Ponds, and into a vacant room, where, feeling something touch his thigh, he put down his hand, and found a letter which had just been written by me in my cell in prison. This is his account of the matter related to me and to others.

I have been asked how I could reconcile it to my conscience to write letters to friends in England, America, and India, when I knew that it was against the rules of the prison to write at all, except at certain appointed times and under supervision.

I answer that it takes two to make a bargain. I was unjustly convicted, unjustly imprisoned. It was brute force alone that placed and kept me in prison. I violated no compact, for I made none. My liberty had been taken from me wrongfully, and all my rights trampled upon. I think, therefore, that I had a perfect right to avail myself of every amelioration of the outrage inflicted upon me which mortals or spirits could offer me.

And why, it may be asked, did not the spirits who did so much for you do more? Why did they not take you out of prison, instead of taking letters, and locks of hair?

The reason they did not was because I would not give my consent. They believed they could do it, and wished to make the attempt. The power of spirits over matter depends upon conditions. Spirits are not infallible or omnipotent. When conditions are favorable, they can do very wonderful things. Close by this prison, in Ashley Place, according to the testimony of the Earl of Balcarres (then Lord Lindsay) and the Earl of Dunraven (then Lord Adare), Mr. D. D. Home was carried out of one window, and brought in at another, floating in the air in a horizontal position, about seventy feet from the pavement. I do not doubt that I could have been taken from my cell over the wall about thirty feet high that encompasses the prison.

A time was appointed to do it. One of my friends was directed to wait for me at a particular place outside the wall, and waited there an hour. The spirit "Ernest" came and unlocked my cell, and wished to take me. I refused to go.

The reason why I refused, under the influence, I believe, of the wisest of my spirit-friends, was this.

My warder and other prison officers would have got into serious trouble. Warders and porters would have been discharged, and perhaps punished. They would have.lost their pensions, and the public would have believed that they had been bribed to assist me to escape. I should have been arrested, or rather I should have gone at once to the home office, and given myself up. I came voluntarily to England to be tried, and I should not have run away from any punishment the "law" thought proper to inflict. I did not come to England to run away again, nor go to prison in order to escape. For all these reasons, when "Ernest" unlocked my cell, and offered to take me bodily over the walls, I refused to be taken. To go ever so far in spirit, leaving my poor body in my cell, did no harm to any one. There is no prison for the soul.

My friend outside wanted the manifestation for the good he thought it would do to Spiritualism. Yes, if any one but a Spiritualist could have believed it. Probably my friends in and out of the prison would have been prosecuted for aiding my escape, and I should have been condemned to a longer and more severe imprisonment. It was better to quietly stay out my time, and do my appointed work. If I had got out of England, I could not have returned. Believing that I had a work to do in England for Spiritualism, and also for prisoners of every grade, I declined to accept freedom at the price of perpetual banishment from a country, which, in spite of much injustice, I still love, and still desire to serve ; for England, no American of the English race can forget, is the country of our ancestors. Her history is our history ; and I, who have seen and felt her hardest, roughest side, can still say with her patriotic poet, —

"England, with all thy faults I love thee still."

CHAPTER XLII

RELEASE OF A PRISONER. — CELEBRATING A BIRTHDAY.

THERE was little chance to get acquainted with my
fellow-prisoners. I could see them at exercise, and
a portion of them every day at chapel; but we were
supposed never to speak to each other. Locked in our
cells, a separate cell for each prisoner, in utter solitude
and silence for twenty-three hours out of every twenty-
four, what chance had we to get acquainted?

None, it seemed to me, for any good; some for evil.
A drunken old creature who had been in prison twenty,
fifty, in some cases more than a hundred, times, could
manage to get beside a girl of fifteen at exercise or in
chapel, and further corrupt her, and arrange for future
meetings.

The prisoners were not all drunken or bad. Our
chaplain, who knew his flock as no other person could
know it, believed that many were " more sinned against
than sinning," and that in many cases of apparent
crime there was no moral guilt. A poor working-
woman, for example, with a drunken husband and hun-

gry children, is tempted to pledge some garment she is making to get bread, and then is not able to redeem it, because her husband spends his wages at the public-house. Under these circumstances she is sent for two or three months to prison. It was an irregularity, an indiscretion, but not intentionally a crime.

We had one poor woman, sixty years old, who had been sentenced to nine months' imprisonment, whom I could not look upon as a criminal. Her quiet behavior, her good temper, and kindness to everybody with whom she came in contact, made her respected and liked.

One day she had a stroke of paralysis, and was taken to the " sick-cells." In a fortnight she came back to her old quarters, considered cured; but we who knew her did not think her well. A fortnight later she was failing visibly, and one afternoon she was taken again to the infirmary. The next day she died. I afterwards heard that the coroner received notice, according to the regulations. A jury was summoned from the neighboring public-houses. The testimony of the physician was given, and, in accordance with it, a verdict of " death from old age " — old age at sixty! We who had watched her knew that she had died from the exhaustion of grief, cold, and an insufficient and inappropriate diet.

[I had for three months been unable to eat brown bread before I was given white, notwithstanding my warder had taken my untasted bread, and reported my case several times to the doctor.]

On the day she died, she was asked if she had any relations or friends she wished to see.

"Oh, dear!" she said, "I *should* like to see my daughter so much; but she is a widow with five little children to take care of. It was trying to get money to pay for her husband's funeral that brought me here. She lives at Norwood. She can't walk so far, and she is too poor to come by rail: so don't send for her."

So, for lack of half a crown or less, the poor woman died without seeing one soul she knew. They asked her what name she would be buried under.

"The name I gave when I came here," she said, "is a false one, but use that. God knows who I am, and it won't matter to anybody else."

Refusing to give her correct name seemed to me a sublime thoughtfulness for the feelings of others, worthy of a higher station and a better fate. Her death made a deep impression on me; and, though she had never spoken to me, I was very sorry for her.

On the night she died I was indeed greatly distressed; and, instead of going to bed at the usual time, I lay my head on my stool, and thought that this poor old prisoner was somebody's mother, and yet that the Christian world, the philanthropic world, the tenderhearted world all about me, was just as merry as if no such tragedies were ever enacted.

While I sat having a little cry all to myself, I heard the cheerful voice of my friend " Joey " saying, " Mrs. Fletcher, how do you do? Rouse up, rouse up! We have brought Willie to see you."

Of course I " roused up ; " and, sure enough, there stood Willie Eglinton — to all appearance the real, living, tangible Willie — in my locked cell. He held out his hand to me, and I grasped it, as solid and real as ever was his own ; and he said, " Well, Bertie, I went to bed and tried to go to sleep ; but I couldn't get you out of my mind. Everybody else has been having letters, and I don't see why I should not have one : so I have come to get it myself."

I smiled, and asked, " Why do you want a letter, now you have got me ? "

He said, " They are talking in Calcutta [where he was at this time] about the ' Mystic Brotherhood ; ' and ' Ernest ' has told me that they are not the only brothers in their doings, but that the power by which their miracles are done is more common than is supposed ; and he wished me to make this experiment of coming to you, and here I am."

" Well, I am sincerely glad to see you. If you want a letter, shall I write it now? "

" Yes, please. I want to take it back with me ; and

to assure myself that I really came for it, and that 'Ernest' did not bring it, I am going to put it in a particular place when I get back, where I shall be obliged to go and get it after I have re-entered my body.''

As I chanced to have the means of writing by me, I wrote a little note, and gave it to him, as he desired. He departed; and, an instant after, "Ernest" appeared. He said, "It was not alone to give Willie this experience of a marvellous phenomenon that we brought him here, but it was more to get strength, and give assistance to the poor, unhappy spirit whose departure has so much grieved you.''

At another time, in October, on the occasion of my husband's birthday, my spirit-friends brought a piece of cake and a glass of wine into my cell, which they wished me to take for the nourishment it would give me, and in honor of the occasion. My teetotal friends will object to the wine; but, as it had probably been dematerialized before crossing the Atlantic, the alcohol may have been left out of the subsequent materialization. It was given me in a glass with a broken stem. When "Winona" brought it to me, she said, "Mr. Fletcher wished this to be brought to you.''

" In a broken wineglass? " I asked.

" Oh, that was an accident! " said "Winona;" " but the wine was magnetized, and we could not wait to get another glass.''

The matter was more fully explained in a subsequent letter from my husband. He wrote : —

" My birthday, as you can well imagine, was not the bright, happy little affair it used to be; and I think that at no time in your whole tiresome imprisonment have I missed you more than I have to-day. I have received many gifts; many have called to wish me 'happy returns;' but your head resting on my shoulder, and your eyes looking into mine, would have been of infinite comfort to me. So at night, after every one had departed, I sat down to have a little cake and wine with you. It may have been a foolish fancy; but I thought that somehow, if I broke the cake, and filled the glass, for your dear sake, you might be able to know of my remembrance of you. So I left the cake and the glass of wine on the table when I went to bed. In the morning they had disappeared.

" If the servants or any one had been in the room, I should have believed that human hands had removed them; but I carefully locked the door, and am quite certain that no one entered the room until I did. And now comes the strangest part of the matter. The night after, just as I was going to sleep, I felt something cold against my face, and heard 'Winona' say, 'Don't be cross. I have taken Bertie the wine; but I broke the glass, and have brought back only the top of it.' And, surely enough, on striking a light, I found, so far as I can judge, the wineglass that was missing, but in a mutilated and cherubic condition."

It was well for me, perhaps, that " Winona " took back the glass, though one cannot see the need of taking it such a distance. It might have been dropped

just over the wall.   I had wondered what I could do
with it, and rolled it up in my bedclothes.   At night
I put it under my pillow.   The next morning it was
gone.   How it came to be broken was never explained
to us.[1]

[1] As there are differences of opinion, even among Spiritualists, respecting these manifestations, I add the following testimony : —

Taking solid objects into or out of a tightly closed room is a common
manifestation, which has been witnessed by hundreds, and perhaps by thousands.   The late Sergeant Cox told me, that sitting with Mrs. Guppy in his
library, with every door and window securely fastened, great masses of
flowers — " a cartload," as he expressed it — had been poured upon the table.
I have often seen such things on a smaller scale.   On two occasions I have
seen a materialized spirit eat cake, and drink wine.   Once at my own house
in Malvern, " Joey," presiding at a birthday festival, sat at a round table in
the centre of the room, in a good light, talking with us, and cut a birthday-
cake, and poured out glasses of wine, which he brought to each person in the
room.   He then, in sight of all, cut a good slice of cake for himself, and ate
it, and then, pouring out a glass of wine, gave and drank " the toast of the
evening," — " long life, health and happiness " to his hostess, adding, " God
bless you, and give you strength to do your work!"   Mr. Eglinton, who
resided with us for some years at Malvern, was the medium.

The other occasion was at a *séance* at the studio of Signor Rondi in Montague Place, London, at which Miss Katie Cook was medium.   The spirit
" Lily," whom I have seen, heard, and felt several times, there and elsewhere, perfectly satisfying myself of her distinct personality, near the close
of the *séance* said, " Rondi, I want some cake and wine." — " Very well,
' Lily :' there is some in my cupboard.   You have only to go and get it." —
" No, Rondi, you must get it for me," said she ; and he went and got her a
glass of wine and some thin sweet biscuits.   She came quite near me, drank
the wine, bit off a piece of one of the biscuits, and handed me the remainder.
" Lily " allowed me to examine her hands, arms, and feet by touch as well
as by sight, to feel her pulse, to place my hands upon her and her medium
at the same time ; and I have her photograph taken by daylight.   Whatever

frauds there may have been in respect to pretended materializations, I have had with five or six mediums, and as to twelve or more spirits, the most absolute proofs of reality, distinct personality, and, as far as possible, of identity. I can as well doubt my own existence as that I have seen, heard, and felt the materialized forms of those whom I once knew in this world, and of others with whom I have become acquainted only as spirits. I hope to be able to give before long a full and circumstantial account of these experiences. — T. L. NICHOLS, M.D.

CHAPTER XLIII.

The first impulse of my friends in America and in England was to appeal to the home secretary, the dispenser of the pardoning-power of the crown, as well as the punishing-power, to release me from prison. Various Spiritualist societies sent resolutions of confidence and sympathy, and memorials or petitions, for which I wish to express my gratitude. But I had at no time the least hope in the success of any effort for my release. Such efforts interested me only as expressions of personal friendship and confidence.

The memorial presented to the home secretary by Dr. Nichols, which he also printed, and somewhat widely circulated, which was also reprinted by a lady-friend, was useful in presenting many new facts to its readers, and in giving some of the suppressed evidence, especially the important affidavits of Capt. Lindmark and Mr. Morton.

The reasons why no memorial, and no amount of proof of the perjuries of the chief witness, could be of any avail with the home secretary, are not far to seek. His subordinates had taken up the prosecution because it was a sensational case, in which the press and the public were greatly interested. The chief of a department, as a rule, sustains the action of his subordinates. The government itself believed me guilty, and had determined to punish me.

The only possible way to get Sir William Harcourt, acting for her Majesty the Queen, to grant me a pardon, was to convince him of the reality of Spiritualism; but I do not expect an avowal of such a belief, at present, from a home secretary, who perhaps aspires to the place of lord-chancellor, — from one who now exercises the pardoning power, and possibly hopes to become the conscience-keeper of the Queen.

The memorial had no effect upon the home secretary: elsewhere it did its work. In the preface to the printed edition, Dr. Nichols said, —

"I propose.to send copies to the witnesses who have volunteered their testimony; to friends of Mrs. Fletcher, in England and America, who in this relentless persecution, and failure of justice, have had entire faith in her innocence; to Spiritualist societies, for the information of their members; to a few liberal members of Parliament, who may see the need of changes in the law, under which the most honest man or woman may be punished as a rogue and vagabond; and to the conductors of public journals, who, in entire ignorance of the facts of the case, took the opportunity to denounce a woman in prison, because she was a Spiritualist, as they would not have done had she been undoubtedly guilty of murder.

"I have taken this perhaps unusual course, because this is an unusual case. The articles in hundreds of newspapers, echoing the charge and sentence, showed how deep, violent, unreasoning, and vindictive is the prejudice against Spiritualism. There was absolutely no proof against Mrs. Fletcher of false pretences. The fact that she was a Spiritualist was enough for the court, the jury, and the press.

"It is, therefore, not enough that the proofs of the innocence of Mrs. Fletcher should be laid before her Majesty's Secretary of State for the Home Department, so that she may be released from prison. It is right that all who have unjustly condemned her should know the real facts of this 'extraordinary' case, and see how easy it is — now, as in past ages, under prejudice and excitement — to use the forms of law to perpetrate cruel wrongs.

"Hear the other side. Read the testimony of Capt. Lindmark, of Mr. Morton, of the other witnesses to facts and to character. Consider, that, among the millions who believe in the reality of spiritual phenomena, there are men and women as intelligent and veracious as among those who doubt or deny it, and that those who testify to the truth of Spiritualism have examined the facts, while those who deny it have refused to examine, and, as in this case, have condemned without a hearing.

"I have been an investigator and a witness of the phenomena called spiritualistic for more than twenty-five years. I am neither a knave nor a fool. I know what I have seen and heard and felt, as I know any other fact in nature. The man who does not know a fact, who has neglected or refused to examine it, has no right to dispute it, or to condemn one who knows it to be true, or believes it upon proper testimony.

"It is the intolerance of ignorance that is the basis of persecution, and has caused the failure of justice in this one of many cases where people are wrongly condemned by public opinion, or in courts of law.

"I ask for simple justice to all Spiritualists, and only for justice to my friend Mrs. Fletcher."

The memorial contains many of the facts I have already related, and was accompanied by the proper testimony. A few paragraphs of the body of the memorial are printed in the Appendix.

The testimony appended to this memorial seemed to me abundant and conclusive. I give the home secretary the credit of never having read one line of it. He was very busy about this time making political speeches, and was nicknamed by " Punch " the " Never-at-home-Secretary." It would have been a pity to deprive great popular assemblies of the benefit of listening to his eloquence; but it seemed to me that it might also be a pity that prisoners unjustly sentenced to penal servitude or the gallows should not have some one to read their memorials or petitions.

With the testimony in the memorial should have been included the following affidavit of James McGeary, *alias* Dr. Mack, who took so prominent a part, as nearest friend of Mrs. Hart-Davies, in my prosecution in America and England; but it came to me too late to be so included.

My friend and former legal adviser, John W. Mahan, Esq., of Boston, wrote to me, under date of Nov. 12, 1881, the following letter : —

DEAR MRS. FLETCHER, — I am informed by your husband that I can send a letter to you by the steamer that leaves on the 15th, and eagerly seize the opportunity to assure you that the cordial greeting you will receive from your friends in America, when once more you are free, will go far to compensate you for all you have suffered in a foreign land.

You know that I am not a believer in Spiritualism, though I must fairly admit that I cannot account for the wonderful phenomena which have convinced so many of its truth; and I can understand the feelings of the opponents of Spiritualism in England: but had the jury that tried you, the judge that sentenced you, the solicitor of the crown who aided in your prosecution, known your real character and that of your friends in America, — had they known how foreign to you was any deceit, how pure, devoted, unselfish, and courageous you are, they could never have sent you to a prison.

I write specially to tell you that Mack (McGeary) has returned to England. He said he was going there to show Madame Hart-Davies to the public in her true character, if she failed to pay him what she owed him.

He signed a statement, which I drew up for him at his dictation, to this effect; viz., that Madame Davies admitted to him that she had testified falsely at your trial in several particulars; that she had committed larceny of articles belonging to you and Mr. Fletcher; and he named a sealskin jacket, a lace shawl, and an overcoat lined with fur, among the articles she had abstracted from your house in London. He said he was ready to go before the home secretary and state these matters under oath, and stated that he had learned her ingratitude, baseness, and utter want of principle, since your trial.

The fact is, Mack and Madame Davies conspired together, the conspirators quarrelled, and now each is calling the other all the vile names to which both are fairly entitled. The truth will be known in the end: but in the mean time you, poor martyr, you are suffering; but the days are passing, and I feel as though your release must come soon. The English people and the English authorities have recently shown some appreciation of America and Americans. If the home secretary will listen to the prayers of thousands of your friends in this country, he will before Christmas allow you to go free, and return to them and your family before another year is ushered in. Until I can hear from or see you, believe me your friend, as I was your counsel. I advised you not to go to England; but you said your honor was at stake, and you did not heed my counsel.

I remain as ever yours,

JOHN W. MAHAN.

The following is the affidavit of James McGeary, *alias* Dr. Mack : —

"I, James McGeary of Salem, in the State of Massachusetts, United States of America, but now temporarily residing in London, Kingdom of Great Britain and Ireland, depose and say as follows: —

"That I acted in perfect good faith toward Madame Hart-Davies (as known and called) both in America and England, as I believed at the outset that she had been injured by Mr. and Mrs. J. W. Fletcher. But during and after the trial of

Mrs. Fletcher I had occasion to consult with Madame Davies; and she admitted to me that she had sworn falsely as to certain facts, while on the witness-stand, in the indictment against Mrs. Fletcher. Mrs. Davies also admitted that she had taken property from the house of Mr. Fletcher in London that belonged to Mr. and Mrs. Fletcher, and declared her intention to keep the same.

"In other respects I learned the true character of Mrs. Hart-Davies, and for this reason I believe that Mrs. Fletcher ought not to suffer further imprisonment. I hereby signify my willingness to appear before the home secretary at any time; and I will then detail some facts of importance, so far as I can judge, bearing upon the question of Mrs. Fletcher's guilt or innocence. I further depose that these facts relate to acts of Mrs. Hart-Davies; and I can satisfy any unprejudiced mind that she is unworthy of belief, that she has committed perjury and larceny, and is utterly incapable of returning friendship, but, on the contrary, is deceitful, and ready to return, for friendly acts rendered to her, falsehood and slander."

Dr. Mack, since his latest return to England, made similar declarations to a friend of mine.

After my conviction, a summons was granted at Bow Street against Mrs. Hart-Davies for perjuries committed in her testimony at the trial; but, as she went to France on the close of the trial, it could not be served. A warrant for her arrest was applied for and granted. The charges of repeated perjuries made by Capt. Lindmark, Mr. Morton, Miss Gay, and others, as well as by her friend and co-conspirator McGeary,

are on record against her. It is just that they should
be known for my vindication. And my first duty, after
my health is sufficiently restored, will be to place these
records before the proper officials, and await the result.

CHAPTER XLIV.

A PLEA FOR PRISON-REFORM.

As the gloomy days and long nights of an English winter wore away in the cold and darkness of solitary confinement in dreary cells, — in that cheerless monotony contrasting with the gayeties of Christmas firesides and Christmas festivities outside, — it is not strange that my health broke down. The cold, the darkness, the horrible character of all my surroundings, the hopeless condition of the constantly changing swarm of bloated, drunken, miserable women, sent to prison for short terms, only to become each time more hardened and depraved, weighed heavily upon my heart. Under such a system nothing could be done for them. If the chaplains could make any impression upon them when they got sober, the moment they got outside the walls, it was drowned in drunken riot. The only hope was in longer sentences, which would not pay the officials as well; but those the magistrates could not or would not give: and what was the good of long sentences in such a place, or under such a system? Cold, darkness, silence, solitude, and the repression of brute force, are not curative, or reformatory, or humanizing influences. They disease the body, and depress, stupefy, and debase the mind. Their tendency is to fill it with gloom, hatred, and desperation. A woman ignorantly, carelessly, yields to the temptations that society and the government itself place around her; owing to badly paid labor and a wretched home, a young girl goes to the music-hall, the public-house, and the brothel; drink quiets remorse and shame; more drink leads to reckless abandonment and disorderly conduct, the police-court, and the prison. The State receives the victims of its own established institutions, — the houses of ill-fame which it tolerates, and the houses of drunkenness it licenses, and from which it draws millions of revenue.

In the absence of any proper classification and separation of prisoners, there can be no reformation. The discipline of the prison is not reformatory. I think it ought to be changed in almost every particular.

What would I have? Above all, the conditions of health, — plenty of light, pure air, pure water, pure, healthy food, sufficient exercise, attractive industry, and humanizing influences.

First of all, there should be perfect cleanliness. It is half the battle to make people clean in their persons, clothing, and surroundings. Plenty of soap and water.

Every prisoner should have a good daily bath. The best arrangement for such a number would probably be a warm shower-bath, into which each one could step for one or two minutes. The spray of warm water, about 100° or 110° F., should end with a momentary dash of cold, to leave the skin in good condition ; then a hard towel, the rougher the better, each bather bringing her own.

Personal and bed clothing should be sufficient for comfort, that is, for health, and always clean, and never inherited, unchanged, as now, by one prisoner from another.

Taken in relays to a model laundry, every prisoner should in turn be taught how to wash ; and in a model kitchen, suited to the preparation of plain, healthy food, every prisoner should be taught how to cook. As books are allowed in all the cells, why not pictures upon the walls, and why not a pot of flowers, adding beauty to cleanliness? I would make a prison for women clean, healthful, womanly, a model home, a model sanitarium for body and for soul. And no short sentences after the first. A prison should be a reformatory school, and for reformation time is a necessary element. Reform is *cure*, and to cure a drunkard of the mania for drink needs at least a year. I hold that the State — that is, all of us — should do for all these poor women — victims of social conditions and institutions, victims of what men do, and neglect to do — what I would do for my sister or my child if she fell into such misfortunes.

Drunkenness and crime are the results of social conditions and hereditary predispositions. Punishments do not deter nor prevent. When people were hanged for theft, it did not prevent stealing. When men and women were hanged in rows in the Old Bailey for passing counterfeit money, it was no perceptible check upon the crime. The Bank of England stopped it by issuing no notes under five pounds, and making these very difficult to counterfeit.

Two great reforms are needed in England.

1. A law reform by means of which innocent persons shall not be unjustly condemned to prison, to penal servitude, nor to the gallows; a better court of criminal appeal than can be hoped for in an overworked home secretary; and a public prosecutor for defendant as well as for plaintiff.

2. A prison reform by means of which those who are justly convicted may have some chance of physical and moral improvement.

It is a comfort to me to think that my trial and imprisonment may have some good effect in promoting both of these much needed reformations. At least, I shall do what I can to beg others to do what they can for the unfortunate and even for the criminal.

CHAPTER XLV.

THE days, weeks, months, wore slowly away. I counted the weeks, days, hours, between me and liberty. My husband could not come to receive me at the prison-gate. He would have been arrested, arraigned, and, without further trial, sentenced, no doubt to penal servitude, on the verdict recorded both against him and my friend Mr. Morton. It would have been a simple formality, without protest or appeal. But there was one who could safely come, my dear boy, Alvah, now in his seventeenth year. My term of imprisonment was to expire on Monday, the 17th of March. The steamer which brought my boy arrived on Sunday.

By applying to the lady-superintendent, I was allowed to leave the prison at half-past nine o'clock A.M., instead of ten, the hour when others would be liberated. For the first time in so many months, I put on *my own clothes*, which, with such things as I happened to have, had been carefully kept for me. I stepped into the little court enclosed by the great iron gates at the

407

entrance, and clasped my boy in my arms, and felt his
hot tears raining on my cheeks; then came the grasp
of the friendly hands of friends, who had come in car-
riages to welcome me to liberty. The morning was
perfectly lovely, and the route from Westminster to
my friend's house in South Kensington lay through
paradise. None but those who have been immured for
months in a gloomy prison can ever know the ecstasy
of freedom. The sensation goes far towards compen-
sating for the deprivation.

Breakfast and friends, cables from my husband,
awaited me at Dr. Nichols's; and there I found a true
home while I remained in England. My friend Mr.
Mengens, who had come from Calcutta, gave me the
refreshment of a week's visit to his family in Brighton;
and as many of my London friends as I was able to
receive called to see me. Others left cards, or wrote.
I was so weak after the first ecstasy, that I could not
see many. And I had my work to do. Every morning, from six o'clock to nine, I worked upon this story
of my life, and my recent experiences, which I wished
to record while fresh in my memory.

In leaving the prison, I had to thank the senior
warder for many civilities, my chaplain for unvarying kindness, the doctor for professional and friendly
care. They were all as good to me as their duties and
the regulations of the prison would permit them to be.

There were some in humble positions whom I wish I could reward as they deserve. Their woman-hearts were full of sympathy. In strict accordance with their instructions they treated me with all the kindness their rules would allow, and with such civility as one would scarcely look for in such a place. To show how warm are the hearts of those whom one might expect to be hardened into heartlessness by such duties, let me give a portion of a letter I received soon after my release, from a woman-warder who cared for me : —

"MY DEAR DARLING BABY, — If I may still call you so, — and I think you will let me, for indeed you are very dear to me, — you don't know how miserable and unhappy I feel, now you are gone. It is not like the same place. It was very bad, but now it is much worse. As I am passing that old cell, I look in. It is empty — no one there. Then I don't know what to do with myself. Oh, *do* forgive me! I ought not to remind you of this dreadful place, but I do miss you so much! I hope you will keep well. Let me beg of you to take care of your-self.

"I was so pleased to see your dear, dear boy; and I love him so much! He has your dear old face, bless him! . . . With fondest love, yours ever."

It is needless to add, that a warder like this did not remain long in the service. ,

With such hearts as the one which dictated that letter, what could not be done for poor women, under

proper conditions and regulation! As to the greater
number of those who are sent to prison, the following
paragraph from a London newspaper, which came under
my eye as I was copying the above letter, gives a sufficient description : —

"WORSHIP-STREET. — A SAD CASE. — *Lucy Brent*, an
'unfortunate,' about thirty years of age, was charged with
being drunk, and refusing to quit the George and Guy public-
house when requested; further, with wilfully breaking a square
of plate-glass, value five pounds.   The prisoner is well known
in the court; and the convictions recorded against her number
nearly a hundred, dating from 1868.   When she first appeared
before the magistrate, she was not eighteen years of age, and
was exceedingly pretty.   She was then charged with drunkenness in the street; and, when she told her history, Mr. Newton
induced her to enter a home for fallen women, under the protection of Miss Stride.   The prisoner, however, soon left the
home, and ever since has refused to listen to any advice.   She
now lives, when not in prison, in the lowest dens of Spitalfields, and on this occasion appeared in the dock with a fearful contusion of one eye, and looking fifty years of age.   She
is a woman of fair education, but whether respectably connected, she would never tell.   She has never been convicted of
felony.   Mr. Bushby said there was nothing for it but to send
her to prison, and ordered her to be kept in jail for two months
with hard labor."

Of course Lucy Brent was sent to Tothill Fields
Prison, where she may have had the good fortune to

fall under the guardianship of the writer of the above letter. But at the end of the two months? The lowest den in Spitalfields again, and then another conviction and sentence.

Surely men who can vote and legislate might do something better than that for their victims. If they really cannot, then let us women try. We could not do worse.

CHAPTER XLVI.

AT LIBERTY IN LONDON. — A FAREWELL SÉANCE, AND
A FAREWELL TO ENGLAND.

I HAVE desired my friend Dr. Nichols, who stood
by me from first to last, to write some account of
our experiences during the weeks I spent in London,
gathering strength for the voyage to America. Especially I wished to have his account of the farewell
séance, attended by some of my friends of both worlds ;
and this last and farewell chapter cannot, perhaps, end
better than with my farewell to England.

" In compliance with the request of my friend Mrs.
Fletcher, for whom I have done what I could do in the
way of friendly service, I will give some account of
her and our experiences before she left us to visit her
family and friends in America, soon to return, we
trust, and complete the work in England, for which
she has had such preparation.

" She came from her Majesty's Prison, Westminster,
with the friends who went to welcome her to liberty,

412

on the morning of March 27, 1882, very cheerful, very happy to meet her friends, especially her good and loving boy, and happy in her freedom as no one can be who has not been in bonds.

"It was evident that her health had suffered. She had lost from forty to fifty pounds in weight, and was often in pain; but the air of freedom was a fine stimulant, and she was radiant and buoyant. After spending a few days with some friends at Brighton, to try the tonic effects of sea-air, she returned to us, and spent her mornings upon the story of her life and its early and recent trials. The triumphs will be, I hope, recorded in a later volume.

"Among those who joined with us in welcoming Mrs. Fletcher to her new-found freedom was Mr. I. E. Mengens, a merchant of Calcutta, who had there received the letters written by her in her cell at Westminster, on the day they were written. Mr. William Eglinton, the medium who had been with Mr. Mengens in Calcutta, and was apparently 'the operator at the other end of the line,' had followed him to London, and was one of our guests. Mr. S——, a New-York lawyer now residing in Paris, had also joined us.

"On Saturday, the 29th of April, 1882, we formed a circle of six persons, — rather the spirits formed it, or re-arranged it so as to place Mr. Eglinton between Mrs. Fletcher and Mrs. Nichols. At a signal the gaslight was turned off, when we saw carried around the table, so as to be read by each one in turn, a message written in letters of pure white light. It was in four or five lines, in a space of about six inches by four, announcing the presence of a spirit-friend of Mr. S——. The vivid metallic lustre of the light shone on the faces of those who read the inscription. When it had gone round the circle, it suddenly vanished.

"Then came our old friend, the spirit 'Ernest,' who gravely saluted Mrs. Fletcher, and all of us in turn. It was the first time some of us had heard him since Mr. Eglinton went to India. Then 'Joey' came, and joyfully addressed us all, and loudly kissed Mrs. Fletcher; then, like a big boy, he wound up the musical box and set it going, because, as he said, he had not heard one for so long a time. Our dear daughter Willie came, and made signal touches upon the hands and foreheads of her mother and Mrs. Fletcher, and on mine. Our spirit-friends joined with us in welcoming our friend to liberty.

"On the afternoon of Sunday, April 30, we made the acquaintance of 'Dewdrop,' professedly the spirit of an Indian-girl who speaks through Mrs. Fletcher when she is in a deep trance. She talked with us for an hour with wonderful vivacity, giving continual tests in remembering persons, facts, and verbal expressions. No one, I think, can listen to or converse with this spirit without believing in her personality, or crediting her medium with very marvellous powers. As one hypothesis is as ' supernatural ' as the other, I prefer to believe the spirit's declaration that she is a spirit. She is the only witness, and I do not see how her testimony is to be impeached.

" On Tuesday, May 2, I accompanied Mrs. Fletcher to the Bedford Pantechnicon, and saw her examine a great mass of property which had been removed from her house, 22 Gordon Street, in her absence, by Mrs. Hart-Davies. Mrs. Fletcher claimed a great number of articles of clothing, jewelry, etc., as her own ; and I saw taken from one of the boxes a packet of letters addressed to Mr. and Mrs. Fletcher. On the examination at Bow Street, and at the trial at the Old Bailey, Mrs. Hart-Davies swore that she had taken no such papers.

" On the night of the 15th of May, 1882, we had our farewell *séance* with Mrs. Fletcher before she went to America. The persons present were Mrs. Fletcher, Mrs. Bower, Mrs. Nichols, Miss Western, Mr. W. Eglinton, Signor Damiani, Mr. S—— (the gentleman before mentioned), Mr. Mengens, and myself. We all sat round a table ; and by signal raps answering to our questions, the spirits, or rapping intelligences, re-arranged us, and the room was completely darkened.

" The first manifestation after this re-arrangement

was a very curious one. A large repeater watch was taken from Mr. S——'s pocket, and carried about the table by the spirit of his brother, as he believed, to whom he had given it, and from whom he inherited it as a keepsake. Several times it was made to strike the hour and quarters from different parts of the table. Mrs. Fletcher's bracelet was taken from her arm, and placed upon that of Mr. S——. All present said they were touched by hands or fingers. Mr. Eglinton was raised bodily so high in the air that the two ladies holding his hands were obliged to stand on their chairs to keep hold of him, while his feet came across the table, and rested for a moment, one on my head, and the other on the head of the lady who sat beside me; so that his body must have been in a sloping position from three to six feet above the table.

" Mrs. Fletcher was then controlled by a very noble, pure, and eloquent spirit known to us as 'Violet.' I express, of course, our belief that she was so controlled. However that may be, I testify that a more beautiful and more eloquent discourse I have never listened to in my life than that in which we were thanked for our fidelity to the medium through her trial and imprisonment. I have a high opinion of Mrs. Fletcher as a woman of ability and genius. She has admirable qualities of intellect and heart; but I am unable to believe that she could of herself have given us the beautifully refined, elevated, and perfect discourse to which we listened in rapt attention. I have heard, I believe, some of the best speakers and actors in the world, some of the best normal and trance speakers, but have never listened to a more perfectly beautiful address than was given by or through Mrs. Fletcher at her farewell *séance*.

" Then followed the most wonderfully beautiful manifestation of the kind I have ever seen. People denounce dark *séances;* but how are we to have the marvellous phenomena of spirit-lights, with gas or candles burning? On this occasion Mr. Eglinton the medium passed round outside the circle, bearing a cross of light about fifteen inches high, — a light indescribably pure and beautiful, like the light of the planet Jupiter. Across the shorter arm of the Latin cross, in beautifully formed capital letters, was the word ' *FAITH.*' The spirit ' Ernest,' in his own direct voice, then spoke to us all, and to each in turn, thanking us for what had been to all of us a ' labor of love ; ' and ' Joey ' did the same, with his own humor and pathos ; and both said good-by to ' Bertie,' and both tenderly kissed her. ' Joey ' was very affectionate in his farewells, and he never says ' goodnight ' to his medium without kissing him two or three times.

" On the 17th of May our friend went with her son

to Liverpool, and sailed next day on the ' Celtic,' of
the White Star Line, for New York, where she was
met by her husband, and welcomed, there and in Philadelphia, by crowds of friends, with a generous enthusi-
asm. When her present work in America is done, we
expect her to come and do what there is for her to do
in England.

"T. L. NICHOLS."

The above statement of Dr. Nichols is accurate, so
far as I can remember. I give it as he has written it;
because, for what he considers worthy of his eulogy, I
am in no way responsible.

And now, dear reader, let me try to answer your
last question as to this book, — *Cui bono?* For what
purpose has it been written? What results do I anticipate?

From first to last it has been my all-absorbing desire
to serve, in every way within my power, the cause of
Spiritualism, — the cause which I espoused so many
years ago, — the cause to which my husband is giving
the best years of his life, — the cause, which, I believe,
is destined, sooner than its advocates imagine, to be a
comfort and service to all who know its phenomena,
and believe in its philosophy.

No one who is unprejudiced can read the report of

my trial without seeing that the difficulty between Mrs. Hart-Davies and myself might have been settled quietly between us at an afternoon tea, had she been disposed. And, if she had been guided by high-minded and well-meaning advisers, who can doubt that this simple and natural course would have been followed? But she preferred to seize the rare opportunity to cast a shadow upon Spiritualism in order to gratify personal revenge.

Every form of religion or philosophy is more or less estimated by the character of its believers and exponents. However unjust this mode of judgment is, we cannot escape its influence. The question of my guilt or innocence should not have affected the moral status of Spiritualism; and yet we see, in the comments of the prosecuting attorney and of the newspaper press, that the question did have a widespread and most injurious influence. The sacred cause itself seemed, to the unbelieving public, to be on trial in my person. And yet I may state here, that from the time I first saw Mrs. Hart-Davies, until some time after the execution of that deed of gift, I never once gave, nor professed to give, her a spiritual *séance*. Her story of the walking coffee-table and the mechanical writing, like the greater part of her testimony, was a sheer fabrication. But if all her testimony be taken as true, when she stated, under oath, in January, 1881, that she had believed and still did believe in Spiritualism, and that she had received communications from her mother through the mediumship of Mr. Fletcher, then she swore, that, to the best of her knowledge, she was prosecuting innocent people.

In giving carefully both sides of this sad case, I have endeavored to show that all the sin and ignorance have been the fault or misfortune of individuals, and that Spiritualism has been an incidental matter, unjustly and maliciously introduced.

My *reputation* has a certain worldly value, and upon it I place due importance; but, as one's reputation is like stock in the hands of a broker with its par value, I have little power over it, and less concern. My *character* to-day differs only as it may have been enlarged and strengthened, or crushed and weakened, by the discipline of the last twelve months. But a sense of justice to my family and friends furnishes sufficient inducement to make the truth known. Out of my experience, so terrible in many ways, has come much good. I know the motives and character of the professing thousands, and the truth and fidelity of the friendly few, as nothing else could have revealed them: those of doubtful and weak natures were wavering in their friendship, while the really upright were strong and true. A literary woman, well known by her popular novels, who was notorious for having been a " natural " wife months before she was a legal one, questioned very much the propriety of recognizing me in the court-room, although she had been previously solicitous for invitations to my house, and had been received by me when nearly every door was closed against her.

Over some of these discoveries I felt like smiling: with others, I was not so inclined. I regretfully confess, that, had the advocates and some of the believers been the only vouchers for Spiritualism, I should then and there have withdrawn my adherence, and taken the first steamer for home. But knowing that the grander the feast, the greater the mob, these discoveries of human frailty only served to strengthen my fidelity.

My next, and surely not less important, desire will be to call attention to the prison system in England and America. Society, as a rule, is more thoughtless than wicked. To inform the indifferent is, in many instances, to convert them. The infinite bounty of nature rapidly increases population; but it does not seem to me, that, of all the millions, we have human beings to spare. Inside our prisons are to be found a considerable percentage of our brightest intellects; and so partisan and unjust has the administration of law become, that to be adjudged guilty is sometimes a compliment rather than a disgrace. Shall we accept as final the judgment of thirteen men, twelve of whom are no more fitted to weigh testimony than many of

our politicians are to hold office? A belief in an ever-
lasting hell as a fit punishment for sin is almost as
kind, and quite as intelligent, as is the lifelong ostra-
cism from the society of decent people for breaking a
statute-law.

Let our prisons be reformatories, hospitals, and
schools, and let the inmates who have paid the penalty
of the law be considered only as graduates from such
humane institutions. What a load will be lifted from
your heart and mine, dear reader, when we can feel
that we are no longer paying, through taxation, for the
torture and brutalization of so many of our blood!

It is laudable to seek the congenial society of those
whose lives are above reproach, but it is better far
to strive to ameliorate the condition of sinners than to
bask in the sunshine of saints.

APPENDICES.

APPENDIX I.

REPORT OF THE CROSS-EXAMINATION OF MRS.
HART-DAVIES BEFORE THE BOW-STREET MAGIS-
TRATE, MR. FLOWERS, WITH THE SUGGESTIONS
OF COUNSEL, ETC.

THE "Daily Telegraph's" report of the cross-examination
on the 10th of February is as follows:—

On the case coming on now, Mr. Lewis asked the learned
magistrate to look at the 17th section of Jarvis's Act.

Mr. Flowers, having done so, said, of course Mr. Lewis had
the right to cross-examine.

Mr. Lewis thought it was his imperative duty. They had
before them a lady who averred that she was in delicate health,
and who wished to go abroad. When the trial came on, it
might be said that she was too unwell to travel, and her deposi-
tion would go before the jury without the modifying effect of
the cross-examination. Such a state of things would place his
client in a very unpleasant situation.

Mr. Wontner suggested, that, if that was the only reason for
Mr. Lewis wishing to go on with the cross-examination, Mrs.
Hart-Davies' evidence was the case itself. Without her, no
true bill would probably be found by the grand jury.

Mr. Lewis still thought it to be his duty to cross-examine
the witness.

Mrs. Hart-Davies was now called, and accommodated with a seat in the witness-box. Cross-examined by Mr. Lewis, she said the letter produced was written from her aunt's residence.

What is her name? — Mrs. Sampson. She is aunt by adoption.

As a matter of fact, she is no relation to you? — No.

When your solicitor, Mr. Abrahams, opened the case, you were present? — Yes.

Did you hear him say that your mother was the sister of the late Mr. Sampson? — I believe so.

Is that statement true? — By adoption it is true.

What am I to understand by that? — I am unable to answer that question.

Now, Mrs. Hart-Davies, your answers will force me to ask you questions I don't wish to. Do you allege that there was any relationship between the late Mr. Sampson and your mother? — As a matter of fact, no.

Mr. Hart-Davies is your second husband, I think? — Yes.

What was the date of your marriage with him? — Jan. 22, 1876. My first husband's name was Ignatius Francis Rickard.

Did you call him Frank? — It might be so, sometimes.

Is he alive? — I believe so. I can't swear to the fact.

Did he obtain a divorce from you? — My family and he did. He presented a petition, and obtained a divorce. I certainly alleged that I did not commit adultery.

Do you mean to swear that you did not commit adultery?

Mr. Wontner objected to the question as being irrelevant.

Mr. Flowers said he did not like to stop the cross-examination unless he felt that it was merely to annoy the witness.

Mr. Lewis assured the magistrate that that was not his object. He merely wished to show the real object the witness had in parting with her property.

Mr. LEWIS (to witness). —Do you assert on your oath that you have not committed adultery?

Mr. Abrahams rose to address the magistrate.

Mr. Lewis objected to Mr. Abrahams addressing the magistrate, submitting that he had no *locus standi* in the case.

Mr. Wontner supported Mr. Lewis's objection; but Mr. Abrahams insisted that he had a right to be heard as a solicitor, watching the case on behalf of the prosecutrix. He asserted that he had a right to protect the lady, and to be heard. He was about to raise an objection, but

Mr. Lewis interrupted, and asked the magistrate to rule that the witness should answer the questions put to her.

Mr. LEWIS (to witness). —Do you allege that you did not commit adultery during your marriage with Mr. Rickard? — I allege nothing. I refuse to answer that question.

Mr. FLOWERS. —But I have understood you to say no? Witness. —Certainly.

Mr. LEWIS. — Pardon me. She has not said no. I repeat the question. —I refuse to answer it.

Mr. LEWIS. — Then I must ask you, sir, to compel her to answer.

Mr. FLOWERS. —I can't go so far as that. And to what does this lead? Supposing she has lived the life of a demon, how will that affect the case of Mrs. Fletcher?

Mr. LEWIS. —I am going to show the real reason for the transferring of this property. What was the name of the co-respondent? —I will not swear.

Mr. Wontner suggested that the file of proceedings would supply the information.

Mr. Flowers ruled that Mr. Lewis could not ask the question. He did not see how it could affect the case, and would only drag the name of some one not connected with it before the public. All this evidence seemed to him to show the immense power the prisoner had over this woman.

Mr. Lewis lamented to hear such an observation from the learned magistrate. He might at once say he intended to call a large number of witnesses to prove his case.

Mr. Flowers still ruled that the question concerning the name should not be put.

MR. LEWIS. — I observe, in writing to Mr. Fletcher, you address him as brother. Is that a Spiritual term ? — I used the term as any lady would who put her trust in a family as I did.

Mr. Lewis repeated the question. Witness. — My heart was too true to make any definition. The term was used in the sense of brother in faith and brother in fact.

When you say brother in faith, do you mean the common faith in Spiritualism ? — I don't understand your definition. I cannot comprehend you.

MR. FLOWERS. — Do I understand you to mean as an adopted brother ? — Yes.

MR. LEWIS. — Is Mr. Fletcher the only man you have addressed as brother who was not your brother by blood ? — I don't remember.

Mr. Lewis handed the witness a letter which commenced "Sweet Brother," and the witness admitted that she had written it.

In what sense did you use the words "sweet brother" ? — In the sense of a true friend.

In 1871, and down to March, 1872, were you living with Mr. Rickard ? — I was nearly always abroad. I don't remember.

Was your marriage subsisting in February, 1872 ? — As we were both alive, I suppose it was. I was abroad at the time. I was called his wife.

Mr. Wontner again asked whether it was competent for his

friend to enter into matters that occurred in the years 1871 or 1872.

Mr. Lewis handed the witness a letter, and asked her if it was written before, or after, the dissolution of her marriage.

Mr. Flowers looked at the letter, and expressed his surprise that it should be in the possession of the solicitor for the defence. But supposing the reading of this letter injured her moral status, and many expressions might be considered unwise, how could it affect the matter?

The witness stated that the letter had been written ten years ago, whereupon Mr. Flowers expressed his opinion that the cross-examination thereon was irrelevant.

Mr. Lewis said he had a number of letters and sketches, which, he ventured to say, if published, would bring the publisher within the provisions of the criminal law. Having quoted from Starkie on Evidence, to show how far the witness was bound to answer questions, he said he was afraid the time had now come when he should be bound to disclose the case for the defence. His case would be to show that the prosecutrix was a woman of no character, that she went into no society whatever, that she was entirely alone, without, so to speak, a friend in the world. It was alleged that she obtained an introduction into the Fletchers' house by stratagem. He (Mr. Lewis) would show that the Fletchers were visited by people of the highest social position, men distinguished in art and literature, and he submitted that it was of vital consequence to the prosecutrix to insinuate herself into such society. He would show that there was a perfect, good, and valid consideration for the gift of this property, and that it was really pressed and forced upon them. The deed of gift was prepared without the knowledge of the defendant; and, when it was submitted to her, she immediately referred it to her husband. It was only ultimately, upon express understanding and bargain that Mrs. Hart-Davies should be received into the house of the Fletchers free of expense, that this property was handed over. In order to establish the defence, he (Mr. Lewis) must show what the antecedents of the prosecutrix were.

Mr. Flowers decided not to admit the evidence of the letters; and Mr. Lewis then asked for an adjournment, during which he would consider whether he should apply for a mandamus to compel the magistrate to admit it.

After some discussion, this course was acceded to; next Saturday being fixed for the further hearing.

On Saturday, Feb. 16, Mr. Lewis said, that, since the adjournment, he had had the great advantage of a consultation with Mr. Day, Q.C., and Mr. Besley; and he might say, with perfect respect to the learned magistrate, that they were of opinion, notwithstanding the ruling, that the questions he desired to put in cross-examination were relevant and admissible; but at the same time they were also of opinion that the magistrate sitting there had uncontrolled power and right either to allow, or refuse to allow, certain questions to be put. Having regard to what had taken place as to the reception of evidence in the memorable case of the Queen vs. Labouchere, and also having regard to what had been thrown out by a learned judge, that the Court would not review a magistrate's discretion, no application had been made for a mandamus. He wished, however, to ask the witness two or three questions the magistrate had ruled to be inadmissible, so that they might appear as disallowed on the depositions.

Mr. Wontner said that there was no occasion to put the prosecutrix to further pain in the matter. The Crown would make no attempt to do any thing against the interests of the defendant; and he personally would guarantee that the evidence of the prosecutrix should not be put in at the trial, unless she was present.

Mr. Lewis replied that he was quite content with that assurance. He could not conceive there would be any advantage in cross-examining any other witnesses there, or to call any; and he therefore reserved the defence.

Mrs. Fletcher was then formally committed to take her trial at the next sessions of the Central Criminal Court, being allowed out on the same bail as before for her appearance.

APPENDIX II.

LETTER OF DR. T. L. NICHOLS TO THE "BANNER OF LIGHT."

To the Editor of the "Banner of Light."—I have thought that some account of the Fletcher case might be of interest to your readers in America and throughout the world. The "Banner of Light" goes everywhere, as is right; and your readers want the truth, no more and no less.

The prosecution of Mr. and Mrs. Fletcher for fraud is one of a series of severe blows to Spiritualists. It is not the first, and will not be the last. We had an almost exactly similar case with Home, when he accepted a gift of three hundred thousand dollars from a wealthy Jewess who insisted upon adopting him, and making him her heir. The trial of that case brought out a great body of testimony to the facts of Spiritualism.

The prosecution of Slade led directly to the investigation of the phenomena by Professor Zöllner and his fellow-professors of Leipsic, and the publication of the splendid results of their investigations. The so-called exposures of mediums in England have been a means of advancing the cause. It is an unpleasant method, but very effectual. The newspapers will not, because they dare not, publish the facts that are or would be offered to them by Spiritualists in favor of Spiritualism; but

432

they give their columns freely to the smallest details of any scandal or prosecution. So the blood of the martyrs was the seed of the church. No doubt the spirits might save their mediums from these prosecutions, but they do not see fit to do so. Probably they have good reasons. Their work is to spread Spiritualism, and they know what will do it.

It seemed to us that Mr. and Mrs. Fletcher committed a grave indiscretion in taking charge of the property and person of Mrs. Hart-Davies; but, after receiving a full account of the matter, I am not disposed to blame them. She appealed to their benevolence. They gave her an asylum, and received her property, the amount of which has been exaggerated. I can have no doubt that the Fletchers acted in simple kindness and good faith. It seemed a good arrangement for all parties that Mrs. Davies should have an asylum, and that her property should be saved for her own benefit. But, from a worldly point of view, it was a great mistake, owing to the peculiar disposition of Mrs. Davies. I will not anticipate the facts that must come out in the cross-examination and in the course of the trial.

Mrs. Fletcher's coming to England under the circumstances was simply and sublimely heroic. She knew precisely what she had to encounter. She left New York with a telegram in her pocket, assuring her that she would be arrested before she left the steamer at Greenock; yet she left her sick husband and family, determined to face a prison, perhaps penal servitude, to meet the charge. On the last day of a most tempestuous voyage she told the captain, to his great astonishment, that the police would come on board to take her to London. She sang her last song with her fellow-passengers, and quietly went on shore with the officer in plain clothes who bore the warrant for her arrest. He did his best to find her decent accommodation in London, but was obliged to take her to Bow Street. The old police-court and lock-up here is one of the worst in London, and in one of the lowest districts, including St. Giles and the Seven Dials. Fielding has left a graphic account of what he had to deal with when he was a Bow-street magistrate. A new court and prison of magnificent proportions are nearly completed; but in the mean time the old ones are at their worst, and Mrs. Fletcher was obliged to stay there one night. Her friends, who met her at the railway terminus, did the best they could, by buying rugs, etc., to make her comfortable; and in the morning, after the formal charge, she was remanded to the House of Detention.

It is a principle of English law that an accused person is to be considered innocent until he is proven guilty: the *practice* is to treat him worse than if he were guilty until he is proven to be innocent. Mr. Flowers, the magistrate, considered the charge, as made by the Jewish police-lawyer Abrahams, so serious, that he refused bail: so Mrs. Fletcher was taken to Clerkenwell. Two persons were allowed to speak to her each day, for fifteen minutes, through a grating. She was compelled to live on prison-fare; and all presents, even fruits and flowers, were rigidly excluded. This, however, did not last long. Mr. Lewis, one of the best London solicitors, was engaged; and when he stated to the magistrate that the property of the prosecutrix had been restored to her and that he had a perfect defence, bail in five thousand dollars was accepted, and given at once by two prominent Spiritualists, one of whom is himself a magistrate and a man of wealth and position.

The remand was for a week. A crowded court welcomed Mrs. Fletcher to her seat of honor in the prisoner's dock in the centre of the court. Her solicitor was ready to cross-examine the prosecutrix, but there was a further delay. A few months ago a reform was made in English criminal proceedings, by the appointment of a public prosecutor. This officer had decided that this case was one of public interest; and he took it out of the hands of Mr. Abrahams, and instructed Mr. Wontner, who, of course, wanted time for preparation: so the case went over to Dec. 21.

Mrs. Fletcher has come here expressly to have a full investigation. Mr. Fletcher's medical adviser would not consent to his crossing the Atlantic. She is quite equal to the occasion, and confident of success. Her friends are perfectly satisfied of her innocence; and those who were disposed at first to blame her and her husband for imprudence are obliged to admit, when they know the circumstances, that they would probably have done the same. It is not possible to predict the verdict of a British jury, perhaps of any jury. I have seen a man convicted, and sentenced to death, whom I knew to be innocent. He received, a few days later, her Majesty's pardon. The red tape .in the hangman's halter could be cut no other way. I have not a shadow of doubt of the perfect innocence of Mr. and Mrs. Fletcher, nor that, in all this matter, they did what they thought was for the best in regard to the woman who is now doing her worst to destroy them. And I have no doubt that this prosecution will advance the cause of Spiritualism more, perhaps, than many years of ordinary effort.

The Fletcher trial was, of course, adjourned over the holidays, and will be resumed on the 7th of January. Mr. Lewis, the solicitor for the defence, will do his best to get justice for his client: but in the higher court, which will try the case if it goes to trial, no solicitor can appear; he can only instruct a barrister. And the cost of legal proceedings, the cost of justice, in this country, is enormous. A solicitor of Mr. Lewis's standing expects a retaining-fee of two hundred and fifty dollars, with corresponding fees for each appearance in court. The barrister will require one thousand dollars, and his junior, five hundred dollars, with daily "refreshers." The chance of a poor man is very small. Happily Mrs. Fletcher has friends on both sides of the Atlantic.

What we want is a full and fair trial, in which evidence shall be given of the facts of Spiritualism. A hundred witnesses of the highest credibility can be put into the witness-box to testify that they have received undoubted messages from their spirit-friends through Mr. and Mrs. Fletcher. Persons as high as any in English society, even the very highest, can give this testimony. Our only fear is, that the case may break down before this evidence is admitted, and published to the world.

Success in any way provokes envy, and of envy comes malice and all sorts of uncharitableness. Spiritualists, I regret to say, are much like other people. Those who make friends thereby make enemies. The chief inciter of the prosecution is a healing-medium, so called; and his most active coadjutor is, I am sorry to say, the editor of a Spiritualist paper. It is not pleasant to see such things, but I remember that Judas was one of the twelve.

The importance of the case to Spiritualism rests upon the fact, that every medium in England who takes two and six-pence for a *séance* is liable to be prosecuted, and sent to prison for three months, under a law passed in the reign of George III. against fortune-tellers.

"Light," a new Spiritualist weekly paper, is to be published on the 8th of January, and not too soon, for we very much need a good organ of the cause in the world's metropolis.

T. L. NICHOLS.

32 Fopstone-road, Earl's Court, London, S.W.,
Dec. 29, 1880.

APPENDIX III.

REPORT OF THE OPENING SPEECH OF MR. MONTAGU WILLIAMS FOR THE PROSECUTION.

In opening the case for the prosecution, Mr. Montagu Williams said he had to lay before the jury a story of fraud and chicanery which had been seldom equalled, and never surpassed, in the history of the criminal courts of this country. Mrs. Hart-Davies, the prosecutrix, was a lady thirty-eight years of age, the daughter of a Mrs. Heurtley, a lady of considerable property, and much addicted to jewelry and finery — a complaint, he believed, very common amongst the sex. In the course of her life Mrs. Heurtley amassed a large quantity of jewels and a collection of valuable lace. When she died, she possessed lace to the value of four thousand or six thousand pounds. In addition, there were jewelry, Indian shawls, silks, and other articles of that description, amounting, with the lace, to something like ten thousand pounds. Mrs. Heurtley had also a good deal of money; and to the prosecutrix, her only surviving daughter, she left the whole of this property. There was a life-interest intervening, but eventually Mrs. Hart-Davies would come into a fortune of many thousands of pounds. Eighteen years ago the prosecutrix married a man named Rickards, by whom she had one child, a boy, now aged seventeen; but the union was not a happy one, and, after much

437

•

mutual disagreement, husband and wife separated. Subsequently Mr. Rickards instituted a suit for divorce, alleging adultery against his wife, who, whilst denying her guilt, was persuaded by her mother that the best way of dissolving the incompatible marriage was to allow judgment to go by default. Accordingly, no appearance was made to the suit, and a rule absolute was decreed. Now, during the time prosecutrix was the wife of Mr. Rickards, she became acquainted, through her husband, with a gentleman of the name of Lindmark, a fact which he only mentioned because it was likely they might hear a deal about him, during the case, from the other side. Some time after the divorce the prosecutrix married a Mr. Hart-Davies. Again the union was not a happy one; but it was during the time that she was living with that gentleman at 79 Farquhar Lodge, Upper Norwood, that she became acquainted with the prisoner and her husband. Mr. Hart-Davies was suffering from some ailment; and the man Fletcher, who was credited with knowing something about curative processes, was called in to attend him. In this way began the intimacy between the prosecutrix and the Fletchers, who were then living at 22 Gordon Square. Shortly afterwards Mrs. Hart-Davies moved to Vernon Place, Bloomsbury, and afterwards went to Tours. On her return she went to live with the Fletchers. By and by a party was formed for a trip to America. It consisted of the Fletchers and a stepson, Mrs. Hart-Davies, and Mr. Lindmark. At New York the company separated, Mr. Lindmark and Mrs. Fletcher going one way, and Mr. Fletcher, his stepson, and Mrs. Hart-Davies, the other; the arrangement being that they should meet at Pleasant Lake, which they did. Up to this time the Fletchers were apparently firm and fast friends of the prosecutrix. He should here tell the jury, that at the very first interview Mr. Fletcher discovered that Mrs. Hart-Davies was a person of "extreme psychic force;" and he told her, that, being a man of spiritualistic and mesmeric influence, he had the power of communicating by media with the spirit-world, wherever that might be. Mr. Fletcher seemed to have discovered this "psychic force" in Mrs. Hart-Davies by taking hold of her hand, which sent him into a trance, during which he had communication with the mother of that lady in the spirit-world. It was by this sort of delusion, and the influence created out of it, that the prisoner and her husband were able to denude the unfortunate prosecutrix of every article she had in the world. The fraud was rendered the more easy because of the deep affection which had existed between Mrs. Hart-Davies and her mother. The Fletchers seemed to have discovered the confiding nature of the prosecutrix, and, from the commencement to the end, to have worked upon the credulity of the unfortunate lady, who really believed that through them she could commune with her dead mother. Now, the jury would find mixed up with all this Spiritualism an unexampled amount of blasphemy. Having made the prosecutrix believe that he was a powerful medium, the man Fletcher induced her to attend several *séances* at Steinway Hall, where she was introduced to Mrs. Fletcher, who with female acuteness soon discovered that she was possessed of a large quantity of valuable jewelry, and was also entitled to the reversion of a considerable sum of money. The Fletchers then seemed to have laid their heads together with a view to deprive Mrs. Hart-Davies of all she had got. They did, in fact, strip her of every thing; and, furthermore, they induced her to execute a deed of gift and a will, making over to them all she was entitled to. For this purpose Mr. Morton, an American, was brought on the scene. He was represented as a sort of secretary or lawyer; and he drew up a document assigning away all

Mrs. Hart-Davies's property. Not satisfied with this letter, it was suggested that the prosecutrix should make a will. She had parted with all her property *in esse ;* but there was a large sum of money, thirty thousand or forty thousand pounds, to which she would become entitled on the death of a lady now living. Of that right, Morton induced the prosecutrix to will away every single shilling to the prisoner in the dock. She had been prepared for this by messages pretending to come from her mother in spirit-land. The following was one of them : —

"Oh, yes, I see it all — all the past! Poor, poor child! You have already suffered far more than the common share of mankind; the body and spirit have been worn by the varied terrible trials which have preyed upon your strength; and more is that you have courageously sacrificed and ruled yourself to keep them shut out from the world's cognizance. Do you know what has been up to this hour your symbol? It has been in the form of a cross, about so high (here the medium held his hand about four feet from the ground). Although you are so wasted by the persecuting reverses of your hitherto sad, sad life, yet have courage; for, my child, I am deputed to tell you that all your experiences are known to Heaven. Yes, God knows all your disappointments, all your hopes made barren, all the unrequited cravings of your loving heart. He knows your secret mental conflicts and your trials. . . . No, he will not count these against you. Take comfort, therefore, and learn that God remembers not against us our poor mistakes of ignorance. Our motives are what he searches, and keeps the records of. Cease to grieve, with fears, lest God's favor is withheld from you. Ah, no! for not one of your ardent longings and searchings after excellence of mind and life are lost to him. He garners them up: they are approved of by him. Know that the Father is with you, and that you are loved by him. Some troubles will yet visit you, but your future will become happier after a time. Strive all you can to place yourself in lively company. Your present life is unsuitable, and is wearing you away; because your nerve-power is continually being thrown off without any return of the necessary vital power to replace that which is lost, and which only can be conveyed to you by influences even more energetic than your own. In your present life and surroundings you fail to receive that benefit. For want of a reciprocal strength imparting force for yourself, the quality you possess, of yielding your nervous power to those about you, will deter all hope of your recovering from the wasting decay which saps up your life, until the necessary support of a strong, inflowing nerve-essence is produced. I warn you, that, for the want of this influence, you are wearing out your life: therefore you really must cultivate the society of lively people, and be fed by the surroundings of highly nervous life. Be in that life. You must be very careful of yourself. You have no disease; but I have told you the cause of your sinking vitality, and it is the result of that cause that your circulation is imperfect. Your blood becomes absorbed unnaturally into the system, and it is now partly water with the blood: hence you complain of languor, and weakness at the heart. I repeat emphatically, that, in your present life and surroundings, you give out to those around you your nerve-force; and, as you receive none in return, this is wearing your life away, day by day, slowly and slowly. When you feel so ill and weary, the spirit of your mother often is with you, by your bed, striving to impart fresh strength to you. This, however, can only be successfully accomplished by the aid of favorable surrounding influences of earth-life. Cultivate them, and get them about you. Be not anxious about your future. Try and get stronger, and so enjoy life in the daily present: it is best so. Again I say, Be comforted and of good cheer, and have no fears that God has ever cast you out of his favor and love. You have a humble heart; and all throughout your life you have truly repented even the slightest faults, ay, even to regretting them so painfully as to have robbed you of much strength. Yet every regret is treasured in heaven, and will become your spirit's recompense hereafter; and your habitual secret aspirations after what is just and good will cause you to become all that you desire, and great will be your reward in the other life. Hope is yours. Live in the present, and ask God's blessing upon your present. Always cultivate your natural longings for spirit-intercourse: it is a necessity to you, and will help to support you. It is almost more than meat and drink to you. Is your mother here now? Yes, dear child. She places her hands over your head. She is often with you. She is your guardian spirit. When you die — oh! I can see. It is your mother who will come with open arms to receive you. She will place a wreath of bright, shining flowers upon your head. You will hear above you angels' voices singing in rejoicing at the birth of another spirit into spirit-life. To see a light afar off. There is the home already prepared for you in heaven. Be at peace, my poor child, and remember all you have just heard. Live in hope, and trust as you have ever trusted, and be happy. Good-by."

The jury would see that there was an amount of blasphemy mixed up in these matters that was perfectly terrible.

This message, I must here observe, had been copied from the note-book of Mrs. Hart-Davies, where she had written it down from memory. Of course I cannot speak as to its accuracy, but it seems very improbable that any one should afterwards be able to record *verbatim* so long a message.

Mr. Williams then read another message, also recorded from memory by Mrs. Hart-Davies, and then said, —

Then there was another message, signed "Mums," which he [Mr. Williams] supposed was short for "mother" in the spirit-world.

THE JUDGE. — It may be another spirit.

MR. WILLIAMS. — I do not suppose it means the "sparkling," my lord. [Laughter.] The learned counsel went on to say, that, when Morton was introduced for the purpose of drawing up the deed of gift, the prosecutrix was on one occasion asked to look into a crystal globe, where, the Fletchers said, a man was to be seen writing. This was done as a preparation for what was to follow. It was suggested that an intimacy of an improper character had existed between Mr. Lindmark and Mrs. Hart-Davies, but the prosecutrix would give an unqualified denial to that imputation in the witness-box. She lost sight of the man for several years; but, when Mrs. Hart-Davies went to live with the prisoner and her husband, he suddenly turned up again. He represented himself as a materialist, and, getting introduced to the Fletchers at their *séances*, became a constant visitor at Gordon Square. There was no doubt that he was on terms of the greatest intimacy with Mrs. Fletcher, as was shown by the fact that she accompanied him by herself in America. Previous to starting on the voyage, Mrs. Hart-Davies had noticed this intimacy; and, when the party got on board ship, the prisoner treated her with a certain coldness. As the intimacy of Mrs. Fletcher with Lindmark increased, the intimacy between the two women declined. Mrs. Hart-Davies noticed that the prisoner had with her on the steamer a large number of boxes, which they now knew contained the bulk of prosecutrix' property; and, by the time they had met at Lake Pleasant, she had come to the conclusion that she had been swindled. The law was appealed to, and a portion of the property recovered; and, on her return to England, Mrs. Hart-Davies managed also to repossess herself of a quantity of goods which had been left behind at Gordon Street. In consequence of the proceedings that had been taken, the deed of gift was declared null and void, and the will was cancelled. He was at a loss to know what defence could be raised to the indictment. Would his learned friend contend, as a matter of fact, that the property was left with the prisoner for safe custody? If so, why did she not deliver it up when it was demanded? and where, in that case, was the necessity for the deed of gift, or the will? In all probability the defence would be, that the property was made a free gift by Mrs. Hart-Davies to prisoner and her husband, and that she was not induced to execute that gift by fraud. That would be the exact point, which he believed his lordship would leave to the jury; but he should submit, upon the evidence he had to call, that under the false pretence that these people had the power of communing with the spirit-world, and of bringing this unfortunate lady into communication with her dead mother, the prisoner and the absent defendants induced Mrs. Hart-Davies to part with all the property she possessed. The jury, he thought, would have no hesitation in coming to the conclusion that the prisoner and her husband, and the man Morton, were jugglers, and that they confederated and combined to cheat the prosecutrix out of her property.

APPENDIX IV.

CHARGE TO THE JURY BY JUSTICE HAWKINS.

THE learned judge proceeded to sum up. The indictment, which consisted of nine counts, charged, he said, the prisoner with obtaining by false pretences a quantity of jewelry, wearing-apparel, and other goods, and also the execution of a deed of gift. The substance of the false pretences was, that the prisoner, in connection with her husband and a man named Morton, represented to the prosecutrix that the spirit of her deceased mother had desired that these gifts should be made, and the deed executed; and the prosecution alleged that these pretences were false *to the knowledge of the accused person*. Then there were other counts, charging the prisoner with conspiring with her husband and Morton in respect to the same property and the deed of gift. There was a count charging conspiracy to steal; but upon that point he should direct a verdict of not guilty, there being no evidence to support the allegation. There was yet another count, charging that the prisoner, in company with two other persons, pretended to witchcraft, sorcery, and enchantment; but he considered that part of the indictment so utterly bad, that he had taken upon himself to quash it. Before dealing with the evidence that had been adduced in support of the various charges, his lordship laid before the jury a general history of the case, commenting upon various points as he proceeded. The object of the cross-examination of Mrs. Hart-Davies in reference to her divorce was to disparage the credit of the prosecutrix; but it would be for the jury to say whether, after the explanation they had heard of that case, — viz., that Mrs. Hart-Davies put in no answer to the charge of adultery, not because she was guilty, but because she desired to dissolve an unhappy marriage, — sufficient remained to induce them to withhold credit to the lady's statements. Again: it had been suggested that the estimate of ten thousand pounds, which Mrs. Hart-Davies put on her property, could not be true, inasmuch as she had herself sworn her mother's estate under a hundred pounds. Of course it would be a serious matter if it could be shown that the prosecutrix swore the property below its proper value in order to defraud the revenue by avoiding legacy duty; but whether it would disentitle her to belief in this case was a question entirely for the jury. Mrs. Hart-Davies, however, had explained that the property was given her by her mother during her lifetime. In one part of her evidence the prosecutrix said that the Fletchers got from her, not only her jewels and clothes, but also the greater part of her income of three hundred pounds a year. Whence that income was derived, they knew not. They knew there was a Mr. James Penrose Hart-Davies, that he had been a sailor, and that his wife desired him to be treated with respect, but beyond that they had no information as to the gentleman. Whether, in the end, it would be desirable to have some further introduction of Mr. Hart-Davies was for the jury to consider. In regard to the relationship of the pair, there was no trace of disagreement between them during the time they were at Farquhar Lodge. Whilst there, they had it in contemplation to visit town together; but, from the moment Mrs. Hart-Davies left Vernon Place on that journey, they did not seem to have been again in communication. How and why the relationship was broken, the jury might possibly divine for themselves; but it was only right to say that it was not suggested that Mr. Hart-Davies had been guilty of any cruelty or impropriety that caused his wife to separate from him. Now, as to the persons who were represented as the criminal actors in the scene, — the Fletchers and their friend Morton, — it was necessary that he should explain, that, although they were jointly charged in the indictment, it was open to the jury to find all of them, or either of them, guilty or not guilty. He must say, that, in regard to some of the charges, *he had failed to find any evidence fixing criminality on Morton.* Of Mr. Fletcher's antecedents they had no information whatsoever, except that he was an American and a Spiritualistic doctor giving *séances* and lectures at Steinway Hall. Of Mrs. Fletcher they had scarely any more information. Whether she was English or American by birth, they knew not. All they knew was, that she got a society around her at Gordon Street, and that she took a great deal of interest in her husband's Spiritualist proceedings. It was whilst the Hart-Davieses were at Farquhar Lodge that the acquaintance with the Fletchers commenced, first of all by the introduction of the husband as a Spiritualistic doctor. The prosecutrix, at that time, was an imaginative, excitable sort of person, already *admitting herself to be somewhat of a believer in Spiritualism, inasmuch as she affirmed that she had seen her dead mother in her dreams and her waking visions.* It was alleged that the prisoner and her husband, finding the prosecutrix to be a weak, flighty woman, inclined to believe all that was told her concerning Spiritualism, laid their heads together to deprive Mrs. Hart-Davies of her property by communicating to her messages purporting to come from her dead mother, but *which they knew to be false.*

The question was not whether the Fletchers got the jewels by representing that the spirit of the dead mother had really communicated to her that which induced Mrs. Hart-Davies to part with them; the question was, ay or nay, *did the prisoner honestly believe the truth of what she told the prosecutrix?* Did the Fletchers honestly believe that they were in communion with the spirit of the mother? Did prisoner believe the dead mother had in words communicated, through the medium of Mr. Fletcher, an order that her daughter should part with her jewels and clothes, or did she avail herself of the credulity of Mrs. Hart-Davies to tell her that which she knew to be untrue, with the view to induce her to part with her property? *It would be shocking to suppose that an honest belief in Spiritualism was a crime according to the law of this country.* People had a right to believe that which they thought fit. As he had said, the question was not whether a hundred thousand or more of persons believed in Spiritualism, or in communion with the departed, but whether fraudulent concoctions had been passed off upon the prosecutrix as messages coming from the spirit of her mother. That was *the sole question the jury had to determine,* and their verdict would not in the slightest degree affect the conscientious belief of those interested in this inquiry. Now, they would remember that Mrs. Hart-Davies, in her evidence, stated that she told Mr. Fletcher at the first interview that she had been more than a common sufferer, but that she did not enter into details. In the message she then received she was told by "Mamma," "You have suffered more than the common share of mankind." The message was couched in generalities. There were no references to particular persons, places, or circumstances. The only person referred to was the prosecutrix' mother, about whom her daughter had always been anxious, and of whom she was always speaking. There was no mention of any one whom the mother had known in life, and to whom she could refer her daughter for that counsel and advice of which the message alleged she stood so much in need. This fact was worthy of remembrance in connection with the fact, that, at that time, the medium through whom the message came knew very little of the prosecutrix' life. At the introduction at Upper Norwood, where Mrs. Fletcher intimated that she was so attracted to Mrs. Hart-Davies that she desired to become as a sister, the jewels were shown to the prisoner. That was important to recollect. Some short time afterwards, during one of her trances, Mrs. Fletcher communicated a message from "Mamma," to the effect that her daughter should not wear the jewels too often, because the magnetism in them was so strong that it might help to take her out of the world before her time. "Mamma," in fact, directed that her daughter should hand the jewels, for affection's sake, to Mrs. Fletcher, to hold as if they were her own. After that, they found Mrs. Hart-Davies taking an amethyst brooch and a diamond suite (the jewels prisoner had seen at Farquhar Lodge) to Gordon Street, where the table rapped out, "Dear Juliet, do as I have instructed you;" the message being written on a piece of paper by Mrs. Fletcher.

A JURYMAN. — Has the handwriting been identified?

MR. WILLIAMS. — Mrs. Hart-Davies said the prisoner wrote it.

THE JUDGE. — *Of course the whole of this case depends upon whether you believe the evidence of the prosecutrix, or not. If you do not, the whole fabric of the case comes down. If Mrs. Hart-Davies has not spoken the truth, if she has concocted these letters for the purpose of convicting the prisoner and her husband, then her machinations would be of so diabolical a charac-*

ter that she would herself deserve to stand in the dock. But here you have her evidence that she saw Mrs. Fletcher write the message, and the paper bears the printed heading of Gordon Street. The learned judge went on to say, that he was bound to direct the jury that the offence, if offence there was, was completed when the amethyst brooch and the diamonds were handed over. The question was, Did Mrs. Fletcher, having seen the jewels at Norwood, make up her mind to become possessed of them? and, if so, did she invent a pretended message from the mother directing them to be handed over? If so, did the jury believe that it was in consequence of these representations the jewels were handed over? If they came to that conclusion, they would have further to consider whether Mrs. Fletcher knew the pretences to be false, and put them forward for the purpose of cheating and defrauding Mrs. Hart-Davies of her property. They would remember that the prosecutrix left the interview with Mrs. Fletcher under the impression, inferred from the message, that she had disobeyed her mother's injunctions, whereupon she packed up the remainder of her jewels, and as soon as possible conveyed them to Gordon Street. Going down upon her knees, she placed the jewels in Mr. Fletcher's lap. That gentleman then went into a trance, and delivered a message purporting to come from the mother, who said, "Bless you, my child, for having obeyed my instructions," and expressed a hope that "Bertie" would have no compunction as to wearing the jewels as if they were her own. It was for the jury to decide what construction was to be put on those incidents. He now came to the question of the wardrobe. Mrs. Hart-Davies had told them that she contemplated going to Tours, and that the Fletchers had urged her to send her property to their house, as they had plenty of room, and could take care of it during her absence. The pris-

oner had previously seen the wardrobe of Mrs. Heurtley, and
had remarked to the prosecutrix, that it would be harmful for
her to touch her mother's dresses, because of the magnetism
that was in them. In consequence of that, the prosecutrix
had informed them that the prisoner packed the things herself,
and they were taken to the house in Gordon Street. Mrs.
Hart-Davies said she had no objection to this, because it
brought her nearer to her mother. The things remained at
the Fletchers' house until the rupture took place between the
parties, except those, however, which were taken to America.
*It was given in evidence by Mrs. Hart-Davies that there was an
honorable understanding that the goods should be returned when
they were required.* That might be so, but the jury must
consider the matter. They must not, however, find the main
turning-point there; because, although there might have been
an honorable understanding, notwithstanding the magnetism
in the things, that they should be returned, the jury must
consider whether there was an intention on the part of the
Fletchers, at the time the wardrobe was received, honorably
to perform such an engagement, or whether the understanding
about the magnetism was simply a trick to induce the prosecutrix to part with her property in the way described. He next
came to the third charge, and that was with reference to the
deed of gift. The evidence upon that matter was to the effect,
that, before Mrs. Davies left Farquhar Lodge, she was introduced to Col. Morton by the Fletchers at their house in Gordon
Street. She was informed that he was their lawyer, and an
American; but she subsequently ascertained that he was a
lodger in the house, paying two guineas a week. After the
first interview with Morton, Mrs. Davies saw him constantly.
On one occasion the prosecutrix was alone with the prisoner
in Gordon Street, when the latter took up a crystal ball, and

said, " I see a man with a brown beard sitting at a table writing, and you appear to be sitting beside him." Mrs. Davies thereupon said she recognized the man with the brown beard as Mr. Morton. The prisoner told her, that, since she had received the jewels, she felt anxious about the responsibility of them, for fear of what the outside world might say when the prosecutrix had gone abroad. She then asked Mrs. Davies to give her some protecting document; and, for the purpose of having this document drawn out, she had an interview with Col. Morton. It must be remembered that the prisoner had recommended Mrs. Davies to go to Morton, and he [the learned judge] thought it right that he should here state with reference to Morton, although he was not now taking his trial, what was the evidence which affected him. Although it was charged against him that he induced Mrs. Davies to sign the deed, there was another count charging him with conspiracy. Mr. Addison, so far as the conspiracy counts were concerned, had raised a point to the effect that husband and wife alone could not, in point of law, conspire, and therefore, although the jury might come to the conclusion that Fletcher and his wife did conspire, they could not indict them jointly for conspiracy, because husband and wife were supposed to have only one mind, and one mind could not conspire with itself. The learned counsel drew from that, that, unless Col. Morton was associated with the Fletchers as a conspirator, the charge of conspiracy against husband and wife could not be sustained. That objection was not in his opinion a good objection in law. It would be revolting to common sense, if it were shown that the wife was the instigator of the crime, and compelled the husband to join her — it would be revolting if the law were in such a condition as this, that a woman, in such a case as he had instanced, should be allowed to go scot-free, because she was married to the man whom she by her influence had forced to join her in the conspiracy, and that the husband should be left to bear the whole brunt of the charge. He had not really determined the point raised by Mr. Addison; but, for the purposes of that day, he had come to a decision, and he saw no reason why the indictment for conspiracy should not be urged against the prisoner. But upon that matter he must take their verdict. If they found that the prisoner did not conspire with Morton, then it would get rid of the legal point that had been raised; but they must not, merely for the sake of getting rid of the legal technical objection, strain or allow the evidence as against Morton to carry them beyond the fair and legitimate effect of that evidence. Although Morton was not upon his trial, it was necessary that they should inquire whether he joined in the unlawful conspiracy and combination. With regard to the original false pretence, he had looked in vain to find any evidence that Morton was one of those who took part in it. There was nothing to make him a joint participator in obtaining the jewels and wardrobe by false pretences. But the next question arose, Was he a conspirator to an unlawful deed? and did he, by unlawful means and by false pretences, combine with either the prisoner, her husband, or with both, to induce Mrs. Hart-Davies to sign the deed of gift? It might be that the Fletchers induced the prosecutrix to go to Morton under false representations, but of that they would have to inquire. The main question was, *Did Morton himself know that he was preparing a deed which was of a fraudulent character?* That was the point, so far as it affected the conspiracy between the Fletchers and Morton; and the jury would have to consider whether the conspiracy existed between the Fletchers and Morton, or between the Fletchers alone. The deed which was drawn up by Morton gave the property to

Mrs. Fletcher to be hers absolutely; but it was stated by Mrs. Hart-Davies, that the prisoner requested that the things which she had in her possession should be made more binding upon her. For the purpose of carrying out that wish, Mrs. Davies again sought an interview with Morton, who made out a draught letter, requesting that she should put her own head and tail to it, and copy it out at home. The prosecutrix stated that she took the letter home, copied it upon her own note-paper, and sent the copy to the prisoner. That letter made over to the prisoner, as a humble and free gift, the property which belonged to the prosecutrix; and the jury must form their own conclusion upon the whole of the circumstances. His lordship next directed attention to the events which took place after the prosecutrix left Norwood for Vernon Place. Vernon Place appeared to have been taken for some temporary purpose. The prosecutrix had contemplated, shortly after her removal there, a visit to France; and, that being so, the subject of the will was introduced. *It appeared from the evidence that the will was made at the suggestion of the prosecutrix herself.* She sought another interview with Morton upon the matter, and he suggested that she should leave her property where it was most useful. Thereupon she expressed a desire that it should be left to the cause of Spiritualism in its highest phases. Morton advised her that her intention could only be carried out through individuals, and remarked, in the words of the prosecutrix, "Who could be better than my brother and sister?" meaning the Fletchers. Mrs. Davies had stated that she had several conversations with the prisoner about the will, and said that she spoke to her mother, through the prisoner, upon the subject, receiving the answer, "Go to Col. Morton, and he will recommend a good solicitor." She obeyed what she believed to be the command of her mother, delivered through the prisoner, and went to Col. Morton, who accompanied her to the firm of Field, Roscoe, & Francis, as they had heard. It was perfectly certain, that, if it was intended that the property of the prosecutrix should be disposed of so as to promote the interests of Spiritualism in its highest phases, there was no such suggestion made in the will itself: on the contrary, the will was prepared in such a way that it was evidently intended that the property should be realized, received, and enjoyed by the Fletchers individually; because it was to be divided between them in equal moieties, and Mrs. Fletcher was to enjoy her share separately, and apart from her husband. Whether there was a conspiracy to bring about that state of things by fraudulent means, was a question for consideration. He would have them understand that there was no crime in a man endeavoring to win any person over to leave him property. If undue influence was used, a will could be set aside; but the mere exercise of civility, affection, or persuasion, with a view of prevailing upon a person to leave property in a certain direction, was not a crime. The charge here was not that there was undue influence exercised, but that there were fraudulent practices. In his opinion, *the evidence upon that point was much slighter than upon any other part of the case.* They might say that it was wrong to exercise undue influence; but it was another thing to say that that constituted a criminal offence, unless the execution of the will was procured by fraudulent misrepresentations. In that case, of course, a charge of conspiracy might be maintained. The evidence of any criminality in regard to this will was very weak; though, at the same time, no human being could look upon the document with any thing like favor.

The Court at this point adjourned for luncheon. On the resumption of the proceedings,

The judge proceeded to read a number of the Fletcher letters, which to his mind threw considerable light on the question of the *bonâ fides* of the prisoner and her husband. The word "scrunch," which appeared so frequently, did not seem to have been used in any indecent sense: in fact, it was part of the sheerest nonsense in the world. In one of the letters Mr. Fletcher spoke of a box of linen sent to Gordon Street, which had an influence about it which he at once recognized as coming from "Julie." It turned out, however, that it was a box of servants' dirty linen: so how it could have possessed an influence, either of "Julie" or her deceased mother, was difficult to understand. There was no doubt that Mrs. Hart-Davies did spend some time in Paris with Mr. Fletcher, and she admitted having sat by him, and laid her head upon his breast; but she indignantly denied having courted any immorality, and afterwards resented what she thought a disposition on the part of Fletcher to treat her otherwise than as a brother should a sister. The jury, perhaps, would be able to judge from the letters whether there was any such disposition on the part of Mr. Fletcher. It was not quite clear why the party went to America, — it might have been some magnetic influence which attracted them, — but there was no doubt that on the way out this lady, who was to have represented "Affection in the Trinity," considered that she had been neglected; and the film having, as she said, dropped from her eyes, she came to the conclusion that she had been swindled. It was important the jury should not overlook the words of Mrs. Fletcher when the demand was made in America for the restoration of the jewelry: "If you take those jewels, there is certain and speedy death before you." It was immaterial whether the property which Mrs. Hart-Davies claimed was worth five thousand pounds or only five pounds. No doubt in a civil action a great deal more of evidence of value would be required: here, however, all the jury had to decide was whether false pretences, known to be false pretences, were used to induce the prosecutrix to part with her property. In regard to the point raised by the counsel for the defence, — that the prisoner, being a married woman, was presumed to be acting under the coercion of her husband, — he had to point out that it was open to the prosecution to call evidence rebutting such presumption, and showing that there was independent action on the part of the wife. The evidence of Mrs. Hart-Davies went to prove that the first mention of the jewels did not come from Mr. Fletcher, but from the prisoner at that interview in Gordon Street, when the message came from the mother, "Do as I have instructed you." If there should be conviction on the conspiracy count, he would desire the jury, for the purpose of considering the point raised by counsel for the defence that husband and wife could not conspire, to give their opinion as to whether Morton with the Fletchers, or either of them, conspired to obtain the deed of gift or the will.

APPENDIX V.

WHAT PRISONS ARE, AND WHAT THEY MIGHT BE.

Aside from the experiences I have given, my life in prison was very monotonous. Once in three months, three times during my year's imprisonment, I was allowed to have a visit from three or four of my friends.

The reception-room is a large cell, divided by strong iron bars into three cages similar to those in which very savage beasts are kept in menageries. In the central cage sits a more or less grim-looking warder in a chair, looking at a clock opposite her, which marks off the twenty minutes allowed for each visit, and to see that the conversation is kept within proper limits, also that there is no smuggling of forbidden luxuries, especially spirits or tobacco. At two of these visits I was allowed, when my friends were leaving, to put my hand through a little hole made for the purpose to be shaken and kissed. The last time, and perhaps because it was the last, the warder graciously unlocked the door, and allowed me to clasp some dear friends in my arms. This was granted by the matron as a special favor.

In a few cases, friends who had some special and satisfactory reasons, business or otherwise, applied to the home

458 · ·

secretary, and were allowed to see me, but under the same conditions. My friend Mrs. Nichols wrote to Sir William Harcourt that she wished to see me about my health and about a memorial to him which she was preparing; and as she was over seventy years old, and in feeble health, she begged that she might be placed where she could have a chair to sit in while talking with me; begged this grace for the sake of Him who said, "*I was in prison, and ye came unto me.*" Her prayer was not granted. She came, however, and talked with me through the two gratings as long as she could *stand*, or the woman who *sat* keeping watch and ward, permitted. The last time Mrs. Nichols visited me she was allowed a wooden chair.

Of my personal treatment in prison I have much to be grateful for, and little to complain of. The "hard labor" which my friends thought so cruel a part of my sentence was a great resource and a great happiness to me. It took me out of the solitary confinement in my close, dark cell. As it was, my health suffered severely, perhaps permanently. The prisons for convicts whose terms are less than five years are admittedly far worse than those for penal servitude.

Dr. Nichols, in his monthly paper, the "Herald of Health," treating the matter from a sanitary and moral point of view, embodied the information I gave him in the following articles, which I copy because the facts seem to me to be clearly and justly stated, and because their publication led to some agitation in the press, and even in Parliament, and, but for the more important and exciting subjects of Ireland and Egypt, would probably have obtained wider notice.

HER MAJESTY'S PRISONS. — Formerly the prisons of England were horribly unhealthy, and in many ways utterly disgraceful. To "rot in jail" was no figure of speech, but a dreadful reality. Men and women were kept in dark and dirty holes, with no regard to cleanliness or ventilation. When transported to Virginia, or the longer distance, to Botany Bay, the transport-ships, like the hulks in harbor, were "floating hells," and half or more of the convicts died on the passage of bad air, bad food, and lack of water. When the government, besieged by philanthropists, made it for the *interest* of contractors to land prisoners at their destination, instead of dropping them into the sea, simply by paying only for those so landed, the mortality of the Botany Bay passage was reduced from sixty to five per cent. So much for making it the interest of men to do right, which is the real duty of all government.

Our prisons at this time are said to be fairly well managed and healthy: so they should be, since good health and good morals go hand in hand; and every prison should be reformatory in every way, — a school of all the virtues, making men and women healthier and better. They should be and do all this for many reasons, one of which is, that many innocent persons are sent to prison, — some, because unjustly accused and convicted; some, because unfortunate and poor. Thousands of persons are imprisoned for debt. We supposed such imprisonment was abolished; but it appears that every one who cannot obey the order of a county court-judge is considered guilty of contempt of court, and shut up in prison.

We have had occasion during the past year to take some personal interest in one of her Majesty's prisons, the one in Tothill Fields, between Victoria Station and Westminster Abbey and the Houses of Parliament. This is a very large prison, entirely devoted to women, placed under the charge of a lady superintendent and female warders. At the gate are two male porters and a clerk; but, save when policemen are called in to quell disturbances which the robust and resolute female warders are not able to manage, the only men inside are the two chaplains (Protestant and Catholic) and the physician. Since there are now many regularly educated, diploma-ed, and registered female physicians, why are they not appointed to female prisons?

In this prison are confined an average of five or six hundred women, nine-tenths on short sentences for drunkenness, disorderly conduct, and petty thefts. The prison-vans bring them, fifty or sixty a day, from all the police-courts of the metropolis, as well as from the criminal courts and sessions. So many come in every day: so many are discharged, mostly to come again. What a work for the chaplains! What a work for reformers!

On the arrival of the prisoners, — numbering at times fifty or sixty a day, of all characters, and in every imaginable degree of filth and disease, — all are *compelled to wash in the same water!* The delicate lady, accustomed to her daily ablution, and the drunken and diseased street-walker, must enter the same bath. Does her gracious Majesty know of this utterly abominable regulation?

After this beautiful introduction to prison sanitation, each prisoner is allowed three quarts of water a day for all purposes, and, once a week, an ounce of very nasty yellow soap, — all her Majesty's government can afford.

A clean chemise and towel are allowed once a week — clean by courtesy; for as the hundreds of pieces are mixed together, and passed through the prison laundry, there is a distribution of filth rather than an achievement of cleanliness. Each prisoner in the laundry is expected to wash sixty chemises a day.

Sheets, summer clothing, and stockings are washed once a month in the same fashion, and distributed hap-hazard. Woollen clothing is worn from October to May without washing.

Blankets are never washed the year round, and are necessarily filled with filth and fleas, with the chance of worse abominations. Prisoners inherit the blankets of their predecessors, with all the filth and vermin they leave behind them. The lowest dregs of the slums of Westminster, Seven Dials, Drury Lane, etc., settle here.

The sanitary condition is made worse by lack of light. Half the cells are too dark to read in: all are badly ventilated, close, and suffocating in summer. The prisoners are kept in these cells day and night, except one hour a day for exercise and chapel. The necessary vessels in the cells become very offensive. The food of the prisoners is brought into, and must be eaten in, these close and nasty cells.

There is one water-closet for fifty-five women, — the average number in each section of the prison, — in which they must all empty their slops. When the small-pox was in the prison, during the recent epidemic, one of these got choked, and the yard was flooded with sewage for four days.

There is no classification. The most refined ladies, rightly or wrongly convicted of some misdemeanor, are mixed with the most horrible drunken prostitutes and female roughs and ruffians, who get the best treatment, because the officers dare not offend them. The silent system is carried out as well, perhaps, as it can be among five hundred women, who cannot be prevented from shouting to each other at night, and relating their not always edifying adventures.

The usual work is picking oakum; but a certain number are told off to sort the paper brought by scavengers from dust-holes and gutters, filling the prison with dust, stench, fleas, and other vermin, and who can say what germs of disease? The prisoners condemned to this filthy labor, covered thickly with dirt, have no change of clothing, and daily mingle with the others in chapel, so that all this filth may be fairly distributed.

The walls of the cells are whitewashed twice a year; this is well: but in the sick-cells the beds are never changed or cleansed.

The diet of prisons, though considered by many as too meagre, seems fairly sufficient for the average. A pint of gruel is served morning and night, and three four-ounce loaves of bread a day. For dinner, a pint of soup, three potatoes, bread, and suet-pudding. The beans are not well cooked (they are seldom cooked enough anywhere), and the bacon is very offensive. On one day in the week, Friday, each prisoner gets six ounces of Australian meat.

There are diet-papers in all the cells, showing what should be given according to the government regulations; but this diet is never furnished, has not been in the memory of the oldest inhabitant.

The diet actually provided does not suit all stomachs. One poor old woman who could not digest it took to her bed, turned her face to the wall, and resolutely starved to death, and so got out of it.

This is the account, intelligent and accurate we have no doubt, which we get from a lady who has had a year's observation and experience of this prison. She makes no complaint of personal ill treatment, but only of the conditions of uncleanliness and unhealthfulness from which all must alike suffer. She was treated by every one, as was natural, with the consideration due to her position and character, and with all the favor the regulations would allow. As kindness is the habit of her life, and it was misplaced kindness that gave her this experience, she had some opportunities of doing good to those around her, and was rewarded, as we know, with the tenderest love of those who had the best opportunities of knowing her.

Prisons, you may say, are for punishment. Yes: but are filth and darkness, foul air and diseasing conditions, lice and fleas, proper punishments or reforming influences? They harden and debase. And what of the innocent — the victims of our constant "failures of justice"? What of the considerable number, who, as one of the chaplains of this prison assured us, are rather unfortunate than criminal, and really free from moral guilt? What of the thousands of prisoners for debt, who for their misfortunes are subjected to all the demoralizing influences of prison-life? Do we not need another Howard, and another Mrs. Fry, to preach another prison crusade, and carry out another prison-reformation?

We shall send this paper to her Majesty's home secretary. Possibly one of his subordinates may read it. We cannot expect that it will catch the eye of a much bothered and over-tasked prime-minister. We may, perhaps, hope for a few moments' attention from two or three members of Parliament; and we ask our many thoughtful and philanthropic readers, and especially kind-hearted, generous women, whether something better cannot be done for five or six hundred female prisoners — several thousands every year — than such abominably vile and unhealthy conditions as we have felt obliged to notice. Other prisons may be as bad or worse. It is certain that in this one there is need of reformation. — *The Herald of Health*, May, 1882.

In the June number of his periodical, Dr. Nichols had occasion to return to the subject, in an article on unsanitary prisons.

Our article on the condition of the great prison for women in Tothill Fields, Westminster, in the May number of the "Herald of Health," may do some good. It has already had the advantage of a parliamentary notice. The "Times" of May 3 contained the following:—

TOTHILL-FIELDS PRISON.—Mr. Broadhurst asked the secretary of state for the home department whether his attention had been called to an article in the May number of the "Herald of Health," giving a description of the condition of prison-life in the Tothill-Fields Prison for Women, in which very grave charges were made as to the insufficiency of clean linen, both in respect to wearing-apparel and bedding, also to the bad light and bad ventilation of the cells, and to the want of more sanitary conveniences, and to the occasional bad condition of those at present provided; and whether he would cause inquiries to be made into the truth, or otherwise, of the charges in question; and, if they were found to be true, whether he would order the prison-authorities to make better arrangements for the cleanliness of the inmates of that prison.

Sir W. Harcourt said he had caused inquiries to be made into the case, and the reports of the medical officer and the lady-superintendent satisfied him that the charges were not well founded.

This is precisely the usual proceeding. When abuses are pointed out in any department of government, the chief inquires of his subordinates, and they never fail to satisfy him that the charges are not well founded. That is what they are for. We repeat the charges we brought, not against the officers of the prison, but against its construction and regulations. We are ready to prove that it is a place, not of healthy and moral restraint and reformation, but of unhealthy, demoralizing torture. Give us the opportunity, and we will prove every item and more. Probably this is not the only defective and unsanitary prison. Coroner's inquests are far too frequent in the Coldbath-Fields Prison, which is for men what the Tothill-Fields Prison is for women. Since our article was written, an inquest has been held there on the body of Edward Woodhouse, aged twenty, a printer. The father of the deceased, while exonerating the warders, said that he believed his son had been virtually murdered by the cruel system under which the warders were compelled to act. The coroner, observing that such a charge was a very heavy one against any public institution, offered to order a post-mortem examination if the father wished it. The father left this in the hands of the coroner. The jury, after a private deliberation, expressed a wish to view the cell in which the prisoner had been confined. After the inspection they returned a verdict of "Death from inflammation of the lungs, of a very acute and sharp nature." Woodhouse, who was sentenced to four months' imprisonment for an assault, was said by his father to be "a strong, healthy young man" when he was sent to prison.

Let us look at the facts. The hundreds of women in the Tothill-Fields Prison are locked up singly in cold, damp cells, many of which — about one-half — are too dark to read in, for twenty-three hours out of every twenty-four. These tombs are badly ventilated, with uncovered vessels, and in winter cruelly cold; while the inmates, wearing out month after month in this dreary solitude, are thinly clothed, sleep on hammocks which give almost no protection, with only two blankets in winter, and one in summer, washed once a year, and meantime, with all they gather, the inheritance of each successive prisoner, and of those moved from one cell to another.

The passages or corridors of the prison are warmed, and made comfortable for the warders. Some of this warm air filters into the cells, and its moisture condenses on the walls, and runs down upon the cold stone floor. Here the poor women eat their hearts out for twenty-three hours of every day with fleas and rats, and perhaps the germs of fatal diseases.

We are glad to learn, that, since our article was published, drains have been inspected, and some cleansing and white-washing done. So far so good; but that will not give air, light, and the conditions of health, which are the rights of every human being. We agree that a prison is for restraint and for salutary punishment: above all, it should be for reform. It is right that prisoners should be deprived of mere luxuries and sensual indulgences. But cold, darkness, bad or insufficient food, filth, and the dreary monotony of silent, solitary confinement in living tombs, can only demoralize, and shorten life.

Some years ago this system was vigorously denounced in "The Weekly Dispatch." It was asserted that no prisoner could endure more than two years of such confinement, and that it was far worse than penal servitude. It is made bad, and kept so, to prevent crime. Is it deterrent? If it were, would the same prisoners come up twenty times, a hundred times, in one case two hundred and forty times, over for sentence? As the gallows does not prevent murder, and did not prevent theft when men, women, and children were hanged for stealing a few shillings, so no amount of cruelty of punishment deters from crime.

There is another difficulty about this prison. It is not only not reformatory, not educational in any way, beyond the influence which may be exercised by the two chaplains, but there are demoralizing influences. Abandoned women find means of communicating with young girls, and offer them induce-ments to become inmates of houses of ill-fame when they leave the prison. Possibly they manage to get sentenced a month for no other purpose. They gather round the gates, and offer hospitalities to those whose terms have expired. There are other things we cannot go into. The prisoners are completely in the power of the warders; and " who is there to watch the shepherds " — or the shepherdesses? A warder may be as drunken and depraved as any prisoner.

We have made no charges against the officers of the prison. No doubt the lady-superintendent, the physician, and the chaplains do their best under the system and regulations which define and limit their duties. It is the system and the regulations, and the very structure and arrangements of the prison, and of prisons generally, of which we complain. Our informant, who has simply given us her own experience and observations, had no motive but that of pity for suffering, and a desire to benefit her fellow-sufferers. She had no complaint of a personal character to make. From the moment of her arrest to the termination of her sentence, she was treated with the greatest possible kindness and consideration that conditions and regulations would admit of. A failure of justice may have the effect of bringing about much needed reforms. Two thousand years ago it was a work of charity to visit prisoners. A hundred years ago Mrs. Fry was allowed to preach to the female prisoners in Newgate. Under our present regulations the words "*I was in prison, and ye came unto me,*" have lost their meaning.

A prison should be in every way a school of healthful, orderly, industrious life. It should be full of inducements to good conduct, and free from temptations to evil. A prison should not lower health, or shorten life; and it should be a training-school for every inmate. Every prisoner should be able to pay the cost of his imprisonment. Some American prisons bring a net profit to the State. We think the State might well divide the profits of labor with the prisoners. There should be every encouragement to work, and none to idle and shirk.

And no short sentences after the first. The third should be for life, or "during her Majesty's pleasure." What a wretched farce it is for our magistrates to sentence a woman a hundred times ! A year is the shortest time to cure the habit of drink. If it recur, either the patient should be kept out of the way of drink, or the drink, by local option or otherwise, out of the way of the patient.

Yes, "the *patient*." A great poet has said, —
"All crime is madness : madness is disease."

Then every prison should be a hospital to cure it. And a hospital should have light, warmth, pure food, pure water, all the conditions of health, and all possible incitements to industry and virtue.

First a hospital, and then a school, — a school of life.

Can all criminals be cured of crime? Certainly not. Crime is almost always hereditary and constitutional, and it is sometimes incurable. There are hospitals for incurables. Men are born liars and born thieves, and all such should be humanely taken care of. But the majority can be cured by the adoption of a reasonable and scientific system of education and discipline.

We thank Mr. Broadhurst for his question to the home secretary, and we are sorry that Sir William Harcourt could not give a more satisfactory answer. He has too much to do. There should be a special minister of justice responsible for the treatment, health, education, and reformation of prisoners.

And we beg our readers not to imagine that we write from Utopia, or of any thing impossible. There has been in France for half a century a prison so educational, so truly reformatory, that the fact of any one having been trained in it is a letter of recommendation. A man who wants a situation of trust cannot give a better reference than to say he is an *enfant de Mettray.* There is a similar-training school for young convicts in Belgium. We do not pretend that the old are as easily trained as the young; but we do know that men and women at all ages may "cease to do evil, and learn to do well," and that the best work in this world is to help all who need our help to live honest and useful lives. We must despair of none, and give real help to all who need it. As a hospital should be the best possible place to cure disease, a prison should be the best possible place to reform the immoral and the criminal. — *Herald of Health,* June, 1882.

Mr. Dillon, M.P., complained bitterly in the House of Commons that he had been locked up in his cell twenty-two hours out of twenty-four, which he thought enough to destroy the health of any one. We poor women at Tothill Fields were locked up an hour longer.

With Dr. Nichols, I see no reason why every prison should not be a school of life for culture, training, and improvement in bodily health and intelligence and morality. With a proper classification of prisoners, all could be taught, and all could be more or less improved. If there are any so demented or depraved as to be hopeless, what is wanted for such is something like an insane-asylum, or hospital for incurables. where they could be humanely treated, and made to pay by their industry the cost of their living. It seems to me to be an awful farce for London magistrates, and magistrates in all the towns of England, to send men and women scores and hundreds of times to prison, to come out each time more hardened and more degraded.

APPENDIX VI.

MEMORIAL OF DR. NICHOLS TO THE HOME SEC-
RETARY, ASKING FOR THE RELEASE OF MRS.
FLETCHER.

The Memorial of THOMAS LOW NICHOLS, M.D., *of 32 Fopstone Road, South Kensington, London, S. W., in behalf of* MRS. SUSAN WILLIS FLETCHER, *a prisoner.*

To the Right Honorable SIR WILLIAM HARCOURT, BART., M.P., *her Majesty's Secretary of State for the Home Department.*

SIR, — I am a citizen of the United States of America, by profession a physician, author, and journalist, for twenty years resident in England. In the exercise of what I presume to be my right, and what I feel to be my duty, I make this appeal in behalf of my countrywoman and dear friend now confined a prisoner, violently parted from her husband, parents, child, and many friends, because unjustly, and, I think, also unlawfully, convicted.

Your prisoner, Mrs. Susan Willis Fletcher, came to England with her husband, Mr. John William Fletcher, both respectable citizens of the United States of America, about the year 1877, to follow their recognized and lawful calling of spiritual mediums and trance-speakers for a large and intelligent body of the people of America, England, and other countries, calling themselves Spiritualists. In America these Spiritual-

471

ists, a growing body for more than thirty years, have been estimated to number several millions, having numerous societies, great lecture-halls, licensed speakers and mediums, and several newspapers, one of which is said to have a circulation of a hundred thousand copies weekly. In Great Britain there are also many Spiritualist societies, several in London, and one or more in most of the provincial towns, with four weekly newspapers, a monthly review, and many registered halls or chapels, speakers, and mediums.

In 1878 Mr. and Mrs. Fletcher established themselves as spiritual mediums at 22 Gordon Street, Gordon Square, London; and Mr. Fletcher held religious services, and gave addresses on Spiritualism on Sunday evenings, at Steinway Hall in Lower Seymour Street, Portman Square, which were attended by a large and fashionable congregation.

Belief in Spiritualism, or the existence of the spirits of men and women who have lived in this world, and their power, at times and under favoring conditions, to communicate with the living, has been and is, I need scarcely remind so accomplished a student of history, common to nearly the whole human race. It was and is the basis of the religions of Egypt, Greece, Rome, India, China, and is the faith alike of Jews, Christians, Mohammedans, Buddhists, and Brahmins.

The manifestations of the presence and power of spirits of departed men and women, which have become common in America, Europe, and over the world, during the past thirty years, have been witnessed by many thousands of intelligent observers, and been carefully examined and rigidly tested by many scientific men, as Professor Hare, Professor Mapes, Judge Edmunds, Professor Denton, Mr. Epes Sargent, and others in America, by Mr. William Howitt, Dr. Robert Chambers, Professor De Morgan, Mr. S. C. Hall, Mr. William

Crookes, F.R.S., Mr. Alfred Russell Wallace, F.R.G.S., the late and present Earls of Dunraven, the Earl of Crawford, and many more in England, and lately and notably by Professor Zöllner of the University of Leipzig, an astronomer of world-wide reputation, who, with his fellow-professors, most carefully examined and tested the manifestations made in presence of two celebrated mediums, — Henry Slade (American) and William Eglinton (Englishman)', with both of whom I am well acquainted, as I have also been with many mediums during twenty-five years of careful examination of the phenomena of Spiritualism.

I assert, and am ready to prove by hundreds of unimpeachable witnesses and by experimental demonstration, the fact and truth, or objective reality, of Spiritualism. There is no need to prove the strong and violent prejudice against it. Materialists and religionists, from different motives, deny its facts, and refuse investigation. On the trial of Mrs. Fletcher all testimony to prove its reality was excluded by the presiding judge, while the jury was asked by the government prosecutor to crush Spiritualism as a pestilent heresy; so that religious persecution became the animus of the trial, and motive of the verdict.

Under these circumstances, you, as a liberal and enlightened minister of the crown, standing in the place of her gracious Majesty, to whose clemency and justice I am making this appeal, will pardon me if I give a brief yet faithful history of this prosecution of Mrs. Fletcher, under the direction of a department of the government of which you are the responsible minister.

[The history of the case is omitted, because it has been more fully given elsewhere. After a brief recital of the facts, the memorial says], —

Had the Fletchers been Methodists, Baptists, or Plymouth Brethren, the matter in dispute would have been settled in a court of equity. The property formally given to the Fletchers had been in great part restored. No injury had been inflicted. Mrs. Hart-Davies was really indebted to the Fletchers. Nothing had been converted or concealed. When the Fletchers went to America, they took their friend, as well as a portion of the property, with them. Mrs. Fletcher had come from America expressly and solely to meet the charge of fraud against her, expecting a fair trial, and not doubting that she would have a triumphant acquittal.

After hearing all the evidence offered on one side, and declining to hear any on the other, the Bow-street magistrate committed Mrs. Fletcher for trial at the Central Criminal Court. The grand jury did not hesitate to find a "true bill." It appears to be as easy in our day to indict and convict and imprison a Spiritualist, as it was some time ago to burn a heretic, or hang a witch, or whip or imprison a Quaker. It being a government prosecution, the various counts of this wonderful indictment were spread over sixty skins of parchment, so that the unrolling of one hundred and twenty feet before the eyes of an Old Bailey jury might have gone far in itself to secure a conviction.

Practically, as the presiding judge, Mr. Justice Hawkins, told the jury, the whole case rested upon the testimony of Mrs. Hart-Davies. There was not offered one word of evidence, either of the non-existence of the spirit of Mrs. Heurtley, or that she could not communicate with her daughter, or that she did not actually make such communications through Mr. and Mrs. Fletcher. The only false pretences alleged were these communications, and no evidence was given of their falsity. It is believed with religious faith, or recognized as a scientific fact, by millions, that spirits exist, and that they can communicate with mortals, and do so communicate. There was no evidence to show that Mrs. Fletcher did not believe in such communications, or that they might not, or did not, come to or through her, or that she had not acted in simple good faith. Her coming to meet her trial, and her remaining on bail to the end, when she saw that the trial was utterly unfair, that all her witnesses were shut out, and that the Court, and probably the jury, were against her, are strong proofs of her sincerity.

A hundred witnesses could have been called to prove the reality of spiritual manifestations, among them men of the highest rank and position; but the Court ruled that no amount of such testimony would be of any avail. Surely this was wrong. Surely it was important to show that the pretences charged as false might be true, or at least that Mrs. Fletcher, like thousands of others, might honestly believe in such communications.

["Well knowing them to be false" is the phrase repeated throughout the indictment; yet this knowledge was assumed, and in no case proven. Spiritualism is false; she must know it to be false: therefore she is guilty. Two centuries ago it was, witchcraft is wicked; she is a witch, well knowing it to be wicked: let her be hanged or burned accordingly. Under judges like Sir Matthew Hale, hundreds of poor women suffered horrible deaths for witchcraft. Ought I to complain of a year's imprisonment under the equally enlightened sentence of Sir Henry Hawkins?]

The jury was exhorted by the government prosecutor to "crush a pestilent heresy," or, as otherwise reported, to "give a death-blow to a great danger."

At the close of the trial, if that can be called a trial in which only one side is heard, the presiding judge occupied five hours in his charge to the jury. I beg to call your attention to a few sentences in this charge. His lordship said, —

"Great excitement had been manifested during the case by persons who had come forward to give the prisoner a character for honesty and integrity, and to say that she and her husband were enthusiastic believers in Spiritualism and in the doctrine of communion with departed spirits. Now, he must take leave to say, that it was absolutely immaterial to the issue they were trying, whether or not there might be in this world several millions of persons devoutly believing that communion might be had with departed spirits."

I was present in court during the whole trial, and I saw no evidence or manifestation of such excitement; also I think the fact that millions of persons devoutly believe in communion with departed spirits renders it not improbable that the Fletchers held that belief.

His lordship said, —

"Of course the whole of this case depends upon whether you believe the evidence of the prosecutrix, or not. If you do not, the whole fabric of the case comes down."

Yet he resolutely and persistently excluded testimony affecting the character, and therefore the credibility, of this witness; apparently agreeing with the Bow-street magistrate, that, though she had led "the life of a demon," she might be believed when she charged another person with fraud.

"It was given in evidence by Mrs. Hart-Davies, that there was an honorable understanding that the goods should be returned when required."

The goods had been so returned: then, why these criminal proceedings?

I am quite aware that the entire press, almost without exception, approved the verdict. The "leaders" of the London journals, daily and weekly, were echoes of the charge and the sentence; but I am too old a journalist not to know what such clamor is worth. It was simply an embodiment of an ignorant and prejudiced public opinion, taking the place of the pillory, to which good and bad men were subjected in a ruder age, when the populace threw their own dirt, because they had no "leader" writers paid to do it for them.

I give you my opinions freely; because I think you wish to know how intelligent and fair-minded men look upon such a failure of justice, and triumph of prejudice, as this trial and its result.

But the charge to the jury and the sentence were as remarkable for what they omitted as for what they asserted. Just and humane judges are eager to place before a jury any evidence or circumstance which may tell in favor of a person accused of crime. In this case, the fact that Mrs. Fletcher came across the Atlantic in midwinter, solely to meet this accusation; the fact, that, during four months at Bow Street and the Old Bailey, she had regularly surrendered to her bail, when she might have kept away, or taken her departure, — were not so much as hinted at. The fact, that no article of the property had been sold, secreted, or made away with; that Mrs. Hart-Davies, with a portion of it, was taken with the Fletchers to America; that the remainder was left where she herself had placed it, — these most important facts were left unmentioned, as if they had not existed.

I appeal to you, right honorable sir, as to the one man to whom the administration of justice, and also of the royal clemency, in these realms, is confided; to the one whose functions are, to a vast number, the most important of those of any of her Majesty's ministers, — whether I have not shown reason why this case should be reviewed in the only tribunal before which it can be brought; and I respectfully ask you to consider some of the evidence which ought to have been given at the trial.

But, besides the grave doubts that every one must feel as to the motives and evidence of the prosecutrix, there remains the fact that there was no *proof of fraud or false pretences.* It was a matter of inference or opinion. There was no proof given that one word spoken or written by Mrs. Fletcher to Mrs. Hart-Davies was untrue. The charge of the judge and the verdict of the jury were based upon preconceived opinions. Mrs. Fletcher, perfectly innocent, as I and thousands more believe her to be, upon this mere opinion, based upon no actual proof, might have been sentenced to penal servitude. Some years ago she might have been transported or hanged, as I much fear thousands of innocent victims have been, when there were no home secretaries to revise the verdicts of prejudiced juries, and the sentences of judges who condemned poor women to death for witchcraft and sorcery, for pretending to which Mrs. Fletcher was gravely indicted in a count which Mr. Justice Hawkins condemned as bad in law, and unsupported by any evidence. The charge of false pretences, I contend, was equally unsupported; and conviction without proof is contrary to law.

Submitting what I have said, and what I have appended, to your wise, just, and merciful consideration, I have the honor to remain, with the highest respect,

Your most obedient servant,

THOMAS LOW NICHOLS.

32 Fopstone Road, South Kensington, S.W.